Hailey Edwards writes about questionable applications of otherwise perfectly good magic, the transformative power of love, the family you choose for yourself, and blowing stuff up. Not necessarily all at once. That could get messy. She lives in Alabama with her husband, their daughter, and a herd of dachshunds.

Visit her website at www.haileyedwards.net

By Hailey Edwards

The Foundling Series

Bayou Born
Bone Driven

BONE DRIVEN

Hailey Edwards

piatkus

PIATKUS

First published in Great Britain in 2018 by Piatkus

3 5 7 9 10 8 6 4 2

A CIP catalogue record for this book
is available from the British Library.

ISBN 978-0-349-41707-3

Typeset in Goudy by M Rules
Printed and bound in Great Britain by
Clays Ltd, Elcograf s.p.A

Papers used by Piatkus are from well-managed forests
and other responsible sources.

Piatkus
An imprint of
Little, Brown Book Group
Carmelite House
50 Victoria Embankment
London EC4Y 0DZ

An Hachette UK Company
www.hachette.co.uk

www.littlebrown.co.uk

For Aunt Barbara, who showed me
life is better with a book in my hand
(and romance on the pages).

She taught me how to love a child with my
whole heart and what it means to be family. I
wouldn't be the person I am today without her
guidance and support. I love you, Bob!

CHAPTER ONE

The first notes in my favorite country song plucked the air as sweat rolled from my hairline into my eyes. I wiped my damp face on the long sleeve of my shirt then squinted at the sixteen-penny nail I had pinched between two fingers. Picturing Geoffrey Timmons' smug face as I swung the hammer in a punishing downstroke was cathartic after spending half the week down at the station playing star witness in the internal affairs investigation guaranteed to dethrone the current chief of police. But he was one small nail in a box of hundreds, and I had more dire concerns on my mind. Fresh worries pressed into my thoughts with every strike until the wood splintered beneath each brutal impact.

Demons were real. *Bang.* I was one of them. *Bang.* I was amongst the worst of them. *Bang.*

And those very real demons had trashed the farmhouse I shared with my dad, who was in no shape to be out in this heat working on repairs while we waited for approval on our insurance claim. That left me, my phone, and a Bluetooth speaker to get the job done.

A bleating car horn alerted me to the fact I had company coming, and I cursed under my breath.

Vultures were circling again thanks to the recording of Timmons' threats leaking to the press – not helped by Jane Doe checking herself out of Madison Memorial against medical advice in order to avoid more abuse from the media, at least according to the statement Kapoor made on the hospital steps. Add to that my refusal to make a statement on either incident, and I was once again a hot topic around town. Frustration guided my aim through four more swings before car doors slammed and crunching footsteps approached.

"What did that sheet of plywood ever do to you, Bou-Bou?"

A grin split my cheeks as I turned and spotted Rixton heading my way with a squirming pink bundle in his arms. "How's my favorite person on the planet?"

Annette Marjoram Rixton was the cutest baby I had ever seen, and that wasn't just because she was scheduled to officially become my goddaughter in three more weeks, on her one-month birthday.

"I'm good." He winked at me. "Thanks for asking."

I gave him a flat stare, my best cop face, but since he had taught me the look, he only laughed. "Does your wife know you've absconded with her child?"

"Nettie is *our* child," he corrected me. "I can't abscond with my own child."

"We both know that's not true." Sadly, abductions happened all the time, and a parent or another relative was most often the perpetrator. "How long do you have before Sherry calls this in and an Amber Alert gets issued?"

"Sherry trusts me, unlike some people I won't name." He coughed into his fist. "*Luce Boudreau.*"

"Mmm-hmm."

"Tell your godmother to set phasers on stun." Rixton booped his daughter's nose. "We aren't out being nefarious. We went on a diaper run so Mommy could nap, didn't we?"

"That was very sweet of you," I had to admit.

"I learned from the best. Look what Sherry got me." Whipping out his phone, he angled it toward me. The screen showed her curled on the couch under a short, thin blanket she probably borrowed from her daughter. "She bought a video camera that clips on the crib so I can check in on Nettie while I'm at work. Turns out it's also handy as a mommy cam. I'll get an alert when she starts moving around, and that's my cue to skedaddle."

Surveillance truly was the gift that kept on giving. Poor Sherry. She really ought to know better by now.

"Come on in." I set down my tools and waved him toward the front door. "Get that baby doll out of this heat."

"Baby doll, huh?" He chuckled. "Nettie must be the drink and wet variety."

Nettie was little bitty and oh-so-breakable, exactly like the porcelain dolls Granny Boudreau had collected over her life. We had boxes full of them in the attic, which my goddaughter was welcome to when she got older.

I held the newly installed screen door open for Rixton with the toe of my ratty sneaker.

"Auntie Bou-Bou has the best manners," he crooned to Nettie. "See how she held the door for a gentleman?"

Since Rixton was holding the baby I was about to vow to protect as my own, I cut him some slack instead of smashing his face in for calling me Bou-Bou. The more I reacted, the deeper the nickname would root into his personal lexicon, and soon there wouldn't be enough upper body strength in the world to yank it from his vocabulary. Starting today, my new policy would be ignoring him. He hated that. Rixton would rather be shot in the foot than have his antics dismissed. Personally? I could use the target practice.

Plastic sheeting taped over all the doorways and windows gave the kitchen the appearance of a crime scene still under investigation, but it was the only cool room in the house. I held back the thick curtain while Rixton stepped inside my chilly sanctuary.

"Can I get you something to drink?" I palmed a bottle of icy water from the cooler acting as my temporary fridge and gulped half of it down before coming up for air. "I've got water, water, and water."

Everything else had spoiled thanks to the aforementioned demons who had turned the farmhouse into a block of Swiss cheese. The second floor was fully restored, but downstairs was so holey, it wasn't worth turning the central air on yet. Only the kitchen and guest bathroom gave me respite from the blistering heat thanks to the portable window unit whirring on cement blocks stacked in the gap where the back door used to be.

"Hmm." He appeared to give the non-existent selection genuine consideration. "How about . . . water?"

Huffing out a laugh, I passed him a cold bottle, careful to avoid a single drop of condensation splashing Nettie's perfect face.

"She's not actually made of porcelain, Luce. You won't break her." He gentled his tone as he set his drink on the counter. "Don't you think it's time you held your goddaughter?"

"No." I jumped back on reflex, waving my arms to ward him

off, and tripped over the cooler. I landed in a seated position on the lid with my back pressed against the wall. "I'm good with looking. Really. I don't have to hold her."

Holding Nettie meant enduring more prolonged contact with another person than I had allowed in ... ever.

"You haven't changed your mind about participating in the christening, have you?" His brows knitted together. "There's no one Sherry and I trust more than you, but you'll still be Nettie's auntie with or without the ceremony."

I clamped my fingers on the lid and held on for dear life. "I haven't changed my mind but—"

Understanding dawned in his expression, and he glanced at my shirt sleeves as though he could see the rose gold metal of the *rukav* banding my arms under the fabric. I watched him realize that while I might love his daughter, I would never be the auntie who let her curl in my lap while I read her bedtime stories on nights she slept over or cuddled her after a bad dream. I was touch-averse. Always had been. Physical manifestations of emotion required effort on my part. They weren't natural, fluid responses to stimuli for me; they were calculated reactions for all that they were genuine expressions of what I felt for those I loved.

For one fraction of a second, I read his doubt that I was up to the task, and a pang arrowed through my chest straight for my pounding heart.

"I didn't think about ... " Rixton cleared his throat. "Are you sure you can handle ... ?"

"I'm sure. I can do this. Let me hold her." Oxygen deprivation blurred my vision as he knelt in front of me and murmured instructions on how to support her head and neck, and then she was in my arms, her weight so slight I might have been cradling a blanket instead of a small person. "What if I drop—?"

"Look at me." His calm order sliced through my panic. "She's a baby, not a ticking time bomb. Unless you count the explosive diarrhea." He patted my knee to avoid an accidental brush with the metal beneath my skin. "You got this."

Nettie blinked up at me through clear, blue eyes the color of faded denim. She blew slobber bubbles that popped on her chin with each breath while clenching one tiny hand in the air like she was grasping for golden dust motes. The smell of her skin, fresh powder and innocence, twisted something in my chest until I had to glance away to dry the promise of tears from my eyes.

"Remember to breathe." Rixton grinned as he snapped a quick picture on his cell. "You're doing great."

A breathless quality entered my voice. "I'm holding a baby."

"Like a pro."

A dull headache blossomed in my temples, the persistent throbbing a reminder of the car accident that had rattled my brain like rocks in a soda can, but I ignored the discomfort. "Look at her fingernails, the wrinkles on her palms." I marveled at each flexing toe and every curl of black hair, each detail I took for granted in adults rendered in flawless miniature. "How is this even possible?"

"Well, it's like this." Rixton sat back on his heels. "Mommies have lady gardens and daddies have—"

A groan slipped past my lips. "Please stop."

"—magic seeds. When the soil in the lady garden is at its most fertile, the daddy plants his—"

"Rixton." I twisted to one side, shielding Nettie with my body. "Your daughter can hear you."

"She won't remember a thing," he promised. "Besides, I have to practice that speech for when she's old enough for me to explain how I will double tap any gardener I catch aiming his tool at her—" he whirled a hand in the air "—flower bed."

A knock on the door did what my threat had failed to do and shut him up.

"Come in," I called out. No way was I tempting fate and actually walking with a baby in my arms. "We're in the kitchen."

Rixton took over host duty and pulled aside the plastic curtain to admit a tall man with angular features arranged in a polite expression that sat wrong on his face, like polite wasn't his default, and he wasn't sure how it ought to look on him. His build reminded me of an Olympic swimmer, all lean muscle and long legs.

He wore gray slacks, shoes that cost more than the new hardwood floor he walked on, and a white button-down shirt rolled up over his forearms. His thick, black hair had been trimmed in an undercut and slicked back, and his soulful brown eyes drank in every detail of the room before settling on me with a tangible weight that made my bones creak. He smiled first at me and then at the baby in my arms. I couldn't pinpoint why, but the flash of his straight, white teeth in her direction set my heart pumping and propelled me to my feet.

"Luce Boudreau?" His silky voice caressed each syllable of my name with the hint of a foreign accent I couldn't place. "I'm Adam Wu. I work for All South Insurance. I'm here to discuss the claim you filed."

Hairs lifted down my arms in a prickling wave. "Rixton? Would you mind taking Nettie?"

"No problem." He read the tension bowing my shoulders in a protective curve around his daughter and positioned himself between Wu and me. "Is this guy legit? Or is he a well-fed vulture in a nice suit?" Keeping his back to my guest, he lowered his voice to keep our conversation private. "Say the word, and I'll toss him out on his can."

Wu shook his head once in silent warning behind Rixton.

"I got this," I assured him and then cut my eyes to Wu. "I'll be right back. I'm going to walk my partner to his car." I shepherded Rixton and Nettie through the sheeting, paranoid he might trip and drop her, then out onto the front porch in record time. "Tell Sherry I'll stop by tomorrow for a visit."

"Okay. I'll keep my phone on me." His gaze slid past my shoulder into the house. "Call if you need me."

"I will." I waited while he strapped Nettie into her car seat then waved him off, watching for the moment he turned onto the main road before returning to my guest in the kitchen. "All South Insurance went out of business about five years ago. We're with Mississippi Fidelity now." I leaned a hip against the counter, toying with the water bottle Rixton had left untouched. "Who are you really?" I decided against playing hostess for Wu and tossed the drink back in the cooler. "Is your name really Adam Wu?"

"Adam Wu is one of my aliases." His wry smile drew my attention to the unusual curve of his mouth and his slightly larger upper lip, like the bee who stung the top couldn't be bothered to give him a matching set. "Special Agent Kapoor prefers it to my others these days."

"Ah." Curiosity trumped my annoyance for a heartbeat. "This is one of *those* visits."

"Where is your coterie?" The man studied me as though I were an exotic animal he hadn't expected to encounter in rural Mississippi. "Why aren't they here? Protecting you? Helping you?"

Wu hadn't earned the answers to those questions even if I'd had them. "Why are *you* here?"

"You have three weeks left with the Canton Police Department." Wu inclined his head, a birdlike gesture of curiosity. "Are you ready to put in your notice next Monday?"

"Counting down the days, huh?" I cocked an eyebrow at him. "Are you here to help me draft my resignation?"

"If that's what it takes." He cast his gaze around the room once more. "Not all charun embrace our philosophies. Some require—" our gazes locked "—encouragement."

"I accepted the deal." I prowled closer, until the toes of our shoes touched. "I stand by my word."

Kapoor didn't have to send thugs like Wu to twist my arm when I had already shaken his hand on the bargain to join a demon taskforce spearheaded by the National Security Branch of the FBI and made my peace with its cost. Namely, my career.

"Forgive me for not trusting your nature." Wu searched my face, and a frown knitted his brow. "Your kind are not known for their honesty. Otillians are a vicious breed, their females in particular. That you are one of the four in Czar Astrakhan's cadre does you no favors in my estimation."

I smiled at him, flashing my own teeth. "Good thing I don't care what you think about me."

"You will." Wu leaned down until our faces were on the same level, until he could look me in the eye, and the scent of his sun-warmed skin hit the back of my throat. "I'm your new partner."

Wu pivoted on his heel and left me swaying toward him. New partner? Wu thought he could replace Rixton? *Ha.* No chance. I marched after him, slapped the plastic sheeting aside, and stepped out onto the front porch. I was about to light into him when I noticed his attention was focused off in the distance where a plume of dust whirled down the main road. I squinted past the mailbox, and my heart gave a hard thud as a familiar black SUV rumbled up the driveway.

Three men exited the vehicle, and none of them were smiling.

"Cole Heaton, Miller Henshaw, and Thomas Ford." Wu rattled off their names without a hitch. "To what does Ms. Boudreau owe the pleasure of this visit? The house carries no scent of her coterie. How long have you left your mistress unguarded?"

Cole ignored Wu and his accusations, his meltwater gaze fixated on me. "Are you all right?"

The black stubble covering his scalp had been trimmed recently, and his face was freshly shaven. As usual, his square jaw bulged as he ground his teeth against words he would never speak but that seemed forever on the tip of his tongue. The zigzag pattern of his nose, each kink a reminder of the violent life he led, no longer startled me. Neither did the missing tip of his left ear. They were simply sums that made up the whole of Cole Heaton.

I had to moisten my tongue before I could speak. "Fine."

"Who's your friend?" Thom tracked Wu with sharp interest, his narrowed eyes glinting bright emerald, the turn of his head causing a hank of dark blond hair to tickle the golden skin on his wide forehead. All ropey muscle and lightning reflexes, the man looked more like a cheetah than the boxy tomcat lurking under his skin. "He smells . . . delicious."

Leave it to Thom to make things weird. Well, okay, weirder.

"Everyone, this is Adam Wu." I gestured around the gathering. "Adam Wu, this is everyone."

A frown gathered in the tight folds between Miller's eyebrows, and he rested his hand on Thom's shoulder to halt his silent prowl forward. Thom hissed at the restraint but quit his stalking behavior.

"We need to talk," Cole rumbled to me. "In private."

"Sure." He had avoided me like a biblical plague since the night I cost him one of his people, and one of mine too. "We can go around back to the picnic bench." I wasn't sure I could handle being in an enclosed space with him, not after the way we'd left things. "It's in the shade, so it won't be as hot."

"Stay put," he ordered Miller and Thom. "Keep an eye on Wu."

"They aren't yours to command," Wu reminded him. "Neither am I."

Leaving them to finish their pissing match, I circled the house and headed toward the lone oak overhanging a picnic bench in desperate need of sanding and refinishing. I was too fidgety to sit, so I leaned against the tree trunk and waited on Cole to join me.

"The house looks good," he said into the tense silence. "You didn't have to do this alone. You could have asked for our help."

"Miller and Thom are the only ones who have reached out since that night." I shrugged like the snub didn't hurt, like going back to playing human hadn't made me feel like my skin was stretched too tight over my bones now that I knew the truth. "I figured that must mean the rest of you wanted things to go back to how they were before."

"There is no going back." His long gait swallowed the distance between us, and he braced one wide palm on the bark over my head. The snap closure on the thick leather band concealing the metal under his skin glinted in the sunlight. "You don't get to pretend you don't know what you are anymore." He leaned in close. "War is here. Famine will be soon. You can't hide from your birthright."

"I'm not." I had been . . . adjusting. Absorbing. Making peace with the fact my entire identity was a lie. Seven days to stitch the rips in my psyche back together sounded more than fair to me. "I've been here, at home, this whole time. You could have visited. If you didn't want to see me, you could have called. If you didn't want to hear me, you could have texted." I met his gaze and held it even when his cold fury gave me chills. "Who's really hiding here, Cole?"

A growl pumped through his chest, and he didn't bother smoothing its ragged edges. We were past all that. "We are your coterie, your strength. You don't get to abandon us again."

"So that's what this is about." The rough bark tugged on my hair as I angled my face toward him. "You're not just mad at me for avoiding you, you thought I would ditch you again." Cole had explained how the coterie waited years for me to find them, but I hadn't known to look. "I wanted time alone to get my head on straight, okay, I'll cop to that, but when you didn't call, I assumed you were angry over ..."

The deal I'd made with Kapoor. Over Portia. Over Maggie. Everything.

"I'm not mad." The lie flattened his lips into a harsh line. "I don't have the luxury of anger."

"Keep telling yourself that, big guy." I blasted out a frustrated sigh. "Why are you really here?"

"Thom and I are working a case up in Ludlow." He straightened from his lean and lowered his arm. "We found something you ought to see."

"I have to work in a few hours, and I can't go tomorrow. That's when the crew arrives to install the new bay window." I tucked a sticky curl behind my ear. "How about the next day?"

"How about now?" He glanced over his shoulder toward the driveway. "I brought it with me."

I followed his gaze. "Is this something Wu should see?"

"Who is he to you?" Cole sharpened each word until the next question cut deep. "Why is he here?"

"Kapoor sent him to check up on me." I wet my lips. "He's my new partner."

Cole folded his fingers into his palms, clenching his hands into meaty fists at his sides. "I see."

Out of my depth, I sidestepped his quiet anger and returned to the driveway to find the Mexican standoff still in progress. I winked at Miller then grinned at Thom on my way to the rear of the SUV emblazoned with the familiar White Horse logo of a muscular white warhorse stamping its left front hoof. Wu, whose presence I had chosen to ignore, sidled up to me at the exact same moment Cole arrived, and they locked glares over my head.

"Cole," I prompted him. "You said you have something to show me?"

"Brace yourself." He opened the hatch and reached for a lumpy towel. "This is the third one of these we've found." He peeled back the fabric to reveal the mummified remains of a cat. I might have believed the corpse was decades old except for its modern collar with the owner's Twitter handle engraved on its tag. "Natural mummification takes forty plus days depending on environmental conditions. This is the work of forty-eight to seventy-two hours. Two of the animals were chipped, so the identifications are positive, and the timelines are solid."

I got a bad feeling about where he was headed. "Any ideas what caused this?"

"An ubaste is my guess," Wu cut in.

I swung my head toward him. "A who-what-now?"

Cole answered for him. "An ubaste is a low-level charun that feeds on the life force of small animals."

"That's good, right?" Stark relief swirled through me. "That means it's no danger to humans."

Wu pinched a fold of the cat's brittle skin between his fingers, and the desiccated flesh crumbled. "Humans *are* animals."

"Not you too." I popped his hand before he ruined more evidence. "You're with the NSB. Doesn't that mean you value human life?"

"No." He dusted his hands. "All it means is I value my life."

A twinge of conscience almost had me apologizing to him, for what I wasn't sure, but it wasn't my fault he was here. He had made his choice to cozy up to the NSB the same as me, and now both of us had to live with our decisions.

"You're saying this thing is a danger to small people." I checked with Cole. "As in, children."

Grim certainty darkened his mood. "Yes."

"What can we do about it?" We couldn't let it run free.

"We hunt it." Cole bared his teeth in a feral smile he aimed at Wu. "That's what the NSB expects, right?"

"Charun who can't be rehabilitated must be killed." Wu didn't sugarcoat his truth. "That includes you, him, and the rest of your coterie."

Brittle ice swept through my chest as the cold place surfaced in response to his threat. Demanding that my coterie participate in a spay and neuter program for demons, like they were little more than animals, was bad enough. Hinting any insubordination would result in their deaths was a step too far. "Raise a hand against him or any member of my coterie, and I will be forced to put a bullet through your brain."

The smug grin Wu gifted me was somehow worse than his calculated jabs, as though he were rewarding me for giving him the reaction he had hoped to provoke all along. "Ah. There you are, Conquest." His warm fingertips brushed my cheek in a glancing caress. "I thought I saw you in there."

"My name is Luce." I recoiled from his touch and bumped into Cole, who wrapped his heavy forearm across my collarbone and hauled me tight against the protection of his solid body. "I am *not* Conquest."

"I can smell your Otillian blood." Wu flared his nostrils. "Blood never lies." His eyes dilated. "Ask me how I know."

"I am more than a birthright I had no claim to until a week ago."

"I hope you're right." The corners of his eyes tightened. Disappointed, maybe, that I didn't take the bait. I didn't ask. "For all our sakes."

Wu dipped his head in a shallow bow and left me alone with my coterie and the uneasy certainty he had been right all along. I did care what he thought. Maybe my competitive nature was to blame, or maybe it was sheer desperation. Wu might be right about my blood, but I was determined to prove he was wrong about me.

CHAPTER TWO

———◆———

Habit had me raising my arm and knocking on the bright red door of the tidy cottage I was calling home these days. A beanpole of a woman with dark skin and warm, brown eyes greeted me with her fists anchored at her narrow hips. Flour dusted the front of her bright purple shirt, and the mouthwatering scent of freshly baked chocolate chip cookies perfumed her skin.

"Tater tot, how many times do we have to go over this?" Aunt Nancy tapped one bare foot on the welcome mat. "You're our guest. You don't knock on the door of your own house, do you? Of course not. So why would you knock while you're living here?"

I ducked my head and scuffed the toe of my shoe. "Yes, ma'am."

"Get your cute little buns in here." She waved me in, and the red silicone bracelet on her thin wrist caught my attention. Must be a holdover from vacation Bible school. "We're air conditioning the whole neighborhood standing here like this."

Once I'd shuffled across the threshold, I lingered in the short hallway until she joined me. "How's Dad?"

"He's watching TV in the living room, some program on the mating habits of ducks, which I will never feed at the pond again." A shudder rippled through her. "He ate a salad for lunch and napped on the sofa, but he hasn't spoken since you left."

Nodding, I raked my upper teeth over my bottom lip. "Thanks for keeping an eye on him for me."

"You and Eddie are family." She took my hand and squeezed with conviction. "We're happy to help for as long as you need us." A heavy sigh collapsed her birdlike chest, and not for the first time I hoped we weren't the cause of her recent weight loss. Stress was a real appetite killer. "The doctors warned us the risk of a recurrent stroke was higher during the first year. He recovered from the first one, and he's going to beat it this time too."

The reassuring smile I meant to offer her was so brittle it shattered before reaching my lips. I hated lying to her. I hated lying to Uncle Harold even more. But hearing the truth about what had happened to Dad, that he had been attacked by the same demons who had done their best to level our home, was a no-go for several reasons. Starting with their deep Christian faith and ending with me carted off to the loony bin. Dad's symptoms, which mimicked a recurrent stroke, were the result of an allergic reaction to Thom's saliva as near as we could tell, but admitting that was the equivalent of lacing my own straitjacket.

"Yeah," I agreed a beat too late. "He will."

The *ding* of a timer rescued me from another pep talk.

"Oh, that's me. I have a batch of cookies in the oven. There's a fundraiser at the church Sunday, and I promised them six dozen." She hustled into the kitchen. "Only two more to go."

Sucking in a deep breath, I ventured into the living room where Dad sat in a pair of ratty sweats, a T-shirt with a hole in the armpit, and a pair of slippers with *#1 Dad* embroidered across the toes. His rumpled hair was mashed flat on one side, and a line of drool had dried to crust from the corner of his mouth across one cheek. He stared beyond the TV at the blank wall and didn't turn his head when I entered the room.

"Hey, Dad." I stepped between him and the show he wasn't watching. "How are you feeling?"

"Fine," he mumbled without inflection. "I'm fine."

"I finished framing out the wall where the new bay window will go." I watched him for signs of interest that never manifested. "The installers are coming out tomorrow to handle the heavy lifting, but I'll be there to supervise."

With visible effort, he pulled me into focus. "That's great, baby girl."

The moment of lucidity passed all too quickly, and he resumed his staring contest with the sheetrock.

"I need to grab a shower." I pressed a kiss to his damp forehead. "I'll raid the kitchen when I get out, and we can have cookies and milk before I head into work."

There was no response, but then again, I was learning not to expect more than two in a row.

On my way to the sewing room acting as my temporary bedroom, I texted Miller an update on Dad's condition. I had to step over the air mattress to reach a basket of clean clothes, but I gathered what I needed without tripping and made a beeline for the relative privacy of the house's only bathroom. Miller must have read more into the message than what I typed, because my phone rang a heartbeat later. "Hey, I didn't mean to bug you."

"We've been over this," he chided. "You don't have to apologize."

"Are you sure?" I sat on the closed lid of the toilet. "I must be driving you crazy with all the questions."

"You've had a big shock. The things you've learned are stretching the fabric of your reality. It's perfectly normal to want answers, and I'm happy to provide them. But what I can't do is continue acting as a buffer between you and ..." his hesitation stretched to make room for a name, a single syllable he didn't speak "... the others."

"That wasn't my intention." I toed off my shoes. "You're easier to talk to than—" my tongue tripped over the same word, and I finished lamely "—the others."

"We're kindred spirits," he mused. "Both afraid of who we are, and both terrified of what we're capable of doing under the right circumstances. Our self-awareness binds us in ways the others don't understand."

"Yeah," I agreed in a rush. "That."

A knock on the door startled me to attention.

"Luce?" Uncle Harold called. "How much longer will you be in there?"

"Twenty minutes." I peeled off my socks. "Fifteen if I hurry."

"Hurry," he urged. "This old bladder ain't what it used to be, pumpkin."

Footsteps shuffled down the hall as I shimmied out of the rest of my damp clothes.

"Ah, the joys of a one-bathroom household." I chuckled with Miller. "I gotta run. The clock is ticking."

"See you tomorrow."

He ended the call before I could ask what he had in mind, but I had no time to dwell. Armed with a loofah, I stepped into the shower and stood under the scalding water until the mixture of dirt, sawdust, and sweat crusting my throat and face was loose enough to scrub off without taking the topmost layer of my skin along for the ride. As I traced a line across my collarbones, I couldn't help but recall the heavy drape of Cole's arm and wish the remembered touch was as easy to cleanse away as the grime.

Rixton shoved an iced coffee and a bag of warm donuts into my hands the second my butt landed in the passenger seat of our cruiser. The entire car smelled like a bakery, and my mouth watered. Working second shift, two until ten, meant lunch was usually in my rear-view mirror when I clocked in. That hadn't happened today. Neither had the cookies and milk. Dad had zonked out by the time I returned to the living room, and watching his fitful sleep had robbed me of my appetite.

"How's your dad?" Rixton asked around a classic glazed. "I meant to ask earlier but . . . baby brain."

"Still a zombie." I hauled out my treat and picked at the sprinkles. "I hate seeing him like this."

More than that, I hated knowing his condition was my fault. War and her coterie might have inflicted the damage, and I would make them pay for what they'd done, but I was the reason he'd been targeted. There was no tap dancing around that grim truth.

"Your dad is tough, and he's got you." He tugged a wet wipe from a packet tucked in the console and cleaned the sugar from his fingers. "He's going to get through this."

I shoved the donut into my mouth to avoid formulating an answer.

"Unit four-one-six," the radio crackled. "We received a 911 call from Hensarling Farms out on Virlilia Road from an unidentified male. The caller was incoherent, but a second male voice was heard shouting 'the fields are burning' before the line disconnected. Arson suspected. The fire department is en route. Police backup has been requested."

"On our way, dispatch." Rixton powered up the light bar and flipped on the siren. "We'll be there in twenty." He stomped on the gas, and I tightened my seat belt. "Those cotton plants will be as dry as tinder. The whole farm will go up if the water fairies don't get their asses there quick-like and in a hurry."

"Don't mock the whole department just because Captain Estes called you out that one time."

Rixton cut his eyes toward me. "He called me Officer Krispy Kreme."

The problem wasn't the nickname. It was that he had answered to it on reflex in front of a half-dozen firefighters who now catcalled him every time we rolled up on a scene.

"You're right. What was I thinking?" I deadpanned. "Clearly, they're the enemy."

"Damn straight."

Fifteen minutes later, we bumped off the asphalt and hit a dirt road that T-boned up ahead. Straight took you to what appeared to be a cluster of barns. Right put you on a narrow lane already clogged with fire trucks that cut between two fields of ripe cotton and led up to the Hensarling homestead. We kept straight and parked between five pickups belonging either to the employees or neighbors come to lend a hand.

"Canton PD," Rixton announced when no one came running. "We're responding to a call for assistance."

A young girl bolted from between two buildings to meet us. She ran straight up to me and took my hand, ignoring my flinch, and hauled me along after her. "Hurry. Please. It's Mr. Rowland. He's gone nuts. They can't hold him much longer."

Rixton and I exchanged glances then followed the girl

down an alley between two massive buildings overflowing with hulking machines painted in trademark greens and yellows. A dirt lot crowded with rusted out equipment sprawled behind the tidy barns, and a small crowd had gathered in its center.

"Deena, you go on now." A woman dressed in jeans and a tee covered in soot rushed toward us and turned the girl on her heels. "Sit in the bed of the truck and wait for me to come get you. Don't move a muscle." She pressed a phone into the girl's hand. "Play a game or watch one of your shows. Just don't come back here no matter what you see or hear."

The girl's voice wavered. "Momma?"

"It's all right." She gathered her daughter close. "Just do as I say, you hear?"

"Yes, ma'am." The girl dragged her heels, but she didn't look back, and that appeased her mother.

"I'm Detective Rixton, and this is my partner, Officer Boudreau." Rixton took lead while I watched our backs. "We're responding to an emergency call traced back to a landline phone associated with this address."

"I'm Jessica Hensarling. This is my grandma Ruth's farm." Up close I saw a crimson smear across her left cheek that competed with the black smudges. The eye above it swelled with the start of what would become a wicked shiner. "Pete Rowland made the call on the barn phone before he lost his damn mind." She indicated we should walk with her. "He's right over here."

A lump that might as well have been a charcoal briquette lay curled on the ground. Had I not recognized the diamond pattern charred into the section nearest me as roasted cowboy boots, I wouldn't have thought I was looking at human remains. As easy as breathing, the cold place welled up in me, allowing me the distance to filter out the cooked meat smell that explained the fainter tang of vomit.

Careful not to disturb the scene, I walked a slow circle around the body. As I cataloged the location of each twisted limb, I noticed the metal nozzle grasped in one gnarled hand and the silvery canister he had contorted around while in his death throes.

This nutbar had set fire to the farm and then himself using a drip torch meant for controlled burns.

Rixton was modeling the stone-cold cop face I worked so hard to emulate. The laughing man who cracked jokes faster than old timers could shell pecans had blocked his heart behind a wall of ice too.

"His skin is still crackling." He squatted next to Rowland's head. "Based on the time dispatch pinged us and our distance from the farm, he must have turned the torch on himself within seconds of ending the call."

"I tried to stop him," Ms. Hensarling murmured, her voice gone weak. "He clocked me with the base of the drip torch." Her fingers traveled up her face to press against the cut over her cheekbone. "He was sobbing, begging for help and then . . ." Her gaze dipped to his ruined corpse. "I'm going to be sick."

We let her stumble to a nearby forklift where she emptied her stomach on its right front tire. We hesitated long enough for one of the others to break from the pack and comfort her. Rixton and I had retreated too deep into our heads to offer more than placations to the witnesses, and lip service wouldn't solve the mystery of what had happened on this smoldering tract of farmland or why this man had taken his own life in such a brutal fashion. Wearing indifference as a shield, we started the evidence collection process.

Six hours after we arrived at Hensarling Farms, Rixton and I climbed back in the cruiser and pointed her toward the station.

Gone was the bakery-fresh scent that had filled the car. Instead we smelled like death, sweat, and a sickly combination of diesel fuel and gasoline. Our clothes were filthy, our hands blackened, and we had yet to sink back into ourselves. Our bodies were running on autopilot and doing a damn fine job of keeping our minds insulated from the horrors left behind us.

Mr. Rowland hadn't stopped with razing the fields. Our arsonist was also a murderer.

One of the mechanics, Mr. Aguilera, had checked his two sons out of school for orthodontist appointments and brought them back to the farm with him to play with the barn cat and her kittens. The boys had been racing up the rows in the field when the fire started, and their legs had been too short to outrun the blaze.

For as long as I live, I will never forget how the small teeth in those blackened skulls looked strung with fine, silver wire.

"I need a stiff drink and a hot shower," Rixton announced. "I can't go home like this."

"I don't think I'm going back to the Trudeaus'." I sounded far off, miles away from here. "Dad and I always drink a beer on the front porch together on the bad nights. We don't talk. We just sit and listen to the frogs sing." I rubbed the grit from my eyes. "I need that slice of calm after what we saw."

"What we saw is why you don't need to be alone tonight. You want some company?"

"I've got a friend I can call," I said, thinking of Miller, "but you're welcome to the downstairs shower." I remembered the bare shelves in the fridge I had bleached earlier in the week. "I'll have to hit the package store."

"I'll call Sherry and let her know we're up to no good." His fingers drummed the steering wheel. "She'll understand I can't face Nettie with this on my skin."

Too bad the images wouldn't wash out of our heads under hot water, but that was the job. We saw things that haunted us, learned secrets we could never tell, heard nightmares given voice, woke drenched in cold sweat with bile perched in our throats all so innocents might remain that way for just a while longer.

The station was quiet when we arrived. Most units were still out on patrol. The one officer we passed in the hall kept her eyes downcast and her strides long to spare us any obligation to exchange pleasantries.

Word traveled fast, and for once, I was grateful.

We split off and hit our respective bathrooms, scrubbing the grime from our hands and faces. The abrasive paper towels from the dispenser scoured off the top layer of skin, which worked for me. We each kept a spare set of clothes in our lockers, and we changed into those. Neither helped much. We still felt dirty, smelled scorched, but at least we looked cleaner.

Our shift might have started out with a bang, but the end was, thankfully, a snoozer. Rixton and I divided the mountain of paperwork looming over us and spent the last two hours bent over the desk we shared.

Liam Dawson, the arson investigator with the Canton Fire Department, called to request our notes since we beat him to the scene and had first crack at the witnesses. Already in this up to our soot-covered ears, Rixton offered to lend a hand. Eager to put this nightmare to bed, Dawson accepted.

And so the Hensarling case became ours.

We managed to sneak out while Uncle Harold was in his shift meeting, neither of us eager to rehash our day, and I sent Rixton ahead of me so he could get started with his shower. That left me to grab the beer, which entailed making the purchase while in uniform. Something about the knowing glint in the cashier's eyes made me feel dirty, like I had taken a wrong step down a path that dead ended past the edge of a cliff. Shaking off the uneasy feeling, I took my six-pack and returned to my Bronco to find a small mountain waiting for me.

"I'm driving you home." Cole extended his hand for my keys. "Don't fight me on this."

He had the wrong girl. There was no fight left in me. I passed over the keys, climbed into the passenger's seat and strapped in. The vehicle rocked when Cole joined me, and his scent swept through my head, clearing away the burnt hair smell that made my stomach roil each time I caught an accidental whiff.

We drove home in blessed silence, and I used the time to text Uncle Harold and Aunt Nancy with my plans for the night. After Cole parked in my usual spot, he came around and opened the door for me. He had impeccable manners for a rock formation. When I made no move to get out, he resorted to his favorite pastime and loomed over me.

"Go on." His hand lifted of its own accord, like cupping my cheek was its idea, and Cole snarled a warning—to himself?—under his breath. He clenched his fist an inch from making contact and backed away until the darkness swallowed him. "I won't be far."

"Cole?" I stumbled when my feet hit the ground, my knees stiff and unbending. "Thanks."

A pair of crimson eyes set in the leonine face of his inner dragon peered out at me from the forest in answer. The pearlescent tip of his whiplike tail cracked against the earth, the scales catching the moonlight, before vanishing.

"I thought I heard your Bronco." Rixton shoved through the screen door, his hair spiky and wet from the shower. A hint of warmth had returned to his eyes, proof he had spoken to Sherry, and she had pulled him back from the precipice. He noticed the six-pack in my hand and frowned. "Where's the rest?"

"You have to drive home after this," I reminded him. "You get one beer. That's it."

Grumbling the whole time, he dropped into a blue rocker and held out his hand until I slapped a single beer across his palm. I sat opposite him, popped mine open, and drank. It went down cold and smooth and a little bitter. Or maybe that was just me. We sat together until my eyes grew too heavy to prop open, thanks to the four other beers I swilled, and Rixton stood to leave.

"Are you sure you want to stay out here by yourself?" He toyed with the tab on his can until it popped off in his hand. "We've got a spare bedroom with your name on it if you don't want to be alone."

"Nah." I yawned wide. "I want to sleep in my own bed. The upstairs is secure. It's just hot with only the ceiling fan running."

"Keep your phone on you." He flicked the tab at my head and hit me between the blurry eyes. "Call me or Sherry in the morning. Let us know that you're okay."

"Morning," I groaned. "I forgot the installers are coming out first thing before it gets hot."

"Poor Bou-Bou." His chuckle thawed him even further. "I'll text you my hangover cure."

Having been the recipient of his sage advice once before, I already knew it. *Don't get drunk in the first place.*

Smartass.

"Get out of here," I grumbled, cleaning up my mess. "Some of us need our beauty sleep."

"Damn, girl. You really are buzzed." He preened like a parakeet in front of a mirror. "You just implied that I don't need beauty sleep, which, incidentally, is one hundred percent true. I'm as devastatingly handsome with two hours of sleep as I am with eight. I'm just stunned you finally admitted it out loud."

"Rixton, stop, please. I already feel the beginnings of the headache I'm going to wake up with."

"Rude." He walked to the edge of the porch and balanced on the top step. "I'm out."

Through bleary eyes, I watched him pour more than three-quarters of his drink on the grass and felt like a total heel. He had sat there and watched while I got progressively wasted—I was a total lightweight—and let me anesthetize myself while he kept his wits sharp enough for the both of us.

Part of me was embarrassed I hadn't caught his subtle redirections. He and Sherry were a rock-solid unit, and the fact Team Rixton now had three players changed nothing. He kept no secrets from his wife. When he got home, they would talk it out, because he thought best while his mouth was moving, and Sherry would cry the tears he couldn't afford to let fall. She would make what he had seen and done okay. And Nettie? She would remind him there were still vestiges of wholesome goodness in this world, that there was hope for a brighter future, and it would be enough. It had to be.

All I could think while I sat there was how this was ending, we were ending, and he didn't even know it yet. I didn't have the courage to tell him I was quitting the force, that I was moving on. I didn't know what to say, what kind of lie would break his heart the cleanest, without the jagged edges that would cut us both. How did I admit to the man who was my professional other half that I was splitting up with him? He had already lost one partner. How would he deal with losing another? And would he ever forgive me?

I had to drop the news before the christening. Had to. He and Sherry deserved the option of going with their second choice, probably a local, maybe another cop. Someone who was normal, human, safe. Someone whose siblings weren't out to end the world my goddaughter was meant to inherit.

"I love you," I called to his retreating back. "I really, really do."

"Aww. You're a sentimental drunk." Rixton chuckled. "How did I not know this about you?"

"Tell no one." With a grunt, I shoved out of my rocker and collected the empties. "Or I will end you."

"Even your threats are cuter when you're tipsy." He pointed a warning finger at me. "Remember to call. Don't make me drive out here and perform a pulse-check on you."

"Yeah, yeah." I lined up the cans and started stomping them flat. "I'll call the second my eyes open."

"You do that." He patted the roof of the cruiser. "Night, Bou-Bou."

God grant me patience. "Night."

Rixton ducked out before my heel slapped the porch as the last can was crushed. That might have ended okay for me had I not then leaned forward to gather the discs for the recycling bin. The forward motion intensified the sloshing in my head until I tipped forward and landed on all fours.

I must have been picking at my French braid while in my rocker, because a curtain of hair slid forward and carried with it the rancid smells from the crime scene. I didn't reach the edge of the porch before the first heave brought sour mash into my mouth. As I christened the new planks with the contents of my stomach, I caught motion out of the corner of my watering eyes.

Cole did his looming thing again, in human form, standing well out of the splash zone.

I heaved again, but this time nothing came up but regret. "Hey."

The porch groaned as he shifted his weight. "You want to talk about it?"

"No." I shook my head, and my eyeballs swam in their sockets. "I'm good. I just . . ." I caught another whiff of my hair and barked out a wet cough. "It's the smell. In my hair. Making me sick."

Cole hooked his hands under my armpits and set me on my feet. I swayed without his support for the split second before he heaved a sigh and scooped me against his wide chest. Careful to keep his hands away from my arms and the delicate coils of metal between my shoulders, he carried me into the kitchen and sat me on the counter sideways so the basin was at my back.

After cutting the sink on, he held his hand under the stream until he appeared satisfied. One of his massive palms then cupped the back of my skull while his other pressed between my breasts, and he started lowering me down onto the quartz slab.

"What are we doing?" I tried focusing on his face, but his flat expression gave nothing away.

"Hold still." He tugged the sprayer from its holder and started soaking my hair with water just shy of too hot then squirted half the bottle of dish soap onto my grungy curls. His strong fingers massaged my scalp, his short nails scratching in small circles that left me a puddle under his hands. Rinsing took forever, but I didn't complain. And when he wet a cloth and scrubbed my face and neck clean, I didn't fuss about that either. "I don't know how to do that girly twist thing with the towel."

"That's okay." I pushed upright while he fetched a clean towel from the bathroom, then I slid to my feet and twisted the sopping wet length up on top of my head. "Do you mind if I get out of these clothes?"

I got the feeling he wasn't budging until I had been tucked in, which was fine with me, but I didn't want to wear my uniform up to my room. I was too beat to shower, but I wanted pajamas all the same.

"Let me get your boots." He knelt in front of me and untied the laces, and when his wide palm wrapped the back of my left calf to tug the boot off that foot, my remaining knee almost buckled. "Now the other."

Once I was standing in my socks, he escorted me to the laundry nook, a former linen closet Dad had converted into a space wide enough to fit a stackable washer and dryer set. There he pulled clean clothes out of the dryer I couldn't have reached without swaying like a palm tree caught in a hurricane.

"I've got it from here." Cole took all of about two steps before turning his back on me and planting his feet, giving me a view of the muscles flexing in his shoulders while I struggled out of my clothes and into a matching tank and shorts set. "I'm decent."

Without another word, he picked me up and carried me through the sheeting and up the stairs to my bedroom where he laid me down. I didn't bother with cover, just rolled onto my side and basked in the luxurious sensation of having an actual mattress beneath me. The problem was, this position gave me an eyeful of the ancient rotary phone presiding over my nightstand, and its silent accusation kicked my heart into a quicker rhythm. I had left it behind, like anyone would steal the ugly thing, like it did me a damn bit of good having it three hundred and sixty-four days out of the year. And yet ... having Cole and the phone in the same room together set my skin crawling.

No. That was ridiculous. I was not going to allow a hunk of

avocado-green plastic to guilt trip me for having a man in my bedroom. Even if the silver tab on its dial glinted with disapproval under the lights.

I am never drinking this much ever again. Never ever. No way, no how.

"Sleep it off." Cole stuck out his hand, and for a second I thought he was grabbing for the phone, and I forgot how to breathe, but he gestured at the towel. "I'll be outside."

Untangling the twisted fabric from my hair required great effort, and when I passed it over, our fingers brushed. With the phone in my periphery, the wires in my head crossed until the worst possible question popped out of my mouth. "Will you stay with me until I fall asleep?"

Cole stared at the towel concealing our hands like he was visualizing the pinpoints of heat where our fingers touched then dropped it like I'd passed him a bag of snakes. "No."

He breezed out of the room and clomped down the stairs, slamming the front door on his way back into the darkness beyond the porch. I stared at the discarded towel until its blue and white stripes flashed behind my eyelids with each blink and even those stark lines faded to black.

CHAPTER THREE

Pounding woke me, and it wasn't in my head. Or at least not all of it. As I rubbed the sleep from my eyes, I touched a clump of tacky hair knotted at my temple. Raking my fingers through the mass didn't help. The texture was dry and stiff like I had forgotten to use conditioner or . . .

Hazy memories from last night bombarded me, and I shot upright in bed.

Cole had washed my hair and put me to bed. And recalling that dredged up the reason for his kindness, and my gut twisted so hard I had to lean over the mattress and dry heave. Nothing came up. I was on empty. But the memory of those little teeth had etched themselves behind my eyelids, and there was no amount of blinking I could do to escape their silver glint.

Bam. Bam. Bam.

The rhythmic thudding dulled the sharpest edge of my grief, a small mercy, and a headache blossomed when I stood, but I had to get up and investigate all the racket. Surely the crew wouldn't have started without me. I hadn't inspected the order or given approval. They had no right to begin without even verifying if I was at home.

I took the stairs two at a time and skidded to a halt in the middle of the living room.

War had smashed through the original bay window while in her true form, that of a colossal alligator-like demon, and taken a chunk of the wall with her. Turns out demons are good at demo. Interior design? Not so much. I had framed out the section in question yesterday so that all the guys had to do was anchor the supports, pop in the new panes, and go. I had planned on doing the trim on my own to save money, but it looked like I had missed the boat. All I could see were dollar signs superimposed over the energy rating stickers.

The front door had been propped open, not that the AC was running, but the violation of my privacy rankled. I stomped onto the porch, glared at the white pickups parked in the yard, and whirled toward the first stooped male figure I spotted with a snarl on my lips. "What do you think you're doing?"

"What does it look like I'm doing?" He took another measurement and drew a pencil line. "Hand me that caulk gun."

"Santiago?"

"Never mind." He grunted, his dark brown eyes flashing with annoyance, and reached around me. "I got it."

"I don't understand." All my indignation drained out of the soles of my feet as I stared at the back of his tanned neck. "Why are you here?"

"Word is Mommy and Daddy kissed and made up," he said, his thin lips curling in a vicious smile, "so you've been granted visitation rights."

Heat blasted up my nape, and I had to rub the skin to ease the sting. "I didn't kiss anyone."

"He doesn't mean literally." Miller joined us with a fresh box of screws in hand. "He's just trying to get a rise out of you."

Glaring down at Santiago, I noticed the slight hitch in his shoulders that told me he was laughing at me. I was tempted to reach down and yank his hair where the longish ends were starting to curl, black and glossy with sweat, above his collar. He and I had butted heads from the get-go, so I hadn't expected a miracle even after we'd bonded during a late-night fishing trip, but whatever brownie points that had won me must have been lost during my weeklong absence.

"Hey, Miller." I offered him a genuine smile that he returned. "It's good to see you." And since Santiago had stiffened on my periphery, I nudged his boot with a bare toe to include him in the moment. "Both of you." He grumbled about toe jam, but he didn't move away, so hey, progress. "I still don't get why you guys are here. I already made arrangements with a contractor to handle the installation."

"We're your coterie," Miller said gently. "We're here to serve."

Serve. The word coated the back of my throat with bitterness.

"Santiago," I snapped, "put the caulk gun down."

"Nope." He kept his bead even as he traced the seam where the window met the wall. "I have somewhere to be in an hour. I don't have time to argue with you."

"Miller," I pleaded with him. "Let me pay you. Let me help you. Let me do something."

"I told you she wouldn't be pleased," Thom said, sounding smug. "You invaded her *me* space without permission." The tracker joined us on the porch and lifted a hand. A dead mouse dangled by its tail from his fingertips. "I brought you a gift."

"Um, well, okay." Gamely, I accepted the offering in the spirit it was meant. "Thank you, Thom."

"I found a nest of them near the back door." He tracked the

pendulum swing of the corpse and wet his lips. "I took care of them for you."

"I appreciate that." I lifted the mouse. "Would you like to, ah, take care of this one too?"

His gaze flicked up to mine. "You're not hungry?"

"No." Not at all. Not even a little bit. "I'm not big on breakfast."

"You're sure?" He waited until I nodded before shifting to his demon form, a boxy tomcat with midnight fur and a nubby tail. And wings. Can't forget those. His scarred face tilted up to me. "Mmmrrrrpt."

"There you go." I held it down until he took it delicately between his teeth. "Good boy."

Stub tail held high, Thom trotted off with the mouse swaying from his jaws.

"He's on patrol," Miller explained. "We're all safer with him far away from the nail gun. There was an . . . incident . . . when we were constructing the bunkhouse, and Thom is no longer allowed to operate power tools."

"I'll take your word on that." There was one member of the coterie who had yet to show his face, but I would rip out my own tongue and beat myself to death with it before asking about Cole in front of Santiago. "How much longer do you think?"

"An hour tops." Miller grabbed a thirty-gallon trashcan I hadn't seen before and started bagging debris. "We have a new client interview this afternoon in Ridgeland." He wiped his brow with his forearm. "We both need showers and fresh uniforms before then."

"How long did all this take?" I joined the cleanup effort. "I'm not usually such a heavy sleeper."

The crew I'd hired had quoted me thirty dollars an hour

plus the cost of cleanup and the dump fees. I could pull that from the ATM on my way to work and drop the money at the White Horse bunkhouse for Miller and Santiago to split. I would pay myself back out of the refund I got from the installers. Assuming they paid up, given the last-minute cancellation.

"We've been here about two hours." He shrugged. "Cole explained about last night."

That brought me up short. "What do you mean?"

"He was on Luce duty." Santiago filled in the blank, as though the information were a blade, and he knew just how to cut me with it. "He trailed you out to Hensarling Farms."

A snarl twitched Miller's lip up over his teeth, but the cat was already out of the bag, and I didn't mean Thom.

"This whole time?" I aimed the question at Santiago, the one most likely to give me the full truth since odds were good the delivery was going to hurt. "You guys have been rotating babysitting detail?"

"War is still out there." Santiago finished what he was doing and deigned to look up at me. "Famine is coming. Can't you read the signs? Desiccated animals? Burning crops?" His lips thinned. "You're worse than useless to us like this. You can't take care of yourself, and you can't protect us either. Of course we're watching your back. You should be thanking us, not taking us to task because we're doing our jobs."

"What is it you want from me, Santiago?" A cold spot blossomed in my chest. "Do you want Conquest back? Is that what this is about? Are you hoping you'll provoke me into a transformation that will end this world and us along with it?"

"No charun has captured Earth and held it," he informed me. "We aren't walking off this battlefield. The least we deserve is a choice in how we die."

"Santiago," Miller warned.

"No, let her hear this." Santiago stood with lethal grace. "Maybe not today, and maybe not tomorrow, but someday soon this shell of yours is going to crack. When that happens, people are going to die." He wiped globs of caulk from his fingertips with a paper towel he crumpled in his fist. "You aren't here to save this world. You're here to end it."

Miller grasped my hand, one of the few places I allowed contact, and I squeezed him back for all I was worth.

"I can't believe that," I rasped. "I won't believe it."

"You're Conquest—" Santiago began.

"No, I'm not." I released Miller to face Santiago on my own. "I'm well aware you all think I'm a construct, that I'm not real, that I shouldn't be treated as an actual person with thoughts and desires of my own. I get that, and I don't blame you, but I'm not giving up on me. Her ambitions are not mine, and I'm going to do everything in my power to hold onto my identity. So thank you for watching my back, and fuck you for being so ready to bury a knife between my shoulder blades."

For the first time since I'd met him, Santiago was rendered speechless.

Ever the peacemaker, Miller cleared his throat. "I think we should all—"

Santiago pivoted on his heel, hit the steps hard, and strode to the borrowed truck. He got in, cranked up, and spun gravel as he hightailed it onto the main road and out of sight.

I threw up my hands and watched him go. "And here I thought we were making progress."

"You are," Miller said on a sigh. "That's the problem. Hating you is easy. It's as reflexive as breathing. Liking you? Wanting to believe in you? Protect you—from yourself and what's coming? That's hard. Santiago doesn't know what to do with those feelings, and he's not the only one."

The remembered sensation of Cole's fingers in my hair tightened my lower stomach, and I jotted a quick mental note adding my name at the tip top of the list of people figuring out what the hell to do with their conflicting emotions.

"Wait. Let me get this straight." I flexed my toes on the porch someone had hosed clean. "You're saying Santiago passively hated me when we met, nothing personal, but now that he might like me, he actively hates me?"

Miller considered the quandary for a moment. "That about covers it."

I couldn't win with him. Could not win.

"I can finish up here if you need to go." Santiago had finished the exterior work down to the trim while he was sniping at me. "I promised to call Rixton first thing, and I owe Sherry lunch." I rubbed the base of my neck. "I need to call Uncle Harold too, let him know I'm better today." Sensing Miller's hesitation, I tossed in, "Thom can stay with me if he wants. He seems to be enjoying himself."

The cat in question was chasing a bumble bee through a patch of wildflowers. Not pouncing or stalking. He flew after the thing as it visited each cluster of white blossoms.

"All right." He left the trashcan for me. "I'll come back for the tools later. You can leave them on the porch."

With cement blocks filling the back-door slot and the bay window in place, I could actually lock the house for a change. "Hold that thought." I ducked inside and palmed a set of spare keys off the hook and twisted an extra house key free. "There you go." I pressed it into his hand. "I'll put the tools inside the front door. I'm still getting looky-loos who want to see where the super gator attacked." Vultures swooped past on occasion, but those tended to steal moments from my life, not machinery off my porch. "I wouldn't want them to run off with your equipment."

Miller closed his fingers around the key like it was solid gold and diamond-crusted. "Here." He reached in his pocket and returned the favor, removing a key from a black carabiner and offering it to me. "In case you ever want to come home."

The metal hit my palm, and my heart gave a squeeze as I made a fist around the small token of trust. "Thanks."

"Luce?"

"Hmm?"

"I'm sorry what I said earlier upset you." His lips twisted like he was tasting his next words before speaking. "I'm attempting to understand and respect your perspective on the coterie, but could you perhaps do the same?" His fingers traced the ribs of rose gold circling his throat. "Our bonds mean different things to each of us."

Miller had been born a nameless slave to a laundress in another world, another time. His father was a prince, and his father's wife had murdered Miller's mother when she learned of the woman's existence. Of his existence. Miller had exacted his revenge and lost himself to an unquenchable bloodlust. Conquest had slaked his thirst, called him to heel, and he had sworn fealty to her in thanks. He told me once that knowing Conquest could put him down if he crossed those lines again had saved his sanity, allowed him to heal. He cherished that bond between them, between *us*.

The core of what made me the person I am rebelled against what Conquest had done in allowing him to serve her, but he wasn't human, and the longer I applied those ideals and expectations to the members of my coterie, the harder this transition would be on all of us. Miller had told me himself he luxuriated in wearing a collar, but his leash had been slipping through my fingers the past fifteen years. Maybe it was time I picked up the slack. "Installing the window fulfilled that need for you?"

His knuckles whitened around the house key I had given him, and his voice came out raw. "Yes."

"What you and Santiago did for me with the bay window? That, to me, was an act of friendship." I struggled to articulate my thoughts. "Friendship is a type of bond too, right? It's a commitment you willingly make to another person. Friends do favors for one another, like you did today, and it's all good. There's no debt on either side. There's only the joy of offering a person who is important to you a token of your esteem." I extended my arm and waited for him to clasp hands with me. "This is my promise to you. I will be your friend, and you will be mine. We will protect each other, be honest with each other, and care for one another, and we will do these things of our own free will without obligation. And if one of us steps too close to the ledge, the other will pull them back, whatever it takes."

A hard breath gusted from his body as I reaffirmed the connection he craved. "Yes."

"I should make those calls." I squeezed his fingers one last time, the touch soothing him. I waited for the recoil to hit, for my palms to go sweaty, but the rest of my coterie, one by one, appeared to be wriggling through the crack Cole had smashed in my armor. "See you around?"

"You have my number." Serenity radiated from his very pores. "Call anytime."

Miller looked good with a grin crinkling his cheeks and his gray eyes, so often turbulent, softened in contentment. A scorched breeze rustled his usually tidy chestnut hair, and he reached up to brush it back into place with his fingers, mixing sawdust in with the dark strands. The urge to ruffle his bangs surfaced, a first for me, but I curled my fingers into my palm before I acted on the impulse. As the tallest member of the coterie, I would have to half-climb him to reach, and so far, only Mt. Heaton had inspired me to consider picking up that particular hobby.

"Shoo before you're late for your meeting." I flicked the broom at his feet. "Do you really want the client's first impression of White Horse to be Santiago's scowl?"

"Good point." He lifted his hand in a wave. "Later."

While he went to chat with Thom, who was sunning himself on the hood of the remaining truck, I finished balling up the scraps of paper and plastic, discarded the junk pieces of trim, and picked up a few stripped screws and bent nails. Miller was gone by the time I finished sweeping the porch clean, and Thom had moved on to climbing a tree on the opposite side of the yard. I left him mewling on a high limb, pleading with me to fetch him, but I hardened my heart. He would remember he had wings and that he could fly down. Eventually. Shaking my head at his antics, I jogged upstairs to find the second surprise of the day waiting for me.

CHAPTER FOUR

The rotary phone dented my pillow, its weight creasing the note pinned under its wide base. Ignoring the itch in my fingertips to snatch the paper and skim, I did the smart thing and completed a methodical search of my room before locking the door behind me and surrendering to my curiosity.

A rhythmic thudding filled my ears as I sank onto the mattress and tugged out a square of embossed stationery. The paper was heavy, the writing bold, and the message curt.

"This is your new phone," I read aloud. "Use it." Puzzled, I lifted the rotary phone and discovered a slim leather bifold case that opened to reveal a black metal cellphone the thickness of a credit card. There was no brand name, and powering it up gave no hints as to its service provider. "Curiouser and curiouser."

Briiiiiing.

A shocked gasp parted my lips as the display lit up with an incoming call.

Briiiiiing.

Cold sweat trickled between my shoulder blades, the bite of hope so hard it drew blood.

Ezra only ever called on my birthday. Today was not my birthday, and plenty of people used that ringtone. Even Cole had for a while after Santiago stole his cell for a prank. And yet . . .

Briiiiiing.

"Luce?"

The sudden boom of a masculine voice in the lull between rings startled me so hard the phone slid from my fingers and clattered to the floor. I spun toward the door, the *locked* door, and found Thom standing on the threshold. "How did you . . . ?"

"I picked the lock when you didn't answer." His nostrils flared as he sifted through the scents in the room for hints of what had me panicked. "I knocked several times."

"I didn't hear you." I tapped the note against my palm, and his eyes snapped to the paper. "I found this and that phone when I came upstairs. Someone broke into the house and entered my room while I was on the porch."

"May I?" Thom extended his hand for the note, and I passed it over for his inspection. He sniffed the edge of the paper then touched his tongue to the corner. "I recognize this scent." He glanced up at me. "Adam Wu."

"Wu was in here?" I swung my scowl around the room. "How did he get in?"

"I'm not sure." Thom hesitated with his palm above the phone, asking silent permission I was quick to grant him. "He touched this." A long inhale puffed out his chest. "No, not touched. He carried this with him for some time. Days." The edge of his lips curled. "The phone is brand new. I smell that too, the metallic burn of fresh circuitry. Wu marked this on purpose." His gaze traveled to the dent on my pillow. "He left this in your *me* space as a message."

A ball of dread formed in my gut. "What's the message?"

"That you're his." Thom hissed at the screen. "He's staking his claim."

"Is this a demon thing?" In my gut, that ball started bouncing. "He told me I was his new partner."

And that was about the time I started feeling ten kinds of stupid for not calling Kapoor to verify Wu's credentials.

"Perhaps," Thom allowed. "Without knowing his breed, it's impossible to say for sure."

"Give me a second." I held up a finger and dialed Kapoor on my cell while Thom returned the other to its spot on my pillow. He answered on the fourth ring. "Hey, I got a visit from an Adam Wu yesterday and—"

"*What?*"

Thom, who had no trouble hearing both sides of the conversation, winced at the near-shout.

"Adam Wu," I repeated. "He swung by my house."

A door clicked shut in the background on Kapoor's end, and a lock engaged. "What did he want?"

"Mostly? To remind me I have three weeks left before the NSB expects me to pay up on my end of our deal. He also wanted to introduce himself, seeing as how we're going to be partners."

"Partners," he echoed. "He told you that?"

"Yes, he did." I eyeballed the present he'd left me and wondered if Kapoor would apoplexy if I told him about that too. "Why do I get the feeling you had no clue about any of this? Aren't you my liaison with the taskforce?"

"This move is above my pay grade," he said, apology clear in his voice. "I'll have to make some calls to management and get back to you."

"What, exactly, is your pay grade?" This was the second time he'd palmed off big decisions on some nebulous higher authority. "Is there someone else I should be talking to about this? I have people depending on me, and all these half-ass answers aren't going to cut it."

"I'm not a small fish, Ms. Boudreau, but you seem to have landed a whale." Kapoor gusted out a sigh. "Wu is not under my jurisdiction. He works independently, and his position is fluid. Give me a day or so to track him down, and I'll get your answers."

Forget a day or so. I was dialing him up when this call ended. "What is he?"

Kapoor hesitated for so long, I wasn't sure he was going to answer. "I am not at liberty to discuss that."

"Of course not." I snorted. "What was I thinking? The right hand of any organization never knows what the left is doing. Why would this taskforce of yours be any different?"

I ended the call before Kapoor fed me another line.

"He came in through this window," Thom said from behind me. "His scent lingers in the wood." I turned as he tongued the dark stain. "This is an old scent." He glanced at me. "He's touched this wood many times over several visits." He shoved the window open and leaned outside, breathing deep. "The sash is the only exterior part of the window or house he touched, but its scent is multi-layered as well."

There was only one way a person got through a window without climbing. "You're saying he can fly."

Not a revelation considering at least two of the five members of my own coterie had wings.

"Yes." Thom rubbed his nose as though it tickled. "I can't identify his breed, but I have catalogued the scent. I will know it if we come across it again in another charun." Had he shifted, his stub of a tail would have been twitching. "Wu is something new, something we have never encountered."

"How is that possible?" By their own admission, the worlds below had all been conquered.

"I'm not sure." He stared out the window, up at the sky, and removed a phone from his pocket. "I must tell Cole."

"I have calls I can't put off any longer too." I checked the time and grimaced. "Would you mind giving me some privacy?"

Thom stepped out, dialing as he went, and I heard his footsteps on the stairs as I started down the list. I texted Rixton and then Sherry, and then I pinged Uncle Harold before calling the Trudeau landline and speaking to Aunt Nancy about Dad, whose condition hadn't changed overnight. She was quick to assure me he hadn't noticed my absence, but that didn't exactly give me a case of the warm fuzzies.

After we finished chatting, I took a quick shower to fix the hot mess my hair had become overnight and dressed in jeans and a long-sleeved tee that wouldn't suffocate me before padding downstairs barefoot.

Thom was nowhere in sight, and I needed to get a move-on, so I walked out onto the porch to search for him. "Thom?"

No answer.

"Thomas?"

Still no response.

I slid on flip-flops and hit the yard. I didn't have to go far. He was sitting in the same patch of frilly white flowers where he'd been chasing bees earlier. I circled around to get in front of him, jerking to a stop at his glazed expression. His phone rested across his palm, his fingers open, and a deep voice boomed from the speaker. I knelt and scooped up the cell, pressing it against my ear.

"Hey, it's Luce." I winced as Cole geared up for another bellow. "I'm here with Thom. Do you have any idea what happened to him?"

"He was updating me on the situation with Wu, but he started slurring his words then stopped talking altogether."

"He looks dazed." I pressed the back of my hand against his forehead and his cheek, and he pushed into the touch. "He's running a low-grade fever." Contact must have broken through to him on some level. He lay back in the grass and rolled from side to side a few times, a purr rumbling in his throat. Eyes fixed on me, he curled around me, rubbing his chin over my hip like he was marking me with the scent glands cats have below their jaws. Not the most comfortable sensation in the world, but I could manage. For him. Words in that foreign language they all spoke poured from his lips, and then he laughed. Once he started, he couldn't control the manic burst of amusement. "Um, correction. He's not dazed. He's high as a kite."

"Wait there," Cole ordered. "I'll be there in ten."

Ten minutes turned out to be more along the lines of five. I was unable to stand as the bone-white dragon landed in the front yard, due to the man curled around my hips, milking my thigh with the claws tipping his fingers, but my entire being snapped to attention at his arrival. The beast swiveled his rounded ears, and his crimson eyes narrowed on Thom. His whiplike tail thrashed at his side, its barbed end striking far too close for my comfort. His white mane stood on end, framing his lion's face, and he angled his branching antlers toward Thom.

"Cole." I scooted forward to shield Thom as best I could from the ornery dragon. "He needs your help."

The great creature shook his head once as if to clear it, and then he surrendered to the change that left me sitting before an equally irritated man, one that caused heat to pool low in my gut. "Get his hands off you."

I made no move to comply. It wasn't like Thom was doing anything wrong. He was clearly not in his right mind.

I was starting to think he wasn't the only one.

"*Now*," Cole roared with a ferocity that kicked my pulse up about a million notches. "Or I will do it myself."

I jumped to unwind from Thom, who had tuckered himself out and started snoring, and marched over to Cole. "What is your problem?" I shoved him, the contact a dropped match in a puddle of gasoline, and my palms itched from wanting to do it again, to savor his heart pounding wild beneath my hands. "He didn't do anything wrong."

The cold smile lifting Cole's lips promised murder. "He. Touched. You."

I was about to snatch a knot in his metaphorical tail when the cold place crashed into me without warning, dumping ice water over my libido. Something was wrong was me, with him, with Thom, but what? As my head cleared, I examined the area for clues, but only one thing caught my eye.

Lacy petals clung with bees, their sweet perfume a tickle in my nose.

"The flowers." Cole had landed feet away from where Thom had collapsed. "I think we've got a problem." Cole clamped his hands on my hips. "Okay," I squeaked when the hard length of him pressed into my lower stomach, and he thrust once. "We've got a *big* problem."

The husky chuckle threading through Cole's voice did terrible things for my self-control.

"Why don't we take this to the porch?" I wiggled in his grip, which, yeah, probably not my smartest move. His pained groan ignited fresh sparks below my belt. I had to think fast, and then it hit me. "You don't want Thom to see us, do you?" I rested my hand on the flat expanse of his chest. "You don't want to share me with him, do you?"

"*Mine*," he snarled an inch from the tip of my nose. "You belong to me, Luce."

Giddiness swirled through me when he spoke my name. *Mine*. Not hers.

The reckless urge to close the gap between our mouths rocked me forward onto the balls of my feet, his lips one bad decision away from mine. A growl was pumping through his chest, and his grip on my hips turned bruising. The sharp bite of pain heightened the burn until I was ready to go up in flames with him.

The glacier coldness in his eyes stung with their intensity. "Tell me I can have you."

Tell him, as in we were locked in a stalemate until I granted him permission to take this to the next level.

But was the plea one from a man who craved the woman with him? Or from a slave to his mistress?

I didn't know, and since I couldn't tell, I withdrew and sucked in air until my ovaries stopped threatening spontaneous combustion.

Maybe I shouldn't be standing out here either. My grasp on the cold place was always tenuous at best.

"Let's talk about this on the porch." I backed away from Thom, from the field, and Cole stalked after me. "Here." I patted the top step. "You sit right here and I'll go—" I yelped as he yanked me onto his lap. "Okay. This works too."

While Cole nuzzled me, his teeth plucking at the tender skin of my throat, I slid my cell from my pocket and texted Miller with 911. Generic, yes, but he was a smart one ... and crap. He was also supposed to be meeting with Santiago and an out-of-town client this afternoon. Too late to untext him now. That meant it was up to me to figure out how to diffuse the situation, and there was only one quick fix I could think of for a guy in his condition.

"You know what really gets me hot?" I leaned in close and whispered in his ear. "The chase."

A crimson sheen covered his eyes when he drew back to look at me. "Yes."

The little bit I'd gleaned about demons and their feral sides had convinced me the primal hunt for a mate would rev his engine the same as any animal.

Thank you, Discovery Channel.

"Why don't you give me a five-minute head start?" I eased out of his grip. "And then you can chase me."

He caught me by the wrist and anchored me beside him. "I can have you if I catch you?"

Only one answer was unlocking the manacle around my wrist. "Yes."

"Then go." He released me and leaned back, resting his elbows on the porch, giving me an eyeful of the tent he was sporting in his pants. "Run."

He didn't have to tell me twice.

I bolted across the yard, hating to leave Thom unprotected, and hit the tree line seconds later. I pumped my legs as fast as I could, but I was human-slow, and Cole was demon-fast. I wasn't kidding myself that I would win this race. The best I could hope for was luring him away from Thom while using the exertion to burn through the drugging effect of those flowers on him.

No clock was required to inform me when my time was up, a roar that silenced the forest blasted out from the general direction of my house, and my heart attempted to spring from my throat and scurry to safety. Thirty seconds later, I heard limbs snapping, heavy breathing, and punishing footfalls.

I almost sagged with relief when I spotted the stream up ahead and cut a hard right to follow its path. *Almost there.* Panic lent me speed, and I kicked it up a notch until the scenery blurred around me while I ran hell-bent for leather.

Cole paced me so close his exhales painted the back of my neck. His hands brushed my sides, seconds from plucking me off my feet, but it was too late. We had arrived. With a triumphant yell, I hit the crumbling edge of a ravine and leapt, pinwheeling my arms all the way down into the deep basin of the small spring-fed pond.

Icy water closed over my head and stole my breath, shocking me from the cold place. I was already swimming toward the shallows when the entire pond exploded outward as Cole cannonballed into the center. I had a handful of mud, was hauling myself onto shore, when his arms clamped around my middle and hauled me back against the furnace of his body. The sad thing was, under different circumstances, this might have been the singularly most erotic event of my entire life.

"Okay," I panted through the stitch in my side. "You win."

The spell broke with an almost audible snap as his sharp exhale whistled past my ear, and Cole rested his forehead on my left shoulder. "I don't know what came over me."

All that delicious heat flushing my skin from the run, the sting of his teeth, the strength of his arms, snuffed out in a blink as confirmation he hadn't wanted this, hadn't wanted me, pelted my ego like hail in a late summer storm.

"It wasn't your fault." I didn't move for fear of startling him. "Thom was acting odd today, but I didn't put it together until I found him on the phone with you. There are wildflowers in that corner of the yard, weeds mostly. We don't mow that area.

I don't know what all's growing there, but I think we need to find out."

We lingered there a moment longer while Cole sank back into his skin, and then he released me, the rush of cold water chilling after his warmth. We trudged out onto the muddy shore together and started toward home. I stepped on a rock and hissed out a curse but kept going. It was one of many aches and stings in my soles I had been able to ignore up to this point. I could last a while longer.

"You're not wearing shoes." Cole glowered at my toes like they were each personally to blame. "It's my fault you're out here barefoot. I could carry you back."

"Nah." More contact with him would be like splashing alcohol in an open wound. "It's not too far. Besides, I roamed these woods as a kid and survived. I came down here every day during the summers to swim. Maggie and I would . . . " A fist clenched around my heart. "We used to jump from that exact spot to see who could make the biggest splash. Dad almost had a coronary the first time he caught us. He actually hired a local contractor to deepen the basin so we wouldn't break our necks."

"You miss her."

"I do."

"She might not come back the way you remember."

"I know."

"She might not come back at all."

"I know that too."

That was it, the entire conversation. It was nothing fancy. No depths were plumbed. No souls bared. Just a string of bald statements uttered on both sides. He didn't cast blame on me, and I didn't volunteer my guilt. Yet somehow those few lines from him accomplished what Miller, through no fault of his own, had failed to do.

Cole absolved me, not for my decision, only Maggie could do that, but for making the only call I could live with afterward.

The problem with Cole was the man was built like a mountain, and all that strength made me view him as a rock, steadfast in the turbulent seas of my awakening. I wanted to cling to him. God how I wanted him to save me from myself. But I was learning that stones, even the mightiest of them, sank under enough weight. And I was not going to be what pushed his head under the water. Not this time.

This time, I would learn how to swim. This time, after my sisters were defeated, I would set Cole free.

And may God have mercy on me. I was certain Cole would show none.

CHAPTER FIVE

The walk back took forever thanks to the awkward silence that thickened the air until breathing hurt. I led Cole onto the porch and parked him in my rocker, which groaned a complaint as his weight settled. I kept a wary eye on him for a good ten minutes while I picked tiny rocks from the gashes on my feet and plucked hateful splinters from between my toes, but the most adverse reaction he showed was in response to the bloody footprints I left behind on my way to rinse my feet in the downstairs tub before pulling on socks and shoes. With that done, and my feet much happier, I hit the single car garage Dad used as a workshop. I palmed the respirator he used when sanding projects, popped in fresh cartridges, and strapped it on before rejoining Cole.

"Here's the plan." I made the necessary adjustments to get a tight seal around my nose and mouth. "I'm going to attempt to drag Thom to the faucet at the side of the house. The hose is in the garage." Had it already been connected, I could have saved myself the hassle of sprinting for my life. "Can you hook it up for me and then get out of Dodge?"

"I don't like this," he said, the muscles in his jaw popping, "but you seem to have the most immunity to its effects. We can't risk me going off the rails again. Next time you might not make it to that pond."

I wasn't sure immunity was the right word, but I had shaken it off faster than him.

"I got this." I smiled before remembering he couldn't see my mouth. "I'll get out the second I have an issue if the mask can't filter out the pollen or spores or whatever."

With a scowl tightening his features, he stalked off to handle his part of the plan while I braved the walk over to Thom. The plants hadn't affected me until Cole showed signs, as best as I could tell, but I was honest enough with myself to admit I wasn't convinced it wasn't his desire that had stoked my own to blistering heights, with or without the plant's help. Cole all hot and bothered . . .

Mercy.

Shaking those thoughts out of my head, I got back down to business.

Thom hadn't so much as twitched from what I could tell. I watched the rise and fall of his chest while giving Cole a moment to connect the hose and me a chance to test the mask while in close proximity to patient zero. A shrill whistle split the air, and I glanced back as Cole sank into his chair, his hands gripping the armrests until I cringed in sympathy.

It's go time.

"Okay, Thom. Up you go." I nudged him onto his back, hooked my arms under his armpits, and started dragging. "You're a lot heavier than you look." Awake he was all elbows and knees. "Maybe you should lay off the mice."

I was panting hard by the time I reached the faucet, but I hadn't experienced the urge to go rub myself against Cole's leg, so the mask was doing its job. Once I had Thom rearranged, I twisted on the faucet and readied the sprayer. A powerful blast of icy water shot from the end when I pulled the trigger, and I aimed right for Thom's face. The effect was instantaneous.

A mighty yowl ripped from his lips, and he jolted upright spluttering and hissing.

Considering how far under he'd gone, I showed no mercy and hosed down the rest of him until he was soaked to the bone and glaring at me in the way cats had that convinced you they were plotting your bloody murder. Water dripped into his eyes and plinked onto his lap off his chin. He looked utterly miserable.

Thom shook a hand through his soggy hair, spraying droplets. "Was that necessary?"

"'Fraid so." I killed the water. "It worked on Cole, so I figured it would work on you too."

"Cole is here?" He lifted his chin and sniffed the air, his head swinging in my direction. "I see."

"No." I thanked the mask for hiding the heat in my cheeks. "You really don't."

Thom swayed as he stood, and his jaw cracked on a yawn. "How long was I out?"

"A half hour or so?" I walked him to the front porch. "Cole will fill you in on what you missed while I collect samples." A storm cloud gathered in Cole's expression as we approached, proving he had heard me, but I ignored the far-off rumble. "We need answers, and I'm in the best position to get them. Can you make arrangements with your lab to get the specimens tested?"

"Yes." He palmed his cell. "We can drop off the materials tomorrow on our way to Ludlow."

Ludlow? Oh, yeah. Right. Our demon hunting expedition kicked off in the morning. Fun times.

White Horse had better equipment than what the department issued us, but the thing about winged demons was they tended to rocket into the air first and ask questions later. That meant using what I had in the trunk of my Bronco instead of the tricked-out kit stowed in his black SUV.

Uncertain what exactly in this corner of the yard was sending our demonic natures into hyperdrive, I bagged soil samples, entire plants, and even scraped bark off the tree where Thom had gotten himself stuck.

About the time I was done sealing the plastic baggies, we had company. A black SUV barreled down the driveway and ejected Miller and Santiago. They took one look at me and started in my direction, but I threw up a hand and stopped them in their tracks. I stabbed the air in Cole's direction, and Santiago hooked an arm around Miller's shoulders before giving his stomach a firm pat and leading him onto the porch.

While they got current on events, I filled an old cooler with the samples, loaded it into my Bronco, and wiped down the areas I had touched. I popped the used cartridges off the respirator, making a mental note to grab spares, but left the mask in the trunk. To avoid teeing off another round of hot flashes, I circled to the back of the house and gave myself a cold shower with the hose before sloshing my way back to where the others had congregated.

Cole prowled toward me. "How are you feeling?"

The driving urge to play adrenaline junkie and climb Mt. Heaton without a harness had yet to resurface. Well, no more than usual. "Normal."

"Thom." Cole waved the medic over to me. "Check her out."

I submitted to a quick exam then waited to hear the results.

"Her eyes are dilated," he murmured, nostrils flaring. "There is a subtle trace of desire, but it's nothing like the aphrodisiacal response you described."

Mortification ignited my cheeks into flamethrowers. So paranormal romances had gotten that tidbit right. Great. Just peachy. "I'm going up to my room, where I'm going to die of humiliation."

Halfway up the stairs, I had an attack of paranoia and ducked into the downstairs bathroom, where I bagged up the clothes I had worn in the field then took another shower just to be on the safe side. In my rush to put a locked door between me and the knowledge each of them had known every time I looked at Cole and had a dirty thought, I hadn't remembered to grab fresh clothes.

The rap of heavy knuckles on the door felt like someone driving nails into my coffin.

There was no question in my mind who waited for me. Only one person would have followed me after I made it clear I wanted to be left alone, and I bet he planned on giving me an earful. That was kind of our thing. I did anything—breathed, spoke, blinked—and he bellowed at me for having the gall to exist.

Figuring I might as well face the music, I opened the door wearing a ratty, blue bathrobe.

"I'm having trouble making eye contact with you right now." The wall behind his head was looking good, though. "Can we do this later? When I have on more clothes?"

"I take it as a compliment," he rumbled over my head, his voice booming in the tight space, rolling like thunder off in the distance.

A compliment. *Ouch*. Talk about getting parked in the friend-zone. Better than him wanting to bleach out his nostrils, but still. Yeah. *Ouch*.

"I need to get dressed." I shuffled past him. "I promised Sherry I would visit her today, and I would like to drop in on Dad too before I head to work."

"All right." He held his ground and allowed me to retreat. "Be ready to leave at eight."

"Sure." I kept addressing my toes. "See you then."

Closing my bedroom door behind me had never felt so good, and that was saying a lot considering all the times I had slammed it after fighting with Dad over teenage drama. Some things never changed it seemed. My hormones were right back to getting me in trouble.

The black phone sat undisturbed on my pillow, and I eyed it warily like it might sprout fangs and bite me. I woke it and checked the contacts. There was only one number saved. No name. I scrolled through the call log and found the call I had missed earlier. No surprise, it matched the digits from its address book.

I almost hit redial just to give myself an excuse to vent, but Wu was an unknown, and I wouldn't live long if I poked too many bears without first filing down their teeth. That decision made, I left the phone behind and dressed for work. I had a couple hours left to burn, but I would rather run my errands in uniform than come back home to change.

Downstairs, all was quiet. The coterie had vacated the premises, and I sent up a prayer of thanks I didn't have to endure a walk of shame to reach the Bronco. I checked to ensure the cooler was secure then headed into town.

The visit with Dad wouldn't take long. Our interactions never did these days, so I made the Rixtons my first stop.

I pulled into their driveway and turned off the Bronco. The engine was still ticking when my phone rang, and I answered as Rixton stepped out of his house. He was dressed for work too, and the sight of him wearing his cop face on the front steps of his home chilled my blood. I still held the phone to my ear, like the filter of technology might soften the blow of whatever news he was about to deliver.

"We've got another victim. Same MO. This time off Hart Road."

"The Culberson cattle ranch." Uncle Harold had lost a bet on the Super Bowl three years ago and paid up in the form of an entire side of beef that Dad and I had to haul from the farm to the freezer. "It's a small operation. They do everything in-house, and there's a farm-to-fork restaurant on the premises."

"Leave the Bronco in the drive." He slid behind the wheel of the cruiser. "I'll bring you home with me after work."

The trip out to Culberson's took about twelve minutes. We spotted the thick, black smoke long before we hit the dirt road leading up to the pasture. Cattle huddled together in the corner of the fence nearest the road, their eyes white with terror, and their screams punching through the blare of the siren. Two gangly teen boys, probably the owners' kids, worked to separate individual cows from the herd and then load them onto a waiting trailer.

"Stop the car," I barked at Rixton when we got even with them. "Shut that gate, boys. I'm radioing in for backup. You can't handle that many cattle alone. It's too dangerous."

"This is our livelihood." The taller one stiffened, his chin jerking high. "We have to save what we can."

"I agree." I stared him down. "Starting with your own skins."

"She's right, Hank." The other boy hooked his arm around the tall boy's shoulders. "We gotta be smart about this, bro. Mom and Dad have enough to worry about." He nodded at me. "We'll wait, ma'am."

"Good call." Rixton keyed up the radio so I could call in the promised backup. "Those kids are brave, but there's a thin line between brave and stupid."

I finished the call and was ready to hit the ground running when we parked in front of the roaring bonfire that used to be a sprawling plantation-style home. A portion of the downstairs had been dedicated to the family restaurant and other business pursuits while the living quarters were upstairs. None of it would survive. I read it plainly on the faces of the firemen working to keep the blaze from spreading to the western fields. The eastern fields, where the trapped cattle bellowed for salvation, was being devoured on the whims of the breeze.

Three men and a woman dressed in jeans and matching tees looked on with grief in their eyes. The oldest of the group, a man of around forty, noticed us and limped over to offer his hand.

"I'm Peter Culberson." He favored his left side, but I could tell the EMTs had been and gone thanks to the missing lower leg of his jeans and the bright bandage wrapping his shin. "Guess you're here to talk about Boris Ivashov."

Rixton handled the introductions then asked, "Is he the arsonist?"

"Yeah." The man ruffled his hair. "I guess." He shook his head. "I can't believe he did this. He's been with us for years." He glanced up, a hint of shock dulling his eyes. "You think you know someone, right?"

Telling him you could never truly know another person was counterproductive, so I shepherded him back on topic. "Where is Mr. Ivashov?"

"They took him to Madison Memorial." He shifted his weight, grimaced. "He's in bad shape. I'd be shocked if he survived the night." He scanned the fields around us through bleak eyes. "Hell, I'd be impressed if they got him there alive in the first place."

Despite the wall of heat roasting my cheeks, I shivered with the knowledge we would have to stop by the hospital at some point, assuming the man survived. "Can you tell us what happened?"

"We're trying out a new lunch menu, so the restaurant was open earlier than usual. I was in the back with our chef when customers started screaming. I ran into the dining room in time to see Boris smash out the front window with the butt of a drip torch, one of those metal canister deals we use for controlled burns on the back forty." Mr. Culberson rubbed his face with the heels of his palms. "He set fire to the tablecloths first, and once the customers started scattering, he got serious about lighting up the tables and chairs.

"We focused on distracting Boris long enough for everyone to clear the building, but he got riled up when he lost his audience and started chasing folks to their cars. I took a shovel and beat him back, but it was like he didn't feel it." A harsh chuckle moved through him. "Guess I did my job a little too well. He started running after me then. Scared me so bad the way he was waving that torch around, I tripped over my own damn feet and fell through a busted-out window. I got my shin cut up pretty good, but I've had worse. Working on a farm, we've all had worse. I got out of there, but Boris walked right into the house, sat down at one of the tables like he was waiting to be served, and didn't budge until one of the firemen hauled him to safety."

"Thanks for your time, Mr. Culberson," Rixton said, ending the interview. "I hope you make a speedy recovery."

"I'm glad no one else was hurt," I added. "You were all very lucky."

"Tell me about it." He looked back at the others. "We're all alive. That's what matters. We can always rebuild."

The others corroborated Mr. Culberson's version of events. We chatted up the fireman responsible for hauling Ivashov out, and he confirmed the victim had been ready to sit at his table until the flesh melted from his bones. He didn't put up a fight until the fireman made it clear he wasn't leaving him to finish roasting.

According to his co-workers, Ivashov exhibited no signs of depression and had expressed no suicidal thoughts. His rampage had been an unintelligible litany of snarls and growls, so no light bulb moment there, either.

Hours later, after the fire had been contained, Rixton and I got in the car and hit a fast food joint. We parked and let the car idle while we crammed burgers and fries into our faces then washed down all the delicious grease with cold milkshakes too thick for our straws.

"We need a make and model on those drip torches." I swirled a salty fry through my chocolate shake then popped it in my mouth. "We also need to find out if there's any connection between Boris Ivashov and Les Rowland."

"Or between the Hensarlings and the Culbersons," he added. "I can't see a tie between cotton and cattle, but there might be overlap on the administrative side or a less obvious link."

"Loans through the same bank." I picked up his thought process. "Policies through the same insurance company."

"Speaking of insurance companies." He slurped on his strawberry malt. "How did your chat go with the suit? Any progress on your claim?"

"The chat was about as much fun as you'd expect." Understatement of the year. "No word yet on when or if they'll be cutting us a check. Apparently, when they wrote up our policy, no one paused to consider the need to hammer out the verbiage for a super gator clause."

Rixton grunted an acknowledgement, or maybe he'd just given himself an ice cream headache.

"No one could have seen that one coming." His frown drilled into the oncoming darkness beyond the windshield. "My guy at MDWFP says they have yet to locate a super gator in the wild. The tracks and slides are all old. Folks got curious and hit the water searching for them, but there have been no civilian sightings either. The general consensus seems to be that Super Gator Fever flushed the beasts from their homes out into the Mississippi."

"Gators on the river, even ones that size, could be anywhere by now." The lie fell from my lips with ease that shamed me. Keeping Rixton in the dark was the smart thing to do, I had no doubts on that score, but I hated withholding information that might one day protect him and his family. "It wouldn't hurt my feelings if I never saw another one."

Too bad the odds of that happening were zero.

War might have beaten a strategic retreat, but she was far from defeated.

"Unit four-one-six." The radio fuzzed to life. "We received a 911 call from a driver involved in a single car accident on Peace Street. Emergency services are en route."

"We'll be there in five," I told dispatch while cramming our trash into its original paper bag. "We can clean up this mess then head back to the station. We need to pull everything we've got on the Hensarlings and the Culbersons. I'll take the Culberson file with me, and you can have the Hensarlings. I could use the reading material on the drive tomorrow."

I bit my tongue, but it was too late to call back the words. Exhaustion had made me slip up and bad.

"A drive, huh?" He threw the car into gear and spun out on the street. "Where are you headed?" I'm not sure what he saw from the corner of his eye, but it had him cackling with glee. "Or am I not asking the right question? *Who* are you heading there with? *Who* is freeing you up to read?"

"You sound like a damned owl."

"Owls are wise, and they also deliver acceptance letters to kids who get into witchcraft and wizardry school. I'll take it." He waggled his eyebrows. "Now about this drive . . ."

Cole was the obvious answer to the real question Rixton was asking. He'd met Cole, and thanks to him defending my honor against that photog turd Moses Franke in Hannigan's, more than a few of our coworkers assumed we'd had a fling during the Claremont case. But I wasn't up to the scrutiny while I still sported bandages on my toes from my sprint through the woods.

"I'll let you know if things get serious" sounded like an ideal compromise.

"My BS senses are tingling." He tapped the side of his nose. "You're being evasive. That means you know I won't approve, which means I've met him or I know of him." His hands tightened on the wheel. "Tell me you're not seeing Heaton."

"Cole and I are not dating." That much was the God's honest truth. "Stop fishing. You're not going to catch anything."

"Oh, Bou-Bou," he lamented. "I trained you. I molded you in my image. I am the process behind every thought you have. That air current swirling under your pits? It's not the vents. That's me. I am the wind beneath your wings."

"Do you hear yourself?" I twisted in my seat. "Does what you just said make any sense to you? I'm honestly curious if what I'm hearing is actually what you think you're saying."

"The point is this—" A solid minute lapsed during which I wondered if he had forgotten his point, or if he had ever known it in the first place. "You have insulted my powers of deductive reasoning, and for that you must be punished."

"Let me guess." I saw where this was heading. "Punishment involves you discovering who I'm going out with and exposing me, probably in a public forum. Let's say the breakroom. Probably after you've chummed the waters with a dozen cherry-flavored jelly donuts to ensure your audience is primed to chomp at all the juicy details."

On a slow news day, my love life was worth a column and obligatory grainy photo in the local paper. Most guys didn't enjoy seeing their private business splashed across the gossip pages, particularly when the articles insinuated they were dating a cryptid, but the few who caught a thrill got booted before the ink dried.

"Aww." Rixton mimed wiping away tears. "You flatter me, but no. I would never waste a dozen donuts on breakroom letches who were only in it for the sugar. I will, however, unmask your boyfriend in front of my wife, who will do the rest of my dirty work for me. Name, description, likes, dislikes, the whole shebang."

The unspoken chastisement that I would even kid about him outing me in any way etched frown lines on either side of his mouth. The only person who hated vultures more than me was Rixton.

Misery swelled behind my breastbone until the pressure shot bolts of agony straight through my heart.

How was I going to tell him I was quitting? How was I going to justify my choice without getting into the whole *I'm a demon with badass, world-ending sisters out to wipe your species off the planet* specifics? And if he pushed me for details, well . . . yeah, Detective. How was I going to admit that as horrific as that sounded, I had brought them here?

CHAPTER SIX

❦

As much as I wanted to head home at the end of my shift, that had Bad Idea written all over it. Even if Wu hadn't issued himself an open invitation into my bedroom, which was damn creepy considering how often the house had sat unoccupied during the last week, leaving him free to rummage through the debris of my life, there was still the mystery of the plants to solve. I didn't have much pride left after this morning, but I wasn't about to risk stumbling through the yard in the dark and contracting another round of the *come to mammas*. Once I got hot and bothered, I had no doubt who my lust would target. I could imagine how well that conversation would go if I wound up sweating it out on his doorstep.

So, Cole, I get that Conquest enslaved you, slaughtered your people, and laid waste to your empire, but do you think I could rub against you for a little while? Just until my skin stops itching? What's that? You can't actually tell me no because of the whole enslavement thing? So I can use your back like a scratching post or nah?

No. Just no. Me and my libido were not his problem.

Far safer for me to head back to the Trudeaus' where I could check in on Dad. Bunking with my uncle guaranteed tomorrow's pickup would be awkward since White Horse had left town as far as he knew, but the location would protect the coterie from exposure. If my desire had been a thread, Cole's had been a noose cinched around my throat, choking off all oxygen except for what he allowed me. I wouldn't put him through that again.

Air mattress it is.

"Earth to Bou-Bou." Rixton waved a hand in front of my face, drawing my attention to the fact we were parked in his driveway. "Are you coming inside to see the missus?" He jabbed me in the ribs with his elbow. "We can order pizza. Watch a movie." He licked his pinky finger then smoothed his eyebrows. "You can babysit while Sherry and I—"

"I can't be in the same house as you while you're doing . . . that." I slapped my hands over my ears. "I have a long day ahead of me, and I don't need the nightmares."

"That's right," he mouthed in front of me. "You have a date tomorrow."

Me and my big mouth. "Say it with me: *scenic drive.*" While hunting for cat-mummifying demons. "Natchez Trace Parkway is gorgeous this time of year." I lowered my hands in defeat. "You should take your girls on a picnic or something."

He fluttered his eyelashes at me. "Is that an invitation to join you?"

"The fall colors won't be out in full force until mid-October," I countered sweetly. "For maximum romance, you should wait until then."

His eyes almost vanished in their crinkles. "So you admit it's romantic."

"I'm out." I left him to choke on his smugness and got in my Bronco. "What the—?" I reached under my butt and pulled out a thin piece of metal. "You've got to be kidding me." Self-conscious as all get-out, I inhaled the way Thom always seem to be doing, but I didn't pick up any peculiar scents. I sniffed the phone itself, feeling ten kinds of stupid, but all I picked up was leather from the bifold. "So much for my demonic super powers."

A rap on the glass startled me into dropping the thing in the floorboard. I cranked the engine and lowered the window while Rixton gave me an expectant look I couldn't interpret. "What?"

"Are you having second thoughts about—" he winked four or five times in a row "—you know?"

"Helping you get laid?" Jabbing the button, I waited until the glass almost sealed before chirping, "Nope."

"You're a cold woman, Boudreau." He clutched his chest. "Dare I say heartless?"

"What?" I cupped a hand around one ear. "Did you say something? I can't hear you."

The porch light flicked on, and I spotted Sherry moving behind the window. If I wanted to make a clean getaway, this was my only chance. I tossed a wave at Rixton, put the Bronco in gear, then backed out faster than Sherry could take the stairs while also pretending not to see her. A low move, yes, but she would talk my ear off if I let her, and I wanted a little quiet time to gather my thoughts before bed.

Briiiiiing.

I sucked in air through my front teeth while my heart slammed against my ribs, a Pavlovian response that made my fingers itch for the rotary phone on my nightstand. Not answering was next to impossible. Had the cell not been sliding beneath my feet, I would have caved to years of conditioning.

Briiiiiing.

Of all the ringtones in all the apps in all the world, Wu had to select that one.

The tang of copper in my mouth was the first sign I had let my anxiety gnaw a layer of skin off my bottom lip. Cursing a blue streak, I turned in to the first fast food chain I spotted and scooped up the silent phone. This time I hit redial before my brain caught up with my thumb.

"How did you know?" I demanded the second he answered. "Who told you about the ringtone?"

Wu chuckled in my ear. "Who do you think?"

The phone cut into my fingers, but I couldn't seem to loosen them. "How do you know him?"

"It's a small world."

Compared to my world as of a week ago? This new world of demons and infinite hells was freaking endless. "Does he work for the NSB too?"

Wu let the silence do the heaving lifting for him.

Yet another thing he had in common with Ezra.

"Answer me, or I'm taking a hammer to this cell when I get where I'm going. I'll do the same to the next one and the next one and the next one until I find you and shove the carrot you're dangling in front of my nose straight down your throat."

"Why does he matter so much to you?"

I clamped my mouth shut until my raw lips tingled and numbed from the pressure.

"Show me yours," he coaxed, "and I'll show you mine."

"I used to think he had all the answers, that he knew me, okay?" For the longest time, some small corner of my heart had been convinced I mattered to him. Why else call? Why else make a connection? Why else spare me the agony that pressed in on me every year on my birthday? Without his intervention, I clawed at the unquenchable itch like I might rake the skin from my bones and reveal what lurked beneath. Only Ezra could stay my hand, his voice more soothing than calamine lotion. "I want to look him in the eyes, put a face to the name, at least once. He owes me that much. I deserve an explanation."

"An explanation for what?" Wu's curiosity burned. "What is it you think he owes you?"

"Ask him."

Fifteen years' worth of phone calls, and all I had was a name. *Ezra*. Maybe I ought to come clean to my coterie. They were my best source of information, and their lives were directly tied to mine. They had no reason to lie to me. Not about something that affected my health and wellbeing, my ability to fight.

Except . . . What if they did know about my condition? We were still feeling each other out at this stage. They might be withholding critical information that could be wielded against me in the event I turned on them, and I couldn't blame them for wanting to protect themselves if that was the case.

Miller had sold me on one point. Living with your inner demon's potential for destruction was easier when someone else held your leash.

As much as I wanted answers, I would content myself with discovering them on my own to protect the coterie and any secrets they carried. Ignorance was a flimsy protection, but it was all I could offer them. The potential for them to rally and take me down was a comfort. And, I had to admit, I was curious.

Ezra wasn't a member of my coterie. The math didn't support him belonging to War either. Had she breached during those early years, bringing him with her, I had no doubt she would have killed me after discovering my defect. Yet he nursed me through those inexplicable pains rather than letting me suffer alone.

Following that logic, my mystery caller must be enrolled in the NSB's demon program. As close as Kapoor claimed they watched me, there was no way those calls had gone unnoticed all these years, meaning Ezra had to be a remnant from an earlier cadre or the descendant of one.

That made him old, dare I say an antique, but if he was registered with the NSB, there must be a paper trail to follow once I got inside and gained access to their records.

Well, what do you know? This put a new shine on the deal Kapoor made me.

"Be careful tomorrow." Wu yanked me from my thoughts. "Ubaste might be lower charun, but they're still vicious."

Weren't we all? "I didn't know you cared."

"I want you in one piece when they turn you over," he said, "otherwise you're useless to me."

At least he was honest. "Thanks for the pep talk."

"Anytime." I heard his grin. "Remember your phone next time."

"About that—"

He hung up on me before I could read him the riot act.

I really had to work on my people skills.

I made it to the Trudeaus' just after Uncle Harold had left for work, so Aunt Nancy was still up and about. Dad was on the couch dressed in fresh clothes and staring at the same spot on the wall. After a quick shower, I joined Aunt Nancy for cookies and milk in the kitchen then sat with Dad through a documentary on a pod of dolphins who had circled an endurance swimmer for over an hour to protect him from the jaws of an intrigued shark.

"Time for bed." I killed the TV and shuffled Dad into Uncle

Harold's recliner while I folded out the sleeper sofa. Tucking him in was the work of minutes, and I left him with a bottle of cold water on the coffee table and a goodnight kiss. "Love you, Daddy."

"Love you too," he said, his stare drifting toward the ceiling. "Baby girl."

The darkened hall concealed me as I watched over him until sleep claimed him.

We had long ago synchronized our off days so we could spend time together, which meant Uncle Harold, who shared his partner's schedule, would be at the house with Dad all day tomorrow. That didn't give me the morale boost I expected. More and more, I seemed to be dumping his care in the Trudeaus' laps.

I was his daughter. It was my duty to tend him, but I had so much else to do. The house had to get repaired before the elements got in and caused us even more expensive problems. Work was the biggest time-suck, but he would understand that. While I could turn in my notice and coast through my last two weeks using vacation days, freeing up plenty of time to play nurse, I couldn't bring myself to bail on what little time Rixton and I had left together.

Selfishness, thy name is Luce.

CHAPTER SEVEN

———◆———

Thanks to the super gator, I had been forced to purchase a new laptop. As much as I missed the previous model, this one weighed half as much as its predecessor. With help from the nifty padded backpack I picked up while shopping, I now had a go bag prepped for coterie business.

Dressed in jeans, a long-sleeve tee, and boots, with my hair twisted into a high bun, I was as ready to hunt demons as I was likely to get. With my pack slung across one shoulder, I hit the kitchen for breakfast and smashed into the first obstacle on my way out the door.

Uncle Harold sat at the table with a steaming mug in front of him. The local paper was folded in quarters just how he liked it, but he wasn't reading the sports column. No. He was staring at the lean man sitting across from him. Or, I imagine, that's how it looked to Uncle Harold. Thom didn't do chairs, and his butt wasn't touching the seat of this one. Posed in a perpetual squat, I could hear his whipcord muscles screaming from here.

What I didn't hear—or see—was any sign of Cole. Considering the man was basically his own mountain range, he would have been difficult to miss occupying the cozy breakfast nook. I took his absence to mean he had palmed me off on Thom for the day. Given our last encounter, I told myself I was grateful I wouldn't spend the next several hours cooped up in a car with him smelling me. But not even I believed me.

"Morning, fellas." I skipped the coffee and poured orange juice into a travel mug. "I hope I didn't keep you waiting long, Thom."

"Only ten minutes." Thom rose to his full height with a fluid grace I envied. "Not long at all."

Ten minutes? How were his thighs not quivering mounds of jelly? Would he even be able to walk out?

"Thom?" Uncle Harold snapped his fingers like he'd just connected the dots rather than been lying in wait for an opening. "You're with White Horse Security, aren't you?"

"Yes."

"I thought I recognized the logo on your shirt." His good-natured chuckle was meant to convince Thom he was a harmless, old man. That his facilities had dulled with age when, in truth, his mind remained as diamond-sharp as ever. "You work for Cole Heaton, correct?"

"Yes."

Casual as the day is long, Uncle Harold leaned forward. "What are Mr. Heaton's intentions toward my niece? Let's make that answer non-monosyllabic, eh?"

"He requested her assistance on a case, and she agreed to consult."

"Will Cole be joining—?"

"We should go," I butted in. "We have a long drive ahead of us."

"All right." Uncle Harold tapped his cheek. "Lay one on me, pumpkin, and then promise me you'll be safe."

I palmed a few muffins leftover from breakfast yesterday then bussed his cheek. "I'll be as safe as I can be. Promise." I picked at the wrapper with my thumbnail. "Are you sure you don't mind keeping an eye on Dad?"

"I'm going to fire up the grill around lunch, and we're going to watch the game." He grinned. "I asked Eddie if he wanted a beer with his football or more milk for his cookies, and do you know what he told me?"

My heart gave a hard thud as hope swirled through me. "What?"

"I told him I'd give my left—" Dad cleared his throat. "I told him I'd kill for a longneck."

I whirled toward the archway leading into the living room and spotted Dad standing there wearing a smile stretched too thin to be genuine. He had changed his clothes from last night, and his hair had been combed. He was pale, and he shook from the effort of remaining upright, but his eyes—

Thank God, they were clearing.

"You look amazing." I dropped everything onto the table and ran to him. Afraid a hug might topple him, I settled for kissing his freshly shaven cheek. "How do you feel?"

"Fuzzy, like someone stuffed my head full of cotton balls while I was asleep." He wiggled a pinky in his ear like that might help relieve the pressure. "It's like I'm waking up from a dream I can barely remember." He beat his fist over his chest. "I told you if this ever came back, I'd kick its ass, and I did."

"Damn straight." Uncle Harold slapped his palm on the table. "We never doubted you for a minute. Nancy wrote your name on the prayer cards at every service. The whole church was calling for your healing."

"Mr. Boudreau," Thom said, "I'm glad to see you're back on your feet."

"Thomas." Dad shuffled forward with his hand extended. "Thank you, son."

A shiver of dread coasted down my spine as Thom cocked his head to one side. "What for?"

"I don't rightly know." Dad chuckled, low and steady. "I saw you and had to get that off my chest."

Relief blasted through me in a quick burst that left me sagging. "I can stay if you'd like."

"You heard Harry." Dad swayed on his feet, and Uncle Harold leapt up only to bump into Thom, who guided Dad down into his vacated chair. "We've got a game to watch and a grill to light." He nodded a quick thanks to Thom. "You don't have to fret over me. Harry won't let me get into too much trouble."

"Okay." I gathered my things to get them out of his way. "Are you sure? I can—"

"You heard the man." Uncle Harold pressed the muffins into my hand. "Go on."

Part of me felt certain if I just kept standing there, Dad would hold onto his lucidity and everything would be okay. But the other part knew that nothing I did would affect this outcome, and it was cruel to steal his thunder by hovering when he had made it to the table dressed, neat, and ready to eat on his own.

"Have fun." I backed out of the room, hating to take my eyes off the hopeful tableau before me. "Save me a cheesy brat."

"Luce." Thom stepped in front of me and cut off my line of sight. "He won't vanish if you take your eyes off him."

"Are you sure?" Physically, yes, he would still be there. Mentally . . . I hated bailing while he was coherent. "I don't want him to slip away again."

Thom guided me out the door, and we didn't speak again until we had fastened our seat belts.

"I wish I could give you more assurances," he said, "but I will not lie to you. I have never treated a human, but I did a thorough study of them to ensure the bodies we constructed for ourselves were sound. Based on what I learned, I had no reason to believe my saliva would cause an adverse reaction in your father. The dose I administered should have knocked him unconscious and softened his memory of events. Without conducting an examination, though, I can't make you any promises other than he will recover. Eventually."

Rubbing my forehead, I massaged away the tension headache sparking between my eyes. I trusted Thom's skills. I trusted his abilities. Hell, I trusted *him*. But Dad was . . . Dad. I wanted him back to one hundred percent, and I wanted him to stay that way. "How much will he remember?"

"Not enough to endanger himself, if that's what worries you." Thom fidgeted in his seat, uncomfortable holding still even behind the wheel. "I expect, if he dwells on the event, he will recall his heart racing, his palms sweating. Thanks to what we have told him, he will frame those sensations as the warning signs of another stroke instead of his fight or flight reflexes kicking in."

"He's a target because of who he is to me, and that's not going to change." I peeled the wrapper off one muffin and passed it to Thom. "Maybe we should have left his memories. Ignorance has its perks, I know that, but knowledge might keep him safer."

"There's a real danger that a human of his age, in his health, would fracture if we allowed him to keep what he learned." Thom nibbled the edge of the muffin like he had never had one and wasn't sure what to make of the thing. "Your decision is the same one I would have made in your place."

"Thanks." I picked at the blueberry crumble on top of my breakfast. "So, why am I really here?"

Talk about ignorance. I had only seen three demon breeds in their natural state. I had no idea what was out there, what was possible, what we were up against. A crash course in demonology was exactly what I needed. The opportunity to observe one in the wild, when it wasn't actively trying to murder me, would be educational, but Cole wouldn't have invited me without a secondary purpose.

He was like the onion Portia had used to explain the terrenes to me. Layers upon layers upon layers.

"Santiago views the ubaste as a portent," Thom admitted. "They're a rare breed, and while they aren't a threat to midlevel or high charun, they aren't without their uses. Still, it's unlikely an Otillian would welcome a nonlethal species into their coterie. Therefore, its sudden appearance is suspect."

"Could it have breached this world on its own?"

"Given there have been two breaches by higher charun and their coteries in the last fifteen years, it's possible." He bit into the muffin, having decided it was worth the effort after all. "The odds of an ubaste deciding to do much of anything other than eat are slim, though. A more likely scenario is that War brought it through with her to unleash when it would benefit her most. She has made use of similar diversion tactics in the past."

"Why does Santiago believe otherwise?"

"The demon is making no effort to conceal its kills, and it hasn't increased its range. The pets have all been taken within the same zip code, the bodies left for anyone to find."

"That seems to support your theory," I mused. "Not detract from it."

"The NSB kept a close eye on us. We weren't unaware of

Kapoor's interest, but we had no inkling of the depth and breadth of the program the human government has initiated for charun. The first thing any midlevel or high charun does on a new world is learn the food chain so that they can integrate at its peak. The lower charun, in turn, do the same, so they know what to avoid.

"An ubaste killing indiscriminately in a residential area makes no sense. They would never venture so close to humans, and they're smart enough to discern the link between a human and its pet. They would grasp that the fastest way to haul down wrath upon its head would be to take what belongs to another. Basic predator/prey behavior.

"For the ubaste to have survived any length of time in this world, say if it were a remnant of a previous coterie, it would have had to fly below the radar or the NSB would have picked it up and killed it. There would be no reasoning with it. It could be tamed, like any wild animal, but only to a certain point. Kapoor doesn't strike me as the kind of man to waste manpower on such a venture."

"Its behavior indicates it's new here and hasn't figured out who the top predators are yet. The fact the NSB hasn't captured it supports the idea it hasn't been here long." I lost my appetite and set my muffin on my knee. "That would mean Famine has breached."

"We'll know more once we capture the creature. If it's new, the smell of other worlds will be on its fur. And if Famine had her coterie carry it through, for whatever reason, it would bear traces of her as well."

"Are you familiar with her scent?"

Thom shuttered his expression. "Yes."

That explained his assignment to this case. "The plan is we find where she emerged and . . . then what?"

"We don't know why or how you came back as you are," he said slowly. "You are unique. The person you've become is . . . soft. War used your kindness to her advantage, and Famine would too if given enough time to acclimate."

"You're talking about confronting Famine before she gets a chance to study War's CliffsNotes."

"War will be searching for her too. She'll want to claim the first ally since you defied her. There's a chance, if Famine has breached, she's already been compromised. She and War are close. Conquest has always preferred working alone, as has Death. But each new world brings with it a new set of rules. The first one to learn them wins."

"Maybe we'll beat War to her." I blew out a long breath. "We at least have to try, right?"

"No, we don't." Thom flicked crumbs from his shirt. "We will, though. For you. Cole has ordered it so."

While I wanted to ask where and when and if he was meeting us, I had to accept that him volunteering Thom to pick me up sent a message that he needed space after what had happened.

"How far to the lab?" The persistent itch between my shoulder blades wouldn't stop until we'd unloaded our cargo. "The cooler is light enough I can handle the drop while you wait if you can get me clearance."

"You already have clearance to access and use any and all of White Horse's resources."

"Oh. Ah, thanks." The lab access alone made me giddy, not that I would need it except for private case work like this since I would soon have the NSB's resources behind me. "When did that happen?"

"It's always been that way. Your name is on all the deeds, all the policies, all the accounts. All of it." He heard my gasp and glanced at me. "Our duty is to provide for you. The business

Cole imagined, that we helped him build, was only ever meant for you."

Gold dots winked in my vision. "I don't need any of that. I don't want it."

"We did the best we could on our own," he said on a soft breath. "Are you not pleased?"

First Cole and then Miller and now Thom. How did I always end up with my foot in my mouth?

"You all worked so hard," I explained. "The company, the properties, the money, all of it, should belong to the coterie."

His ears twitched, the muscles pulling taut so that had he been shifted, they would have flattened against his skull. "That's not how this works."

"Maybe it's how this should work."

A long sigh parted his lips. "You don't want anything from us, do you?"

"I want your friendship, your knowledge. I want to not be alone in my otherness." I tore the wrapper containing my muffin to shreds. "I want the best for you, and from everything you've told me, that means the old power structure has to go. I understand Miller needs me in ways the rest of you don't, and he and I have come to an understanding, but I can't play over-lord and pretend I'm okay with that. It's wrong. You're asking me to abandon who I am, the core of what makes me *me*."

His shoulders rounded until I had to keep going, had to make him understand.

"I'm not going to abandon you, any of you. I accept that you're mine to care for, mine to protect." Conquest had brought them here, spirited them away from their home worlds, and that burden was mine to bear. "And I understand that means I'm yours too, and that your ideas about protecting me are different than mine."

"I wish you could stay," he said softly, and his meaning was clear. He believed Conquest was in me and that she would prevail. "Perhaps you're the reason why I made this journey. I wanted to witness miracles, to experience wonders, to understand the fundamental reason for our existence, and I have beheld echoes of all those things in you.

"When I return to my people, I will possess a vaster knowledge than any who has come before me, and I will tell them of the two-souled Otillian who fought against her nature and won the loyalty of her coterie through bonds stronger than the bands implanted beneath their skin." Satisfaction gave his eyes a glint. "It will make a good story, I think."

My gut clenched like I'd been kicked. "You're leaving? When? I didn't think that was possible."

The alarm in my voice accomplished what my speech had failed to do and put a satisfied grin back on his face. "You don't want me to go."

"We need you." By all accounts, the worst was yet to come. "We can't survive this without you."

War had savaged him and Santiago, and that was during her opening salvo.

Puffed up to maximum capacity, he allowed, "I won't return until you no longer require me."

As to the *how*, he kept that nugget of information to himself. I couldn't say I blamed him.

Thom executed a series of quick turns that dumped us out into a paved lot beside an industrial building. The logo painted on the side was a variation on the one I was used to seeing on White Horse's vehicles. I must have missed the memo where Cole admitted the private lab they used belonged to them, but the setup made sense. I didn't see him contracting work out to the general public. He wasn't that trusting. There was also the fact some of the compounds he required tested were not of this world. On the heels of that thought stumbled another. "Does this lab employ humans?"

"No." Thom eyed my muffin so hard I passed it over to him. "All the employees at this facility are charun. There was no other way to ensure our privacy."

"I wonder how many are in the NSB's pocket?" I fiddled with the door handle. "Kapoor would have planted a mole here, maybe several, and they would have dug in deep."

"You've partnered with the NSB," Thom reminded me. "There's no point weeding them out now that we are aware they must exist. It would only cast suspicion on you. We'll isolate them instead and make sure none of the more sensitive materials pass through their hands."

I popped open the door and stepped out. "What do I need to tell them?"

"Bring the cooler to the front desk." Thom began picking the blueberries from the muffin and tossing them out his window. "They know who you are. They know why you're here."

Sucking it up, I left him to finish his breakfast while I grabbed the cooler from the trunk. I backed through the front door of the building and approached a circular desk. The lobby was as sterile as it got without being a hospital, but what had I expected from a lab?

The dowdy receptionist who had been lost in conversation goggled up at me, and the phone slid through her fingers. It clattered across the linoleum, and she joined it, going down on her knees and planting her palms before her. She didn't stop there, either. She bent forward until her forehead touched the floor and held the pose until I cleared my throat.

"You, ah, don't have to do that." I glanced around like maybe she was bowing to someone else who had crept up behind me the way it happens in the movies, but we were alone. "Really. You can get up now."

"Mistress, blessings upon you." Her voice came out muffled. "I had heard we were to expect a visit from you. I would have prepared the rites, but Master Cole forbade it."

"I'm in a bit of a hurry." I backed up a half-step. "Can I leave this with you and ...?"

"Yes, Mistress." She didn't budge from her position. "I will see it is taken in for processing."

"Thanks." I rubbed the base of my neck. "I, ah, appreciate your assistance."

"It is nothing, Mistress."

Unable to peel my eyes off the prostrate woman, I inched out the door before rejoining Thom. "That was uncomfortable."

"Veronica still bows to Cole after all these years." He got us back on the road. "Breaking etiquette would shatter the foundation of her world."

There was a message there, a blunt one, and I received it with a sigh. "What about you?"

"What about me?"

"Does she bow to you?"

"No."

Getting answers when he wasn't in a giving mood was like pulling teeth. "Why?"

"The gesture is done out of respect for his station."

I should have packed pliers. "As leader of the coterie?"

Thom cranked up the radio, and that was the end of that.

CHAPTER EIGHT

———————

I spent the rest of the drive absorbed in the Culberson file, pausing now and again to ping Rixton with questions. Mostly I got baby pics in return. I didn't mind the trade. Plus, Nettie's adorableness meant her father had trouble forming cohesive non-baby thoughts long enough to tease me.

Thom dropped his gaze to the phone in my lap. "Are you going to answer that?"

"It's not—" the display lit with a number that left my palms sweaty "—ringing." I narrowed my eyes at Thom, wondering how the trick worked. "Boudreau."

"Wu filed the paperwork to establish your partnership the night you agreed to join the taskforce." Kapoor cut right to the chase. "You two will be working together unless or until the higher ups are convinced the match isn't working." His sigh blew across the line. "Sorry, Luce, but what Wu wants, Wu tends to get."

That solved one mystery. Our partnership had been his

bright idea. No wonder he'd shown up on my doorstep with an ultimatum. His was more than professional courtesy; it was personal interest. "Why does he want me?"

"You'll have to ask him that."

"Is this how it's always going to be with us?" I gazed out the window as the rolling scenery slowed. "I ask a question, you get back with the answer after careful consideration, and raise four more questions while you're at it?"

"Nah." The edge of amusement crept into his tone. "Sometimes I'll raise five."

Thom cut his eyes toward me. "We're here."

"I have to go." I peered through the window. "Thanks for getting back with me."

"Luce . . . " Kapoor made a ticking sound behind his teeth. "Let me know if Wu gives you problems. He might be a whale, but I'm in management. They issue us harpoon guns for a reason, understand?"

A sliver of grudging respect for his willingness to confront Wu cut through my annoyance with him. "I'll let you know if I can't handle him."

Kapoor signed off with a huff of laughter that implied a better trick would be if I could.

After tucking away the phone, I began flipping through the Culberson file again. I skimmed the whole thing, front to back, without experiencing a single *ah-ha* moment. Frustrated, I took stock of our surroundings. "How much farther?"

"Another pet was discovered a half mile from this location." Thom threw the SUV into park while I stuffed my gear back where it belonged. "I tracked it to that house on the right last night."

Blinking away the dancing lines of text from my eyes, I focused on our surroundings. "This is not what I was expecting."

Thom had guided us into a warren of a subdivision and parked in the driveway of a half-finished house at the end of a row dappled with homes in various stages of completion. Pallets stacked with shingles waited on the road, and some yellow, mechanical monstrosity was frozen mid-scoop over the manmade pond it was creating.

"The site has been shut down until bills owed by the development are paid to its construction partner."

"Are ubaste nocturnal?" I swept my gaze over the area. "Are we hoping to find where it's denning?"

"Yes." He lifted the rear hatch and removed a carpeted square that revealed a hidden weapons cache. Three knives and a gun disappeared on his person that I noticed. I'm sure there were more. The last Glock got pressed into my hand, and already I felt better about life. He also passed me a six-inch dagger I slid between my belt and jeans for safekeeping. "Hunting them is easier during the day."

A detailed map of the subdivision was only a few clicks away online. The developer wanted the plots sold ASAP, and there were at least two dozen listings that outlined the layout of the entire development. The cell signal wasn't great out here. I almost whipped out the black phone to check its reception, but I decided to make do with what I had.

"Let's use a standard search grid." I checked the gleaming road signs until I located the ideal starting point. "We'll start on Cypress Lane, work our way down Dogwood Court, then finish on Magnolia Circle." I scanned the nearest houses, both skeletal outlines left exposed to the elements. "Do we stick together, or do we each take a road and meet in the middle?"

"You aren't at full strength, and it will capitalize on any perceived weakness." Thom sidled up to me. "I'm not sure how susceptible you are to an ubaste in your current form, but we can't risk finding out. We do this together."

Full strength meant going demon, a thing I wasn't certain I could do. After all, if Conquest hadn't stirred to save herself from her sister, I doubted she would care much if an ubaste snacked on us. "Works for me."

As we moved from shell to shell, we cleared every room on each floor. No sod had been rolled out, so the yards were patchworks of dirt and weeds that made it obvious nothing had tunneled down into the earth or was otherwise using the ground for cover. We made it three houses down Dogwood Court before a fetid stench launched me into a coughing fit.

"What is that?" I lifted the collar of my tee over my nose, but it didn't help much. "It smells like week-old Chinese food and dirty diapers."

"We're getting close." Thom flared his nostrils, his expression tight. "That reek is indicative of a den."

House number four came up empty, but we struck pay dirt on house number five. It was more than three-quarters finished inside, and it was one of the few homes that had a full basement. Claw marks had ruined the cherry hardwood floor, and thick clumps of gray hair made dust bunnies in the corners. We cleared the first and second levels then regrouped by the door leading underground.

"Cover me." Thom gripped a dagger in each hand then vanished down the stairs.

"Thomas," I hissed. No electricity meant no lights, and no lights meant he had disappeared on me. I couldn't see him to cover him. I couldn't perceive anything at all beyond the fifth or sixth step. All was pitch black. "Fall back."

A high-pitched yowling pierced my ears a second before a massive ball of mottled fur plowed me down on its way out of the darkness. I hit the floor with a grunt and aimed my gun at its retreating back, but Thom flew past in a whir of black feathers and ruined the shot for me. Glass exploded as the beast shattered a window in its frantic bid for escape, and Thom zipped through the opening, wings blurring with their speed.

"Don't worry about me." Groaning, I got my legs under me. "I'm fine. Thanks for asking."

I jogged through the house, out the front door, and trailed the thing from where it crash-landed. The ubaste, in daylight, with its low hind quarters and higher withers paired with its spotted pelt reminded me of a hyena, but its face was utterly alien. Rather than a jaw lined with teeth, the tip of its nose tapered down into a proboscis similar to what came standard on mosquitos, except the ubaste swung its limber snout with the ease of an elephant curling its trunk.

Unlike Veronica, the ubaste wasn't humbled by my appearance. Given its rabid expression after waking up on the wrong side of the basement, I'm not entirely certain it knew what I was or cared. Still, it would have been handy if it had fallen at my feet instead of scuffing its paws in preparation for a charge.

I settled into a comfortable stance and steadied my aim. I couldn't outrun the creature. I had to stand my ground. One deep breath in, one out, and it was thundering toward me. I popped off six rounds that hit center mass and caused green blood to blossom across its chest, but it didn't slow. I got in a few more shots before impact slammed me flat on my back. Pinned under its paws, I was stuck as the ubaste aimed its needlelike snout at me.

"Thom?" I called. "Little help here?"

Black wings came into view over the ubaste's shoulder. Thom had landed on its back and was walking the length of its spine. No time to wonder what the cat was up to, not when the ubaste was stabbing at me like I was an iced coffee he wanted to slurp.

Whatever Thom was up to, he wasn't doing it fast enough. The puckered end of the ubaste's snout brushed my cheek, and white-hot agony ripped through my limbs. The pounding of my heart slowed, and my lungs forgot what they were supposed to be doing for the span of a few tortuous beats.

The cold place surfaced before true panic sank in, and it was as if my body moved on autopilot. I retrieved the knife Thom had given me and sliced through the creature's snout in a clean arc. Its shriek of rage was more of a gurgle as its proboscis hit the dirt, and I almost pitied the ugly thing.

"*Mmmrrrrpt.*"

Over the ubaste's thrashing head, Thom locked gazes with me. I read the look to mean *you better get while the getting's good*. Scrabbling backward, I managed to wriggle out from under it seconds before its dazed thrashing morphed into drunken imbalance. Thom hovered out of range until the ubaste's knees liquefied, and it collapsed in a heap of fur and stink. I flopped on my back a safe distance away and caught my breath.

"Thanks for the assist," I panted. "Is it dead?"

The boxy tomcat landed on my chest, turning breathing into a workout, and proceeded to lick his right front paw.

"Good talk." I rolled onto my side, startling the cat into flight, and pushed myself upright to get a better look at the demon. "Did you get what you needed?" Already the smell was worse. Must be all that green blood slicking its fur. "What do we do with the body?"

Once the cat finished cleaning his face, he deigned to notice me and shifted back onto two legs.

"It's not dead. The narcotic in my saliva has rendered it

unconscious." Thom left me where I sat and approached the creature. He squatted beside it, ran his palm over its mottled fur and inhaled the scents he stirred on the air. He dipped his fingers in its blood and tasted that too. "There is no hint of Famine on this beast. The taint of the other worlds has gone too."

"Then it knew the rules." I frowned at the hulking mass. "It's been here long enough to figure out how to blend in, how to survive. What caused it to go rogue? It must have known it would be hunted down."

"I can't say. An illness perhaps?"

"I have an idea." I stood and tested everything out to make sure I hadn't twisted a knee or an ankle during the takedown. Relieved when everything worked as it should, I dusted off my hands. "Are you good here for a minute?"

Thom stood. "Where are you going?"

"I need something from the SUV."

"Okay." He retrieved the ubaste's proboscis. "I'll get started here."

Cursing my stubborn refusal to carry the black phone, I jogged to the SUV and thumbed redial on my way back to Thom.

"You're out of breath," Wu observed. "What are you doing?"

"Jogging." Not a total lie. "I hear it's good for what ails you."

Wu made a noise too dignified to pass as a real snort. "To what do I owe the pleasure?"

I imagined him sitting at his desk, elegant fingers steepled in anticipation, a hungry spider in his silvery web. "I have an ubaste on my hands, and it got me thinking."

"How can you possibly think past the stench?"

Putting distance between myself and the corpse had done wonders for my cognitive abilities. "Does the NSB catalogue lower demons? Is there any way you could identify this particular one?"

"The NSB maintains records of each charun who is spayed or neutered." A bitter note flavored his accent. "We all have files in the system. Photos, blood, and tissue samples."

Ignoring his sharp response, I kept pressing. "So that's a yes."

"Yes."

"Great." I reached Thom, who eyed the phone with unease. "I'll owe you a favor."

He waited the span of a heartbeat. "I'm ready to call in my favor."

I laughed. He didn't. "You're serious?"

"Have dinner with me, and I'll get the information for you."

"Dinner," I echoed. "You've got to be kidding me."

"I want to get to know you." The silk in his voice caressed my ears. "We are partners, after all."

"Not yet we aren't." I pinched my bottom lip in consideration. "Aren't there fraternization laws in the NSB?"

"Charun are, at their core, primal beasts. Sterilized females no longer experience heats. They no longer throw off the scent to entice males. Without that call to mate, males are far less interested in sexual relationships. The impossibility of creating offspring withers the urge. So, no, there are no fraternization laws. There's no point to them."

The relief I expected to cascade through me never manifested. I hadn't been sterilized. I hadn't been outfitted with a demon-friendly IUD yet, either. The heat thing . . . yeah. I wasn't touching that with a ten-foot pole.

"Fine." I avoided eye contact with Thom. "I'll have dinner with you."

Wu was a gateway to the information we required. There was nothing for me to do but walk through it.

"Excellent." His mood audibly improved. "Photograph the body, take hair and blood samples. I'll text you the address of the lab we use. You can drop off the materials there for processing, and they'll send them direct to me. I'll call with the results once I have them."

He ended the call and left me staring at the screen, wondering what kind of bargain I had just struck, but I couldn't afford regrets. "What do we do with the ubaste?"

Thom would have overheard my conversation with Wu, so he knew we had to collect samples, but that still left us with a whole lot of butt-ugly demon we couldn't leave out for humans to find.

"We employ a team for cleanups." Thom didn't elaborate on the specifics, and I didn't ask. We had left the ubaste breathing, but I didn't kid myself that it would remain in that condition. Any demon drawing attention to its species would be put down before humans got involved. "I'll place the call once we've finished. Where does Wu want the samples taken?"

A text notification pinged, and I swiped my thumb over the icon. I read the address, re-read the address, and then I laughed.

Oh, yes, the NSB knew all about the White Horse lab. Wu had, after all, just directed me to them.

During our second trip to the lab, I let Thom do the honors. To further avoid any awkwardness with Veronica, I ducked low in my seat and used my phone as a shield to deflect her stare. With her nose pressed to the glass front door, she reminded me of a doggy in a pet shop window who just knew she would be chosen if only she performed the right combination of tricks.

Five demons already depended on me, and I wasn't about to add another into the mix.

Rubbing my face with my hands, I hid in the blessed darkness of my cupped palms for a moment.

I'm a demon. A nightmare given substance. A plague upon humanity.

For the most part, I was adapting. Okay, *adapting* might be a strong word for putting one foot in front of the other, taking this new life one day at a time. But sometimes reality crept in on mouse feet then lowered the whammy and left me with my ears ringing.

Hunting the ubaste, confronting yet another alien breed, had been one of those times.

Desperate for a breather, I lowered the window, closed my eyes, and sucked in fresh air heavy with the scent of oncoming rain.

"Are you all right?"

A lesser woman might have squeaked at Thom's voice so near her ear, but not I. I was developing a sixth sense where he was concerned, which maybe should have worried me. I glowered at him. "Keep that up, and I'll buy a bell for you, mister."

His left ear gave a decided twitch. "I'm no house cat."

No, he was the back-alley brawler that kept the neighbors up all night yowling. "Are we done here?"

His eyebrows rose when he noticed my slump. "Are you hiding from Veronica?"

"No." I hauled myself upright. "I was just getting comfortable."

"She unsettles you," he surmised.

"A touch, maybe." The reverence thing bugged me a surprising amount.

"Most charun you'll encounter share a similar worldview as their new human neighbors. Earth is their home. They want to protect their families and the lives they've carved out in this terrene, and they're willing to coexist with mortals to do it. Recent events are stirring unrest within the charun popu-lace. Two cadre have been spotted, and they know what that means." He hesitated. "Those who thrive on chaos and darker things are more inclined to embrace your return."

"I'm guessing Veronica falls into that category."

"Yes." He studied me. "Does knowing that make you see her differently?"

There was no way I was falling into that trap when I had just gotten the taste of foot out of my mouth.

"What she does to get by is her business as long as she doesn't harm anyone in the process." I had to imagine there must be a yin and yang happening where she could feed or indulge her desires without drawing the NSB down on her head. "When she crosses the line? That's when it becomes my business."

"Do you apply the same values to charun as you do humans? The same worth?"

"Yes." I reached through the window to ruffle his hair, as shocked by the impulse as the fact I enjoyed the contact. Again, I wondered if the coterie bonds were to blame, if spending time with them had activated some strange magic, or if Thom's animalistic nature trumped my usual aversion to touch. "I've spent enough time around you guys to know not all charun are evil or, you know, bent on world domination. Regardless of species, the vow I made when I pinned on my badge was to protect the innocent."

For a long time after that, Thom stayed put, letting me pet him. And then he said, with no small promise, "I'm going to find a way to keep you."

"I am not opposed to being kept." A cramp in my arm ended the petting session, which, yeah, sounded dirty, but touch appeared to be a platonic requirement for Thom. Plus, he seemed onboard for Operation Luce Is A Real Girl, and I would take all the help I could get holding on to my identity. "So we're done?"

All in all, my first day of demon hunting hadn't been so bad.

"We're done." He circled the SUV and got in beside me. "Are you in a hurry to get home?"

Cat he might be, but Thom wasn't as slick as he thought. "Are you asking me about Wu?"

Demon hearing left zero to the imagination. Thom already had the skinny on the deal I'd brokered with Wu. He just wanted to drag the gory details out of me.

"You deserve any happiness you can find" was his response.

The gnawing pit in my gut kept me chewing over the ramifications of dining with a guy who wouldn't require quickdraws or rope to scale, but facts were facts. I was bad for Cole. He didn't want me in a romantic way, I wasn't sure if he wanted me at all, and not knowing his limits meant he was off the menu. Though crossing out his name hardly penned Wu in. Thankfully, he had spelled out dinner was more of an interview process. No code words, hurt feelings, or unmet expectations required. That alone made the prospect refreshing.

"Wu is working an angle, but I haven't figured out what it is yet. This dinner is a ploy of some kind. The object is most likely to get in my brain, not my panties."

Thom made a huffing noise under his breath. "Do you believe everything that male charun tell you?"

"You guys don't exactly come with instruction manuals." I snorted out a laugh. "I have to believe that when a guy says he doesn't want my hands on him, he means it." *Damn it*. This was not about Cole. This was about Wu. And boundaries. "For that reason, I'm willing to extend a little faith and believe when a guy says he doesn't want to put his hands on me, he means that too."

"You are so young," he mused. "I forget that sometimes."

Crossing my arms over my chest, I restrained myself from sticking out my tongue at him, but it was a near thing. "The reason I'm in a hurry to get home, if you must know, is because I want to see Dad. We finished up early. I might be able to catch the fourth quarter of the game. I wouldn't say no to a brat hot off the grill either."

He made a noncommittal noise.

"Do you have any plans for tonight?"

He rolled his shoulders. "I have to brief Cole and the others."

The mention of Cole sucked the air out of the cabin, and we cruised the rest of the way to the Trudeaus' in silence.

I saw smoke curling over the roof and cracked a window to breathe in the smells. Thom parked at the curb, and I gathered my things. "Are you sure you don't want to come in?"

"I wouldn't want to intrude."

"Uncle Harold won't interrogate you again. Yelling at the TV will keep him occupied."

"Thank you, but no." He shook his head. "It's Miller's and my turn to clean the fleet and handle scheduled maintenance."

All those SUVs . . . I didn't envy them the job.

"Tell him I said hello." Backtracking, I amended to, "Tell everyone I said hi."

"Enjoy your cookout." Thom glided away from the curb and rolled down the street at a sedate speed.

After hiking my bag up on my shoulder, I let myself in the house and dashed toward the living room. Dad was asleep on the cushions, and a frayed pink blanket covered his legs. Football played on the TV, but someone had muted the game. I dropped my stuff beside the coffee table then went in search of my uncle. I found him manning the grill with a beer in one hand and tongs in another.

"I see your partner in crime didn't make it to the fourth quarter."

"He dropped off around the second." Uncle Harold lifted the foil covering a pan filled with simmering beer and brats. "He started fading about two hours after you left. He lost interest in the TV before the game started, but I sat with him until I had to start dinner or go hungry."

"He walked out of the fog once." For those precious moments, he had been his old self. "He'll do it again."

"From your lips to God's ears." He plated a thick cut rib-eye charred to perfection, Aunt Nancy's favorite treat. No doubt an enticement to get her to eat more. "How did the case go?"

"We wrapped up today, actually." I took the plate to free his hands. "Looks like I get to sleep in tomorrow. And before you ask, no. Cole did not join us. It was just me, Thom, and our—" *target* "—suspect."

"Any particular reason why you're padding your résumé with odd jobs, pumpkin?" Uncle Harold did casual well, but the beer had roughened his usually smooth delivery. "Anything you need to tell us?"

"It's not my résumé I'm padding. It's my pockets." The white lie burned going down, but the truth wasn't an option. "You should see all the toys White Horse has at its disposal. I found out today they own stock in a private lab. I've got to say, it's an impressive operation. It makes what we have down at the PD look like we're coloring with crayons while they're whipping out calligraphy sets."

He grunted. "That's the power of money."

"You ever consider working for the private sector?" I repeated the question Thom had once asked me. "Better pay, better hours, better toys. It's not a bad gig if you can get it."

"I'm a cop, Luce. I don't know how to be anything else."

He sounded okay with that. "Besides, I'm too old to learn new tricks. Branching out is for the young. I'm content to stay right where I am until I retire."

Retire. Yeah, right. Pretty sure we'd be hauling his corpse out of his cruiser. "When will that be?"

"Depends on Eddie, I guess." He took another long drink. "I'm not interested in working solo, and I don't have the patience to train up another partner. He might decide this is it for him, and if he goes, I go too."

Actual retirement hadn't crossed my mind. It's not like Dad had been in any shape to make that call.

"You make it sound so noble," I teased, "but I know the truth. You can't stand the idea of working every night while you know he's out on the water spotlight fishing without you."

"Pumpkin, you know me too well." Uncle Harold chortled. "Do me a favor and light that bug candle? The mosquitos are eating me alive out here."

"Sure thing." I held out my hand. "Matches?" He dropped a box on my palm, and I crossed to the outdoor dining table. A hodgepodge of white cotton discs, chunks of candle wax, a casserole dish, and a few tiki torch refills cluttered one end along with a weathered crockpot. I had to set down the plate to dig out the candle he mentioned, and then I had to clear a space before lighting it. "What's going on here?"

"Nancy's cooking up some of her famous Waxy Wonders." He grinned with pride. "The guys love them. She makes batches for the fishing club a couple times a year."

As if hearing her name, Aunt Nancy popped her head through the sliding glass door leading into the backyard. She spotted the steak on the table and waved tinfoil at me before I could think to question him about the Waxy Wonders' purpose. "Hurry up before it goes cold."

Scooping up the steak, I pointed at his grill. "Do you need me to grab another plate for the brats?"

"Nah." He lifted a dish rag to expose two more stacked in his prep area. "I got it covered."

I hustled into the kitchen and passed over the steak. "What smells so good in here?"

"Bacon wrapped onion rings, green beans with bacon, and my signature baked beans with pork belly."

Water flooded my mouth. "So . . . bacon."

"Don't sass me, Miss Priss." She passed me an onion ring snug in its crispy bacon suit. "Go keep Harry company so he doesn't burn the brats."

"I like mine charred." He always set a few on the grill after their beer bath for me.

"You're the only one." She hip-bumped me out of her way with a fraction of her usual oomph. "Oh, and your phone's been ringing."

I pulled my cell from my back pocket and woke the display. "I'm not showing any missed calls."

"That's odd. I could have sworn I heard a phone ringing over here." She indicated my backpack. "It must be your laptop. Do you use that Internet call app?"

Oh. That explained it. Not my phone, the black phone.

"The app came preinstalled on my new laptop." That much was true. "It's probably another prompt to activate the service or something." That much was . . . not so true. "I'll go mute it so it doesn't bother us again."

With purpose in my stride, I stalked over to my backpack, unzipped the front pouch, and pulled out the phone. Sure enough, Wu had called me while I'd been out back. Hiding the phone against my thigh, I locked myself in my temporary bedroom before hitting redial. "What's up?"

"I'm ready for that dinner now," Wu said without missing a beat.

"You can't already have the results," I spluttered. "The lab has only had the material for an hour."

"There's only one way to find out."

"Can we do this tomorrow?" I could still smell charcoal burning. "We're having a family cookout."

A smile shadowed his voice. "I can wait until then if you can."

"Why don't you tell me now," I gritted out, "and we'll go out tomorrow?"

"I'm sorry, Luce, but I don't know you well enough to take you at your word."

Right then having world-ending powers sure would have come in handy. "Thanks for the vote of confidence, partner."

"We don't know each other yet. I'm trying to remedy that."

Yeah. Sure. Mr. Altruistic. "When do you want to meet?"

"How about now?"

Goodbye, hot-off-the-grill feast. Hello, gelatinous goo reheated in the microwave.

"Sure." Defeat rang through the word. "I need to shower and change. What should I wear?"

"Something nice."

I had one dress hung in the closet, its matching flats tucked under the sewing table, and that was only so I had an outfit ready for church. "This isn't a date."

"I never said it was." That smile was back, and I wanted to wipe it off his face. With my fist. "I'll pick you up in an hour."

I ended the call before saying something I probably wouldn't regret but that might make the hour or so I had just agreed to spend in Wu's company even more onerous. Trudging into the kitchen, I located my aunt and broke the news. Uncle Harold would have to find out through the grapevine, otherwise he wouldn't let me out the door without giving Wu the third degree. There was no way I could shrug this off as a work thing like I had with Thom earlier. Me flashing ankle on a day other than Sunday would send my uncle into a tizzy.

With that in mind, I rushed through a shower, cursing Wu for the necessity of shaving my legs twice this week. I dressed, wove a French braid into my hair, then sneaked past my sleeping father to wait at the curb. The sizzle of burgers hitting the grill made my stomach rumble, and I pressed a hand over my abdomen like that might quiet its complaint.

Whatever Wu had to tell me, it had better be good.

CHAPTER NINE

———❦———

Wu arrived seconds before I decided *to hell with it* and went inside to fix myself a to-go plate. He parked a sleek sedan at the curb and joined me on the sidewalk. He had paired expensive shoes with another white button-down shirt, this one fastened at his wrists and open at the collar, with black slacks. The matching jacket waited on a hanger on a rod strung across the backseat.

I couldn't have stopped my eyes from rolling if I'd tried. And I didn't.

"Ms. Boudreau," Wu greeted me. "You're lovely this evening."

Compared to his city slicker good looks, I was dressed in petal pink flats with flecks of mud staining the sides that screamed country girl. The flowy dress was a skosh better. Its floral pattern was a nod to summer, and its gathered elastic waistline modest underneath a braided leather belt. The round, pleated neckline was easy to dress up or down with the right necklace, and the full sleeves fastened with pearl buttons at my wrists.

"What I am is starving." I cast one last, pitiful glance over my shoulder. "You couldn't have called an hour later?"

"You would have already eaten if I had." He opened the passenger side door and held it for me. "I would have missed my chance."

I leveled a glare on him. "How did you know?"

"I have my ways."

After he ensconced me in his ride, I waited a full thirty seconds before pouncing on him. "What did you find out?"

A hint of a smile curved his lips. "We'll talk about it over dinner."

A smarter woman would have snagged another bacon-wrapped onion ring for the road. "Do you really want to talk about bodily fluids over a meal?"

"You're a cop. Your father is a cop." Wu snorted, and even that sound managed a lyrical elegance. "You can't tell me this would be the first time you discussed a case over dinner."

He had me dead to rights, but I wasn't done yet. "That's different. Dad and I are co-workers. We share a vocation. It's only normal to discuss work and office politics for us."

"You and I are partners," he reminded me. "Both of us have ties to the NSB. Using your own logic, that means we can discuss work, that it's normal for us."

"That is future you and me." A future that was three weeks away, and so distant, so alien from the life I led now, I had trouble imagining it. "Present you and me are barely acquaintances."

"Then consider this a team-building exercise."

"Yes. About our team." I pegged him with a look. "Kapoor seemed downright shocked that I had been assigned to you."

"Kapoor is not my immediate supervisor," he said, sounding like this was an argument not worth repeating. "There was no reason to consult him on the matter."

"So he told me."

The car accelerated. "What else did he say?"

"He called you a whale." *And promised to harpoon you if you try any funny business.*

"Why would he call me a whale?" Wu glanced down at himself as though checking for signs of a blowhole. "That makes no sense."

The urge to indulge in ocular gymnastics made my eyes twitch. "He meant you're a big deal."

Wu nodded in clear agreement. "I am."

"Maybe what he meant was you have a whale-sized ego," I muttered.

If he heard, and I'm sure he did, he let the potshot pass uncontested. "Why not ask me your questions?"

"I don't know you, which means I don't know if I can trust your answers." The coterie was aware of Kapoor, they respected his tenacity, which was more than I could say for Wu. "Kapoor, on the other hand, has done me a solid. He has protected my coterie. Multiple times."

"He protected them at a cost," Wu reminded me. "He did you no favors."

"I'm well aware." I gusted out a sigh. "That doesn't change the fact that their lives and safety are my responsibility, and I've been falling down on the job. Until I can manage on my own, I'm not going to bite the hand that feeds me."

"You've become possessive of them in a short amount of time," he observed.

"They risked their lives protecting Jane Doe. I had no idea who or what she was, but they did, and they still kept her safe. For me." Thom and Santiago had almost paid for that protection with their lives. "Thom saved my dad after War revealed herself, and Portia . . ."

She had risked it all transferring her essence into Maggie in the hopes she could revive my best friend.

The way it had been explained to me was some charun, like Cole and the guys, could manifest their own skins. Others, like Portia, required hosts to survive foreign terrenes and function within those societies. The latter were divided into two groups: viscarre and emocarre, or parasitic and symbiotic.

Portia fell into the latter category, the connection to her host a mutually beneficial one. Otherwise, I never would have entrusted Maggie to her. Not that I'd had a right to bargain with Portia as though Maggie's life were my own in the first place. Desperate to save her, I had struck the bargain demanded of any host without first asking permission. I wasn't sure Maggie would ever forgive me that.

"I don't deserve their loyalty," I told him, "but I have it. Now it's up to me to earn it."

"I expected it would take longer for you to accept them." He angled his head sharply to one side. "Perhaps it shouldn't surprise me. Some ties run too deep to sever, even the ones you attempt to carve from under your skin."

There was only one member of my coterie who had taken to self-mutilation to free himself of me.

The reminder was not welcome.

Wu, who must have noticed the shift in my mood, redirected our conversation. "Have you been able to locate War?"

"No." Miller was hot on her trail, but she was covering her tracks well. "We've shifted our focus onto anticipating Famine's breach. We hope to reach her before War sinks her hooks in her."

"Are you hoping to reason with her?" Curiosity spiked his tone. "Do you think you can win her over?"

"There's a chance she might come back like me, right?"

"There has never been an Otillian like you," he said with utter conviction. "Expect treachery. Famine might come into this world blind and deaf to its facets, but she'll learn them fast. Any weaknesses she senses in you, she will exploit."

"Tell me something I don't know."

"One bolt of lightning contains enough energy to toast one hundred thousand slices of bread."

"You did not just say that." A surprised laugh bubbled up in me. "Are you serious? Is that a real thing?"

"Yes, I did. Yes, I am. And yes, it is."

The rest of the drive passed in a flurry of animal trivia that would have bored another man to tears. Wu, however, appeared to have a near-eidetic memory. He also seemed to have filled his brain vault with a crap ton of useless informational tidbits that made me wonder how he spent his downtime.

We arrived at our destination, a rustic lodge-style restaurant located three towns north of Canton. The line backed out onto the wraparound porch, and music poured through the parking lot from speakers mounted under the eaves. Wu opened the car door for me, and the air smelled delicious. While I was starting to drool, he grabbed a thick folio from the trunk.

"It tastes even better than it smells," he promised. "Come on. I have a reservation."

"Of course you do."

Wu cut straight to the front of the line, and I followed with my head ducked to avoid the glares cast in our direction. Oblivious to the disturbance he'd caused, Wu bent the ear of the hostess exchanging names for pagers at the door. Her eyes brightened at the attention, and she honest-to-God giggled at whatever line he dropped to convince her to seat us on the spot.

We ordered drinks, both of us opting for sweet tea, no

alcohol lest this seem date-like, and she returned thirty seconds later with chilled glasses filled with amber liquid and a silver tray of lemon wedges with a small mesh strainer for catching errant seeds.

Once she left, I cocked an eyebrow at him. "You had a reservation, huh?"

"Yes." He lifted his menu, flicked it open. "I made it under another alias." His lips twitched. "Benjamin Franklin."

"You dropped a hundred dollars on a table? Here?" I surveyed the cozy dining area, the overall décor that of a bait shack on its last leg. It was an illusion, of course, and you didn't have to stare hard to see through to the pristine tabletops with their pressed linen napkins stuffed with polished silverware. The vintage advertising signs hung on the walls weren't reproduction. They were originals, a little rust-eaten, just enough to fit the theme, but gorgeous with their bright pops of color. "What do you like about this place?"

"Their snow crab legs." He noticed me soaking up the ambiance, and what I hesitated to label as approval suffused his features. "The surf and turf isn't bad either."

"No, it's not the food," I decided. "You like that this place is one thing masquerading as another."

Fine dining in a dilapidated cabin. The caliber of diners spoke to the quality of the food and the appeal of the environment. The more I studied the staff in their pressed tees and starched shorts, casual but not, and the drinks breezing past, craft beers with hand-printed labels, no household names in sight, the more certain I became that it had cost Wu more than a C-note to charm his way past the head of the line.

After selecting a perfect wedge, he squeezed lemon into his tea. "Is that so?"

"Tell me I'm wrong."

"You're wrong." His smile blossomed at my immediate scowl. "I was only following orders, Ms. Boudreau."

"Cute."

"Thank you."

I counted backward in my head from ten. "I didn't mean—"

"I know what you meant." He sipped his drink and deemed it worthy of his taste buds. "Do you want to talk now or after dinner?"

"Now is good." I didn't want to give him a reason to linger over coffee and dessert.

"As you wish." He produced the black folio and flipped it open on the tabletop between us. "I believe this is all the information you requested."

Several pages of printed material, including photographs and X-rays, had been paperclipped together, and a clear evidence baggie the size of a Post-it note had been stapled to the top sheet. I rubbed my fingertip over the plastic, rolling the tiny cylinder inside to get a better look at the device. About the size of a grain of rice, I had a good idea of what it was before I flipped it out of the way and read the first page of the report.

"These results didn't come from the lab." I kept skimming page after page. "The NSB is microchipping charun like animals. I'm guessing that happens during the mandatory examination. They're already digging around in us, so who's going to notice an extra lump?"

When Wu didn't contradict me, I knew I was on the right track.

"You've got a mole on the White Horse cleanup team." That made the most sense. "All they had to do was use one of those handheld scanners you see in animal shelters to read the chip. After they located the registration number, the data was at your fingertips."

Wu sat back and let me stumble through the rest.

"The ubaste we hunted wasn't a recent breach. It was part of a litter born to a female who was brought here during the last Otillian reign of terror." I scratched my nail on the paper. "This information clears Famine. The creature was either sick, or someone set it on this path."

"Ubaste are low-level charun. Their cognitive function is on par with a pig or similar animal. It's smart enough to figure out how to survive, and it's trainable, but it has very little agency outside of meeting its basic needs."

"You ruled out sickness quickly. Is that not a possibility?"

"Unlikely. Charun are hearty. We're immune to most human viruses and diseases."

"So either this guy developed a case of agency or someone set him up with a hunting ground and told him to go hog wild."

Thom's idea that the ubaste might be a distraction seemed most likely. We already knew War had been here far longer than the coterie had realized. There was no telling how she had spent her time outside of the procreation required to fill her coterie's roster. This seemed like just the type of red herring diversion she would favor, a confusion tactic, and it's not like she didn't have plenty of time to plan. She was no doubt several steps ahead of us.

Wu read far too much into my silence. "What are you thinking?"

"This guy was a gift from War."

"You believe she used the ubaste to distract your coterie." He figured it out so quickly I had no doubt he had already been thinking along the same lines. "What would she gain from that?"

"Other than distracting us from the search for her and Famine? I'm not sure. White Horse got involved thanks to a small contract set up by distraught pet owners—*Crap.*" I dug my phone out of my pocket and started texting Miller. "We need to send someone to check and make sure those concerned citizens weren't actually members of War's coterie dressed in human skin suits."

"I've been following the arson investigation in the papers."

Done with my warning, I set the phone aside to play attentive co-diner, and that meant replaying what he'd said to catch the change in conversation. "Santiago thinks the fires are portents of Famine breaching."

"You disagree?"

Santiago had history with Famine that caused him to jump at shadows, and his hatred of her was well deserved, but that was a coterie matter. Wu hadn't earned the right to hear the heartbreaking details of how Santiago had lost his wife to Famine's machinations, and I wasn't about to betray his trust to satisfy Wu's curiosity.

"No one has set me down for Cadre 101 classes yet, but it seems to me if Famine was going to start a fire to wipe out crops, she would focus on the destructive aspect. That's her gig, right?" I tried putting what had been bothering me into words. "What's happening with those cases isn't just arson. People with no history of mental health issues are clocking in to work one day, their psycho switch is flipping without provocation, and they're burning everything down around them before committing suicide. It's too staged. It's almost like . . . "

Wu leaned closer. "Yes?"

"It's almost like someone is using Famine's MO to commit crimes, like they're trying to convince us she's already breached, and they're wiping out any evidence that links those acts to the true perpetrator in the process." And they were doing a damn fine job of it. The scope of destruction was truly worthy of Famine and her coterie. "It's War. It has to be." I could even guess how she'd managed the trick. "Her coterie has to bargain for skin suits. They could have infiltrated those farms at any time through employees with desires big enough to gamble on a demon's ability to deliver."

"Skin suits." He chuckled. "Talking to you is endlessly fascinating." His amusement tapered. "You should be aware 'demon' is derogatory. I figured an upstanding citizen such as yourself would want to know."

"I can't get the word out of my head," I admitted without throwing Santiago under the bus for making the comparison in the first place. "I mean to say charun, but my brain clashes with my tongue sometimes."

While he was graciously accepting my apology for my political incorrectness, our server arrived to take our order. Wu reached across the table and closed the folio, but he didn't draw it back to his side. That might have had something to do with my death grip on the leather, but I liked to think he would have afforded me the courtesy of reviewing the material had we not been interrupted.

"How is the infant?" he asked once our waitress bustled away to put in our ticket.

"She's a baby." Had a member of the coterie asked me that, I would have whipped out my cell and started scrolling through the digital equivalent of a wallet full of pictures. But I remembered the flash of his teeth so near Nettie's tender skin and nixed that idea. "She sleeps, drinks, and fills up diapers."

"In that," he mused, "all young are the same."

Something in his tone set my cop senses tingling. "Do you have kids?"

His lips parted before he moistened them. "I have friends with young children."

That was not a *no*. Interesting. There should have been zero hesitation given the prohibition on charun breeding, and yet . . .

Maybe Wu had sired offspring before joining the taskforce.

"How did you come to work for the NSB?" I meant to be smoother, but I was too curious. "How long have you been with them?"

"I followed in my father's footsteps." His lips twisted. "You and I have that much in common." He tipped back his head, staring at the ceiling. "I can't remember when I joined. Several decades ago. Six or seven. I was a freelance consultant before that. Not much has changed in how I operate except now I have an office and benefits."

"You're talking sixty or seventy plus years of service." I slow-blinked at him. "How old are you?"

I had gotten used to thinking of my coterie and me as contemporaries, even though deep down I was aware they were as timeworn as Conquest. But they had traveled so far. It made sense they were ancients. Wu talked like he had been born here. For whatever reason, that made my head throb.

"I lost count."

For a second, I thought someone had tripped the fire alarm, but no. Based on the calmness of our fellow diners, the ringing was in my ears. "What does your father do for the NSB?"

"That information is classified."

Smashing into that brick wall didn't bother me much, considering how disoriented his admission had left me.

"Not everyone is as fortunate as you." Wu chased condensation down the side of his glass with a fingertip. "Not all fathers are as worthy of a child's trust as yours."

All of a sudden, his soft spot for kids was starting to make a whole lot more sense.

"I did get lucky," I acknowledged, "but I didn't have to rely on genetics. My dad chose me. I have an unfair advantage. I wasn't an amorphous life about to pop into existence. I was a scraggly girl with big eyes and an even bigger stomach. He took one look at me and knew I was his little girl." A flush tingled in my cheeks. "That's what he says, anyway."

Wu crossed his arms over his chest and plucked at his fuller, upper lip while staring at me.

"What?" I hated mirrors, but I almost wished for one now. "Why are you looking at me like that?"

"You're really you." He rubbed his jaw. "I wasn't convinced before, I can see the echoes of Conquest in you, but you're Luce too."

"How can you tell?" I hated the wounded throb in my voice, the need to be reaffirmed as my own person.

"The cadre don't love the way humans do. Charun don't love that way, not with our whole hearts. It's biology, instinctual, to mate and to procreate. It's hardwired into some to mate for life and others to mate for a season, for some to raise their offspring and for others to abandon them to fend for themselves, but you feel beyond depths I thought possible for your kind."

Like a top spun, my thoughts whirled back to Cole, to our connection. And I wondered if he cared, if he *could* care, or if lust was the extent of his emotional range where I was concerned. That and his deep-seated hatred of Conquest.

"You're thinking about Heaton." Wu sounded disappointed in me. "Thinking about him always changes your scent."

"Uh, let's not go there." I cringed. "I'm well aware of the scent I throw off around Cole."

"Sadness." His nostrils flared the slightest bit. "Thinking about him makes you sad."

Relief swept through me, but on the heels of that came regret. That was what he scented on me. Not sadness. Unhappiness maybe. Grief. A wish that things could have been different between him and me, that I wasn't standing so deep in another woman's shadow he couldn't see me through the gloom.

"We can't have it all, right?" That was the closest I had ever come to acknowledging I wanted Cole out loud, and it stunned me that Wu, of all people, had coaxed that truth from me when I did my best to avoid thinking it, let alone admitting it. "What about you?"

He sat back, palms braced on the table. "What about me?"

"I assume, based on our fraternization talk, that you're single." Though the idea charun wouldn't seek out emotional ties when reproduction was off the table struck me as sadder than my unrequited whatever it was. "No lucky charuness has caught your eye?"

"No," he said, and for no good reason whatsoever, I was convinced he had just told me his first lie. "As I said, without the urge to mate, the other urges fade away too."

And that was his second.

Interesting.

Maybe dinner had been a good idea after all. The longer I spent with him, the easier I read him. An open book he was not, but I could make do with flipping a few pages of frontmatter for one night.

Our food arrived before I got to the good stuff, but my stomach couldn't care less about his past when I could practically hear the hushpuppies barking on my plate. I stole one before the waitress set my plate before me and popped it into my mouth. Judging by Wu's quiet astonishment as I demolished my meal, he'd had no inkling his future partner was three-quarters stomach, but he didn't seem to mind. Even if he couldn't keep up.

Dessert was served as the main course vanished, and we didn't get a say in the matter as we were each handed a swirl of gray ice cream served in a black cone. Twisting it in my hand, I took a delicate sniff. "Do I want to know what flavors make these color combinations?"

"The cones are made with almond charcoal, and the soft serve is made with black sesame seeds."

"You are a peculiar man with peculiar tastes." I gave a tentative lick, and my eyes rolled closed at the savory flavor. Nutty, toasty, with a slight crunch thanks to the seeds sprinkled on top. "Lucky for me, I seem to share them."

Wu's grin was cut short by my phone ringing. "You can answer it. I don't mind."

"Thanks." I brought it to my ear. "What's up?"

"Jones scheduled a press conference in a half hour if you want to tune in. Should be on all the local channels. Word is she's going to address the fires and ask the public to step forward with information if they've got any."

"The tip line will be lighting up like a Christmas tree." Too bad asshats with more time on their hands than sense made half those calls. "I don't envy whoever lands phone detail." And the unenviable task of weeding out the genuine tips from the crank calls. "This will be the first time Jones steps up to the podium as interim chief."

"Jones is good people. She's not going to lose her cool or go glory hog on us."

Roberta Jones resembled everyone's favorite auntie, the persona one she had cultivated during her years on the force, but she had been known to chop the legs from under a suspect with the sharp edge of her bright smile, and she had never once raised her voice to be heard. Respect did that for a person.

"Yeah." I gave myself an internal shake. "You're probably right."

"Bou-Bou, one thing you ought to know about me by now is that I'm always right."

I snorted so hard I almost choked on the lick of ice cream melting on my tongue. "You're something all right."

Rixton hesitated. "What's with the music?"

"Music?" I played dumb. "You must hear the TV."

"Unless you're watching Food Network for a change, then no. I'm not. You're out somewhere. I can hear the conversation around you and the clink of dishware." Glee rang through our connection. "You're on a date. Hot damn. A second date. Or wait—the drive was this morning. Does that make this part two of the first one?" He gasped. "Will this be a trilogy?"

"Keep this up, and I'm going to get a complex." My eyes met Wu's briefly. "I'm not on a date. I wasn't on a date earlier. I will never be on a date at the rate you and Uncle Harold are going."

That didn't begin to touch on Dad and his free tours for prospective suitors of his sprawling acreage and his shovel collection.

"Tell you what. You supply me with a list of candidates, and we'll handle the rest. I'll perform background checks on them, Trudeau can interrogate them, and then your dad can compile the data and select the best man for the job."

A groan eased past my lips. "You three are not in charge of finding me a man. Ever. Even if I wanted one, and I don't, no. Forever no. Infinity no."

"You never let me have any fun," he pouted. "Now that I have a daughter, I understand the requirements better than ever."

Oh God.

"A stable job, a fat bank account, a clean psych eval, a nice house in a good neighborhood—" he ticked off his requirements with gusto "—no chemistry, no touching, no kissing, no sex, no procreation without a surrogate . . ."

"As Nettie's godmother, I'm using my veto powers on at least half those items. Mostly the second half."

"Godmother veto powers are not a thing."

"We'll pick this up tomorrow, okay?" I shot Wu an apologetic glance. "I gotta go."

"'Cause you're on a daaaaate," he sing-songed.

I ended the call with a jab of my thumb and muted the ringer to block his redial, which . . . Yep. Right on time. Vibrating, my phone buzzed its way across the table. Ignoring Rixton, I gave up on my ice cream and placed it on an empty dish. "I would apologize for my partner since I'm sure you heard every word of that, but once I started, I would never stop."

Wu watched my ice cream melt for the longest time. "I can see I have even bigger shoes to fill than I first thought."

"Honestly, it's best if you don't try." The sentiment flashed his eyes up to mine, and I winced. "What I mean is Rixton is Rixton. I've already bought stock in him. What you have to do is sell me on you."

"I can do that."

He sounded so very certain he could that I questioned the sanity of offering him the advice at all. Maybe that's why I pressed harder. "What do you want from this partnership?"

"I want to break the cycle of violence that plagues this world," he said with such earnestness I had no choice but to believe him. "I think you and I can do that. Together."

A month ago, world peace would have sounded like a beauty pageant answer. Now it sounded pretty damn good if you asked me.

"Can we get the check now?" I stole one last scoop of

melting ice cream with my spoon. "I hate to rush, but I need to go face the music. I didn't exactly tell my uncle I was going out again, and he's likely to be cleaning his shotgun on the porch when we get back."

"I've already paid." He tossed his napkin on the table and rose. "We're free to leave."

"I might have spaced out while I was on the phone, but the waitress didn't bring our ticket. I would have noticed."

"They have my card information on file. They'll add the usual tip and charge me accordingly."

I pulled a fifty from my purse. "That ought to cover me."

Wu accepted the bill, wrinkled his forehead, and then folded it into a paper ring he slid onto my pinky. "I invited you out. This was my treat. You can pay next time."

"I'll hold you to that." I should have taken the ring off, but it was such a cool trick I left it on my finger.

During the return trip, I read the ubaste file from front to back, having no illusions about Wu letting me take the information with me. I was on my third re-read when he glided to a stop at the curb in front of the Trudeau home and came around to open my door. I let him, because it was kind of nice, and it sent the right message to the man waiting on the welcome mat for me wearing a Canton PD shirt over his faded flannel pajama bottoms and #1 Dad house shoes.

"Wait a minute," Dad called as Wu attempted to make his escape. "I'd like to have a word with the man who took out my daughter."

"Oh boy," I muttered then escorted Wu to his interrogation.

CHAPTER TEN

The dad who spent a solid ninety minutes extracting a fascinating—if totally fabricated—life story from Wu was absent at breakfast the next day. His clarity lasted a few hours after my *un*date ended, and we spent them on the couch watching a documentary on Torres Strait Islanders while munching popcorn and skimming SportsCenter in the hopes of catching the final score on the game he had slept through.

Glued to his side, I kept him company until cloudy-eyed exhaustion dragged him under before climbing in my own bed. The spaced-out look hadn't left him when I sought him out and found him staring at the same spot on the wall as usual.

Around the time I noticed I was gazing off too, a text came through from Miller assuring me that he and Santiago had vetted the clients with missing pets to ensure they were human. That didn't eliminate the charun element from the equation, given someone had riled up the ubaste, but it meant the clients had been victims and not cohorts. Now we just had to determine whether the same could be said for the arsonists.

Today was my last day off, and I had no plans. I ought to be working at the house, but I was hesitant to return until we received the lab results on the plant samples and isolated the cause of our episodes. The arson cases would keep another day. The ubaste situation was handled. Miller had a bead on War, so I wasn't needed there either.

A month ago, faced with a clear schedule and a surplus of energy, I would have dropped hints until Maggie declared a girls' day out and kidnapped me for lunch and an early movie. She would have paper, rock, scissored me into watching her choice, and I would have sucked it up and lost myself in the latest dramedy to hit the big screen.

One thing would have led to another, and she would have ended up calling her fiancé, Justin, and inviting him to join us in town for a late dinner. He would pass, and we would hang out until dawn or exhaustion drove us back to our homes.

But my best friend was in isolation, in an unknown location, while Portia attempted to bargain with Maggie for the use of her body. That was assuming Portia had already healed the multitude of life-threatening wounds that led to her offering to merge with Mags in the first place.

Maggie returning with a dual personality was daunting enough. Factor in the possibility Portia might return in control of my best friend's body while there was no spark of her consciousness behind those bright, hazel eyes? I wasn't sure I could handle looking at her, talking to her, without a hint of Mags in her body language.

Maggie was going to despise me for the choice I'd made, for ruining the life she'd built, but as long as she was alive to hate me, there was a chance at redemption. I had to believe that. I would go crazy with guilt if I didn't.

"You look thoughtful this morning." Aunt Nancy joined me at the table carrying a bowl full of cereal with sliced fruit layering the top that she set in front of me. "Did that nice young man put this look on your face?"

Wu was not nice, young, or a man. "I was thinking about Maggie."

"Oh, tater tot." She reached across the table and covered my hand, hers chilled from the cold bowl. "You didn't get bad news, did you?"

"No." There had been no updates on the case. Kapoor was handling the fallout, which meant he would soon meet with Portia and Maggie to discuss what lie he could feed her family while causing the fewest ripples. More than likely, her case would be marked cold or an unclaimed body would be used to fake her death. Either outcome would gut her family, but one offered hope that normalcy might one day return while the other was a permanent solution. "I'm just missing her. Rixton is doing his best to fill the gap, Sherry is too, but they've got Nettie. They need to be focused on her, not me." The truth of it was, "I wish there was more I could do."

"We're keeping her in our prayers, and Special Agent Kapoor is doing his best to find her. That's all any of us can do."

"At the risk of being put to work if I admit I'm bored—I'm bored." I dug into the breakfast she'd made me. "I have work I could be doing, but I want to get out of my head for a bit."

"You can't work at the house today?" Not an ounce of censure threaded her voice. She wasn't cracking the whip to get us gone. It was only natural that she would ask, considering I had spent all my spare time making repairs, which backed me straight into a white lie. "I'm waiting on an order to arrive.

There's not much left to do now that the bay window is in without those supplies."

"Well, in that case, you can help me with the garden." A broad smile stretched her cheeks. "If I had known I'd have a worker bee with me today, I would have picked up supplies yesterday. Would you mind driving me down to Mervin's? I have the worst headache today. I don't want to chance getting behind the wheel."

Between shoveling in bites, I reassured her, "I'm happy to play chauffer."

Migraines were no joke, and Aunt Nancy had suffered from the vestibular kind all her life.

"I bought some Confederate jasmine plants earlier this week. I would love a trellis for them to climb. Your eyes are better than Harry's these days, your hands steadier too." She indicated I should carry my bowl with me into the backyard as she outlined her plans. "The man won't wear his glasses, and the last time I asked for his help, I ended up with the Leaning Tower of Pisa for tomato cages." She indicated a few plastic trays filled with white flowers stacked on the porch. "Come smell these for inspiration."

I did as I was told, and the perfumed sweetness filled my lungs. "They're lovely."

"Jasmine is my favorite flower. Always has been." She smoothed the peeling label with its mason jar logo back in place. "When I saw these at the nursery, I couldn't resist."

A day of hard labor, where I could turn off my brain and follow orders, was just what the doctor ordered. We finished breakfast then hit the home improvement store, where I grabbed the supplies for what she had in mind.

More than a dose of much-needed normalcy, I relaxed into the work, feeling like I was earning my keep for the first time since arriving at the Trudeaus'. While neither my aunt nor uncle would see it that way, Dad had raised me to pull my own weight. While he might have meant it metaphorically, I was pretty sure as Aunt Nancy transformed her simple trellis design into a full-scale pergola, I hauled enough lumber to make it literal.

That night I fell into bed aching, sunburned and exhausted, and I slept better than I had in weeks.

Ungluing my eyes required more effort than I was willing to expend. So when my cell lost its damn mind around three in the morning, I groped on the floor until I hit cool plastic and brought it to my ear. "Hmmph?"

Rixton greeted me with "There's been another fire."

"Where?" Canton was running out of real estate fast.

"Madison."

That woke me up enough to slit my eyelids. "That's not in our jurisdiction."

"Jill Summers, the arson investigator for MFD, heard about the Hensarling and Culberson fires and gave Dawson a call. He returned the favor, and I agreed we'd meet them."

There was a weary resignation to his tone that set the hairs on my nape prickling. "What aren't you telling me?"

"There are five bodies. Four kids." He cleared his throat and started again. "The mother locked them in the basement with her, and the house burned down around them."

All vestiges of sleep evaporated. "I'm getting dressed now." I climbed to my feet and started looking for a clean uniform. "Where do you want to meet?"

"I'll pick you up. I'm ten minutes out."

Ending the call, I tossed the phone on the air mattress and suited up for work. A quick twist of my wrist got my hair out of my face, and I stomped on my boots. Unsure what we were about to walk into, I slung my backpack with the Culberson file and my electronics over my shoulder.

Dad was snoring as I crept past the living room and backed out the front door into a wall of hard muscle. I jumped at the unexpected contact.

"You're leaving early," Cole rumbled when I whirled to face him. "Rixton called?"

"Yeah," I said, voice tight. "There's been another fire. This one in Madison."

"Anything we can do to help?"

Reflex prompted me to demur, but I was learning demons—*charun*—got huffy when their help was declined. "We're trying to source the manufacturer on the drip torches used in the first two fires. The labels were burned off, but there should be serial numbers stamped on the bottoms. I'm not sure if the same device was used to start this fire, but it seems likely if we were called. I can get you that information in a few hours if you're interested."

"Text me when you know something. Any photos you can spare will help Miller pinpoint connections between the three."

I worried my bottom lip between my teeth, aware I was crossing lines. Sharing information on an ongoing police investigation was a big no-no, but the department brought in consultants all the time. Human laws wouldn't help us combat an inhuman crime spree. For that, we needed the charun perspective and all the help they could give us.

"I'll do one better. I'll email him copies of our notes." Not that he needed them. Miller was a research fiend. "That will save him a few keyboard strokes."

"All right. I'll let him know to be on the lookout." Cole paid the road particular attention. "I'll be close if you need me."

I used his distraction to study his profile, and my fingertips itched to trace the lumps down the bridge of his many-times-broken nose. "You drew babysitting duty tonight, huh?"

"We rotate." Cole returned his attention to me. "Would you have preferred Miller?"

"No," I blurted. "It's nice. Seeing you."

Nice was probably not the best word choice. Every single time we bumped into each other, one of us left the confrontation raw.

Shifting his weight onto his rear foot, he gave me breathing room between him and the door at my back. "I should have told you I was sending Thom in my place."

"I was—" *relieved, disappointed, relieved, disappointed, relieved* "—not expecting him. It all worked out, though."

"He told us you handled yourself out there." What looked an awful lot like pride lit up his face. "He said you went straight for the snout."

"More like the snout went straight for me." A shudder rippled through me. "It was like a bad first date where the guy is convinced the cost of dinner has purchased him a goodnight kiss."

His voice grated. "Speaking from experience?"

An unwelcome realization dawned on me. Since Cole was on guard duty tonight, he had tagged along on my dinner *un*date with Wu. He must have sat in the parking lot, idling in his SUV, while I tried black sesame ice cream for the first time and made nice with the man who was about to become a stylish fixture in my life.

"A little," I admitted, thinking of Joey Tacoma and the horror stories Maggie had shared with me over the years. "Most boys were too scared of Dad to put their hands—let alone tongues—on me." After Joey, none of them even tried. "Now Mags, she could tell stories that curled your toes. She was the social butterfly." Use of the past tense caused the words to get hung in my throat. "One upside to discovering I'm charun? I can blame all those failed first dates on interspecies incompatibility."

Much to my surprise, Cole laughed. A soft huff that managed to sound as startled as the smile I gave him in return. That's when it hit me. We had been carrying on a conversation, one spiked with landmines of personal information, yet he wasn't grinding his molars into dust.

All those words he always seemed to be chewing over, the ones stuck in his craw, well, maybe a few had escaped in my yard the day we clocked that six-minute mile to the pond.

"I read your report." He eased back another step, and I followed him to the curb. "I had no idea the NSB was microchipping the lower charun. That's valuable information. It will make identifying them easier in the future."

"You already placed an order for top of the line chip readers, didn't you?"

"Santiago is hacking their systems as we speak," he said, which was answer enough. "He plans on mapping their infrastructure and using it to construct our own information portal."

Hearing that didn't surprise me. "How did he gain access?"

"Thom hunted down another lower charun, tranquilized it with his saliva, then removed the microchip while it was unconscious. Santiago took it from there."

"Well, since it looks like we're stuck with Wu, at least he's good for something." Even if he didn't know it yet. "That reminds me. He and I talked about more than the ubaste. We discussed the fires too. I'd like to bounce some of our theories off you later if you have time."

Cole pulled out his cell. "I'll text Thom and let him know I'm taking his shift."

"You don't have to go that far," I insisted. "We can hash it out over the phone."

"I don't mind."

I fidgeted with the strap on my pack to give my hand something to do besides itching for an excuse to touch him, and the movement caught his eye.

Cole fixated on the strap, no, on my hand. "What is that?"

I looked down and spotted the origami ring. "Oh." I flexed my fingers like I was just as surprised to see it as him. "Wu made it for me out of the fifty I tried to use to pay my half of the bill."

"You're still wearing it," he said flatly.

"It's cute." And I was an idiot for not removing it sooner when any member of my coterie would sniff it out and know who made it and wonder why I had yet to unfold the bill and return it to my wallet. Whimsy was not an excuse they would buy. "I shouldn't have worn it out, though."

"No," he agreed, "you shouldn't have."

"It's not a mark of ownership." Though, according to Thom, Wu was all about marking his territory where I was concerned. "It's just a fun thing."

"With charun, it's never just a fun thing. Gifts carry meanings."

"There." I slid off the ring and put it in my pocket. "Better?"

Without answering, he popped the snaps on his leather bracelet, exposing the thick ridges of heavy scar tissue built up around the rose gold band that circled his wrist. Holding out his offering, he waited until I extended my arm in acceptance before securing it in place. The band was four inches wide and sized to fit him. On me, it looked more like an archery bracer. His heat still warmed the metal fasteners, and his scent was engrained after so many years of wear. It was all I could do not to bring it to my nose and inhale the potent combination of leather and man.

Gifts carry meanings.

What did this one say?

The leather bracelet and his matching watch kept his bands, Conquest's mark of ownership, concealed. Exposing them could mean so many things. That he was no longer ashamed of the connection, that he no longer cared to hide who and what he was, or simply that he had five more tucked away in a drawer at the bunkhouse and could afford to lose one.

"Cole." I spun it around my wrist. "I . . ."

Headlights flashed in the distance, their familiar shape giving away the driver's identity.

"That's Rixton." I glanced back at Cole and found him fixated on where I had tucked my arm against my chest, cradling the gift he'd given me like it was precious, and it was. Whatever the symbolism to him, it meant everything to me. "Guess I'll see you around?"

"Not if I do my job well you won't."

With a nod, he walked away, leaving me to be eaten alive by my curiosity as he made a quick turn down Burberry Street then dipped into the shadows cast by a hedge acting as a privacy fence on the corner. I was searching for signs of where he'd gone when Rixton slowed in front of me, lowering his window as he rolled to a stop.

He leaned out and followed my line of sight. "Who was that?"

Rixton must be distracted if he wasn't calling me out on the mysterious *who* being Cole.

"A friend," I murmured, tucking my hand behind my back.

Without meaning to, I had set him up to crack a joke at my expense, something along the lines of "Yeah, your *boyfriend*" but he didn't rib me as I joined him. There was too much darkness gathered in the cab for him to dispel it with humor. The numbers struck me again.

Four kids. *Four.*

No wonder Rixton had been rendered mute.

"I spoke to Dawson before I left the house," Rixton said at last. "He's driving down too."

Made sense. He would have to liaise with his counterpart in Madison. "Has he given you anything on our cases yet?"

"The Hensarling Farms fire was started in the southeastern corner of the field. Wind speed and direction must have been calculated for maximum damage. That or Rowland got lucky. The fire swept up and across the property, destroying ninety percent of the crops before the fire department got it contained. The same accelerant responsible for starting the initial blaze was found in the drip torch basin." He shook his head. "For Dawson, it's an open and shut case."

"Or it was until the Culberson fire," I prompted, hoping I wasn't hearing what I thought I was hearing.

"The second fire destroyed a home and a homebased business. Most of the livestock survived, and there were no fatalities. The only injury was the arsonist, and he's expected to make a full recovery baring any complications from his burns." A scowl cut his mouth. "Dawson warned we can't rule out the possibility someone read about Hensarling and got inspired, but a copycat doesn't feel right to me."

"I agree." The incident felt too deliberate considering the previous fire. "Plus, the odds of the Culbersons finding a scapegoat willing to torch himself within twenty-four hours are slim." Even then, it took fanatical devotion or the promise of a fat payoff to prompt that type of sacrifice. "What do we know about the third fire?"

"The body count," he said gruffly. "The rest we'll learn when we get there."

There turned out to be a grassy plot on the edge of town. I counted six industrial greenhouses, each spaced within a dozen feet of each other. A mason jar had been hand-painted on the side of the nearest one, and a cheerful green sprout pushed up through its open mouth. Bold letters spelling out *Orvis Nursery* filled the glass in lieu of dirt. The siding had melted like wax in some parts and warped in others from the heat, but the structures themselves appeared stable. The same couldn't be said for the small home positioned behind the business.

Charred lumber rose like crooked fingers from the cooling ash scattered across the grassy yard. I got the impression the house had been two stories but compact, and it sat on a thick concrete slab. Firemen stood beside their engine, lights flashing, but the blaze had run its course. They were packing up to leave as we arrived.

A short woman dressed in a navy pantsuit stood about three yards away from the house with a camera in her hands. She walked around a spot on the ground, snapping pictures. The shock of red hair identified her as Jill Summers, the arson investigator for the Madison Fire Department. This was her scene.

"Ms. Summers," Rixton greeted her. "Dawson invited us down. I hope you don't mind."

"Sorry to roll you guys out of bed so early, but I heard about the trouble up in Canton and thought you might want to examine the scene." Her pale blue eyes flicked to mine. "Heard you got Chief 'I'm Ready For My Close Up' Timmons kicked out on his wrinkly ass."

"He got himself booted out of office." I drew a circle in the air. "I just painted on the bullseye."

Summers cackled before she rubbed a hand down her face and wiped away her amusement.

"Let me walk you through what we've got. The house had a full basement. One corner was a solid concrete box reinforced with rebar that acted as a storm shelter or—considering the fat stack of incident reports on her ex—a safe room." Mr. Orvis would be the prime suspect, the husband always was when the victim was his wife or kids, and his list of priors wasn't doing him any favors. "There were two ways in or out. One through the basement, and one through the cellar doors." She nudged a set of double doors inset into a cement frame with her boot. The heavy chains wrapping the thick handles jingled with each kick. "Ms. Orvis engaged the locking mechanism behind her once they were all in the shelter. The cellar doors aren't warped from impact or otherwise damaged as far as we can tell."

The chains gleamed, and the padlock linking them did too, a stark contrast to the rusted metal door they guarded. "Do we know if this was intentional?"

"It's too early to tell," Summers admitted, but a somber edge had entered her voice. "The bedrooms were all on the second floor. Each room had a window, but there was no emergency ladder we could find. The first floor had two exits, a front and a back door. Those must have been inaccessible to drive them down."

"The chains and lock are both recent additions." The new hardware bugged me, but Ms. Orvis had had four panicked kids to shepherd to safety. Mistakes would have been made, in judgement and otherwise. "Maybe Ms. Orvis forgot the exit was locked or hoped she could knock the door off its hinges."

"Maybe," she allowed. "Odds are good they succumbed to smoke inhalation soon after the interior locking mechanism was activated. That could explain why there was no apparent damage to the door. They might not have made it that far."

"I don't mean to split hairs," Rixton began, "but if you think this was an accidental fire, then why did you call us to consult?"

Abandoning the cellar, Summers led us to a pile of debris spread out on a white cloth. "Anything look familiar?"

Rixton met my gaze over her head, his expression as tight as my pinched lips. I squatted next to the fabric and got a better look at the rusted hunk of metal, untouched by the flames. "It's a drip torch, similar in size to those discovered at the Hensarling and Culberson fires."

Joining me, Rixton glanced up at Summers. "Where did you find this one?"

"Outside the cellar doors. About where we were standing. I've got photos if you want them."

"We'd appreciate that," he said. "Send us copies of all you've got, and we'll do the same."

Both our arsonists had been caught red-handed, but it was too early to count this as a third incident.

"Rixton," a tight voice called. "Boudreau. Glad you could make it."

We stood and greeted Dawson, but he was quick to move past us to Summers. He was eyeing her like a man drowning in shark-infested waters, his gaze pleading for a hand up into her lifeboat. Clearly, the higher ups were applying pressure to find answers before a third tragedy struck Canton.

Rixton and I left the arson investigators to compare case notes while we walked the perimeter. Nothing stood out as important, but I snapped a few pictures of the area on my phone out of habit.

"Might as well check out the greenhouses while we're here," he said when we'd finished our circuit.

The walk didn't take long. As far as morning commutes went, Ms. Orvis had had a good one. We left the intact buildings alone and focused on the damaged ones. Circular burns in clusters on the walls left the siding as spotted as a ladybug in places, though the worst damage had been done to the wooden tables that held inventory. Several plants were blackened or reduced to ash, withered in their plastic pots or dumped on the dirt floor as their stands collapsed.

A wash of heat swept up my nape, and I tugged at my collar. "Is it hot in here to you?"

"Half the left wall is missing," he pointed out. "It's no worse in here than it was outside."

"Must be the long sleeves." I rubbed my hands up my arms, my skin itching. "I'm roasting in here."

"Bou-Bou." Rixton cornered me near a stand of tomato plants. "You're pouring sweat. You good?"

"Yeah." I mopped my sleeve across my forehead. "I just need some air."

He didn't mention the breeze sweeping through the greenhouse or remind me about the missing wall. He just stepped aside and let me go without comment. I stumbled through a side door that led into a narrow alley between buildings and leaned against the ribbed wall until I could breathe again.

A hulking shadow broke from the gloom. "Luce."

The muscles along my inner thighs quivered at the sound of his voice.

Cole flared his nostrils. "You smell . . ."

"Can we not revisit that conversation right now?" A gnawing hunger sparked by his proximity feasted on my bones. I fumbled within, summoning the cold place, desperate to ice this clawing need, but the heat flaring along my nerves melted away any chance of relief before I could dive in. "Don't come any closer." I threw out a hand to warn him away from me, and the fasteners on his bracelet glinted on my wrist. "I'm having hot flashes." I was cramping, my core spasming, from wanting him. "What the hell is wrong with me?"

"We're at a greenhouse." Low and soothing, he kept his voice calm. "Whatever the plants were at your house, they must grow them here too."

Had my motherboard not been fried, I might have come to the same conclusion. "You're too close."

"I haven't moved." He eased back a few steps anyway. "Is that better?"

"No," I moaned, sinking to my knees. "You've got to leave." A throbbing heat curled up through my middle, and some bastard drove a spike of ice through my left eye. "Please, Cole. Just go. I can't think with you here."

A primal growl vibrated through the space between us, and every inch of my skin lit up as though he had reached out and stroked me. Good Lord, the ache had me crawling toward him on all fours, and he didn't have the sense to run.

Why wasn't he running?

"Bou-Bou?" Rixton skidded to a stop in front of me. "Are you hurt?"

The only answer I had for him was the furious roar clogging my throat at having my hunt interrupted. My fingers curved into claws, and the urge to slash out at him, punish him, left me with the phantom sensation of his blood slicking my fingers. I wet my lips and imagined the hot, metallic taste.

And then I tossed my cookies.

"Shit." He leapt out of range of the vomit splatter. "What's wrong with you?"

"Allergic reaction," I rasped through swollen lips.

Elbows wobbling, I crawled on hands and knees toward
the ruined house and away from the nursery. When Rixton
offered me his hand, I recoiled. I felt sick. Physically unwell.
Mentally ill.

I had roared at Rixton like I had swallowed a lion.

I had imagined the weight of his blood coating my hands.

I had barely restrained myself from committing an unforgiv-
able act of unprovoked violence.

"What can I do to help?" Rixton hovered over me like
a moth. "Should I call your dad? Harold? One of your boy-
friends?"

"Water." I kept crawling, ignoring his jibe, but I was starting
to attract attention. "Need water."

Rixton bolted for the greenhouse behind us and returned
moments later with a hose pouring icy water. He held it out to
me in expectation I would want to drink or rinse out my mouth.
I took the thing from him and held it above my head, showering
my entire body with a shock of frigid liquid that extinguished
the embers of my earlier desire and the rage at having been
thwarted. I sat there under the spray until the weight of several
pairs of eyes fell on me, and the soft clicking noises phones made
when they snapped pictures cleared the haze.

"Put your phones down before I smash them, and give her
some goddamn privacy," Rixton snarled at the gathering. "If
any pictures show up online or in the paper, I'll know one of
you are responsible. I will find that person, and I will make
their life a living hell. Are we clear?"

The group dispersed after that, a few guys flashing their
phones as if to prove they had erased the images, but even more
stomped off pissed at being called out for assholish behavior.
I reached over to rest my palm on the top of his shoe and
croaked, "Thank you."

"Don't thank me for demanding they treat you like a person and not a byline. Jesus, Bou-Bou. Sometimes I wonder what Sherry and I were thinking having a kid. Bringing Nettie into all this ugliness."

Sometimes he wasn't the only one.

CHAPTER ELEVEN

Rixton didn't waste his breath suggesting we go to the hospital. I picked myself up, skin too sensitive for contact, and let him bundle me in a blanket he'd stolen from the back of an ambulance. Once he had me tucked in the cruiser, he made a beeline for the nearest drugstore and carved himself out a parking space in front of the sliding glass doors. He came out swinging a plastic bag and got behind the wheel.

"Drink this." He jabbed a bendy straw through the foil seal on a bottle of Benadryl and passed it over to me. "We've got to get the swelling down."

Arguing with him would get me nowhere. I accepted the small bottle and started sipping. "Pretty sure you're not supposed to chug this stuff."

"We are going back to my place," he informed me. "You are going to shower, you are going to sleep in our guest room, and Sherry is going to mother hen you. I would threaten to cock you, but that sounds both sexual and violent. So just trust me when I say I'll be getting my rooster on too. You are going to allow this, because we love you, and you almost made me shit myself back there."

"Sorry," I mumbled around the straw.

"You've been acting like a long-tailed cat in a room full of rocking chairs for weeks. Jane Doe, Maggie, the super gator attack. Plus the hot mess with Timmons and his pet vulture. Your dad's relapse." A very human growl revved up his throat. "Life is kicking you in the lady bits, hard, and I've got no way of shielding you without ending up embroiled in either a sexual harassment or divorce lawsuit."

"I've got a lot on my plate right now." I smacked my lips, but the fake cherry flavor burned all the way down. "Things will level off soon."

"That's not good enough, Bou-Bou." He slashed his hand through the air. "Tell me you're okay, or tell me you're not, but tell me the truth. If you're sinking, if all this is too heavy for you, I'm sticking out my hand. All you have to do is grab on, and I will haul your ass out of that water before you go under."

Tears welled, threatening to fall, but I couldn't find my voice. All I could do was nod my thanks.

A copper tang soured the cherry aftertaste on my next pull of Benadryl, and I couldn't swallow hard enough to clear the thickness in my throat. The crimson liquid, viscous and rich, turned my stomach when I licked a sticky drop off my thumb.

"Pull over." I clamped a hand over my mouth. "I'm going to be sick again."

"Hold tight." He guided us off the shoulder of the road. "Do you need me to hold your hair?"

"No." I fell out the door and collapsed in the grass on my knees as I voided my stomach.

All those cracks in my façade that had everyone so worried? Pretty sure this counted as one of them.

Sherry fussed over me for a good hour before tucking me in the twin bed in the guest room with a promise she would call Uncle Harold and let him know I was playing houseguest for the morning. She and Nettie were up for the day, but Rixton was beat, and I was too. Tucked under the covers like I was a kid again, I listened to the clink of dishes in the kitchen and the comforting babble of my goddaughter.

I was staring at the ceiling, unable to relax into sleep, when a thump at the window drew my attention.

Cole filled the opening with his wide shoulders, and I turned onto my side to get a better look. I expected him to ask for an invite, but he made no move to raise the glass. Smart man to keep a barrier between us. He brought his phone up to his ear, and mine rang seconds later.

"Hey."

My jaw stretched on a yawn. "Hey yourself."

His gaze swept over me from head to toe before settling on my face. "How are you feeling?"

"Not great." Talk about an understatement. "This time my reaction was off the charts."

"I don't think we have to worry about a cumulative effect. There's a good chance it was the sheer number of plants that overwhelmed your senses." He hesitated. "Has it worn off yet?"

"Rixton made me drink a bottle of Benadryl, which I mostly vomited right back up, but it seemed to help."

"Benadryl is a histamine blocker." The tight bunch of his features eased into thoughtful lines. "That might explain how it brought you down so fast. I'll run the possibility past Thom and see what he can mix up to inoculate us against the plant."

"It's a good thing I can't shift the way you can." I rubbed the heel of my palm over my heart, as though any cracks forming would fan out from that point. "I made a spectacle of myself. Rixton threatened all the wannabe photogs, but I'm not holding my breath."

"That's not what has you shaken."

"I almost hurt him, Cole. I imagined how his pain would feel, how his blood would taste." I pulled the covers up higher on my chest. "Is this how it starts? Are these the first signs of Conquest rousing? What if she's been waiting on her sisters this whole time? Now that War is here and Famine is coming, maybe she's ready to crack me open like a walnut."

"You protected him from the urges. That's what matters."

Never one to utter empty platitudes, Cole didn't say the words I most longed to hear. He didn't assure me I would never hurt Rixton, didn't accuse me of overreacting, didn't promise me Conquest would remain sleeping, but the worst was when he didn't tell me everything would be okay.

"I'm scared to nap," I whispered. "I shouldn't have let Rixton bring me home with him."

"Sleep." Cole's fingertips brushed the glass. "I won't let you hurt anyone, Luce."

"You can't skulk in the bushes all morning. The neighborhood watch will call it in." I thought about it and then decided. "Or they might skip the police and call Rixton direct."

"I have natural camouflage," he reminded me. "I'll be back in twenty. Can you hold on that long?"

Despite the number of times I'd brushed my teeth, I still imagined the taste of copper. "Yeah." Cole turned from the window, and I sat up to watch him go. "How will I know when it's safe?"

With his back to me, I couldn't be sure, but I'd bet money he was smiling when he said, "You'll know."

A half hour later, he missed his deadline, and I tossed off the covers. I was prepared to suck it up and go without rest, but then the roof groaned overhead. Panic surged in my veins as the math of how much dragon a three-bedroom ranch could support tumbled through my head, but the resulting equation went something like this: Cole plus dragon equals safety.

Trust was an invaluable commodity, one that could not be bought, and I realized as I closed my eyes that I had given him mine.

Sherry had washed and pressed my uniform while I slept, eliminating the need for me to swing by the Trudeaus' before Rixton drove us to work. As much as I wanted to check on Dad, I wanted to get out of my head more, and the fastest way to do that was to bury myself in paperwork.

Dawson shot us both an update around dinner, but the bulk of his email contained information gleaned from Summers on the Madison fire that she had already shared with us prior to his arrival.

Over a platter of fajita fixings at our favorite Mexican restaurant, Rixton and I compared our own notes while stuffing our faces.

The Hensarlings and the Culbersons used different banks to finance their farms. Their insurance policies were carried by separate companies as well. No obvious strings tied the two together on a business level.

On a personal level, however, each farm employed several family members. A few of the Hensarling employees appeared to be connected to the Culbersons by blood or friendship, scandal or rumor, but there was nothing malicious in those relationships.

The deeper we dug, the less dirt we had to shovel. The

two crimes appeared to be random, unrelated events. This morning's tragedy was our last hope of catching a whiff of connection between all three.

By the end of the shift, I was antsy to follow up on a hunch, but first I had to shake Rixton. The problem was, he had picked me up, so he was dropping me off too.

"Thanks for the ride." I made to escape the cruiser onto the sidewalk in front of the Trudeaus' house. "And everything else."

"Remember our talk," he warned me. "I'm here if you need me. So is Sherry. So are Harold and Nancy."

"I know." I eased onto the sidewalk. "Night."

Rixton shooed me toward the front door. "Skedaddle."

Luckily, I had already made my peace with this necessary pit stop. Rixton put on a brave face, but I had shaken him earlier. Hell, I had rattled myself.

When I lingered in the driveway, he mimed a walking gesture with his fingers. He wasn't leaving until I was in the house with the door shut behind me. Getting out of there once I got in would be tough, but I needed to change and pick up supplies before I left again.

Thanks to our overlapping schedules, Uncle Harold wasn't at home. Aunt Nancy, however, waited for me in the hallway with a wrinkled brow and a tapping foot. "What happened that was so awful you couldn't face coming home?"

Though part of me wanted to insulate her from the ugliness of my morning, she had been married to a cop long enough to have heard it all by this point.

"Liam Dawson is working the arson cases that have been on the news. Rixton and I are helping." I shifted the pack on my shoulder. "Today we got called down to Madison. There's been a third fire. There were five casualties." I scuffed my foot, but I couldn't postpone the lie. "So, yeah. I wanted to decompress, no questions asked. Rixton offered to let me sleep at his place, so I crashed in his guest room."

Aunt Nancy stopped tapping her foot and raised a hand to her mouth. "I had no idea."

"I'm sorry I worried you, but the next few weeks are going to be rough. We've got to shut this down before more innocents are hurt." I dropped the bag at my feet so it would be easy to grab on my way out the door and put my cop hat on. "Mind if I ask you a few questions?"

Her hand lowered to her throat. "Of course not."

"Did you know Eliza Orvis?" This was going to get messy fast, but every scrap of information helped. "Your jasmine came from Orvis Nursery, right? I recognized the logo tonight and thought I'd ask if you knew the owner."

"Her in-laws go to church with us. That's how I heard about her business. The divorce got nasty over who got to keep it and the name, and they were stuck in the middle. I don't know Eliza except on sight, but the kids attend Sunday school every other weekend." Her gasp made me regret opening my mouth, and her fingers trembled. "You don't mean . . . ?"

"The house was burned to the ground," I said softly. "There were no survivors."

Her hand drifted back up to cover her lips. "The babies?"

I shook my head once.

"Lord have mercy." She spoke through her fingers. "I'll speak to Pastor Waite and see what can be done." She noticed the bag at my feet and sagged on her frame. "You're leaving again?"

"As soon as I change." I didn't expect what popped out of my mouth next. "I can move out if my hours are disrupting your schedule. The house is habitable. I'll still help with Dad, but at least you wouldn't have to deal with me coming and going at all hours."

"You're welcome to come and go as you please, tater tot." Her sigh carried sorrow. "I just hate you have to see so much ugly out there. Though I suppose someone's got to look. Blind eyes behold no injustice."

Eager to get changed and on my way, I edged closer to the living room. "How was Dad today?"

"He had a few lucid spells later this afternoon. They lasted about a half hour to forty-five minutes each. He was foggy again before he went to bed, but he's resting easy." She joined me on the threshold, both of us watching him sleep. "At this rate, he'll be ready for the department's annual bass tournament next month."

"Team Kiss My Bass does have a title to defend," I reminded her. "If anything is going to snap Dad out of this, it would be fear of losing that hideous trophy to one of the rookies."

"I'm just glad Harry lets your father keep it at your house." Her relief rang true. "I'm pretty sure it's an old mount with sentimental value that someone's wife wanted gone. I bet you five dollars the founder established a tournament in its honor as a means of thumbing his nose at the missus."

I snorted but had to admit, "You're probably right. I have to sweep scales off the floor every week."

Of all the chaos that had erupted in our living room, somehow that eyesore had remained unscathed. Bass can't get mange, but this one had the fish equivalent. Paired with the dry rotted board it was mounted to and the plaque held on with Gorilla glue, its value was purely sentimental.

I watched Dad a moment longer before I could tear myself away from him. "I better get going."

Aunt Nancy nodded in understanding. "Will you be back tonight?"

"That's the plan." I reached over and squeezed her hand. "I'll text you if anything changes."

Leaving her to finish her nightly routine, I shut myself into the sewing room and sent a text before changing into street clothes. Shrugging my backpack into place at the door, I headed out to my Bronco where I added the respirator and fresh cartridges to my supplies.

A black SUV pulled up to the curb as I was locking up, but the grin tugging on my lips released its hold as Santiago saluted me from the driver's seat with two fingers. I returned the wave after a slight hesitation then slid in beside him.

"Hey." I stashed my equipment at my feet. "Are you up for this?"

"Yep." The leather bracelet I had yet to remove caught his eye, but he only shook his head, like there was no point in fighting the inevitable. "Unlike Cole, I have a natural immunity to most toxins." As he guided us back onto the road, he curled his thin lips up in a smile that might have made him handsome if he'd kept his mouth shut. "I won't jump your bones unless you ask me nicely."

Thinking back to how things had gone down at the house, I had to ask, "And no one told me this, why?"

"Cole's engine was revved too high for rational thought, and Thom was too sluggish to process more than what was right in front of him. Miller's nose is crazy sensitive. He got a second-hand hit of the stuff, and his stomach growled the way it does before he vanishes into the swamp to make entire deer herds extinct, so I made myself useful and held a claw to his gut. Disembowelment wouldn't have stopped him for long, but it would have given us a chance to run."

Well, that explained his spontaneous show of affection that day. Santiago wasn't a touchy-feely guy, so it had struck me as odd how he'd embraced Miller like two friends having a chat. Threatening disembowelment? Now that was much more in character. "Have you made any progress with your database?"

"Yes and no. I downloaded about half of the information I wanted before a shadow noticed me poking my nose where it didn't belong and booted me. What I've got is enough to get started, but I'm going to have to sneak in again to get the rest." His lips twisted. "When you go active with the NSB, they're going to chip us too, and we're going to have to leave them under our skin so we give the appearance of compliance." The twist ironed out into an almost-smile. "The sooner I finish dissecting the chip we recovered, the sooner I can figure out how to disrupt the signal. Once I know how to ping their towers, we can fake transmissions and falsify our locations. Used sparingly, we can fly under the radar for brief periods of time."

The ability to hide from Wu would be priceless in the coming months. "Color me impressed."

"You might have noticed yanking people's chains is a hobby of mine. I look forward to giving Wu's a good, hard pull one day soon."

I laughed under my breath, well aware I shouldn't encourage him. "We need to teach him some boundaries." I toyed with the hem of my shirt. "Thom said he's been in my room. I'm not officially NSB property yet, and he's already got me carrying a cell that's basically a private line direct to him."

"That's a stopgap measure until you're chipped, I'm sure. He can track you, any calls you make, and any messages you send on that line." A thoughtful expression settled on his features. "It's got to be crawling with NSB bugs. Mind if I play exterminator?"

The offer to mess with Wu was too good to pass up. "As long as you don't hose me with your wand, I'm good."

A wide grin hit his mouth and stuck there. "Sometimes I almost like you."

"The feeling is nearly mutual."

We arrived at the nursery and had our pick of parking spaces. The area was isolated enough we didn't have to worry about neighbors spotting us and calling it in, but I wasn't in a hurry to explain why I had circled back without touching base with Summers if the local cops cruised past to spook looters.

"I'm going to suit up and take a look around," I told him before the mask made speech difficult. "Here's your new toy." I passed over the black phone then tugged on yellow dishwashing gloves pilfered from under the sink at the Trudeaus'. Once I popped in new filters, I strapped on the respirator and pulled out a set of goggles. Overkill maybe, but I didn't want to tempt fate. I had a hunch my lady bits only perked up when Cole was in the immediate vicinity, but I did not want to discover I was wrong only after I'd started dry-humping Santiago's leg while he cackled and filmed my humiliation to share with the rest of the coterie. "Come looking if I'm not back in thirty."

That fast, he had the back off the phone, its guts exposed to his lustful gaze. "Mmm-hmm."

Using the ruined house to orient myself, I located the greenhouse that had given me fits. As I retraced my steps, strolling the main aisle, a prickling sensation skated over my nape. I waited a moment to see if it passed. I still felt itchy, but not itchier. I decided to press my luck and flipped on my cell's flashlight. Three tables surrounded me, and any of the plants on offer could be the culprit, but my gut drew me toward a display in the rear. Written in a child's scrawl were the words: Cat Garden. The printed notecard beneath claimed all the varieties were cat-safe treats.

I snapped pictures of each plant on offer, making sure to get a clear shot of the identification pick stuck in each pot. Catnip, mint, cat thyme, licorice root, cat grass, lemongrass.

I froze over the last row, the white clustered blooms an exact match to the ones in my yard. *Valerian.* The mystery plant was valerian. I selected the heartiest one of the bunch and dropped it into an evidence baggie then sealed it tight. I would let the lab verify the match, but I had no doubt I'd isolated the culprit.

Back at the SUV, I raised the trunk to find a foam cooler awaiting me. I stuck the bagged plant in there, stripped off my equipment, and joined Santiago. He grumbled when the motion sent a miniature screw rolling, but he caught it before it dropped and went back to fiddling with the black phone's innards. A guitar pick stuck to his bottom lip, and an eyeglasses repair kit rested on his knee. Clearly, he didn't need much in the way of tools to be dangerous.

After snapping the shell back together, he turned it over in his hand. His phone had been connected to the black phone via USB since I arrived, and his fingers now flew over its screen.

While he was otherwise occupied, I drafted an email and CC'd in the coterie to save time. I included the snapshot of the plant and a quick note that identified it as the same one from my yard. I was skimming Cole's curt response about dropping the specimen off at the lab when my phone rang. The screen lit up with *private number*, and I flashed it at Santiago.

"Time's up." There was no doubt in my mind Wu was on the other end. "Did you get what you needed?"

"Yep." He closed an app bearing the White Horse logo on the black phone, erased it, did a quick scan, then placed it on my palm. "There you go. Your pest problem has been solved. According to the GPS, you're chillin' on the observation deck of the Empire State Building."

I drew back, startled. "It's that specific?"

"I might have helped the ruse along by implanting pictures I scooped off the Internet." His expression tightened. "I get why you did what you did, the deal with Kapoor, but Wu wasn't part of the bargain. He has no right to tighten the noose around your neck."

"If I balk now, before I've been sworn in, they won't trust me to tow the company line when the time comes. My word is all I've got, and I've given it to them." I stared at the phone blaring in my lap. "I can handle Wu."

The alternative, that our partnership would be a sham, was too depressing to entertain.

"I hope you're right."

Ready to solve at least one mystery, we circled back to the lab. The odds of me running into Veronica again were slim, but I still persuaded Santiago to deliver the samples with the excuse that if he was immune then it made the most sense for him to handle the drop instead of me suiting up again.

High from his shenanigans, he didn't fight me. For once.

On the drive home, he received a call that starched his spine. He carried on a low conversation with the added precaution of using that fluid language that poured in one ear and out the other. Nosy to a fault, I strained to hear, but I couldn't tell if the caller was male or female, and I had no clue about the topic.

Alone with my thoughts for company, I kept circling back to this morning. A niggling doubt plucked at the back of my mind, but it took me a minute to isolate the cause. The victims. Summers had described the scene, but we hadn't examined the bodies.

At the time, it hadn't struck me as odd. Considering I still dreamed of small teeth and silver wire, I blamed my subconscious. I had been so stoked not to have fresh images added to my nightmares that the lack hadn't registered.

As much as I wanted to share my epiphany with Rixton,

I didn't want to admit I had spent my night running around Madison with Santiago. Emailing Summers and requesting copies of the coroner's reports made more sense, so I did that to avoid a conversation about exactly why I had gone back to the crime scene without him.

Santiago ended his conversation before he parked at the curb in front of the Trudeaus'. While I was gathering my belongings, he kept slanting his eyes toward me and working his jaw. Since he wasn't the type to hold back, ever, I held still to provide him with the widest target area for whatever blow he was about to land.

"Spit it out." I braced myself. "I can handle it."

"That was Portia." A grimace twisted his face. "They're back."

They, as in both of them. *They*, as in a successful cohabitation. *They*, as in . . .

Muscles tensed, I braced for impact. "But?"

"Maggie doesn't want to see you." He studied the night beyond the windshield. "Portia said the bunkhouse is off limits to you until further notice."

The news hit me with the force of a Mack truck and knocked the breath out of me. I had expected her hatred. I had prepared for her cutting ties with me. I had earned that punishment and so much more. But acknowledging there was a knife sticking out of your chest didn't numb the pain when it was twisted.

CHAPTER TWELVE

————⊗————

The lab emailed me their report bright and early, not that I thanked them for the notification on my cell waking me. I read their findings through one squinted eye then flipped onto my back. The air mattress rocked under me as I hauled my backpack over by the strap and groped around in its middle. I wiggled my laptop free, placed it on my stomach, and started searching for information on valerian.

According to the Internet, whose medical advice was iffy at best, the root had anxiolytic effects. Its top uses appeared to be treating joint pain, menstrual cramps, anxiety, and sleep disorders. There were also footnotes about it working as an aphrodisiac, in that it lowers inhibitions to open a person up to their sexual cravings. Humans used the stuff as a sedative, but it stimulated cats, giving them a high similar to catnip.

That explained why exposure to the plant had blissed-out Thom, why I had been ready to climb Cole like a tree, and why Cole had been willing to let me. Miller's response was harder to peg, but if the plant lowered *all* inhibitions, that might explain his aggression.

Following that logic chain led me to two distinct and uncomfortable conclusions. Remove self-restraint from the equation, and Miller saw us, his coterie, his fellow charun, as food. Erase that same ironclad self-control from Cole, and he saw me as edible in a far more pleasant, if complicated, way.

Clearly reactions varied across species. Mine had me wondering if my inner charun was more along the lines of a dragon than a winged kitty given how valerian affected me. I could always ask Miller what lurked beneath my skin, he'd offered to tell me once, but I was certain nothing good would come from knowing.

Unable to fall back asleep, I dialed Flavie, a classmate from high school who'd started a weekend lawn care business that had exploded into her adult nine-to-five empire. Chipper as always, she answered on the first ring. "Hey, Luce. I heard about your dad. I hope he's feeling better."

"He's making progress. I'm hopeful." The stock answers annoyed me for no good reason, considering I was the one giving them, but I chalked it up to lack of caffeine. "I was hoping you could help me out with a weed problem."

"Sure thing." Lawnmowers buzzed in the background. "You know I dig landscaping."

I paid her the obligatory chuckle before getting down to the reason for my call. "There's a patch of valerian growing in my yard under that big oak in front." She cut our lawn when we let things get out of hand, so she knew the property well. "Turns out I'm crazy allergic to it. Do you think you could pull it out and comb the yard to make sure there are no more clusters growing?"

"No problem. We'll get you squared away."

"Thanks."

After ending the call, I joined the breakfast in progress in the kitchen. Dad was sitting at the table, and I flung my arms around his shoulders before delivering a smacking kiss to his cheek. The chatter fell off a cliff after my uncharacteristic show of physical affection, but everyone had recovered by the time I plopped down in the chair beside him.

There was no way to tell them that, thanks to the bond with my coterie, I was healing that disconnect between touch and sensation. Not enough to make me normal, maybe, but enough that I could show people who mattered that I cared in a way that had felt unnatural until other charun came into my life.

Dad sipped from his mug, casual as you please. "How's your young man?"

I almost blurted *Cole?* before I remembered he had misinterpreted Wu dropping me off as the end of a date thanks to the dress. "We're just friends." Minus the friendship. "You don't have to show him your shovel collection. Promise."

Uncle Harold grunted once, and Dad returned the guttural disagreement.

I almost felt sorry for Wu.

Almost.

My phone rang as I accepted the empty mug Aunt Nancy passed me from her place setting, and I elected to ignore the caller in favor of soaking up a peaceful morning with family. I muted the ringer, poured myself coffee from the pot on the table, and doctored it up just the way I liked it. The first sip scalded my tongue, but I didn't mind. It wasn't until I set down my drink that I noticed all eyes on me.

"Go on," Dad urged. "You might as well answer."

"The job will just keep calling," Uncle Harold agreed. "At least find out what it is you're avoiding."

"Whatever it is, it can keep until after she's had breakfast." Aunt Nancy pushed her chair back and headed to the stove where all the breakfast fixings had been covered by paper towels. She mounded eggs, bacon, and pancakes on my plate. Usually she only cooked big breakfasts on Sundays, but I wasn't about to complain about my good fortune. "You're skin and bones, tater tot. You need to eat more."

Between her and Rixton, I was far more skin than bones. Living here a week already required me sucking in my gut to fasten my uniform pants. Much longer, and I would have to file requisition paperwork for the next size up.

"Rixton feeds me a steady diet of donuts and iced coffee, and Sherry sneaks me frogurt." I hadn't been back to Hannigan's since the night Cole wrote his hefty check for damages, but she knew what I liked. "I don't think you have to worry about me withering away."

"Junk food doesn't count," she said, adding extra bacon. "You need to eat real food."

"Yes, ma'am." I accepted the plate, bowed my head while she murmured a quick prayer, then shoveled in as much food as possible before the vibration in my pocket guilted me into answering. It was during my second helping of bacon that the knock came at the door. I pushed back my chair. "I'll get it."

"Sit yourself down." Aunt Nancy pointed her tongs at me. "I'll get it. You finish eating."

She didn't have to tell me twice.

"Oh, hello, John. Would you like to join us for breakfast?" Her voice carried down the hall. "We're just finishing up, but there's plenty left over."

"Thank you, ma'am, but no." He cleared his throat. "I hate to break up a family meal, but I need to speak with Luce."

"Come on in." Footsteps preceded them into the kitchen,

and Aunt Nancy stepped aside to reveal my guest. "Your partner's here, tater tot. You can take your conversation to the
living room." She stuffed a paper towel crammed with bacon
into his hand. "We'll stay in here and give you privacy."

Rixton beamed. "Mrs. Trudeau, if I wasn't already married—"

"She would still be mine," Uncle Harold finished for him.
"And don't you forget it."

Chuckling, I guided my chastised partner into the living
room and waited for him to get to the point. "Boris Ivashov is
awake." Four pieces of bacon later, he wiped his fingers clean.
"We've got a short visitation window if you want to bring him
flowers." He crumpled his napkin into a ball. "I understand if
you'd rather I handled this solo."

All the delicious food Aunt Nancy had spent the last hour
coaxing me to eat threatened to spill.

"I have to go back there sometime." I had managed to avoid
stepping inside Madison Memorial since I signed myself out
against medical advice and hitched a ride to the swamp on
the back of a dragon. Sadly, that streak appeared to be ending
today. "It might as well be now."

Rixton left me to dress and grab my things. Aunt Nancy
pressed more bacon into our hands on our way out, and I didn't
blink when I noticed Rixton had already sat a box of a dozen
classic glazed donuts in my seat. I moved them aside, climbed
in, and passed them over as needed during the ride. I was
grateful for the iced coffee he left me in the cup holder since
breakfast kept sneaking up the back of my throat.

Paranoia that War had planted more than one of her coterie
on the staff at Madison Memorial kept my nape prickling as
we crossed the parking lot. Unlike on previous visits to the
hospital, I walked right through the sliding glass front doors
with Rixton. We both knew our way around, so locating

Ivashov's room only required finessing his number from the receptionist.

I entered the room ahead of Rixton, eager to escape the nurses lingering in the hall, and approached the bed. The patient had seen better days. The combination of blood loss, white bandages, and strain had sapped the color from him. He opened his eyes when we entered the room, identified us as cops, and managed to pale even further. But a nominee for Madame Tussauds, he was not. Despite his wan complexion, this guy was no dripping wax sculpture.

Culberson must have been mistaken about the severity of Ivashov's injuries.

"Boris Ivashov?" Rixton waited for confirmation, proving he was weighing Culberson's account against the wan figure reclining in bed too. "We're here to ask you some questions about the fire."

"I want to help," he rasped, "but the last thing I remember was loading the dishwasher."

Rixton made a few notes. "Have you ever used a drip torch?"

"No." Wide-eyed, he glanced between us. "Are they saying that's what started the fire?"

"No." I shifted my weight forward. "They're saying *you* started the fire."

"I've worked for Lacy and Peter Culberson for a decade. Why would I set fire to my livelihood?"

"That's what we're here to determine," Rixton said. "You're not giving us much to go on."

"Atonement requires an acknowledgment of wrongdoing. How can a person ignorant of their own guilt not be considered innocent?"

I shot Rixton a look that warned this guy might have a few screws loose.

"You understand the burden of guilt." Ivashov studied me. "Don't you, Officer Boudreau?"

A chill skittered up my spine. "We didn't introduce ourselves."

"You're wearing long sleeves to cover the markings on your arms," he reasoned. "I've read enough papers and watched enough TV to recognize you." He tapped his chest. "You're also wearing a nametag."

Reaching up on reflex, I ran my fingers across the bar of brassy metal, feeling the engraved grooves of my name.

"I got this, Boudreau." The genial warmth usually found in Rixton's voice cooled. "Wait for me in the hall."

Liquid syllables poured from Ivashov's lips, tugging on threads of forgotten memories, and I moved a step closer as though proximity might spark comprehension.

Understanding the charun language was beyond me, but I would recognize it spoken anywhere, and hearing it now tilted the floor beneath my feet. Suspecting War had a hand in this was one thing, but here was proof our arsonist was a charun wearing a skin suit. That made Ivashov a murderer for all that there had been no bodies at the crime scene.

"Out," Rixton snapped. "Now."

Over his shoulder, Ivashov held my gaze and switched back to English. "I won't harm him. I give you my word."

For some reason, I believed him. That didn't mean I was going very far. "I'll be right outside."

After ducking into the hall, I dialed up Cole and leaned against the wall. The reward for mashing my phone against my ear was a wince as he barked a gruff hello. We hadn't spoken since the dragon catnapped on Rixton's roof, not even to brainstorm, but his curt greeting shook me.

"We have a problem. I'm at Madison Memorial with Rixton." I checked the hall for perked ears. "We came to ask our surviving arsonist a few questions, and he popped off in the language you guys use. What do you call that anyway?"

"Otillian," he answered. "All conquered worlds are required to learn the fundamentals. It's a universal language among charun in the same sense as English is for humans."

I should have expected his answer, but it was a gut-punch all the same.

"Miller is in the lobby," he continued. "Once you and Rixton leave, he'll go up and assess the situation."

"Okay, that works. I'm going to grab Rixton and we'll—"

A woman's voice, husky from sleep, murmured in the background. Cole must have covered the receiver with his palm, because I couldn't make out what he said to her, only that the words were spoken in a gentle tone, more tender than any he'd used with me.

I wondered if I had woken him. I wondered if he was in his room, if she was in his bed. I wondered if War had been wrong about him being faithful to Conquest, to me. And then I wondered if there would ever come a day when I stopped caring what Cole did during the hours and days when he wasn't with me.

"I have to go." I ended the call and ignored the phone when it rang a heartbeat later. I was saved from myself when Rixton exited the hospital room. "Get anything useful out of him after I left?"

"All he wanted to talk about was you." His worried stare pinned me to the spot. "He must be one of the fanatics. Seeing you excited him too much for him to be of any use." His expression shifted into a glare. "Don't apologize. I see the words forming on your lips. We had no idea this guy was a fruitcake." He paused. "Okay, so we had a pretty good idea he was candied cherry crazy going in, he did light up a restaurant then pull up a chair, but there was no way to know you'd be his trigger. We're done here. You ready to go?"

No, I wasn't. I didn't have much choice, though. "Yeah."

Ungluing my heels from the linoleum took me so long Rixton glanced back over his shoulder. I wanted to hang around and wait on Miller so we could take another crack at Ivashov, but I couldn't think of a single excuse that would fly. Ivashov had tweaked Rixton's nose by making his interrogation all about me, and Rixton would no more let me in that room alone than he would toss Nettie into a tank full of piranhas.

The two halves of me kept brushing up against each other these days, and the friction was brutal.

Leading a duplicitous life wasn't anything new. I had always concealed aspects of my nature in order to fake being normal. There had always been the mask I showed the world, and the face I kept hidden.

These days I was elevating navel gazing to all new heights, and the mask I had worn so faithfully had started slipping. I was peering around its comforting edges at others like me, learning more about my new normal, discovering ways to sink deeper into my own skin. The idea of losing an ounce of my humanity terrified me almost as much as embracing the charun side of my heritage, but in order to remain who I was, I first had to understand who I had been.

Reaching that new plateau of enlightenment came at a price, and for me, that cost meant leaving behind parts of my old life to embrace a new one. For the first time since Kapoor neatly boxed me into joining his cause, I looked to the future with a smidgen of anticipation.

There would be fewer lies to remember once I worked with other charun, and I wouldn't have to break my brain in pursuit of two possible outcomes—the human-friendly one and the truth. Then again, that duality of thinking might always be part of my reality. There would always be two answers going forward, the seen and the unseen, and I would forever be seeking what lurked within the latter. It was part of my nature.

We must have passed Miller in the lobby, but I didn't spot him. Ignoring the stab of disappointment at being sidelined, I got in the car with Rixton and left Miller to handle coterie business. He would update me later, and that would have to be enough. With the case against Timmons still making headlines, and Jane Doe a question mark in the public's collective consciousness, I couldn't afford the extra scrutiny right now.

Rixton got a call before we made it out of the parking lot. I didn't pay much attention to his conversation until I saw he had turned left, heading into town, instead of right, putting us on the road home. I waited for him to finish before raising my eyebrows. "What's up?"

"That was Summers. There's a small problem with your request for the autopsy reports."

"What kind of problem?" I checked my phone to see if she'd emailed me, but I came up empty. She had reached over my head to Rixton, which annoyed me beyond reason. Men passing info along to male colleagues was nothing new, but it sucked to see a woman reinforcing those negative behaviors. Summers and I hadn't crossed paths enough to qualify as friends, but we were friendly, or so I'd thought. "Can she not share them?"

"The bodies are missing."

Jill Summers met us at a Waffle Iron off East County Line Road in nearby Ridgeland, the halfway point between her house and her office. She had secured a corner booth, and we piled on the bench opposite her. The waitress filled our mugs with coffee, her expression tightening when none of us ordered more, and she left us alone to pursue more lucrative tables.

"I'm surprised to see you here, Boudreau." She reached for a packet of artificial sweetener and managed to rip the thing in half with twitchy fingers. Fake sugar rained down on the table, and she gave up with a disgusted sigh. "I heard you were on vacation."

The annoyance beating under my skin quieted. "Who told you that?"

"I'm crap with names." She sipped her coffee black like the jolt might kick-start her brain and flagged the waitress down for a refill. Maybe too much caffeine explained the shakes. "Tall guy, early to mid-thirties. Asian. Black hair, brown eyes. A real looker. Dressed well. Slight accent."

Crap on a mother-effing stick. "Adam Wu?"

"Yeah." She snapped her fingers. "That sounds right."

Rixton swung his head toward me, his stare burning a hole through my right temple, but his question was for Summers. "What did he want?"

"The same thing as you," she said. "The coroner's reports on the Orvis family."

"Did he happen to mention why he wanted them?" Rixton rubbed his thumb in the bowl of his spoon. "Who he works for?"

"He works for All South Insurance." She shrugged. "The father, Timothy Orvis, is the beneficiary listed on all the policies. The couple was recently divorced, but they both lived in Madison. Greedy bastard must have cracked the whip on All South."

Rixton leaned forward. "What did you tell him?"

"The same thing I'm telling you. I collected my evidence, MPD collected theirs, and then the bodies were loaded into a transport and taken to the coroner's office for examination." She swept errant granules off the table onto the floor. "They never arrived. I spoke with the coroner myself, and my call was the first she had heard about the Orvises. She checked with her staff, but no one had been told to expect burn victims. They scanned their logs. No one had checked out any of their transports, but the odometer on one vehicle read higher than its last check-in. There were enough miles to account for a trip out to the nursery and back with about fifteen miles for padding."

Rixton's spoon clattered from his hand. "Tell me there's surveillance footage in the garage where the transports are kept."

"I could, but I'd be lying." A wry grin curved her lips. "I can remember when the system went digital, if that tells you anything. We're lucky we've got that much work already done for us. Otherwise, we'd be thumbing through the old log books to find out who was on call."

"We're going to have to pay Mr. Orvis a visit," I told Rixton.

"No, we're not." Rixton shook his head. "There's no concrete evidence connecting our cases. We can't impede MPD's investigation. The Orvis fire occurred within the Madison city limits. That makes Mr. Orvis their suspect, not ours. There's too much riding on us resolving these cases for us to stomp on another department's toes, particularly one who's a close neighbor."

Mentally, I was already composing Wu a scathing text message when I zeroed in on Summers. "How did my name come up in conversation?"

"I was dictating an email to you on my phone when he let himself into my office. He heard your name, mentioned he knew you, and led with that." She twirled her mug between her hands. "He wondered when I saw you last, I pretended not to remember, and I asked him the same to see if he was legit.

That's when he pulled one hell of a scowl and told me you were sightseeing up in New York."

Rixton nudged me in the ribs with his elbow. "Are you going on vacation and forgot to tell me?"

Wincing at how close the accusation mirrored the truth, I grimaced. "I'm not going on vacation anytime soon."

Rixton accepted that as fact and looked to Summers. "Wu must have embellished how well he knew Luce to get you to loosen up. Get it? *Luce*-en?"

Summers cackled while I rolled my eyes. Sometimes I forgot other people, who weren't joined at the hip with him for eight hours at a stretch, found him funny.

"We get it." Looking to Summers, I cleared my throat. "I owe you an apology."

"Who?" She glanced around. "Me? Why?"

"I got miffed when you called Rixton instead of emailing me a response."

"Us girls have to stick together." She lifted her mug, I lifted mine, and we clinked them together. "We have to prove ourselves every day and sometimes twice on Sundays. I would never overlook you based on your sex. Even if I had to ping Rixton, as the senior officer, I would still update you on the situation and not let you fly blind."

I ducked my head. "I appreciate that."

"Working under Timmons was bound to give you a complex," Summers allowed. "I can't say I blame you for looking for shadows where there are none." She pulled out her phone, started scrolling, and flashed me a glimpse of the home screen on her email app as proof. "Since Wu told me you were on vacation, I figured it was faster to just call Rixton and give him an update."

Feeling two inches tall, I mumbled further apologetic noises.

"Not that I don't enjoy meetings perfumed with bacon, 'cause I do," Rixton said, scratching his cheek, "but was there a reason why you wanted to do this in person?"

Summers pulled a manila envelope off the seat beside her. She held it out, leaving it up to us who made the grab, and Rixton murmured, "Ladies first."

That was all the encouragement I required. I pinched the clasp, pried up the flap, and hauled out a stack of crime scene photos that left me staring at five charred masses, all about the same size. "How tall was Ms. Orvis?"

"She was five-six according to her license," Summer supplied. "She weighed about one seventy-five."

I passed one of the photos to Rixton. "How old were her kids?"

"She had a set of seven-year-old twins, a six-year-old, and a five-year-old."

"How sure are we the fifth body belonged to Ms. Orvis?" There must have been a reason why they leapt to that assumption given the condition of the bodies. "What am I missing here?"

"Ms. Orvis contracted a rare gum disease in her early twenties and wore false teeth as a result. Considering one of the victims wore dentures, it was a safe assumption the final body belonged to Ms. Orvis."

"There's no way a hundred and seventy-five pounds cooked down to this but left dentures behind," Rixton said, reading my mind. "Were any tissue samples taken? What about the dentures? Were those bagged as evidence or . . . ?"

"The pictures you're holding? I printed those off out of habit. These days the higher ups want me to stick with digital files for reference unless I'm asked to turn in paper copies of my reports to the various parties involved, but you know how it goes with old dogs and new tricks." Her lips compressed. "The email containing those photos was erased from my account. It's gone. I called my guy over at MPD to ask if he would forward me another set." She lowered her voice. "The files had been scrubbed from the system. Not deleted, wiped clean. This is the only proof those photos existed."

I leaned back in my seat, tugging on my bottom lip. I could think of one organization whose agents were old pros at making evidence disappear. The fact Wu had paid her a visit bolstered my certainty the NSB had gotten involved. Why erase this crime but not the others? What was different about this scene?

The Hensarling fire gave us three corpses, the Culberson fire gave us a burn victim, and the Orvis fire gave us five bodies. The Hensarling dead had reached the coroner's office without a hitch, Ivashov had been admitted to the hospital, and yet these five bodies got lost in transit?

I examined each photo again. "Do you have a copy shop in town?"

"I can make any copies you need at my office," Summers offered.

"No, she's right." Rixton gathered the photos into a neat stack and returned them to the envelope. "You've got a problem. Until you clean house, it's safer if we do this on neutral ground." He tossed some cash on the table. "We can forward you scans if you'd like."

"You sound like you're leaving without me. I can't let those out of my sight. My superiors would skin me alive." She plucked the folder from his hand. "Let's go. I'll feel better knowing there's at least one more set floating around out there."

The copy shop was bright and clean, and the self-serve stations were ideal for our use as we set up an assembly line. I scanned the photos and emailed them to Santiago and Miller, figuring their accounts would be the most secure. As I finished, I passed each photo to Rixton, who printed five copies. Once he was satisfied we had all we needed, he passed off the originals to Summers, who tucked them in her folder. Before we parted ways, he passed her one of his collated stacks so she had a spare set.

While they divvied up the goods, I got an email from Santiago. None of the drip torches were a match. Different sizes, ages, manufacturers. Odds were good each had been found on the property it had been used to destroy, theft being a solid second option, rather than our perp going on a shopping spree down at the local Mervin's. That lead, such as it was, had dead-ended.

Though it must have killed him, Rixton managed to hold his tongue on the topic of Adam Wu until we were on the road back to Canton.

"What do you know about this Wu character?" His fingers drummed the wheel. "Before you answer, you should know your dad called and asked me to run a background check on him since you guys are dating."

"I'm going to strangle him." I dropped my face into my hands with a groan. "We aren't dating, and you can't go running background checks willy-nilly."

"What we learned tonight justifies me whipping out a shovel to dig around him." He tilted his head to one side and then the other, popping vertebrae. "I saw your reaction to him. He makes you nervous, and not in a good way. You all but threw Nettie at my chest then punted me to the curb to get us away from him." He spared me a quick, searching glance. "Talk to me, Luce. Why did Wu pay you a house call? Why did you go out to dinner with him? Why is he sticking his nose in this case?"

Suspicion from Rixton hurt, but I had earned it ten times over. He was too smart, too honest, and too good at his job to let me get away with vague misdirections and mumbled non-answers for long.

"He doesn't work for All South." I placed my sweaty palms on my thighs and gazed ahead while I started laying groundwork for my defection. "He's a recruiter."

"A recruiter?" Rixton did a double-take before returning his attention to the road. "For who?"

"The FBI."

"The FBI," he echoed. "They're looking at you?"

His surprise bordered on comical, except this was no laughing matter. "Yeah."

"Are you looking back?"

"I'm exploring my options." My fingers curled into throbbing fists. "Kapoor chatted me up during the Claremont case and laid out my options." Just not the ones Rixton must be imagining. "He mentioned you applied once."

"I wanted it bad there for a while," he admitted, "but then I started dating Sherry. It was hard enough on her letting me out the door at night to patrol the streets where we grew up. She knew I was toying with the idea, and she told me upfront she couldn't handle the big leagues. It wasn't an ultimatum. It was a statement of fact. She was telling me her hard limits. She had reservations about marrying a cop, and I smoothed them over, but the FBI scared her." He rubbed his thumb over the curve of his wedding band. "I had to make a choice. The girl or the career. I chose Sherry."

My palms smarted from the sting of my nails biting into flesh. "I figured it was something like that."

"Crazy how it feels like I'm right back where I started. The girl or the career. Only this time it's your call, and I'm on the sidelines. I'm also not a girl." He gave his head a shake. "I always figured we'd be like Eddie and Harry, two old timers who don't know when to quit. I had sweet plans for our motorized scooters too. Full decal treatments, light bars, sirens, the whole shebang."

"I'm not sold on leaving." I had no choice but to go. "I'm not sold on any of it." But I didn't have much say there, either. "I haven't said anything to anyone yet. Not you, not Dad, not the Trudeaus."

"We'll support whatever decision you make. That part's a no-brainer." A shrug rolled through his shoulders. "Wherever you roam, you'll always be my Bou-Bou."

"What about Nettie?" I asked in a small voice. "I won't be around as much as we thought if I accept their offer. I would understand if—"

"Finish that thought, Luce, and we're done with or without the new job." His gaze hardened, and I pitied the road for taking the brunt to his glare. "You're my friend. You're Sherry's friend. We don't need a uniform or a paycheck tying us together to still be family. Don't insult me or my wife by implying we only chose you because of proximity or lack of options or whatever the hell else you're thinking over there. We chose you, you agreed, and you're damn well stuck now. I want the best for my little angel muffin, and you, Luce Boudreau, are the best."

A broken exhale that wanted to be a sob choked me.

"Please don't start with the waterworks." He popped open the console, groped around its interior, then passed me a crumpled packet of tissues. "I'll buy you an ice cream cone. Two scoops of made-fresh-daily plus a handmade waffle cone. All you have to do is not leak until I can palm you off on someone more absorbent than I am."

Dashing away the moisture under my eyes with a tissue, I blew my nose. "No waterworks here."

Twenty minutes later, he was placing a warm cone dipped in chocolate, rolled in sprinkles, and topped with two scoops of brookies ice cream in my hand. "What are brookies any way?"

"The lovechild of brownies and cookies," he answered around a mouthful of his own cone as he left the drive through lane. "How do you not know these things?"

I used the spoon provided and dug in. "I live at home, and parents force you to eat real food?"

"A spoon? Really?" He sighed in my general direction, a thick ice cream mustache coating his lip. "This is how those rumors about you being found in the swamp started."

Snorting at his attempt to cheer me, I chewed on a nugget of chocolatey goodness. "Pretty sure those rumors about me being found in the swamp were started based on the fact I was, actually, found in the swamp. Articles were written. There was news coverage and everything."

"Semantics."

We reached the Canton city limits, and I ditched the spoon to finish the job with my teeth.

"The thing about Wu I don't get," Rixton said between crunches on his cone, "is why he would go to Madison, visit with Summers, and drop your name. He had to know that would get back to you."

"I'm in an observation period," I hedged. "He's probably checking up on me."

"Why the Madison fire? There are two in our jurisdiction he could nose around in."

I peeled the paper wrapper down my cone. "Your guess is as good as mine."

"Your performance was flawless at the other scenes," he answered, as if I had asked him a question. "There were a lot of witnesses to your episode at the Madison fire. News must have filtered back to him. It makes sense he might have gone searching for clues, going as far as to chat up officials who had been in contact with you prior to the incident, to figure out what shook you."

Shook me made it sound like my allergy story had been debunked. That couldn't be a good thing. Rixton was whip-smart, and given time and distance for the wheels in his head to spin, he would churn out his own diagnosis for my erratic behavior, and that could get dangerous. For both of us.

"What do you plan on doing with the hot papers we've got in the trunk?" The segue wasn't my smoothest, but the way Rixton had left his thought hanging, like I might want to finish it, wasn't happening. "The Orvis case isn't ours, but we could start a folder and file a set of copies for a rainy day."

"Works for me. I'll leave another set in the car with our hardcopies. That leaves a set for me and a set for you for our personal records." He finished his ice cream and balled up his trash to drop in the mini can I had learned to keep behind my seat since he was forever snacking and would otherwise junk up my floorboard. "Can you forward me a scanned set of files too? We ought to loop Summers in so she can get that information in the right hands."

"The scans were grouped as a single file too large to email. The copy shop sent me a link where I can download them." The real issue was I had to gain access through Miller or Santiago in the first place. "I'll forward you copies when I get home."

"I had no idea you were a budding tech genius," he teased. "No wonder the FBI wants you bad."

"I'm just regurgitating what I was told." And probably getting half of it wrong. "I made nice with one of the tech guys from White Horse. He taught me a few things."

"I bet he did." He got serious on me in a blink. "Do you need to hear The Talk again?"

"Um, no. Thank you, but no. Once was more than enough. Believe me. I will never forget that talk." And, if he sprang it on Nettie when she was older, neither would she. Maybe it was a good talk after all. "Why is it so hard to believe I have other guy friends? You're a guy and my friend."

"I'm what you call a unicorn," he informed me, voice solemn. "We're rare and never spotted in the wild."

"Are you trying to tell me the only reason why I can see you is because you've been tamed?" I fought to smother my grin. "Are the bars enclosing you, allowing me to view your mystical majesticness, your marriage? Do you see your vows as a cage?"

The blood drained from his face, and he cleared his throat twice before he croaked. "You win. I will not pick on you about the guys you date, no matter how many of them there are, and you will never tell Sherry that you mistakenly believed I referred to our marriage as a cage."

"See, I don't know. That jibe about *no matter how many of them there are* makes it sound like you think I'm shacking up with half the town instead of believing me when I tell you I've got a lot of guy friends." I hummed in consideration. "Maybe I should ask Sherry for her opinion on what you meant, since you seem to think I'm so confused."

"You win, no qualifiers." He bowed his head. "I am at your mercy. Use your newfound powers wisely."

Cackling evilly, I rubbed my hands together. "Where would the fun be in that?"

CHAPTER THIRTEEN

⬧━⬥━⬧

Despite the text I'd sent Miller, I didn't hear back from him before my shift ended. Unsure what had gone down when he confronted Ivashov, I decided to give him space. Calling Wu and demanding an explanation for his meddling in the Orvis case ranked high on my to-do list too, but I wanted privacy for that one. The less Rixton ferreted out about Wu and whose shoes he meant to fill, the better for us all.

Thanks to the pickup service this morning, I rated curbside delivery at the Trudeaus' house. Call me crazy, but I was starting to feel like a takeout order, and I missed my Bronco.

Country living made carpooling too much of a hassle. Dad and I had always driven our personal vehicles to the station then rode out with our partners from there. Regulations required patrol cars to remain within the city limits, so it made more sense for our partners, who both resided in town, to keep the cruisers with them.

Letting myself in the front door, I was drawn toward the

living room by raucous laughter. I crept down the hall, listening until I could pick out the individual voices. Each one belonged to one of Dad's fishing buddies, and his voice threaded through the rowdy conversation. Careful to keep out of sight, I leaned my head against the wall and soaked up the atmosphere until the happy chaos made my eyelids heavy.

On soft feet, I backtracked to the entryway and dashed through the kitchen to avoid giving myself away. I didn't want to spoil his fun while he felt well enough for visitors. I scooted into the sewing room, ready to hit the air mattress face-first. As I unsnapped the first keeper supporting my gun belt, I froze when a sixth sense tingled across my skin. The weapon was in my hand, aimed at the far corner, when I reached over and flipped on the light.

"Cole." I puffed out my cheeks then lowered the weapon. "Hiding out in darkened bedrooms is a good way to get shot."

"You hung up on me."

Shrugging, I set the gun on the sewing table and started back on the snaps. "You sounded busy."

His heavy brows furrowed. "I *was* busy."

"I don't need details." Me and my overactive imagination could fill in the blanks just fine. "What are you doing here?" Finished with the fasteners, I looped my duty belt over a chair that threatened to tip backward until I kicked off my boots and sat them on the seat. "What happened with Ivashov? I haven't heard from Miller since I left the hospital."

"He refused to give up his mistress or any details of his operation, even with her stink embedded in his skin, so Miller is taking care of the problem."

Since Miller tended to solve problems by dunking his victims in stomach acid after a short trip down his esophagus, there was nothing to say except, "Okay."

"I thought you might be interested in this." Cole extended a folder toward me. "The lab sent it over this morning."

"I read their email." I took it, careful not to brush his fingers, and flipped it open. "Is this more of the same?" Rather than answer, he stood there and watched until I hit the amendment at the bottom. "This report is on the second plant." I skimmed lower. "The soil mixture from the Orvis nursery sample matched those taken from the roots of the ones planted in my yard." A sigh welled up in me. "Why does this not surprise me after the day I've had?"

Cole accepted the file and tossed it on a stack with others I kept on the sewing desk. "What happened?"

"That's right." I started unbuttoning my uniform shirt. "I lost my shadow. How crazy did that make you?" Cole held his tongue while I tossed the heavy polyester shirt onto my pile of dirties. I still wore a long-sleeved silk pointelle undershirt that covered my arms and hugged my curves. I always kept the farmhouse like an icebox to compensate for the layers I wore, but Uncle Harold and Aunt Nancy weren't used to the cold. "I'm roasting in here. Can you turn around while I slide on some shorts?"

The mountain uprooted itself and pivoted toward the wall to give me privacy.

A shower was mandatory before changing into my pajamas, so I slid on last night's cotton shorts and sank cross-legged onto the mattress with my backpack in my lap. "I'm decent." I patted the carpet. "Have a seat."

With more grace than a man of his mass ought to possess, Cole folded himself into lotus position on the floor opposite me. "You have something to share?"

"I do." I pulled out my hardcopies of the crime scene photos and passed them over. "This is my only paper set, but scans of the originals are floating around in Miller's and Santiago's inboxes."

"These must be the Madison victims," he murmured. "What am I missing?"

"Four are children, all under the age of eight. Ms. Orvis was five-six and weighed one seventy-five."

"Ms. Orvis must have been a long-term host to a viscarre. That would explain why she burnt to a husk."

"It makes sense, given the link between the valerian plants, that Ms. Orvis was a host. I can buy that she was facilitating a Drosera. What I don't get is why this evidence was left for us to find."

"Parasitic charun have, in the past, acted as sleeper agents. Once activated, they complete their mission and then suicide. A charun who has remained in a host for too long won't leave anything but skin behind unless they sacrifice themselves too. The real question is— What was the assignment? And does the presence of a husk indicate a completed mission or an aborted one?"

While those were both perfectly good questions, I had gotten stuck on the mechanics. "Are you telling me that if a coroner sliced open one of these sleeper agents, she would find a charun under its skin?"

"Cohabitation is more complicated than a stack of Russian nesting dolls, Luce. The charun interested in pairing will be absorbed by the host. Cutting open a host would reveal abnormalities in the organs and blood, small adaptations created when two species merge, but there wouldn't be an actual charun folded up inside the host, no."

"That makes no sense." I ground the heels of my palms into my eyes. "How does it work?"

"Call it what you want: thaumaturgy, alchemy, diabolism, magic."

"Let's stick with magic." At least it was less alien than the alternatives. I had never heard of thaumaturgy and would have mistaken it for thermology or another heat-based study rather than dealing with the occult. "Though, after this talk, I'm going to imagine charun in search of cohabitation shrinking down to multivitamin size then getting swallowed by a host."

"I'm not sure that would work." One corner of his lips curled the slightest bit. "The host would digest them."

"Sure, expect me to believe a super gator can merge with a human, but scoff at a magical multivitamin."

The wondering regard he bestowed on me ruched his melt-water eyes into crow's feet. Both fond and amused, frustrated and annoyed, fascinated and apprehensive, it vanished from his expression in a blink, making it impossible for me to glean more from him than the fact an unfathomable magnetism kept attracting us when it ought to have repelled.

"You hung up on me," he said, a lion-headed dragon with a thorn stuck in his paw.

Just as quickly as he resurrected the topic, I buried it down deep where it would be forgotten. To make certain he dropped it this time, I flung out bait he couldn't resist. "Wu was in Madison. He paid a visit to the arson investigator. Summers claimed he wanted copies of the coroner's reports, but when she went digging, she discovered the bodies had never reached the coroner's office." I tapped the papers in his hand. "No official record of these exists. Someone erased them. We're talking dug into private mail servers and scrubbed inboxes clean."

"Sounds like your future partner is working overtime to bury this case." His dedication obviously troubled Cole. "Has he mentioned it to you?"

"We talked about the possibility of an infiltration over dinner that night, but our speculation was prior to the Madison incident. New evidence might have prompted him to act since he was already aware of the situation." Without my permission, my gaze slid to the pocket where I kept the black phone. I would have to woman-up and call Wu at some point to confess my sins. "He's kind of pissed at me right now."

Cole followed my line of sight. "Any particular reason?"

"Santiago dissected the phone Wu gave me and screwed with the GPS for kicks." I scratched my nail over the zippered compartment. "When Wu chatted up Summers, he told her I was sightseeing in New York."

A slow grin wreathed Cole's face, and his deep chuckles did uncomfortable things to my stomach. "I knew we kept him around for some damn reason."

"We have to learn to play nice with Wu. We're stuck with him for the time being." I let my head fall back on my neck and stared at the ceiling. "I have to put in my notice." It wasn't what I'd meant to say, but it was out there now. "Once I do that, this gets real."

Cole palmed my knee and squeezed once, his fingers stretching up my thigh in hot streaks that burned like starbursts. "We'll be with you every step of the way."

Covering his hand with mine crossed lines, but I couldn't resist the scratch of his scarred knuckles under my palm for the fleeting seconds he allowed the contact before withdrawing. "I appreciate that." Cole got to his feet and offered me a hand up, but I shook my head. "I'm tired. I think I'll go to bed early tonight."

"I have something to show you." He kept his arm extended. "The fresh air will do you good."

"I don't know." I stared at my knee, where I still felt the imprint of each of his fingers, and wished I was strong enough to boot him out the same way he got in. "Can this wait?"

"You hung up on me," he said for the third time. "You owe me."

I scoffed at his gall. "I owe you for many things, but not for that."

"Fine." His shoulders tightened. "I'll cash in a different token. Take your pick, but get dressed. You're coming with me even if I have to carry you out of the house barefoot and in pajamas."

I glared up at him. "You're bossy, you know that?"

"Get moving." He snapped his fingers. "I'm giving you ten minutes, and then I'm taking you however I can get you."

Shutting my eyes, I allowed myself a second to hold onto the wish he meant those words differently before releasing them into the ether. "What's the dress code?"

"Wear something comfortable." He tromped to the far corner of the room, snagged my waterproof boots, then dumped them at my feet. "Nine minutes." He turned his back and crossed his arms over his chest, his muscles pulling his shirt taut. "Eight."

"That wasn't a full minute," I grumbled while scurrying to meet his deadline. I stripped down to my underwear, pulled on fresh socks, jeans, boots, and then a shirt suitable for public consumption before knotting my hair at the base of my neck and shrugging on my backpack. "Ready."

Cole raked his gaze over me, assessing my choice of outfit, then nodded. "Let's go."

"How did you—? Ah. Never mind." I crossed the room to the window. "You fit through that?"

"I'm flexible," he deadpanned.

"Is this what you wanted to show me?" I teased. "Your contortionist routine?"

A low growl pumped through his chest as he eased past me and shoved up the sash. "Watch and learn."

"Too bad this show doesn't come with popcorn," I mused as Cole maneuvered until he sat on the windowsill, his back to me. "I could have greased you up with some of that butter-flavored oil theaters float their kernels in." I bit my tongue. "Um, pretend I didn't say that."

"Say what?" Bracing his hands on the jambs, he slid his hips forward until he poured himself out the window. He ended up kneeling on mulch in the front flower bed and shot a daring grin over his shoulder as if challenging me to compete with his exit. "Get a move on."

I was an old pro at sneaking out, and I had the advantage of having less mass than some mountains I could name. All I had to do was throw one leg out the window, brace it on the ground, duck under the sash, then straighten and pull my other leg out to be standing. This was a cake walk compared to the stunts I'd pulled climbing out of my second-floor bedroom back home. Those late-night escapes had required stealth, rope, and sneakers for outrunning Dad's sixth sense for when I was about to get up to no good.

"You're lucky you didn't trample the azaleas." I breezed past him. "Aunt Nancy would have dragged you by the ear to Mervin's to buy her new ones, and then she would have stood over your shoulder and watched while you planted the replacements and redid her mulch."

His long strides overtook me in two steps. "Is that the voice of experience I hear?"

"I might have smashed her impatiens once. And there was an incident with caladiums." I let him keep pace with me since I had no idea where he had hidden his SUV. "I had to buy replacements out of my allowance, and I spent the weekends doing penance. I missed more than one softball game on account of midnight shenanigans."

He palmed his keys. "Where did you go?"

"Nowhere and everywhere." Just me and Mags against the world, against our parents, a united front too stubborn to realize how much better we had it than most. "Usually it was just Maggie and me doing our worst, which was still pretty tame. We drank beers in hayfields, drove too fast, went too far, sneaked into clubs down in Jackson where folks were less likely to know who to call if I got caught. Dumb teenager stuff."

Lights flashed ahead as Cole unlocked the SUV. "Why did you do it?"

"You might have noticed Dad can be guilty of smothering me at times. Busting out of my room and going to hang with my bestie without his permission? It was downright illicit as far as I was concerned. I felt so badass breaking his rules and getting a taste of freedom when I had none. Things are better now that I'm grown and carry a firearm when I leave the house, but we could have fallen out in a big way if we hadn't worked so hard to find middle ground." Patience must be Dad's middle name. It sure wasn't mine. I had the adoption papers to prove it. "Mags was on the run from her parents' expectations. They're old money, and they anticipated she would marry well and young, pop out heirs, then spend her days planning parties and playing hostess."

We reached the SUV, and he held my door open for me. "She broke the mold."

"Smashed it." I smiled through the twinge in my chest as I climbed in and got buckled. "She chose her own path. I've always been proud of her for that. I rebelled enough to fill my quota, but I never made a clean break from my roots."

"I disagree." His hand, where it rested on the doorframe, flexed as though he were fighting the impulse to slam the door in my face before he finished his thought. "The person you are now is nothing like who you used to be. You might not have made a conscious choice to break from tradition, to turn your back on your past, but you created this life all on your own. You have a family who loves you, friends who are loyal to you, a job that serves your community. This person is remarkable."

The door closed before I formulated a response, and he took his time joining me. I hadn't noticed him taking the backpack from my hand, but he stowed it in the rear then got behind the wheel.

Heaviness weighted the air, stretching into infinity before shattering when he flipped on his blinker, and I realized where he was taking me. "We're going to Cypress Swamp?"

"Yep."

We parked the SUV in a well-worn patch of grass that had mostly gone to dirt. While I got out and took a look around to see what held his interest in this part of the swamp, he pulled a cooler from the rear and started walking down to the water-line. We had to pass through a patch of brambles to get the full view, and I hesitated when I spotted White Horse's airboat lying in wait for us.

"We're going on a boat ride?" I hadn't been out here since the night I helped fish Jane Doe from the water. "I hadn't been on an airboat in years until I met you."

"Wait here." Cole took a few jogging steps then leapt the five feet of shallow water between the shore and the deck, landing in a half-crouch that would have done Thom proud. He held his position while the boat rocked, kicking out waves that splashed duckweed onto my boots. "Let me strap this down, and I'll maneuver closer for you."

Once he secured the supplies, he removed a long metal pole from a strap and used it to push the boat closer to shore. Our fingers brushed when he reached for me, and his hand clamped down on my wrist, right along the first metal band. The brush of his thumb along the raised skin would have made me cringe had another man stroked me in such a way, but his caress sparked heat in my veins. I cleared the gap with a hop that slammed me into him, and I rode out the gentle swells tucked against his side while trying to control the scent of desire that clung to my skin around him.

"Thanks." I disentangled from him and plopped down on the bench seat to put distance between us. "Do I get a hint?"

"You'll see soon enough." He cranked the engine, and the propeller mounted in a steel cage behind me whirred to life. "Hold on."

Conversation on an airboat is impossible unless you like screaming, so there was nothing for me to do but sit back and enjoy the ride. The spotlight mounted on the front of the boat cast a spear of light to dispel the darkness, but I didn't worry about the narrow scope. Cole saw in the dark just fine. The light was a concession, one I appreciated since—his keen night vision or not—cruising the swamp past midnight at high speeds was enough to jumpstart my pulse.

Twenty minutes into our ride, he killed the motor, and we coasted to a stop in an area that might have struck a familiar chord had I been able to see more trees to use as landmarks. While I studied the buttressed knees of a bald cypress tree, a sense of déjà vu swirled through me. As we drew closer, I spotted the knot where I had carved a date into the trunk in chunky numbers, a child's remembrance of her unbirthday. "Why are we here?"

"This is where Edward Boudreau pulled you from the swamp." He shifted his angle to the right about a foot. "We breached two yards south of here." He pointed off in the shadowed distance. "Less than a dozen yards east, War staged her grand entrance."

I stood and turned a slow circle, seeing the area through new eyes. I wished we had made the trip in daylight. I had been out here dozens of times to sit and think, but discovering this was a nexus point for us all gave me new perspective on this corner of the swamp.

"Famine will breach here." He knelt and removed a metal panel from a depression in the deck. "The broken seal is a beacon." He removed what appeared to be a thin laptop encased in black metal, not dissimilar to my new phone. "She'll follow its pull to this area when the time comes." He tapped a few keys then set it on the seat beside me, angling so I could view the grid covering the screen. "Each square represents a different live video feed."

Vibrancy was not what I expected from a live feed given the hour. "They're color night vision cameras?"

"There's more." He pulled up a different screen covered in a multicolored graph that expanded as I watched. "Santiago talked me into purchasing an acoustic Doppler current profiler. He's wanted one for years, and this gave him an excuse to write it off as a business expense."

The readout kept inching along, but I had no idea what it meant. "What is an acoustic Doppler whatchamacallit?"

"ADCP is a hydroacoustic current meter similar to sonar," he explained. "Using the Doppler effect of sound waves scattered back from particles within the water column, it measures current velocities over a depth range."

Sonar. Doppler. Particles. Velocities. "Mmm-hmm."

"According to Santiago, that means it measures the speed and direction of water currents."

Ah. Now that I got. "How much current is he expecting out here?" The surface was calm until you reached River Bend.

"Large bodies gliding through the water create wakes the same as boats do," Cole explained. "Santiago is hoping to train a program to spot anomalies so that when Famine breaches, we'll get notified of the disturbance." He flipped through a few more screens. "He mentioned side-scan sonar and something about a trawl, but I shut him down after he asked permission to buy scuba gear and a shark tank."

I brushed my fingers over the keys, switching back to the camera feed, and pulled up the one over our heads that showed a hulking man bent protectively around a slender woman half his size. "This must have taken days to install and connect."

"The order arrived the morning we were set to go to Ludlow." He secured the laptop back in its bin then reclaimed his seat. "Thom was already in town running an errand, so I asked him to go in my place."

"You made the right call." I spared him the need to make an excuse. "We needed a cool-down period."

"Yes," he agreed without looking at me. "We did."

"Thom and I got the job done. That's all that matters." I gestured toward the laptop. "It's not like you were twiddling your thumbs, either. I'd call how things shook out a win."

He turned his head in my direction but kept his eyes downcast. "Can I show you one more thing before I take you back?"

"Sure." I tightened my grip and told myself it was so I wouldn't slide when he accelerated. "I've got time."

"Let me refresh the bait first." Cole cracked open the cooler, and a wall of stank smacked me in the face so hard my eyes watered. "Santiago is using natural alligators as test subjects." Rather than the hooks I expected, Cole threaded a piece of thin rope through the cavity of each whole raw chicken then tied them off on preset anchors floating in the water. "The rope breaks away easily, and we monitor the area to make sure none of the local wildlife is harmed."

That last part was a calculated kindness. The guys didn't give a fig for much outside of the coterie, but they would fake compassion. For me.

"Do you trust me?" Cole killed the light, and we plummeted into velvety darkness.

My response was automatic. "Yes."

This time there was no burst of speed once the engine caught, no wind lashing hair in my eyes. We puttered for about ten minutes before he cut the motor again and used the pole to angle us in position behind a copse of cypress trees. Through a split in the trunks, I spotted a ball of artificial light hitched to a lamppost illuminating the blonde head of a woman sitting on the deck with her back facing us. Even without her signature pencil skirt, crisp blouse, and neck-breaker heels, I would have recognized her anywhere.

"Maggie," I breathed. "She looks so . . . "

Alive.

Cole tapped my knee then brought a finger to his lips. I nodded that I understood and settled in to watch. I'm not sure what held her attention as she stared up at the White Horse bunkhouse. It was peculiar with its staircases that led nowhere and windows in place of doors. The quirky building was nothing like the tidy house she'd shared with Justin, and it stood worlds apart from the sprawling plantation-style home where she had spent her childhood.

Portia seemed to like the place, but I wasn't sure Maggie would embrace the idea of so many roommates or such an isolated location, not that she had much say in the matter. I had taken all her choices away from her. What to wear, where to live, who to love . . .

I started to protest when Cole shoved off and let us drift back the way we'd come, but he had already given me a gift that pulled me down as sure as a pair of cement shoes.

I was grateful for an excuse not to talk on the ride back to the SUV. As it was, the trip was too short for me to blame my tears on windburn. I used the hem of my shirt to wipe my face when we coasted to a stop, but it didn't help. The pain kept pouring out through my eyes from my heart, leaking down my chin to drip onto my knees. I clapped a hand over my mouth to stop the sobs from escaping, but I wasn't fooling anyone.

I ached for what I had done to Maggie, and the fact I was grateful she still lived gutted me.

Until I could reconcile those things, I had no right asking her forgiveness.

Breaking all our own rules, Cole pulled me onto his lap with a sigh of resignation, as though this moment had been a long time coming, and he had grown tired of fighting against its arrival. Though it was wrong of me to accept what he offered, I wrapped my arms around his thick torso and buried my face in the crease between his pectorals. He held me while stroking one wide palm up and down my back, allowing me to shatter in his arms, where he could gather the broken pieces and fit me back together again.

The only man I had ever allowed to hold me was my father, and there was no comparison between those rare experiences and this one. Cole pinned my arms down with his, the contact startling against my banding even with a layer of fabric between our skin. His palm smoothed over the ornate juncture where the *rukav* joined its two halves between my shoulder blades. The faintest rumble under my cheek had me pressing my ear flat against his chest to catch the vibrations.

Cole was ... purring.

The intense physical contact ought to have spiraled me into a panic attack, made me itch to shake him off, turned oxygen solid in my lungs, but that rhythmic sound was drugging. His scent filled my nose, and his heat melted the ice crackling over my heart.

"I was with her when you called," he said, though he owed me no explanation.

Relief to which I had no right punched out of me on a hard breath that blew across his shirt, and he shivered beneath my cheek as though he'd felt it skate over his skin. "You don't owe me any explanations."

"I know."

But he had given me one because it mattered to me, because I needed closure, and because he was the kind of man who knew those things, who did those things, who deserved so much more than anything I had to offer. That didn't stop me from wanting to give him all of me or from wanting to take all of him too.

I closed my eyes when the stubble on his chin caught in my hair, relishing the intimacy of the contact, wondering how the press of his jaw might feel against other places.

The next thing I remembered was waking in the SUV with my head on his shoulder. Legs tucked under me, I had curled across the console to wrap around his right arm. I had almost convinced myself I was dreaming until the SUV came to a stop, and he pressed a kiss to my temple. That brush of his lips, so much softer than I ever imagined them, incinerated the cobwebs, and my pulse set off at a gallop he must have heard.

"We're here," he murmured. "You need to head inside and get some rest."

Knowing all that had happened tonight would be viewed through a harsher lens tomorrow made me reluctant to budge.

Cole would regret softening toward me and begin the patch job on the crumbling spots in the wall surrounding his heart as soon as I said goodnight. But then I would bumble along, right on his heels, and discover each crack left jagged as though rooting out his weaknesses came second nature to me.

Perhaps it did. After all, Conquest had had centuries to perfect the art.

Quick as ripping off a Band-Aid, before either of us balked, I rose up and kissed the prickly underside of his jaw. "Thanks for sneaking me out."

I shoved open the door, uncoiled my legs, and hit the sidewalk before he could shake off his surprise. Unwilling to glance back and catch his molars grinding, I tossed a wave over my shoulder and hustled into the house. The impromptu party was over, and all the lights were off. I heaved a sigh of relief when it hit me I had escaped an interrogation. Creeping into the sewing room, I shut the door on my heels.

Tomorrow would kick me in the teeth soon enough. Tonight I wanted to dream with a smile.

CHAPTER FOURTEEN

———◆———

The good mood I had fallen asleep cradling lasted me through the morning. I'd noticed on my way to raid the orange juice that Aunt Nancy had filled one of those magnetic grocery lists with items, so I tore off the top sheet and decided I would contribute to the household by doing the shopping for her. Flavie called to update me on the status of my valerian-free yard while I was checking out, and the news that I could return home buoyed my already high spirits.

I was humming a song by Florida Georgia Line as I pushed my buggy across the parking lot, but my steps faltered halfway to the Bronco when I spied the tall drink of water reclined against the driver-side door. "Hi there."

"Hi yourself." Wu flung a tight ball of fabric square at my chest. "You look well-rested."

I grabbed the bundle on reflex before it hit the asphalt, shook out the heather-gray material, and failed to cage my laugh before it escaped. The long-sleeve tee featured a vintage photo of an iconic city skyline. A banner reading "New York the Empire State" cut the image in half, and the tag hanging off the sleeve proclaimed *Made in New York City.*

"Aww." As I smoothed the shirt against my chest, he noticed the leather bracelet that was fast becoming a wardrobe staple and scowled all the harder. "You brought me a souvenir. You didn't have to, but thanks."

"I flew to New York." His clipped tone highlighted his accent. "I bought a ticket and walked the observation deck at the Empire State Building. I saw the entire city at a glance, but the one thing I didn't see was you."

"I've never been to New York. Too much of a homebody." I rubbed my thumb over the grayscale image. "I hear it's one hell of an experience. Did you enjoy your trip?"

"Do *not* play games with me." A flush warmed his face as his temper rose. "I contacted Santiago Benitez to verify your whereabouts."

Leave it to Santiago to take a joke ten steps too far. God only knows what other evidence he'd planted to make the trip appear authentic. For all I knew, he had forwarded Wu a fake itinerary complete with purchased tickets for tourist attractions I planned on visiting along with a number for a concierge bribed to demur when asked if a Luce Boudreau was a guest at his hotel.

"I'm going to strangle him." I opened the tailgate and started loading my bags. "It was a joke. He just got carried away." I tried for a winning smile. "I'm glad you're here, though. You saved me a phone call."

Immediately suspicious, he shoved off the vehicle with his shoulders. "What do you need?"

"Ouch." I clutched my chest. "You act like I have to need something to want to talk to you."

"I'll ask again—" one of his perfect eyebrows arched "—what do you need?"

"What were you doing down in Madison?" I checked the cart to make sure I hadn't left anything behind. "A little birdie told me you paid Jill Summers a visit." I cast him a thoughtful glance. "The funny thing is, you asked about the Orvis case. Well, okay, so that's not the punchline. After you made that long drive and nudged Summers into checking her records, which I had already requested, as I'm sure you know, she discovered—wait for it—that the bodies had never reached the coroner's office."

His black mood lifted a bit, and a smile twitched in his cheek. "Are you accusing me of something?"

I pulled on my cop face. "Where are the bodies?"

"I have no idea, officer," he said, playing along. "I would tell you if I knew."

"Wu, this is not the hill you want to die on." I bumped his hip with my cart. "Trust me."

He wiped imagined dirt from his slacks. "More hills have died under me than the reverse."

I barked out a laugh. "Did you really just call yourself old as dirt?"

His lips pursed. "I am old."

"Snappy comeback." I returned the cart to a nearby corral. "How good are you at making things you don't want humans to see disappear?"

"Very good." He narrowed his eyes. "Why?"

I flashed him the other bit of information that had filtered to me overnight. "Do these photos look familiar to you?"

"Where did you get those?" he demanded while studying my phone screen. "I erased the files."

"The digital files, maybe." I grinned up at him. "Senility isn't a good look on you. There's this thing us youngsters call *paper*. The Chinese invented it in like 105 A.D. or something. You were probably a toddler at the time." I pocketed my cell. "Have you ever heard of a printer?" His lips flatlined. "No? Then this will blow your mind—"

Wu loomed over me, but I had been loomed over by the best and wasn't intimidated. "Who has the prints?"

"Lots of folks at this point." I hooked my thumbs in the belt loops of my jeans. "What does it matter without the bodies?"

"We don't leave evidence behind," Wu growled with all the fervor of an oft-repeated mantra. "Photos are evidence, *paper* or not."

Still annoyed he had been sneaking around behind my back, I saluted him and jumped in the Bronco. "I wish you the best of luck retrieving them."

"Oh, no," he crooned, catching the door before it shut. "This is your mess too. You're going to help clean it up."

"No thanks." I wrenched the door from his grasp. "I've got a full plate."

"That wasn't a request." He tapped on the window. "We'll meet at your house after your shift."

"I'll pencil you in," I lied. "Later, gator." I hesitated. "You're not a gator, are you? I'll be honest, Droseras freak me out, and that was before one almost ate me."

"It's rude to ask a charun their species," he informed me primly. "Most prefer to keep their true selves hidden."

That was certainly the case with my coterie, and, I had to admit, ignorance was my personal preference as well. "How can species remain secret with so many being bagged and tagged?"

"Consider it doctor/patient confidentiality. Charun of the same species are often grouped together to receive their physicals or are kept in the same facilities to make catering to their biological needs easier, but most are grateful to find kin on this terrene. This is one instance where a shared secret is more often kept than individual ones."

"I suppose this means I'll be in isolation when the time comes." Sterile environments gave me the heebie-jeebies, so worries over my future thirty-day vacation at Hotel Hysterectomy had been shelved too high for my brain to reach them. "Are there other Otillians in the program?"

"Most would rather die than forfeit their honor by aiding an enemy terrene."

"I'm a traitor no matter how you look at it, huh?" I scanned the bright blue skies stuffed with fat clouds, tuned in the laughter of children racing buggies across the asphalt, their parents shouting warnings to look both ways before crossing, and had zero problems with wearing that label. "Either I betray my heritage, or I betray my family."

"You have three sisters," he pointed out. "Aren't they also family?"

"Blood doesn't make a family." Heart and home did that. "War almost killed my dad." My throat tightened. "She did kill my best friend." The Maggie who had been carried out of my backyard wasn't the same person who depended on paper, rock, scissors to make her life choices. "I won't paint Famine or Death with the same brush until I've met them, but War is my enemy, and if they side with her, that makes them my enemies too."

He picked at the rubber seal cupping the window. "Your coterie supports your stance?"

"They don't think I'm going to stick around, if I'm honest." I gave a tired laugh. "Maybe they're right. Maybe I don't exist. Maybe I am a construct." I turned over the engine. "But right now, I feel real. I feel like I'm a person. I feel like I have everything to lose, and I'm going to hold on for as long as I can."

"You're a brave woman," Wu said quietly. "We're lucky to have you."

The more time I spent with Wu, the more he confused me. Most of the time, he was a well-dressed pain in my ass who was too imperious for his own good. But when he talked about things that mattered, he wiped off the gloss and left what appeared to be a real person exposed. Matte finish was a good look on him. "Luck would have been not meeting me at all."

Without Conquest, this terrene and all its inhabitants would have known peace.

"You're buying into your own propaganda," he chided, stepping back. "Conquest is a title, not a person. If it hadn't been you, it would have been someone else." He let that sink in before adding, "You're the best chance this terrene has at finding a more permanent solution. You could save hundreds of thousands of lives, maybe even break the cycle."

My palms went damp where they gripped the wheel. "No pressure."

"Until tonight," Wu said, and he made it a dare.

Okay, so in hindsight it might not have been wise to spread photographic proof of charun existence to the humans desperate to solve murders, but destroying evidence went against everything I had been taught. Had I understood what I was seeing, the larger implications for charun, I would have called Wu sooner. Crime scene preservation, chains of evidence, these were my defaults, but it looked like they were about to get reset.

*

The eight hours I spent sitting across the desk from Rixton passed at a snail's crawl. There was no point in us putting in legwork on the Hensarling, Culberson, or Orvis cases when there was charun involvement, but it's not like I could unveil the existence of what humans would consider demons. The only choice I had was to lie, and I did, in ink and in voice, until I choked on them.

The one respite from my guilt came when I drafted my letter of resignation. I printed it off, folded it up, then slid it in an envelope and scrawled Chief Jones's name on the front. I should have turned it in right then and there, but I wasn't ready yet. I might never be. But that wouldn't change the inevitable.

In search of a hard push that would send me tumbling over the edge, I caved to Wu's request and met him at my house around midnight.

The glass on the bay window sparkled in the headlights as I pulled into my usual parking space. I couldn't tell where Flavie had pulled up what, but I trusted she had gotten the job done. The new siding gleamed as I hit the stairs, punched in the alarm code, and let myself in.

Another ugly truth I hadn't wanted to confront reared its head as I inspected the place for livability. Dad couldn't bunk with the Trudeaus forever, and I would have to leave for a solid month after my two-week notice played out at the department. This place had to be move-in ready for when Dad got steady enough to fend for himself. Not that he would have to, considering I planned on hiring a part-time nurse. The reality was in-home care or a nursing home, and I wasn't about to check Dad into one of those.

Following a hunch, I took the stairs up to my room and found Wu sitting in the open window across from my bed. His black tactical pants, heavy boots, thin turtleneck, and tight beanie all followed a similar theme: stealth mode. "Is that really what all the super-secret agents are wearing on covert ops these days?"

"I brought you a set." He flicked his wrist toward a chair in the corner. "Now we can match."

"That was almost a joke," I accused. "Don't tell me you actually have a sense of humor buried in there."

"I would have strangled you for the stunt you pulled otherwise," he stated matter-of-factly.

"Nah. I'm a valuable commodity. The worst you would have done was huffed and puffed and blown my house down." I gestured around us, indicating the space as a whole. "Right now, it wouldn't even take much effort to knock the old girl to her knees."

"I'll give you some privacy."

"Thanks." I crossed to the chair and rubbed the stretchy shirt material between my fingers. "I appreciate—"

Movement caught the corner of my eye as Wu executed a seated backflip out the freaking window. I rushed over and leaned out, but he had already stuck the landing and was walking away. "Show-off."

Wu spun around then and executed a neat bow in acceptance of the compliment.

Learning he was stalking me wasn't a surprise. Thom had already speculated as much, and the guy wasn't being subtle about it either. After the trick Santiago had played on him with the phone, I couldn't blame him for wanting to put eyes on me to make sure I was where I was supposed to be considering War was on, well, the warpath.

None of that bothered me. No, what I resented was that his demonstration hinted he had witnessed the playful exchange between Cole and me. Wu wasn't flamboyant by nature, and backflipping from windows was not his style, but men got flashy as peacocks when it came to one-upping each other.

Last night had already taken on a dreamlike quality, the memory a faded photograph I kept taking out and examining in the hopes of recapturing the significance attached to the moment. The fine details of those precious, unguarded hours I'd spent with Cole were evaporating like mist exposed to sunlight. That was bad enough without Wu's attempt at superimposing himself over the mental snapshot.

Yanking the curtains shut, I changed into my burglar gear and met Wu in the yard. He had traded out his sedan for a compact SUV in standard black. "I know you like to accessorize, but you coordinate rides to match your outfits too?"

"Black SUVs are common." The subtle dig at White Horse got ignored, so he pressed on. "No one will notice one more."

"What's your plan?" We loaded up and headed out. "I have no cat burgling skills if that's what you're thinking. For that matter, I have no cats and have never burgled."

Wu appeared unimpressed with my lack of résumé. "Would Summers keep the prints in her office?"

I almost played the *I didn't say Summers kept the prints* game with him, but I resisted. Score one for my maturity level. "I doubt it. She's aware someone has taken a magic eraser to all the digital files. She would hide the hardcopies to protect them. Her office is small. There's no room for a safe unless it's the fireproof kind you can carry out by the handle, which would defeat the purpose. That leaves her vehicle or her house."

He nodded along with each point. "Where does she live?"

"I have no idea." I glanced over at him. "We've always met on scene or in public."

"Call your coterie and have them locate her address."

"You expect me to believe you don't already have that nailed down?"

"Can you ever follow a simple order?"

"You said we're partners. You're acting like this is a dictatorship."

"Humor me," he said dryly. "I'm curious how good your people are, how well you all work together."

"Fine." I dialed Santiago since Miller was still giving me dead air. "Hey, can you tell me where Jill—?" I got out a pen and pad of paper from my backpack. "Give me that again." I scribbled down the address. "Thank you much."

Santiago grumbled at me, which I took as progress. Maybe we were past out-and-out name calling.

"Here you go." I handed Wu the sheet of paper. "Are we good, or did you need something else?"

Wu skimmed the information, which made me all kinds of panicked since drivers ought to keep their eyes on the road, then balled up the paper and tossed it in the floorboard. "That'll do."

I almost tacked on "pig", but I figured he wouldn't get the *Babe* reference Rixton was so fond of using.

"That's it?" I waited for him to explain. "I hassled Santiago for that?"

Granted, Santiago had clearly expected me to pester him at some point since he'd had the information cued and waiting on my call.

Wu cut his eyes toward me. "I expected you to call Miller."

I clamped my mouth shut.

Scenting blood in the water, Wu verbally circled me. "Where is he?"

I strapped on water wings and got ready to paddle for my life. "He's not answering his phone."

"Miller wouldn't leave town without checking in with Cole or you first." Wu hummed an interested sound. "He was last seen at Madison Memorial around the time you and your human partner interrogated Boris Ivashov. Both men vanished shortly after that."

"You remembered all those names, but you reduced Rixton to 'your human partner'?" I kicked back in my seat. "You can do better than that, Wu."

Streetlights whipped across his angular face. "Where is Miller Henshaw?"

"I have no idea." I spread my hands. "I haven't seen or heard from Miller in over twenty-four hours."

"Ivashov is a loose end in need of cauterizing," he said at last. "Will Miller finish the job?"

A sour taste rose up the back of my throat. "Call it a hunch, but I don't think you'll have to worry about Ivashov."

"It bothers you that Miller would kill to protect you," Wu observed.

Miller had already killed for me. All of my coterie had in the aftermath of War's failed coup.

"How could it not bother me?" I massaged the tight spot between my eyebrows. "It's not only that a charun will die, but his host will too. Two deaths for the price of one is hard math."

"The host is already dead." Wu gentled his tone in an unspoken reminder the host had bargained for that death. "That's what the body in Madison meant, why it had to be collected, why the evidence must be destroyed. Viscarre slowly eat away at their host. The process takes time, but death is inevitable, and the shell must be disposed of before humans get their hands on them."

"I understand." Going forward, I had to be more careful. For all our sakes. "What's your plan for when we reach Summers' house?"

"The plan is to comb over every inch of her residence until we've acquired each piece of evidence she's got on the Orvis fire, anything that could be linked to charun involvement, and then we destroy it."

"What do we do if she's home?" I scratched my scalp under the beanie meant to conceal my hair. "What about an alarm system? What if the documents are in a safe?"

A dark chuckle moved through his chest. "How often are you home?"

"Okay, so I'll allow that people in our profession don't get as much downtime as most." For instance, the lack of sleep from the past week had left me with sandpaper discs for eyeballs. "That still doesn't explain how you're going to handle the infiltration or acquisition portion of the program."

Wu made a hard left then pulled into the circular driveway of a modest ranch-style house. Summers' car was nowhere in sight, so that was good news. Neighbors snugged up to her property on either side and in the rear, which wasn't ideal.

"Stick with me." Wu slid out, gathered a bag of supplies from his trunk, strolled up to the front door like he had every right to be there, then frowned back at me, who was slinking from shadow to shadow in the manner of a crafty cartoon character. "Luce." The amount of exasperation packed into that single syllable impressed me. "Come here, please."

Head down, certain one of the neighbors would call the cops at any moment, I hustled to his side. "Hop to it." I bounced from foot to foot. "We're drawing too much attention."

"No one has noticed us," he assured me while he got to work ripping an adhesive strip off the back of a metallic disc he slapped onto the siding above the doorbell. "This will disrupt the signal from her alarm. Once the light turns green, we're good to go." He glanced at my hand-wringing. "Put on your gloves."

After what felt like thirty years later, the tiny red light switched to green, and Wu started picking the locks. Nape prickling, I squirmed behind him in an approximation of the potty dance, desperate to burst inside and shut a door between us and the rest of the neighborhood. A cold sweat broke across my shoulders and rolled down my spine. Stubborn lungs refused to inflate, and gold spots glittered in my eyes.

"Breathe," Wu murmured. "I've got this. We're almost in."

Metal clicked in his hand, and he swept me inside before closing it behind us.

"I'm not cut out for this." I wiped my forehead dry on my shirt sleeve. "I'm three seconds away from a panic attack." I puffed out my cheeks and bent over to brace my palms on my knees. "You might want to reconsider this partnership thing if B&E is a job requirement."

"You are nothing like what I expected, Luce Boudreau."

"I get that a lot." I squinted up at him, thankful for the nightlight illuminating the hallway. "One day the peer pressure is going to get to me, and I'm going to embrace my inner psychopath so I can start living up to everyone's expectations."

"As entertaining as it is to watch you hyperventilating over breaking the laws you're sworn to uphold, we don't have much time. We need to locate the files and make our exit." He gave me a measuring look. "Can you handle this, or do you need to wait here?"

Glaring at him, I straightened. "Pardon me for being a law-abiding citizen."

"We'll remedy that in time," he promised as he skulked deeper into the house.

Sucking up my pesky morals, I set off in the opposite

direction. The house was a modest two-bedroom, one bathroom, and the number of spaces where she could have hidden items of value were finite. I lucked across the converted home office and started riffling through the papers scattered across her desk. Nothing caught my eye, so I started pulling out drawers and then moved on to the file cabinets.

Warm breath fanned my ear. "Find anything?"

"*Wu.*" I clutched my chest. "Do *not* sneak up on me."

"Apologies," he said without sounding sorry at all. "Well?"

"Nothing." I noticed his hands were also empty. "What about you?"

"No luck so far." He drifted to a bookcase and started leafing through the pages of a hardback thriller. "Why don't you check the bedroom? I'll pick up where you left off in here."

The dismissal irked me, but it wasn't like I enjoyed snooping. "How long were you watching me?"

Wu lifted his head but didn't answer my question. He didn't even come close. "I can smell what you've touched. I can tell where you've been."

Heat sizzled across my nape in reminder of exactly how well charun noses worked. "I'll just . . . go do that."

The bedroom was crammed with furniture and the detritus of life. There was a queen-sized bed, a squat nightstand, and a walk-in closet in place of a bureau. I tackled the bed first, but Summers hadn't hidden anything under her mattress or the frame. The nightstand was stuffed to overflowing with fast food receipts but not much else. I checked the underside of each drawer but came up empty there too. The closet was full of nice pantsuits for work, and there was a basket of faded tees and shorts in the bottom. I shuffled everything around, but nothing caught my eye. I returned empty-handed to the office and found Wu examining the contents of a folder.

I leaned a shoulder in the doorway. "Have any luck?"

He glanced up, his expression unfathomable. "She has a file on you."

"What?" I snatched it out of his hand and skimmed it front to back. "Phew. You had me worried there for a minute. This is nothing malicious. Just newspaper clippings."

His expression indicated he begged to disagree. "It's an invasion of your privacy."

"Says the guy who outfitted me with a phone for the sole purpose of stalking my every move." I handed it back to him. "Privacy is an illusion, and it's getting thinner and thinner these days."

"That was not my only reason." He returned the incriminating papers where they belonged. "I gave you a direct line to me. Only three other people on this terrene can say that."

"Keep spoiling me, and I'm going to feel obligated to make you a friendship bracelet."

Wu sighed, a sound I was coming to enjoy provoking, and crossed to me. "She must have kept the prints on her person. We'll check her vehicle next. The digital copies can be wiped as soon as we have the hardcopies in hand."

We cleaned up after ourselves and left the way we came. Wu caught me studying the disrupter thingy and walked me through disengaging it. Ready to be on his way, he didn't notice when I pocketed the nifty device. Leaving him in my dust, I sprinted to the SUV, climbed in, and breathed a sigh of relief that we had made it in and out without getting caught. I was still luxuriating in our success when he joined me.

"When do we search her car?" I strapped in, ready to *Flintstones* this SUV out of the driveway and back into nice, anonymous traffic. "Please tell me we're not going to stakeout her street until she comes home."

"All right, I won't tell you." He backed out, found another empty driveway, and parked there. "We need to wrap this up tonight. We'll take shifts. I'll go first."

Grateful I hadn't had coffee for hours, I reclined the seat. "Wake me when it's go time."

"You would trust me to watch over you?" A mixture of surprise and pleasure and some undefinable something that fled too fast for me to identify splashed across his features. "You would leave yourself defenseless against me?"

"What a very charun thing to say. I don't trust you too far, but I'm pretty sure you're not going to murder me in my sleep." Leave it to him to twist a simple nap into an exercise in trust he hadn't yet earned. For one thing, murder would stain his fancy shirt. For another, he had made the mistake of letting me know my value. He wouldn't harm a hair on my head. Not unless I stepped out of line. "Okay, how about this? A member of my coterie is out there right now, watching us. Lift a finger against me, and they'll break it off and beat you to death with it. Does that make you feel better?"

"Actually, yes." Proof I retained some sense of self-preservation coaxed a smile from him. "That explains why I smelled fur."

"Thom's on duty tonight?" I yawned so hard my eyes watered. "He's bitey. I wouldn't recommend pissing him off if I were you."

"I wouldn't dream of it," he murmured. "Sleep well."

Putting another skill Rixton had taught me to good use, the ability to sleep anywhere and at any time, I linked my hands at my navel and dozed.

CHAPTER FIFTEEN

A hard jostle knocked me awake, and I blinked up at a tan ceiling in confusion. The tingling awareness I wasn't alone had me cranking my head to the left, and I yelped when I spotted Wu behind the wheel.

He didn't so much as flinch. "Bad dream?"

"What time is it?" I blinked until the blurry numbers on the clock made sense. "I was out for five hours? Why didn't you wake me?" I pulled the lever on the seat and sat upright. "What about Summers?"

"Do these look familiar?" He reached between the seats and produced a file with the single set of prints Rixton had given her along with the glossy originals. "When we wipe her this time, it should fix the problem." He angled his head toward me. "Right?"

"Wrong." I rubbed my face. "Rixton has a few more copies. I'll disappear those tomorrow."

His fingers wrapped the gearshift until his knuckles

whitened. "Do you think he would have distributed them yet?"

"Usually he's on the ball, but we're juggling a hellacious caseload. He's working long hours, and he has a newborn at home." Rixton didn't believe in doing things half-assed, so he would wait until his head cleared before making his case about the possible connection between all three fires. "There's a better than good chance he'll wait until the shift meeting to make his move."

The tension in his fingers lessened. "Did you give anyone else prints?"

"I emailed copies to Miller and Santiago, but their computers are vaults." You didn't do the type of work they did without making sure all the doors you kicked down in pursuit of information wouldn't fly open on your own computer. "You don't have to worry about them. I promise if I need to reference the photos, I'll do it online in a secure environment. I won't make more prints. Deal?"

"Let's deal with the other sets first. Then we'll discuss the need for you to possess your own."

A small victory, but I would take it. "Are we done then?"

"For tonight, yes." Headlights washed over his face, and his eyes gleamed golden as twin suns. The otherworldly sheen made me intensely curious what he hid beneath his suit. "Other loose ends might need tying off before all is said and done."

Maybe Wu had been a sailor in a previous life. He sure was a knot enthusiast.

"I still can't believe you flew to New York." I tried not to laugh but failed. "Santiago is going to be full of himself for weeks after this."

A resigned sigh escaped Wu. "I don't suppose I could persuade you not to mention the trip to him."

"*Nope.*" Dirt on Wu was worth too much to squander. "He and I are like oil and water most days. Ratting you out will earn me some much-needed bonus points with him."

"What will you tell your partner about the photos when he notices they're missing?"

"I'll lie to him." The acid taste of regret burned up my throat. "I don't want him near any of this. He's got a wife and a kid and a whole, normal life ahead of him. He's already in this up to his neck, and he has no clue. I'm not letting him dig himself any deeper."

"You're doing the right thing," he assured me as he turned up my driveway. "Humans are fragile, and they break easily."

"What about Kapoor?" I found myself asking. "He's human. The taskforce must have some human oversight."

"Kapoor is a demi, but he chooses to identify as human." Wu sounded mystified by that mindset, humanity as alien to him as my heritage was to me. "They are an unavoidable staple in higher management. This is their terrene, after all." I couldn't tell if he was joking, and he moved on before I could ask. "The bulk of our taskforce are charun, though there are a few demi among them."

"Demi," I clarified, "as in he's half charun."

"Yes." Wu parked his SUV, and we sat there staring at my house. "He didn't know until his mother was captured by the NSB and quarantined. He was eighteen, a senior in high school. The mandatory testing required of all mixed blood children exposed his heritage."

I hazarded a guess. "He joined up to right the wrongs against his mother?"

"I've already told you not all fathers are as worthy of a child's trust as yours. The same can be said for mothers." His fingers tightened on the gearshift until his knuckles punched against his skin. "He hated her for a long time, for making him what he is, but mostly for not telling him what he was." A sharp inhale moved through his chest, and he released his grip. "Kapoor joined to play exterminator. He was a smart kid, driven, and we needed people like him. He lasted a decade before he burned out on all the death he was dealing."

I swallowed hard. "How nervous should I be that the NSB sent an exterminator after me?"

"He wasn't there for you, not in that way." Wu didn't bother assuring me Kapoor wouldn't have offed me if I hadn't agreed to cooperate. "He's been reclassified to what the taskforce calls a janitor. All cases and public disturbances with suspected charun involvement land on his desk."

"That explains why he was cleaning up after us." And why his reach exceeded his grasp on occasion.

"White Horse has been a special project for him," Wu admitted. "Kapoor expressed an interest in you early on, no doubt expecting us to put you down. When no kill order was issued, his fascination shifted onto your coterie." A growl revved up my throat that earned me an interested look from Wu. "He's loyal to us. He won't harm your people so long as you keep them in line."

Gravel churned in my voice when I asked, "How do I know where the line starts and where it ends?"

"The academy will cover the basics, and I'll tutor you on the laws involving coterie creation and sustainment."

"Coteries are a thing outside the cadre? Other charun form them too?" I reflected on how it had been explained to me. "Miller told me each coterie is led by a high charun, that the groups vary in size and species, but the only true limit is how far their master's control extends. I assumed that meant only cadre."

"We've covered enough for one night." He shut me down fast. "Call when you've finished with Rixton."

"All right." I slid out and stretched, the elastic fabric moving with me, and I plucked at my top. "Hey, do you want these clothes back or ... ?"

"Keep the outfit." He cast me a knowing look. "You'll need it again."

Well, wasn't that a comforting thought. "Night."

"Goodnight."

A deep ache in my bones for home had me mounting the stairs after Wu left instead of heading back to the sewing room at the Trudeaus' for the night. With that in mind, I texted Uncle Harold to let him know where he could find me. I pulled up short when the front door opened under my hand. I was paranoid about locking it, always had been, since folks had a nasty habit of inviting themselves into our house.

On reflex, my right hand brushed my hip but found nothing. I hadn't gone to see Summers armed. There had been no point with Wu and a member of my coterie on the fringes acting as backup. And it's not like I would have shot her for having the nerve to bust me for breaking into her home.

Since Wu had been so helpful as to out my babysitter, I sent Thom a text then had to wonder if he would receive it if he was on all fours as Wu had implied. Still, I meant to back out and wait on him, I really did, but the moonlight chose that moment to glint off a puddle on the floorboards, and all my good intentions evaporated.

Shoving the door open wider illuminated boot prints tracked through the living room headed in the direction of the kitchen. I crept inside, avoiding squeaky planks, and let myself into the gun safe masquerading as our hall closet. I reached in, retrieved my shotgun plastered in screamo band stickers, and loaded her as quick as a heartbeat. With the weapon braced against my shoulder, I started clearing rooms, saving the kitchen, where the tracks vanished beneath the sheeting, for last.

Pulse thumping in my ears, I stepped through the slit in the plastic. There was so much blood ... and then I spotted the source. I rushed over to the body and hit my knees, the gun smacking the floor under my hand. "Miller?"

Curled on his side, he rested his head on an outstretched arm. Blood pooled under him, pouring from a ragged wound above his hip. His breaths came short and hard, and he flinched when I touched him, but he didn't answer.

"It's okay." I smoothed the damp hair from his forehead. "Thom's on the way. He'll know what to do. Just hang on until he gets here, okay?"

Miller gave no sign of hearing me over the incessant chattering of his teeth.

Footsteps echoed beyond the plastic, and I nestled the butt of the gun against my shoulder. "Show yourself."

"It's only me," Thom said, parting the folds and entering the space with his hands held up where I could see them. "What happened?"

"No idea." I lowered my weapon and shook my head. "I found him like this."

"He's lost a lot of blood." Thom knelt beside Miller and checked his vitals. "I'll do what I can to stabilize him, but we're going to need to transfuse him. See if you can reach Cole."

I pinged Cole, got no response, and cued up Santiago.

"You better be dying," Santiago grumbled, "and not interrupting me for a home address you could Google."

"I'm not dying," I rushed, "but Miller might be. We need help."

"Tell him to bring the full medical kit," Thom instructed, his eyes flipping up to mine, "and tell him to come ready to bleed."

"I heard him." Santiago dropped the attitude. "I'll be there in fifteen."

"Where's Cole?" The question slipped out before I checked the urge and winced in anticipation of punishment for my lapse.

Santiago didn't disappoint. "Not here."

He hung up, and I pocketed the cell. "What can I do?"

"Bring all the towels you've got. A pillow and a quilt aren't bad ideas." He brought Miller's wrist to his mouth and bit down until fresh blood painted his lips. "That will ease his pain." He palmed one of Miller's curved shoulders and pushed it straight. "Can you help me turn him onto the opposite side?"

"Sure." I hooked my fingers through Miller's belt loops, and together we flipped him onto his back. "Just one more," I told him, though he was past hearing. "Here goes nothing."

Thom and I wrestled him so that his injury faced the ceiling, and then we got busy peeling back the fabric. The material was frayed and caked with blood. I sacrificed a pair of poultry shears from a nearby cabinet to cut the shirt free of him. The gaping bite mark wept, the ribbons of skin tattered.

"Don't get sick over him." Thom nudged me away. "Get back if you can't stomach this."

Forcing my lids closed, I drew in gulps of oxygen through my mouth, its metallic taste registering on my tongue with cold familiarity as I spiraled inward. The arctic well of rationality deep in my core roused, its frigid calm spreading ice over my emotions in a sheet that trapped them from surfacing.

"Towels, pillow, quilt," I said smoothly, the bite of frost in my mouth. "I'll be right back."

Thom whipped his head toward me, and his administrations faltered. "Luce?"

"I won't be but a minute." Knees that had failed to support me when I first spotted Miller had no trouble locking now. "Call out if you think of anything else."

Thom's hesitation lasted until I reached the sheeting, and he asked, "What about your gun?"

"I don't need it." I heard myself talking, but I was divorced from the words coming out of my mouth. I was still caged in human flesh and had no charun powers, so I had no idea what the cold place expected me to do if whoever had taken down Miller came back for seconds, but the beauty of embracing this headspace was its efficiency, the ability to function without panic over seeing a friend bleeding out on the kitchen floor. I reached the front door as it flung open under Cole's hand. "Thom's in the kitchen."

His charge halted midway, his feet and brain pulling him in two different directions as he stared at me.

"Miller's bleeding out," I told him, and I might as well have been reporting on the weather. "Santiago's on his way with supplies."

With visible effort, Cole wrenched himself away from me and stormed off in their direction.

I gathered the supplies Thom had requested, adding a few extras, and then I hit the stairs. I met up with Santiago, who carried a black duffle large enough to double as a body bag on his shoulder, and held the plastic aside so he could get to Thom. Following him in, I circled around Miller then knelt on Thom's left side across from Cole, who sat with his back to the cabinets.

Miller's head was deadweight when I lifted it and slid the pillow in to support his neck. I worked in tandem with Thom, blotting the wound clean as he stitched it closed. Shock blasted through me when he sniffed the wound before licking the length of it clean, but there was too much insulation between me and what was happening for the disorientation to last.

When the time came for him to pierce Cole's thick vein, I was running on autopilot again. Needles, which usually made me squirm, didn't bother me all that much at the moment, even when Thom started the IV on Miller. A bag of saline came next, and Cole hooked that onto a cabinet drawer pull. While Thom checked the line for patency then moved on to tweaking the clamps and hooking up tubes, I existed in the white noise of my own head.

The process lasted two hours during which no one spoke or moved except for Thom, who vacillated between his two patients.

"I can make a bowl of soapy water," I offered into the quiet. "Miller needs to be cleaned before he rests."

Otherwise he might wake glued to the floor.

"No." Cole removed the needle from his arm with practiced ease. "I'll bathe him. Can you turn on the shower?"

"Sure." Out of clean towels, I pulled another quilt from the shelves in the laundry room and left it folded on the sink while I turned on the water and adjusted the temperature. Cole was standing in the doorway when I finished, his gaze empty when it fell on me. "It's ready."

"Go wait with the others," he ordered, shuffling through the doorway with Miller lolling in his arms.

Numb to my toes, I did as I was told. Santiago and Thom both stopped what they were doing to look at me, but I shook off their stares and mixed soapy water in a mop bucket. I sopped up the mess staining the floor, dumped the pinkish water down the sink, then washed my hands.

I was fine until I noticed the blood staining my nailbeds, until I really thought about how it had gotten there. Shakes spread from where my hands gripped the edge of the sink through my arms until chills brushed across my shoulders and spread up my nape. The cold place melted as if it had never been, the horror of what I had seen rushed back, and I heaved into the basin I had just scrubbed clean.

"Thank God," Santiago muttered.

Thom appeared at my elbow, a silent comfort, and I smiled weakly at him. "What's with the face?"

"You went away." He leaned across the space and rested his forehead against mine, his need for reassurance that I was me again too great for me to deny him. "Don't do that again."

"I'm sorry" was the best I could manage when some days that numbing cold was all that got me through. "I'm better now."

Santiago shouldered Thom out of the way. "Did you leave by choice?"

"Yes." I slumped forward, too tired to argue. "I made the call, but it's instinctive for me to reach for that part of myself when I need to shut down fear or panic. I've done it all my life."

"You can't give her an inch," he snarled, so close his spittle hit my cheek, "or she'll take a mile."

"I'll work on it," I promised, because seeing Santiago rattled shook me too. "Hey, I almost forgot. I got you a present." I patted down my pants until I located the small device I had stolen from Wu. "Merry Christmas."

"You're early," he said, peering at my palm with avarice, "but I'll take it."

"It's a signal disrupter of some kind. Wu slapped it on a house we broke into tonight."

Santiago cocked his head like he hadn't heard me right. "You did *what?*" He wheeled on Thom. "What the hell were you thinking not telling us Wu threw a B&E party and only invited her?"

Thom held his ground. "I wonder where she got the address."

"Wu already had the address," I chimed in. "His plan was to trick me into calling Miller, so he could get a bead on his location, but Miller hasn't been in contact with me for days."

A vicious edge serrated Santiago's voice. "What did he want with Miller?"

"He wanted to know if he had to clean up after Miller when he got done with Ivashov. I told him no." I rubbed my chapped fingers together, the faint stickiness from using too much soap reminding me of other tacky fluids I had been wrist-deep in tonight. "That was before I found Miller collapsed in my kitchen. I'm not sure how he got here, but it's not like I've had time to go explore the yard for clues. I doubt anyone followed him. The blood in the foyer was congealing. He'd been here for a while. They could have attacked him before we arrived to finish the job."

"Unless they used him as bait."

I whirled toward Cole's voice and found him drenched, dripping water onto the newly cleaned floor. I yanked open a drawer and tossed him a ratty dish towel. It was that or paper towels, and neither was going to do him much good considering his surface area. Miller was nowhere to be seen, but that didn't stop me from craning to see past Cole's shoulder into the living room.

"He's on the couch," he told me before I got a crick in my neck. "The wound is already sealed. He won't get blood on the fabric."

"I don't care about that." I had scrubbed out worse. "How's he doing?"

"He's breathing easier." He rubbed his face and head dry with quick, hard strokes. "We shouldn't move him again."

"I'm staying the night." Or the next six hours, whichever came first. "I'll keep an eye on him."

"We can't leave you both unprotected in case whoever started this tracks Miller to your house." Cole let his scowl deepen. "I'm staying. Thom, you're with us. Santiago, head home."

Leaving Portia unprotected overnight was unacceptable as well, so I was grateful Santiago had been dispatched.

"I can rest in your father's recliner," Thom declared as he shifted into his boxy kitty persona.

"You can take Dad's room." I rubbed the base of my neck. "I put fresh sheets on the bed a few days ago while I was cleaning the upstairs." I snapped my fingers. "Don't leave yet, Santiago. I'll be right back."

I jogged out to the Bronco to retrieve my souvenir and met him in the living room. He stood with his boots planted far apart, annoyance vibrating through every tensed muscle. Taking a page from Wu's book, I lobbed the ball of fabric at Santiago's face. He caught it mid-air and shook out the material.

"What the hell?" Brow furrowed, he scanned the image. The instant its meaning registered, he broke out in a grin so twisted with evil satisfaction he rivaled the Grinch. "Tell me this is real."

Pleased with my decision to sell Wu down the river, I smiled back with all the wicked intent I could muster. "Check the tag."

Cole and Thom chased our exchange back and forth with their gazes like they were watching the US Open.

Santiago read "*Made in New York*" aloud and whooped with unmitigated joy. "That dumb SOB believed me." He pumped his fist. "I'm damn good at what I do, but I hid you from the NSB. Do you realize how huge that is?"

"Your happy dance clued me in, yes."

"Maybe I was wrong." Santiago wiped under his eyes with the hem of the shirt. "Maybe it *is* Christmas."

"Mmmrrrrpt." Unimpressed, Thom swished his stump tail as he leapt onto his perch for the night.

Shaking his head, Cole started climbing the stairs.

"Does this mean you figured out the blind spot?" Santiago had mentioned finding a way to conceal us from Wu should we ever need one. "Will you be able to hide yourself and the others too?"

"Damn skippy." He tossed the shirt over his shoulder. "I'm in their system now. The chips won't matter. I can make us invisible." He patted the wadded fabric. "This proves it."

"I thought you were just being an ass," I admitted, "but you were actually being a useful ass."

"Yeah, well, I can multitask." Santiago sidled past me. "Thanks for the trinket, and for helping me stick it to that prick."

"You're welcome." I escorted him out, locked up like it mattered when charun weren't known for knocking, then followed in Cole's footsteps. He forked left into Dad's room, and I was smart enough not to follow him in to offer a guided tour. "Night, Cole."

When he made no reply, I kept walking until I stood at the foot of my bed. *Home*. The Trudeau house was nice, and it was filled with love, but there was nothing quite as wonderful as being in your own space with your own things.

I passed on a shower, though I needed one. I was too tired to trust my legs to prop me upright for fifteen more minutes. As a compromise, I peeled off the vintage quilt covering my bed, a gift to Dad from his mother, and collapsed facedown on the mattress. The sheets would cost me thirty bucks to replace if bleach couldn't remove the bloodstains. At this point, I was willing to make the sacrifice if it meant I didn't have to move again.

Shampoo and fabric softener wafted from my pillow, and I breathed in the comforting scents. I was boarding the sleepy train when heavy footsteps in my open doorway caused the conductor to withhold my ticket. Using maximum effort, I twisted my head to the side and glanced over my shoulder.

The familiar outline of Mt. Heaton blocked the doorway. "Goodnight, Luce."

Brain muzzy, I watched through drooping lids until he vanished around the corner. I considered getting up and closing the door to discourage another such incident, but that would require working legs and motivation, and I was all out of both. Plopping my face back down in my pillow, I closed my eyes and scrambled after the train, praying I caught up before it left the station.

CHAPTER SIXTEEN

I snapped awake to a symphony of masculine voices raised in heated debate. I rolled out of bed, rolled too far, hit the floor, decided the floor was an okay place to be, crawled on all fours to the bannister, crawled too far and busted my nose on a spindle, finally peered down into the living room and cursed.

Rixton stood in the foyer dressed in his uniform. His service weapon was trained on Santiago, who had planted his feet apart, barring my partner entrance to the house. Thom blocked off the staircase while Miller watched from his spot on the couch with his lip curled over his teeth.

"What's going on down there?" I demanded, hauling myself to my feet. "Rixton? Santiago?"

"When you didn't show up for work, I came looking for you." His aim didn't falter. "That's when I discovered your house has been infested. I saw the Bronco and assumed you were home, but this fella refused to answer any of my questions."

"Work?" As I plodded down the stairs, my stomach dropped into my toes. "What time is it?"

"Almost five," Rixton supplied. "I gave you a few hours in case you were tracking down a lead and forgot to give me a heads up."

"Put the gun down," I sighed. "They aren't holding me hostage. I fell asleep upstairs last night. I didn't realize it was so late. I didn't think I'd sleep so long. I didn't even set an alarm."

Rixton spotted me, and the color drained from his cheeks. "What the hell happened to you?"

I glanced down at the clothes from last night, which did an admirable job of concealing the bloodstains, but Rixton wasn't a detective for nothing. "Miller had an accident." Lucky me, I didn't know what had happened, so I couldn't tell him what I didn't know. "I made sure he didn't bleed to death while he was getting stitched back together." *On the floor, in my kitchen.*

The weapon hung limp in his hand for a full thirty seconds before he put it away and shoved past Santiago to inspect Miller. His eyes rounded then bounced back to me. "What kind of accident?"

"The kind that's none of your business," Santiago informed him. "If we wanted the cops involved, we would have called them."

"Luce is a cop." Rixton stabbed the air in my direction. "Therefore, cops are involved."

"Luce isn't a cop," he snarled. "She's—"

"She's a friend," Thom finished for him. "She didn't render aid in any official capacity."

"I need to speak to my partner." Rixton started walking toward the porch. "Alone."

On my way past, I ruffled Thom's hair. The bruised skin under his eyes spoke to the long night he'd spent watching over Miller. Briefly I wondered if I'd looked that dead on my feet last night. "I'll be right back."

Rixton's mood failed to improve when exposed to fresh air. "What's going on in there?"

Lord knows I had earned his suspicion, but God it hurt when he directed it at me, considering I had never given him cause to doubt me until now. But what good would an apology do if he offered me one? None. The worst was yet to come.

I curled my toes under me. "I told you—"

"You lied to me. Do you think I can't tell?" He scoffed at the very idea I might fool him. We were too close, knew each other too well. "Why are those men in your house? What is your connection to White Horse?" When I didn't answer quick enough for him, he kept hammering at me. "You didn't show up for work. You didn't call. You screwed up, Luce." He glared at the bay window where I noticed Santiago watching with quiet menace from the living room. "I thought White Horse left town after the Claremont case ended. I know you had a thing for Cole, but I thought that was over when he ghosted on you. What is this? A family reunion?"

He had no idea how close his barb had come to hitting the truth. "White Horse is . . ." *think, think, think* ". . . working for me."

Comprehension sparked behind his eyes, and he hissed out a curse. "Maggie."

"Maggie," I agreed, and I didn't have to fake the spike of agony the name conjured.

"Let her parents foot the bill," he said gently. "They've got the cash to run this type of operation full-tilt. You don't. I'm sure they've already hired someone. Did you ask them first?"

"They won't talk to me. They were never big Luce fans, and they see this as proof of my bad influence over their daughter." I let slip a fact I had refused to dwell on. "They blame me for what happened to Maggie. When I kept calling the house, Lila, one of the maids, gave me an earful about the harm I had caused the family."

"A psychopath targeted her." Again, he was right on the money. "That wasn't your fault."

"I don't care if they blame me." They should. I deserved every hateful thought that popped into their heads and some they lacked the imagination to conjure. "All that matters is we bring her home."

"It's been two weeks" was what he said, but what he meant was "she's dead".

An overwhelming majority of abductees were murdered within the first twenty-four hours, and we were well past that narrow window.

"I made a deal with Cole. I'm helping them work some minor cases, and in exchange he's cutting their rate for me. I hired them for a month. After that . . ." I would be gone, and my coterie would be too. "I'll talk to the Stevenses at that point if White Horse unearths any leads worth following. They can make the call to hire them to complete the job or maybe just pass the information on to their people."

"Let me know what the final bill runs you," he said. "Sherry and I will pay half."

"Thanks, but I can't let you guys do that. You've got Nettie to think of." There was no way I was lying to his face *and* stealing from his family. "Let me handle this. She's my best friend. It needs to be me."

"If this is what will bring you closure, then I fully support it." He hesitated a moment before adding, "Just don't renew after the thirty days, okay? There comes a point where you're going to have to let her go. You can't run yourself ragged and spend every penny you've got chasing a ghost."

A normal person would have hugged him then, but I had never been normal, and a hug would only convince him he was right about me teetering on the brink. There was no good way to explain the coterie was healing my touch aversion, that perhaps the lack of contact with my own kind had been the problem all along, without sounding one bump short of a pickle.

"I promise you, when the thirty days are up, I'll let it go." An easy promise to give considering I had no say in the matter past that point. "I'm sorry about flaking today. You know that's not me." Or it didn't used to be. "Miller was tracking a lead in the swamp and got himself bitten. He came here seeking help. He's lucky I came out to check on the house, or he would have bled to death before anyone found him."

Rixton angled his head toward the doorway. "How did he get in?"

"I gave him a key." I rushed to explain myself. "The guys came out to help with the bay window to save me a few bucks on installation. I offered to let Miller leave his tools here since the job ran late, and he was due in a client meeting that afternoon. I gave it to him so he could let himself in if he needed his equipment before we could meet up again."

"Make sure you get that key back," Rixton warned. "You can't have an open-door policy with these guys, Luce. They could be ax murderers for all you know."

Murderers, yes, but they required no axes. Their teeth worked just fine. "Dad approved of them."

"For a job, yes." Rixton's glare nailed me in place. "Does he know they crashed in his house last night?"

I cringed. "Not exactly."

"You need to call the shift office." Rixton backed off a few paces. "Let them know you won't be in tonight." He took the steps. "If you need a day or two to get sorted, take them. You've got the time."

No, I really didn't. Two weeks. Fourteen days, give or take. "I'll touch base with Albertson."

"See that you do." He crossed the yard. "Oh, hey. I found that note on your desk. I turned it in to Chief Jones during the shift meeting." He winked. "You can thank me later."

The spit dried from my tongue. On my desk? *No, no, no.* I had put that letter in a drawer. Right? *Right?*

I wasn't ready. Not yet. But it was too late. My partner had just tendered my resignation.

Rixton would be crushed if he found out before I told him. Sleeping in had bought me a good sixteen hours before I was expected at work again. I would tell him then, I had to, in case the chief started sizing him up for a new partner before his old one turned in her badge.

God, the thought of Rixton with someone else was eating me alive. We were a team. A damn good one.

Why couldn't I be normal? Live my small-town life, work my small-town job, have my small-town friends? Why had fate selected me for the destiny lotto? I had zero aspirations for greatness. I just wanted to do my job, come home, watch Discovery Channel, and imagine all the places I would never visit because they might be nice, but they weren't Canton, Mississippi.

"Hey, Rixton, wait a sec." Guilt soured my gut, made it churn with regret. "I need to grab a file."

"Help yourself." He popped the trunk with the key fob. "Do you think your house guests will want the rest of these donuts?

I bought a dozen vanilla cream-filled, but I can't finish them alone. Even I have my limits, few though they may be."

"I have nothing edible in the kitchen." I would have to remedy that if Miller required another overnight stay. "I'm sure they'd be thrilled to take a few thousand calories off your hands."

Checking to make sure he got in the car and stayed there, I shoved up the lid on the trunk and started sorting through the heavy-duty plastic box we used as an on-the-go file cabinet. I didn't have to search far to spot the envelope with the photos. One stack was missing, probably his personal set, but I took what was there and tucked them between the pages of the Hensarling fire report to hide them until I could secure them elsewhere.

"What's on your agenda for tonight?" One manila folder looked like the next, but I tucked the file under one arm with the label facing inward to mask what I had taken. "Are you going to hit a burger stand and make bad life choices since there will be no witnesses?"

Gut roiling from my deception, no matter how necessary, I doubted I'd ever eat again.

"Burgers will probably happen. And fries. Maybe a hotdog." He passed over a box that must have weighed three pounds. "I have to flush all the sugar from my system, and I bet those buns are super absorbent."

I hated bursting his bubble but . . . "I don't think that's how it works."

"Do you ever read those medical articles in magazines? What they claim will heal you today they swear will kill you tomorrow. Who's to say I'm wrong? And if I am, by some miracle, wrong—" he shrugged "—give me twenty-four hours."

All those articles were hooey, in my opinion, but Rixton was a magazine connoisseur, and I wasn't about to pick a fight with him over his choice of reading material. "What about those thirty-two-ounce sodas you knock back with your meal?"

"Shh." He mimed zipping his lips. "We don't talk about that."

Sagging under the weight of the donuts, and my guilt, I let him off with a warning. "Be careful out there."

"I always am." He pointed at me. "You be careful in there. Take my advice. Pry that guy off your sofa before he asks for his own toothbrush to keep in your bathroom."

"Yeah, yeah."

"Later, Bou-Bou."

The annoyance usually sparked by that particular nickname never surfaced. Its days were numbered after all.

Santiago held the door open for me, hoping to relieve me of my burden, but I carried the box straight to the couch. Sinking down beside Miller, I passed him the first of nine donuts. "Would a sugar coma be a step up or a step down from where you are now?"

"I'm willing to find out." He smashed the whole thing in his mouth and pleaded with his eyes for another, which I had prepped and ready to press into his hand. "Thom? Santiago? You guys want to grab one before they're gone?"

Thom accepted one, careful to pinch it between two fingers. Sniffing around its edges, he licked the icing off the top, then sat the otherwise untouched pastry on the coffee table while he cleaned his hands with a moist towelette he pulled from his pocket.

Santiago polished his off in two bites. Without missing a beat, he scooped up Thom's and finished it too. When he caught me staring, he wiped his hands clean. "Do you have any idea how much of his saliva I've had in my body at this point?

He could probably transfuse me with the stuff. Sharing food with him won't kill me."

"Have you guys already hashed out what happened?" I passed Miller his third. "What did I miss?"

"We waited for you," he said around a mouthful of dough. "Cole ordered a late breakfast for four from the Waffle Iron. He ought to be back any minute."

I cued up another donut. "Am I one of the four, or should I take what I can get?"

"You're one of us," Thom assured me. "Cole would stay, but he must return to Portia."

I mouthed *thank you* for telling me what I couldn't help wanting to know without making me ask.

"What's in the folder?" Santiago nodded toward my side. "You're going to cut off circulation in your arm if you don't ease up on the clamp action soon."

"They're crime scene photos from the Orvis fire down in Madison." I placed them on the coffee table. "Wu *requested* I obtain all the copies Rixton and I are responsible for so I can hand them over to him."

"Same ones you sent us?" Santiago waited on my nod of confirmation. "The adult female is a textbook example of how viscarre clean out their victims. I can see why he'd want those out of human hands, not that pictures will do them much good without the bodies to go along with them."

Thankfully, that threat had already been eliminated. "The bodies never made it to the coroner's office."

"Way ahead of you." Shades of his Grinchiest smile returned. "They were incinerated about six hours ago according to the timestamp on the security feed I was watching."

"I'm not going to ask." I pinched the stretchy fabric of my cat burgling pants. "I'm a cop for a couple more weeks. Let me enjoy walking the straight and narrow while I can. After Wu gets ahold of me, I get the feeling my moral compass will be spun."

"To accomplish any good in this world or any other," Thom said, "you sometimes must do bad things."

"Listen to the fortune cookie." Santiago swiped a donut faster than I could pop his hand. "The only way we stay alive on this terrene is to keep hidden. Someone blabs, and we're toast. Most terrenes are tolerant of other charun, if not welcoming, but this one is peculiar in that there are no native charun. There are only humans and what comes from mixing species."

"Why would Earth be the exception?" I wondered. "Are there other . . . beings . . . here?"

The men all got busy looking somewhere else.

Lucky for them, the front door chose that moment to open, and a tailor-made distraction waltzed through looking better than anything that might be in the bags he carried.

"Cole," Miller called in welcome. "Glad you're back."

"Food," Santiago echoed. "I'm glad you're here."

Thom ducked his head in apology for the evasion, but I didn't have time to dwell because breakfast was incoming, and the guys were falling on Cole like lions on a gazelle. As he pressed a box in my hands, my stomach growled its own welcome to him.

"I got you a breakfast bowl with double meat and added cheese in your grits." He made a second trip onto the porch and returned with a drink holder brimming with a variety of lattes, black coffees, and other assorted wake-up juices. Saving me for last, he passed me a nondescript cup. "It's a surprise."

Intrigued, I took a hesitant sip, moaned, then licked an icy sweetness from my lips. "What is this magical creation?"

"The barista recommended it for coffee drinkers with a sweet tooth." He sipped his—plain black—and watched me have another taste. "Cold-brewed iced coffee mixed with espresso granita and topped with homemade vanilla bean ice cream."

"It's delicious." A thought struck me, and I set my goodies on the coffee table while I darted up to my room. I came back down and pressed a fifty-dollar bill into Cole's palm. "There's your tip, delivery boy."

Cole looked like he might protest until he noticed the crisp lines where the intricate folds used to tuck. "Are you sure you want to give this up?" Rough, his voice was so rough. And uncertain. I both loved and hated having that effect on him. "The bracelet was a gift. You don't owe me anything."

I gave his words from the swamp back to him. "I know."

But taking that ring from Wu, letting him slide it on my finger, had injured Cole in the same way hearing a woman's voice, soft from sleep, had wounded me.

Expecting him to pocket the cash, I gasped when he shredded the bill into confetti then dusted his hands over the dregs of his coffee. I got the feeling if I'd had a fireplace, he would have tossed the whole thing in there for good measure.

"What did Ulysses S. Grant ever do to you?" I couldn't fight the laugh hitching my chest. "Was that really necessary?"

"Yes," he said, tossing back his cup and drinking it all down. "It was."

So this must be the modern day equivalent of when dragons of old scorched their enemies' bones before grinding them to dust between their teeth. Maybe it aided digestion. Or maybe Cole was caving to his instincts in a way that left my new partner breathing. For now.

Settling back into my spot on the floor next to Miller, I

took a sip of my drink and noticed all eyes on us. "Do you guys want a sip?"

"Nope," Santiago said, making a popping sound with the P.

"I don't enjoy coffee." Thom shook his head. "I prefer milk steamers."

Miller was the last man standing, well, laying. "I'm good with my orange juice."

"All right." I dug into my meal and let their stares bounce off me. "Don't say I didn't offer."

Done exacting his revenge, Cole sank into Dad's ancient recliner, which groaned in panic at its current circumstances. I really had to invest in some Cole-friendly furniture for the place. Not that we would be around long enough to get much use out of it, but I would visit often. That much I could guarantee Kapoor. He would get his month, but after that, I wanted regular off days and vacation time nailed down so I could coordinate with Dad.

"I don't have much time," Cole said, kicking off the conversation. "What can you tell us?"

"Ivashov was a plant." Miller shoveled in his eggs faster than he'd hoovered the donuts. "He let me take him from the hospital without a fight, and he endured the—" he focused on his meal to avoid eye contact with me "—*interrogation* for several hours. There wasn't much left of the host when he snapped. That's when all hell broke loose."

Cole leaned forward, planting his elbows on his thighs. "Thanases?"

"No." Miller crunched on his bacon. "War's mate was nowhere in sight."

"Well," Santiago drawled. "Don't keep us in suspense."

"Sariah." Miller let his announcement sink in. "She must have worn a tracker of some kind. There was no indication we had been followed, but she hit a certain point, and the weak act dried up in a hurry. She bared her teeth, ripped out of her host, and attacked. I could have taken her, but three of her siblings answered whatever distress call she was throwing out."

"War is trying to take us out one by one," Santiago decided, "weaken the coterie."

"Starting with Miller was ambitious," Cole countered then checked with the man in question. "Did she give you anything?"

"Nothing." He closed the lid on his empty container. "She didn't crack." He sipped his juice. "She's worse now than the last time our paths crossed. Whatever happened to her during the last century, it's totally unhinged her."

"Three of her *siblings*?" I swore I smelled smoke as my brain kicked into high gear. "Drosera siblings? As in born from a Drosera pair?" There was only one I could name: War and Thanases. "This Sariah is War's daughter?" That's what they meant. What they hadn't said was that made her my niece. Conquest's niece. "And you've known her how long?"

"Sariah is the only surviving child from War's first clutch with Thanases," Thom informed me. "She hatched first, and she ate her siblings as they emerged. None of War's other children have survived as long. Sariah won't allow it, and her parents approve of her ruthlessness. Sariah is War's third, second only to her father. Her appearance portends nothing good."

"Where has she been?" Santiago asked. "That's what I want to know. That's what we need to find out."

"War exposed herself publicly," Thom explained when it became obvious to him I was lost as to why her arrival was such a big deal. "Sariah ought to have been there, but she wasn't. Thanases was the only senior coterie member we encountered. The others were young, inexperienced, easy to kill."

That was easy? Dad almost died, Maggie lost her life as she knew it, and Cole had been held hostage at knifepoint.

"Cannon fodder," Cole agreed.

"I'll start digging," Santiago volunteered. "Sariah wouldn't have gone with Miller without a reason. We're missing something."

"You do that." Cole rose, and the recliner sagged with relief. "Report back on what you find." His gaze touched on me. "I need to get back to the bunkhouse. Portia is still weak from her transition. If Sariah is singling us out, she'll start with the weakest link."

Santiago scratched his jaw. "Portia would eviscerate you if she heard you say that."

"Notice I said it where there's no risk of that happening." Cole scrubbed his palm over his bristly scalp. "She's a top-notch fighter and a major asset to this coterie, but facts are facts. She needs more time to regain full strength. She's a liability until then. We're going to have to close rank and make sure she gets what she needs to recover."

Having nothing to add to this portion of the conversation, I stood and started cleaning up the trash. I was dumping the containers in a trash bag in the kitchen when a tingling awareness swept over me, and I turned to find Cole camped out near the fridge, the point farthest away from me.

"Santiago told me there was trouble this morning."

"I overslept and missed work." I tossed an empty cup with more force than necessary. "Rixton drove out to check on me and bumped up against Santiago. It wasn't pretty, but I've smoothed it over for now."

When I didn't elaborate, he prompted me. "What did you tell him?"

"More lies," I huffed out on a tired laugh. "What else? He

thinks I hired you to find Maggie's remains. That seems harmless enough, so I let him believe he was right."

"You had to explain us away somehow. We had no reason to still be in town unless we'd picked up additional work in the area."

"Maggie used to pick on me because I sucked at lying. She could always tell." I shuffled to the table and sank onto a chair. "Now I'm an old pro." At this rate, I would have to start making notes to keep up with all the yarns I was spinning. "Every time I open my mouth, I betray someone. All those little white lies sure add up fast."

"Things will be easier when you're working for the NSB. Everyone will be on the same page there."

So I kept telling myself, but I was starting to wonder if it got easier or if you simply got used to it.

"The things that make me human, that make me *me*, are the very things I'm leaving behind." I voiced one of my greatest fears. "What if severing those ties gives Conquest a stronger hold on me?"

Cole kicked up his chin. "I'll bring you home if you start backsliding."

The promise held an edge. "The NSB isn't going to let me leave every time I get homesick."

"You're an asset to them." He stated the fact. "They're going to do whatever it takes to hold you together. You're the best weapon they've got in the coming war, and it does no one any good if you go off prematurely."

Thunking my elbows on the table, I dropped my face into my hands. "I wish someone would pull the pin already."

Footsteps pounded out a furious cadence across the room, and I gasped when my chair wrenched away from the table. Cole spun me around, got down on his haunches so I didn't have to break my neck looking up at him, and shoved his hard face in front of mine.

"You've asked me to accept you're more than a vessel for Conquest. You've asked me to trust that you will resist her control, fight against your own nature. You've asked me to have faith, when I lost mine so long ago I doubted ever finding it again." He placed his palms on my knees, engulfing them in his warmth. "You say you're Luce Boudreau." His thumbs stroked the insides of my thighs. "Make me believe it."

The subtle caresses short-circuited my brain. "What if I can't?"

I hadn't exactly had much luck so far.

"Conquest always gets what she wants at any cost." Fluttering muscles chased the skin across his jaw. "One of those things has always been . . . me."

"Oh, Cole." I covered his hands with mine. "You don't have to tell me."

"Everything about her from the way she walked, the way she laughed, the way she smiled, reminded me of all I lost, all she took from me. I couldn't stand the sight of her, but she couldn't bear to be parted from me." He extended his bare wrist, the scars a stark reminder of how bad I was for him, and offered himself up for my inspection. "She cuffed me with these and strung chains from them that she wore wrapped around her hips as a belt so that I was forced to follow wherever she led."

Unable to glance away, I stared at the glimmering rose gold, hating we shared such brutal history.

"Her touch dirtied me. Her voice poisoned me. Her taste . . . " He flexed his fingers. "I tried to kill her. Many times. She grew to anticipate our battles." His breath sawed from his lungs. "I sold her my soul, gave her dominion over me, and I had no recourse. She owned me, and she never let me forget."

I rolled my lips in to stop from begging not to hear when I had to learn our history in order to understand our relationship.

"I've known you desire me from the day we met. You wear your need as perfume on your skin." His thumbs started their slow circles again. "You could have taken me that day in the woods while I was mindless to get inside you. You could have allowed me to pleasure you, and no one would have blamed you."

"You would have blamed me." I rubbed the pads of my fingers over his rough knuckles. "And you would have blamed yourself. The first I can handle, but the second . . ." I broke even that small contact. "Consent matters, and you couldn't give yours." I cleared my throat, the skin flushing across my cheeks and throat. "I'll see what I can do about the, ah, smell."

A rhythmic purr filled the space between us as he covered the bracelet I wore with his wide palm, his fingers tightening around my wrist until he chained me in place. "I already told you." His meltwater eyes thawed precious degrees. "You complement me."

All the while a blush swept up my throat, I attempted to pinpoint what made this time different, why this felt like *he* was the one complementing *me*.

"Are you two done yet?" Santiago called from behind the plastic sheeting. "Portia's not getting any less alone the longer you two bump gums and gods only know what else in there."

There was no mistaking Cole's reluctance to rise. "I have to go."

"Me too." I got to my feet. "I have a mission to accomplish for Wu."

"Wu is dangerous." His gaze dipped to my mouth as though assessing other, equally lethal risks. "Make sure you take Santiago with you wherever you go."

"He can't play escort. Not after this morning. Rixton would burst a blood vessel." I held up a hand to forestall his protest. "I have to visit Sherry. Rixton has the last copy of the Orvis documents in his home office. I need to finesse that from under her nose, and that can't happen if Rixton comes charging in like an enraged bull."

"Be safe." He lingered, but he didn't add more. "I'll see you later."

As much as I wanted to ask how much later, I was aware of both Santiago listening at the doorway and Cole weighing the challenge he'd laid down for me. I wasn't willing to push either. Especially since it looked like Santiago was playing backup for me while Thom kept watch over Miller.

"Santiago's got my back." Probably. "I'll be fine." I rocked a half-step forward. "Take care of—" I bit off the name I had no right to speak "—yourself."

"I won't let anything happen to them," he promised me, proving one of his super powers, in addition to super strength and the ability to fly, was reading me like a book. "I won't let them out of my sight."

While he made his exit and said his goodbyes, I got busy securing an invitation. "Hey, Sherry."

"Oh, God. An actual adult person. Keep speaking. Full sentences. Whole words. Come on. Talk to Momma." Her groan lasted forever. "Did you hear that? I baby-talked you. I am losing my mind."

"You've been a mom for like two weeks." Shame sneak-attacked me that I no longer tracked Nettie's age in daily increments. "There's no way you have cabin fever already."

"Let's be clear—" She was quick to correct me. "Nettie isn't the problem here. It's my husband. He's lost the ability to communicate like an adult, and I don't think I'm telling you anything you don't already know when I say he was iffy on the whole mature conversation thing to start with."

"Well, it just so happens my night is wide open." I braced a hip against the counter. "You feel up to having company?"

"I'll even brush my hair." She squealed. "How soon can you get here?"

"Two hours?" I had to shower and run a few loads of laundry first if I hoped to salvage my stealth mode outfit and towels. "I would offer to bring Thai over when I come, but Rixton mentioned you're on a special breastfeeding diet. What are acceptable substitutions?"

"Pick up the Thai," she pleaded. "If I can't eat it, at least I can smell it."

Poor Sherry. Responsible adulting sucked. "What about you?"

"How about a veggie plate from Pansy's? I've been craving collards for whatever reason, and that would really hit the spot. Extra cornbread, please and thank you."

We chatted a moment longer before I ended the call and started the clothes. I figured I would wash the black outfit first since I was going to have to bleach the hell out of the towels if I wanted to save them.

Leaving the boys to entertain themselves, I jogged upstairs, ducked under the shower, and started scrubbing dried blood off my stomach. Considering where I was about to go and what I was about to do, I felt dirtier when I stepped out than when I got in.

CHAPTER SEVENTEEN

————◆————

Sherry greeted me on the porch with a cooing Nettie in her arms. I thought she was coming in for a kiss on my cheek and wondered if that was a new symptom of mommyitis, but nope. She was leaning over to stick her nose in the bag from Thai-Thai For Now. After a long inhale that must have sucked half the flavor off my noodles, she straightened with a sigh. "That's the stuff. Come on. We'll eat in the living room like heathens."

"I eat in the living room all the time." Dad had enforced the oldie but goodie *eat at least one meal together as a family* rule when I was a kid. As far as rules went, it was a good one, but it didn't hold up as well now that we worked different shifts. "As a matter of fact, I ate a late-late breakfast on the floor in front of my couch."

"Scandalous." She led me to the living room and placed Nettie in a bouncy seat she kept going with the tip of one toe. "Clearly, you're the heathen queen."

"I was found in a swamp," I reminded her. "You're lucky I use silverware instead of my bare hands."

"Oh, please. Your lack of table manners has nothing to do with where you were found and everything to do with you being raised by a bachelor." She patted the cushion beside her. "How about you sit next to me and blow on each bite in my general direction? I wouldn't want you to burn your tongue or anything."

"Will I get in trouble for exposing you to secondhand Thai?" Eyes narrowed, I clutched the bag to my chest. "Rixton is already pissed at me."

"You've been acting weird for weeks then one day you're a no-show at work, and you think he's going to take that well?" She snorted, an utterly inelegant sound that still came out daintier than when I let one fly. "He's worried about you. I'm worried about you." She pegged me with a sad look. "I never see you anymore."

"I miss you too," I said by way of apology. "I'll try to do better."

"I don't mean to guilt trip you." She accepted the bag I passed her and dug in. "Okay, so I meant to guilt trip you a little. That's what friends are for, right? I'm just asking you please—for the sake of your goddaughter—don't give her father a heart attack."

"He told you." There was no other reason why me missing work, with or without a call, would have merited him ratting me out before he got home tonight. "About White Horse."

"He might have mentioned finding you dressed in a cat burglar special, covered in blood, and surrounded by men of questionable ethics. He might have also mentioned the guy camped out on your couch resembled a shark bite victim." She accepted the can of sugar-free, dye-free, caffeine-free soda with a curled lip, but it had been the least offensive option on the menu. "What he didn't mention was if a certain hunk a hunk of burning love was there."

"*Cole*—" I emphasized his name "—was not there, thank you very much."

His earlier presence and his eventual return were beside the point.

"Mmm-hmm." She pointed at herself then drew a circle in the air. "This is my *I believe you* face."

"You're fixated." *Pot, meet kettle.* "Objectify your husband for a little while, why don't you?"

"I would," she agreed on a sigh, "but it's more fun when it's a hands-on experience."

Eww. Eww. Eww.

"Speaking of hands-on—" I twirled more noodles around my fork "—I'm not touching that comment."

A mewling sound rose from the bouncy seat, and Sherry set down her food. "What's wrong, sugar lump?" She lifted her daughter, wrinkled her nose, then turned her head to cough. "You are *so* your father's daughter." Eyes watering, she cuddled her baby closer. "We'll be right back. This won't take but a minute."

"Take your time." I placed my foot on the coffee table and went through the motions of popping the tab on my own drink. "There's no rush."

Singing an old nursery rhyme, Sherry carried Nettie down the hall to her bedroom for a change. I waited a heartbeat to see if the door would shut, but it didn't. Nothing for it. I set the can on a coaster and stood in a rush, making my way down the opposite hall to where Rixton had carved out his office in the formal dining room.

Stacks of papers, electronics, and bills littered the glossy oak behemoth functioning as his desk. Six ladder-back chairs, their seats buried under a mishmash of overflow, tucked beneath the table. Two bookshelves crowded one wall, both stuffed to capacity, and a file cabinet on wheels sat abandoned in one corner.

Hands trembling, I started a quick and methodical search through Rixton's belongings, the invasion of his privacy unsettling the Thai in my gut. Nothing. There was nothing here. I scanned the room again, slower this time. Where had he ... ?

Years spent exploring the labyrinthine twists of Rixton's mind popped the answer into my head.

Below the window was an outlet that didn't match the style of the others. It was larger, plainer, and the color was one shade lighter. Those were sins Sherry would never forgive without good reason. I crossed the room and knelt, running my fingers around the raised edges. There was a bit of give, but not enough sway to be useful. I tested the screw in the center with my thumbnail only to discover it was fake. The entire rectangle was one solid piece of molded plastic.

Springing back onto my feet, I scoured Rixton's desk for the letter opener I'd spotted earlier and carried it to the wall where I used the flat edge to pry the whole contraption forward a fraction of an inch. With my fingertips, I pulled the cover out farther until the dummy outlet fell into my hands. Through the narrow opening, I spied several sets of rolled-up papers secured with rubber bands. Tucked into the gap between the wall studs, nestled between other scrolls, was the bundle of prints.

Before I lost my nerve, I finagled the photos from their hidey hole. Once I popped the cover back in place, I unrolled the stack, checked to make sure they were all there, then folded them until they fit in my back pocket. I'd worn an extra-long, extra-loose shirt to make the contraband less noticeable. It was the best I could do on short notice.

Tearing the images to pieces and flushing them would be more satisfying, a fitting outlet for my guilt, but my gut warned me Wu would accept nothing less than the originals. After going through all the hassle of securing the copies, he would want to destroy them in the manner he saw fit.

With that done, I rolled back onto my feet and examined the outlet. Everything looked good from here. As I backed out of the office, I returned the letter opener and checked to make sure I had righted everything I'd touched. Certain I had covered my tracks, I dashed back into the living room and ran smack into Sherry and Nettie.

"You're not leaving already, are you?" Sherry strapped Nettie back into her seat. "I promise she won't drop another bomb for at least three hours."

"There were no napkins in our bags." I gave her a wide berth and kept my back to the wall. "I was going for paper towels." Excuses made, I bolted for the kitchen where I stood with my palms braced on the sink and hung my head. "I am so not cut out for covert ops."

"Luce," Sherry called after a few minutes, "a piece of your chicken jumped off your plate into my mouth. You better hurry up in case the others attempt an escape. I'm only one woman here. I can't stem the tide."

I tore off a few paper towels on my way back into the living room, but I couldn't stomach another bite. I had betrayed Rixton, Sherry, and Nettie. In their own home. The one place meant to be a safe haven, and I had shaken that foundation of their trust and love and welcome with my deceit.

Rock, meet bottom.

I sat and talked with her for hours, like I might never get another chance, which was a real possibility after Rixton realized what I had done. I even fed Nettie a bottle while she

luxuriated in the safety of her bouncy seat, but I couldn't stop
fidgeting. I was ready to crawl out of my skin by the time Rixton
called to ask Sherry if she needed him to pick anything up from
the store on his way home.

That was my cue to exit stage left.

With the prints tucked safely in my back pocket, I said my
goodbyes and hit the steps at a gallop. Holed up in the Bronco,
I brought the black cell to my lips and spoke two damning
words. "It's done."

But whether I meant the job, the friendship with Sherry, or
my partnership with Rixton, I wasn't sure.

Wu met me in the same grocery store parking lot where I
saved Sherry all those years ago, and it got me thinking about
how life moved in circles. Free will creating endless ripples in
a cosmic pond. This was where it all began for me and the
Rixtons, and this might very well be where it ended.

With my hip braced against the Bronco's tailgate, I watched
his approach, his every move screaming *top of the food chain,
baby* and marveled at how charun blended so well among
humans. They were apex predators, and they wore us like dressing as a sheep might hide the wolf salivating behind their eyes.

"You're unhappy." Wu studied the heaviness in my shoulders,
the drooping of my spine. "You should be pleased. You got what
we needed without getting caught."

"I invited myself over to my partner's house tonight. I
brought his wife dinner and pretended I was there to visit
her and the baby, my goddaughter, and then I broke into his
personal files while her back was turned." The copies in the
car had at least been held in a communal area, not that theft
of community property was better than personal. I shoved the
prints at him, eager to wash my hands of them. "I accept the

necessity of what had to be done, but I take no satisfaction in what I did. He's my friend. He deserves better than this. They both do."

Wu mimicked my posture. "How is Miller?"

"Ready to leap tallish buildings in a single hop."

"So protective." His chuckle raced over my skin. "I'm not interested in exploiting his weakness."

"Mmm-hmm." Survival of the fittest got real when charun were involved. "Do you ever get tired of spying on me?"

"You fascinate me." His shoulders twitched in a shrug. "So, no, I don't."

Can't blame a girl for trying. "Can we agree to leave my coterie out of this?"

"Since you're one and the same, no." He shoved off the Bronco. "Miller, in particular, is a high risk. His unflinching loyalty to you is the only reason he's not kept in chains. While he's weak, he'll have difficulty holding onto his skin. Either we monitor him from afar, or we check him into a facility until he's recovered."

"He stays where he is," I warned him. "Miller will be back on his feet within the next twenty-four hours." I had overheard Thom tell Cole that much. "He's healing well. There's no reason to think he's going to explode into ... whatever it is that scares the pants off everyone."

"He hasn't told you?" Wu wiped all expression from his features. "You haven't seen him?"

I opened my mouth, and then shut it. "We all have our secrets. I'm not going to twist his arm to get at his."

"I can understand why he would want you to look at him and see the face he's chosen instead of the one he was born wearing." Wu ruffled his thumb over the top corner of the papers he held. "Your human mentality is as much of an asset as it is a hindrance. Your mind would bend if you beheld his true face in your current state."

"Enough." I slashed my hand through the air. "Just enough, okay?"

Wu ducked his head. "I am sorry for what you had to do tonight."

"That makes two of us." I shoved him out of my way. "I'm going home."

Standing under the shower wouldn't make me feel any cleaner, but at least it would camouflage my tears.

Back at the farmhouse, no one spoke to me on the way upstairs to my room. The ability to smell emotions must have told them what was doing, and they let me handle the fallout on my own terms. I scrubbed until my skin turned raw before giving my hair the same callous treatment.

The brutal events of the past few weeks slipped from my eyes and down the drain until I was spent.

Dressing in pajama shorts and a baggy tee, I braided my hair back then headed down to check on Miller. I made it halfway before pounding started on the front door. The patient craned his neck to see who had come calling, but Thom shook his head once, and Miller reclined. Santiago was less circumspect. He took up position behind the door and nodded, clearing me to open it, which I did.

"Rixton." Cold sweat broke across my spine in a chilling wave. "What's up?"

"We need to talk." His gaze slid past my shoulder to Miller. "Alone."

"Let's go out back." I led him onto the porch and around the house to where the old oak tree overshadowed the picnic bench. Too wound up to sit, I braced against the trunk and opened myself up for what came next. "What's on your mind?"

He wasted no time. "Where are the photos?"

"Rixton—"

"You took the spares out of the trunk." He bulldozed over me. "I was too busy losing my shit over where you were and why you weren't answering your phone to pass them out during the shift meeting, so I put it off until tonight. Except when I went to get them out of the trunk, I came up empty."

"Rixton—"

"I checked on the prints before I left the station, so I know they were there when I arrived at your house. This was the only stop I made that wasn't drive-through. You were the only person who got near that trunk other than me." He slapped his open palm against the tabletop. "The worst part is, I told myself it didn't matter, that I had one last set squirreled away someplace safe. I could run off more copies and let that be the end of it. Except, when I got home, those had vanished too."

Aware of what came next, my chin hit my chest.

"That's when I remembered what Sherry told me when I called to ask if she needed anything before I got home. She told me that you had spent the afternoon with her. That gives you the means and the opportunity, but what was the motive?" Fury crackled in the air between us. "Tell me what's going on. Explain this to me in a way I can understand."

"I can't."

"You tampered with evidence. You better have a damn good reason, or I will report this. I won't have a choice. I have a family to support, and I can't lose my job, not even to protect you."

There was nothing I could say without digging my hole deeper. Summers would contact him when she realized her copies were missing. Of that I had no doubt. And together they would realize that all digital traces of those photos, as well as anything else Wu felt the need to scrub, had vanished too.

I was the only common thread, and Rixton would yank on me until the whole story unraveled.

"I'm sorry."

"I'm sorry too." The fight drained out of him. "Until you can present an argument that changes my mind, I'm going to have to ask you to stay out of my home and away from my family. You violated my trust tonight, and you abused Sherry's hospitality. You're giving me nothing to help me put your betrayal into perspective." He took a breath and tried reasoning with me again. "I want to trust your reasons for doing this. I want to believe you did what you did for a purpose I can understand. But you've got to meet me halfway."

That last bit was an olive branch extended, and I batted it away one last time. "I understand."

"Chief Jones read your letter," he said in a quiet voice. "She ordered me to talk you out of leaving for the department's sake. The mess with Timmons stirred up enough bad publicity, but your leaving before he's sentenced makes it look like you're getting forced out."

My arm was being twisted, all right, just not by the department. "I don't have a choice."

"Seems to me you had plenty of them. You could have told me you'd decided to accept the offer from the FBI. You could have told me you had written your letter of resignation. You could have kept your sticky fingers off the evidence." The chill in his expression stung. "You've been sinking since Maggie, and this latest stunt will force me to watch you drown."

"I wasn't ready to turn in the letter," I protested weakly. "I wrote it but . . ."

"No, Luce, you don't get to blame that on me. I might have

played messenger before you were ready, but you wrote it, signed it, and addressed it to the chief. You made your choice. You just hadn't screwed up the courage to go through with your decision."

I couldn't look at him, not his feet, not the ground beneath his feet. I was so much lower than that. "What will you do now?"

"I'm going to sleep on how to handle this." His sigh whistled out in a long note, like the stab of my betrayal had punctured a lung. "You want my advice?" He didn't wait for me to answer. "Let the resignation stand and use your comp time to ride out the notice." He raked his fingers through his hair. "I'm going to request for the Hensarling and Culberson cases to be reassigned before your association taints what evidence we do have. The only chance we've got at a conviction is pinning down Ivashov, if we can find him, and I won't risk losing him on a technicality."

Ivashov was a literal dead end, but that was yet another detail I couldn't share with him. "Do what you have to do."

Without another word, Rixton left me standing there alone in the dark.

I sat on the tabletop and stared off into the distance until the sun rose.

CHAPTER EIGHTEEN

In order to avoid any and all discussion about the fallout with Rixton, I left the coterie at my house after dawn and sneaked into the sewing room at the Trudeaus' to crash for a few hours. Word traveled fast in law enforcement communities, and ours was smaller than most. I was on borrowed time if I wanted Dad to hear my side of the story before Uncle Harold overheard any gossip about me making the rounds, and I had to scrape them both off the ceiling using one of Aunt Nancy's spatulas.

"Afternoon, baby girl." Dad glanced up from the crossword puzzle he was working at the table. "You got in late."

"We need to talk." I joined him, grateful I had hit the sweet spot between breakfast and lunch so we could sit alone. "There are some things I need to tell you."

"All right." He set down his pen and linked his fingers on the table. "Shoot."

"I resigned from the force." Palms braced on the table, I

waited for him to go nuclear. When his eyes failed to round, and his mouth remained shut instead of gaping like a carp, I feared he might have zoned out again, but I pushed on before I lost my nerve. "The FBI expressed interest in me after the Claremont case, and I've decided to accept their offer."

"I see." His shrewd eyes narrowed. "Will joining the FBI make you happy?"

Happy was so far away I couldn't see its tail lights to chase after the glow.

One more lie spilled over my lips without consulting my brain. I was training myself to cover my ass first and ask pesky moral questions later. Wu would be so proud. "Yes."

This must be the road I'd heard so much about, the one paved with good intentions that landed you in hell. Or, in this case, a special taskforce full of charun.

"It's about damn time." A wide grin split his lips, and his eyes twinkled. "You were always meant for bigger and better things. I'm surprised it took you this long to figure out this town is too small for you."

A wave of dizziness swirled through me. "This town is home."

"Yes, it is, and it always will be," he agreed, "but you'll never grow into your full potential here."

"You don't sound . . ." *upset your only daughter is flying the nest* " . . . surprised."

"You've been searching for answers your whole life, and there are none here or you would have already found them." He sipped tea from his glass. "You're restless; you have been for years." He wiped his upper lip dry with his thumb. "You might have settled if not for Jane Doe. She's the proof you've waited on, the mystery solved, and I like to think I know my daughter well enough to understand she won't know peace until she's dealt with her past."

How prophetic his words were for reasons he would never understand. "You're right."

"I'm your father," he said, "of course I'm right."

"I planned on making this my life, on retiring from the force." It felt important he understand that. "The idea of leaving home, leaving you, is so new."

"You've been through hell the past few weeks." Absently, he rolled the pen across the page. "A fresh start, a clean break, might be what you need to heal from it all."

"What about you?" Recognizing the nervous habit, I reached over and stilled his hand by covering it with mine. "I've been working on the house. It's almost as good as new. You can move back in once the doctor gives you the all-clear."

The second I hire a part-time nurse to keep an eye on you.

"Well, here's the thing. I had already made up my mind to sell the place before you moved back home last year. I don't want to spend my golden years riding my lawnmower across all that acreage, and I can't afford to bring Flavie on to tend it full-time. I don't want to knock around that big house alone either."

Sweat gathered in my palms, and my fingers went limp in his grasp. "Where will you live if you sell the house?"

"Elm Place," he said with satisfaction. "I went on the tour last year after Dr. Brenner expressed concerns about me living on my own."

"Elm Place," I repeated. "That's the assisted living community behind Edgewater Baptist Church."

"Yes and no. There are several levels of care available. I qualify for what they call *independent living*. I would have my own apartment, one bedroom and one bathroom. A cleaning service comes in twice a week. Laundry facilities are on-site. Continental breakfasts are served each morning in the lounge, and they offer room service options for lunch and dinner if you're not up to cooking. The restaurant around the corner caters to the facility." He winked. "Residents get a discount."

"Why didn't you mention this sooner?" I reclaimed my hands so he wouldn't notice them trembling. "I thought you wanted to stay at the house. I gave up my apartment so I could help with the upkeep. I thought that was what you wanted."

"You cancelled your lease and showed up on my doorstep. How was I supposed to say no to that?" His expression softened. "With you there, I didn't mind staying put. You were a huge help, and you took good care of me, but you're young. You've got dreams of your own to pursue. I don't mind being left behind, that's how it's supposed to go, but I do want to remain on my own terms."

Woozy, I braced my forearms on the tabletop to hold me upright. "This all seems so sudden."

"Not at all like my daughter announcing out of the blue that she's resigned from a job she loves to pursue a new career without once hinting she might level up?"

Okay, so I had no handy comeback for that one. "The farmhouse has been in our family for generations. Your parents died there. You were born there." I couldn't imagine a world where that country lane no longer led us home. "Are you okay letting all that history go?"

"You're my only child, and Harry and Nancy are all the family I've got to speak of." He scraped his thumbnail over the etched design on his glass. "Letting the old girl go will be hard, but this second stroke was a wakeup call for me. I'm not getting any younger, and neither are you." He sucked on his front teeth. "There's something else I ought to tell you while we're being honest."

"Hit me." I locked my muscles in anticipation. "I can take it."

"Looks like CPD will be losing not one but two Boudreaus." His shoulders squared. "I've decided to retire."

The floor disappeared from under my chair. "What about Uncle Harold?"

"Harry saw the writing on the wall months ago." Dad let his gaze travel across the room as though expecting words to materialize on the floral wallpaper. "Nancy is hinting at wanting to buy an RV and do some traveling. Both of their boys live out of state, so there's that too." He swirled the contents of his glass. "I did my adventuring when I was younger. I'm ready to spend my days on the lake and my nights in a recliner."

A fillet knife slid between my ribs would have hurt less than this. Losing our home, the only one I had ever known, gutted me.

Focus on the upsides.

Never in a million years would I have considered placing Dad in any type of assisted living facility, but that meant he wouldn't need the nurse I had been considering for him. The staff there could handle his medications and be warned about his dietary restrictions. Plus, having neighbors meant someone would come running if he called. The fact those neighbors were also human insulated him even more from War and her coterie. While there wasn't much a few dozen geriatric humans could do against immortal charun, their presence would still act as a deterrent.

Aware Dad was watching me, waiting for a reaction, I forced my lips to move. "I think I've gone into shock." I sat back in my chair. "This is not how I expected this conversation to go."

"I'm right there with you." His lips pursed in a shrill whistle. "My baby girl is going federal. Hot damn."

And my dad was checking himself into a retirement home. Woo-freaking-hoo. "We're two crazy kids, all right."

The flatness in my tone sent him ferreting out the cause. "How is Rixton handling the news?"

"We talked it out. He thinks it's best if I go." And never look back. "I'm going to miss him. Sherry and Nettie too."

"He's still your friend even if he's not your partner," Dad soothed. "You can call him up whenever you want, and you'll be able to visit. Plus, you can do that video chat thing with your phone. That works over the Internet too, right?"

"Yeah, it does." Desperate to redirect the conversation, I pointed out, "That means you'll have to learn how to video chat too. We might have to upgrade your tablet."

"Let's save that as a last resort." The corner of his eye twitched, and I almost laughed at his technophobia. "It took me six months to figure out how to turn on this one."

Back on solid ground, we passed the rest of the afternoon together in blessed lucidity. His keen mind was once again blade-sharp, and he cut more answers out of me than I had intended to give, but I healed a little more each time he lanced those wounds.

Noticing the time, I excused myself and headed down to the station. The Bronco sat lower under the weight of all my gear, or so I imagined. Bags of uniforms, boxes of ammo, my bulletproof vest, my firearm in its plastic case, my badge tucked in its leather wallet with the CPD crest stamped on the front, boots, and a dozen other tiny items tossed into a plastic bin along with my active case files.

An entire career condensed into three trips from the trunk to the shift office.

Thanks to my careful timing, the station was as empty as it ever got when I arrived. None of the officers on duty stopped me to ask what was doing or offered me help with my burdens. Odds were high they figured I was schlepping for another

Boudreau and had no words of condolences prepared for the ending of an era. Add to it the fact I wasn't much on hugging it out, and pretending I was invisible was more comfortable for us all.

On my way past the chief's office, I lingered in the doorway, expecting the framed newsprint to still be hung on the wall but knowing better. All of Timmons' belongings had been boxed and dropped off at his house to make way for Jones.

I earned a few raised eyebrows when I dumped my supplies in the shift office since there was no hiding who the equipment belonged to at that point. I made sure to get full credit for each piece then pocketed my slip so that I couldn't be accused of stealing from the department on top of everything else. While I was there, I sat down with Sergeant Albertson and got approval to ride out my notice using vacation time.

"Your comp and sick time will both show on your last check." She handed me a printout, the last copy of the shift schedule I would ever receive, and it blocked out my name. "Take it up with payroll if the numbers are off." Her hard eyes raked over me. "Good luck, Boudreau."

"Thanks." I escaped out the front and sat in the Bronco while my heart slowed its racing then dialed Wu. "Just giving you a heads up that Rixton is onto me. He pressed me for deets, and when I withheld them, he suggested I not show my face down at the station."

His exhale tapered into silence. "I'm sorry, Luce."

"I dropped off my gear just now and cleared two weeks of leave through the shift office." I dashed my fingertips under my eyes. "After that, I'm all done here."

"I'm in town if you need company," he offered. "I can meet you wherever you'd like."

"You don't want that. Trust me. I'm in a mood, and even I

don't want to be around me." Wu reminded me of what I would never have with Rixton again, and I doubted I could keep a civil tongue when it would be so easy to lash out at him for helping land me in my current predicament. "Raincheck?"

A fist pounding on my window shocked a curse out of me. A young girl, early teens, was hammering away, the front of her shirt drenched with blood, her eyes wide.

"There's a man," she sobbed, her voice muffled through the glass. "He grabbed me when I walked past, and I . . . I . . . "

"I have to go," I snapped out to Wu. "There's a situation here."

One I was no longer qualified to handle, but I wanted an outlet, and she had provided me one.

"Who is that?" Wu demanded, his keen ears missing nothing. "*Luce.*"

Ending the call, I slid out on the asphalt beside the girl and pocketed my phone. "Can you show me?"

Her head wobbled on her thin neck, and she clasped my hand. As much as I wanted to snatch it back, I let the kid have her anchor while she hauled me to a shadowed nook between two buildings.

Crimson flecks dotted the sidewalk, and a larger pool spread from under the head of a downed man. I was about to call for backup when I recognized his profile and dread ballooned in my chest.

Forgetting about the kid, I ran to Santiago and dropped beside him. "Santiago?"

"I don't think he's going to wake up," the girl informed me. "I hit him pretty hard."

The comment snapped my head up, and I forced myself to look beneath the careful application of blood and grime, to see past the innocence to evaluate her as a potential threat.

There was no way a kid had done this much damage to him. Meaning either she was charun, and I was screwed, or she had help, and I was still screwed.

"With what?" Her empty hands gave me no clues. "Never mind. Doesn't matter. I'm calling this in."

"Mom won't like it if you do that," the child sing-songed. "She taught me to protect myself at all costs." The wispy quality to her voice evaporated, leaving behind cold maturity. "Our parents share similar philosophies, it seems."

Twisting my upper body toward her, I carefully worked the cell from my back pocket. With one hand behind my back, I fumbled to mash redial before she caught on. "You must be Sariah."

"I am." The girl plucked at the frayed hem of her cutoff shorts. "And you're my auntie."

Using the family angle was low, but it was my own fault for exposing that weakness in the first place. "You hurt my friend."

"Your friend hurt me first." She pushed out her bottom lip in a pout while pointing to her elbow, abraded and crusted with blood. "Want to kiss my boo-boo?"

Eyes on Sariah, I pressed two fingers to the steady pulse at Santiago's throat. "What do you want?"

"I came to introduce myself." She jerked her chin toward Santiago. "He tried to stop me."

"That's it?" My eyebrows popped up into my hairline. "You expect me to believe you just wanted to say hi?"

"I missed introductions." She rocked back on her heels. "I was out playing, and Mom didn't call me back in time."

"Here's an idea." Ending the call to Wu, I brought the phone out and dialed up Cole. Thanks to her charun senses, she would have heard Wu's voicemail recording. There was no point in hiding my SOS now. "The next time you play, how about break out the sidewalk chalk instead of someone's skull?"

A short laugh shot out of her and ricocheted off the nearby buildings. "Okay, I'll cut the crap." Her demeanour shifted yet again, stretching the boundaries of what looked natural on the girl. "We need to talk. I hung out in that hospital forever waiting on you, but your human partner is a bulldog. He refused to give us a moment alone, and Miller caught up to me before I could go after you."

Recalling my brief interaction with Ivashov, I had to wonder if Sariah had been testing me by speaking Otillian. Unlucky for us both, I hadn't understood a word she'd spoken, so whatever chat she'd wanted to instigate over Rixton's head never happened.

"I didn't mind the change in venue. The swamp is quieter, and it leaves fewer witnesses." That explained why she'd gone along willingly. It fit her agenda to use him as bait. "I'd hoped you would play knight in shining armor to Miller's damsel in distress when my sibs and I ambushed him, but no matter how close I pushed him to the edge, he refused to call for help. He smashed his cell and tossed it in the water."

All those unanswered texts explained away at last.

"I wanted to have this conversation on neutral ground, but that's not going to happen. I see that now. You're too well protected. But the fact remains I've got a proposition for you and intel you're going to want."

"What kind of proposition?" Against my ear, the phone rang and rang and rang. "The only information worth the risk would be intel on the cadre." Sariah knew where her mother and father were hiding, what their plans entailed, but she wouldn't give them up easily. That left me with one tempting alternative. "You know when Famine is coming."

The call connected in my ear at long last. "Luce?"

"There's only one way to find out." She spun on her heel and walked away. "I'll be in touch."

"We've got a problem." As much as I itched to track down Sariah, to exact vengeance for Miller, I would never leave Santiago vulnerable. Even if he was an ass ninety percent of the time, he was my ass. "Santiago is down a block from the station."

"What happened?" A growl reverberated through my cheek where I pressed the phone. "Are you hurt?"

"I'm fine." A chill danced in the exposed juncture between my shoulder blades. "Sariah paid me a visit."

"I'll be there in fifteen minutes." A feminine voice rose in the background, in protest or encouragement, I couldn't tell. He snapped back at her using liquid syllables that poured through my ear. "Don't move."

"What about Portia?" It had been her voice I heard. "You can't leave her unguarded."

"I won't leave you unguarded either." Icy finality glazed his vow. "Thom and Miller can stay with her."

"I hate to break it to you," I said while examining Santiago for injuries aside from the knock on his noggin, "but it's going to take longer than fifteen minutes for them to get there and you to get here."

"They're already en route to the bunkhouse," he explained. "They hoped that removing themselves from the equation might help smooth things over with Rixton."

Heart a lead weight in my chest, I sank onto my butt on the concrete. "That's no longer a concern."

Cole remained silent for a beat too long. Sometimes his no-platitudes policy really sucked.

"I have to go." I tunneled the fingers of one hand through Santiago's hair and applied pressure as best I could without stripping off my shirt or his to use as a makeshift bandage. "I need both hands for this."

Before I killed the connection, a bloodcurdling roar announced his dragon had cracked his chest wide open in a fit of righteous fury.

"Head . . . hurts," Santiago hissed. "You . . . good?"

"I'm fine." I kept my hand right where it was and dared him with a glare to fight me over playing nurse while I tucked away my phone. "It's you that worries me. You got your brains scrambled, and you're already one egg short of an omelet."

Glazed eyes narrowed on the mouth of the alley. "What did she . . . want?"

"To introduce herself." I repeated what she told me, doubt slathered on thick, burning the minutes until help arrived. "She played me like a banjo. She showed me a young girl with blood on her shirt, mentioned a guy trying to grab her, and I couldn't get out here fast enough."

His lids drooped. "Sucker."

Irritated, I zinged him. "You suck."

Okay, so *zing* implied I had rocked the comeback when it was more of a pebble, but come on.

A sudden heaviness in the air had me craning my neck to search for Cole, but his camouflage was flawless when he chose. There was no way to disguise the wind gusts, however, or the air displaced by his massive wings. Not to mention the deep-throated rumble that poured from his muzzle and helped me locate his exact position.

Warm scales brushed against my outstretched hand, his lips plucking at the skin of my palm the way a horse might as it searched for a sugar cube. An inquisitive noise rose in his chest while he curled the length of his serpentine tail around my ankle.

Headlights blinded me before I could raise a hand to shield my eyes, and I shot to my feet, placing my body between

Santiago, the invisible dragon, and whoever had jumped the curb. Doors opened and shut, and Thom appeared carrying a med kit with Miller tight on his heels.

"We need to get him out of this alley," Miller said in lieu of *hello*. "Sariah cherry-picked her spot to make sure any stink you raised would bring the cops running."

"What are you doing here?" I almost tripped where Cole had manacled me. "I thought you guys were sitting with Portia."

"Cole texted us about Sariah." Miller looked me over, his gaze snagging on the odd way I stood with my ankle cocked to one side. "We got a late start, so we were closer to you than the bunkhouse. I texted back to let him know we'd handle the pickup, but I got no response." His nostrils flared as his chest rose and fell in quick pants. "Now I see why."

Thom, who had gone around us, was binding Santiago's head with gauze when I turned to check on him. "The injury is minor," Thom announced, "but he'll heal faster in the water."

That bumped the farmhouse out of the running. "You're headed on to the bunkhouse?"

"That's best for now, yes." Thom met my eyes, his seeing too much. "You should go home too."

With no help from me, they loaded Santiago onto the backseat. Thom tossed me a packet of wet wipes to clean the blood from my hands then pulled away from the curb. I stared after them for a few minutes before noticing I had more company.

Wu stepped from the shadows into a pool of light. "Did you really think they'd leave you unprotected?"

The weight around my ankle tightened, assuring me I was far from alone.

"Thom has two patients onboard." Our medic was getting a workout these days. "They're the priority."

"You're the priority," he corrected me with a shake of his head. "I hope you grasp that before it's too late."

The air beside me wavered, a moonlight mirage taking shape, and in its place stood Cole dressed in his White Horse tactical gear. As usual, my heart gave a wild kick, the sight of him always good for my daily dose of cardio.

The edge of Cole's lip snarled up over his teeth. "We're well aware of where our priorities lie."

"Are you?" Wu crossed his arms over his chest and plucked at his upper lip. "Sariah gained access to Luce. We could have lost her tonight."

From the corner of my eye, I saw Cole flinch as if struck either by the insult to the coterie or the thought of losing me. "Luce can take care of herself."

"Not yet, she can't." Wu dared him to disagree. "She's too human, and you know it. You allow it. You all do." His gaze dipped to my ankle, where I still felt the absence of the dragon's tail. "No, you encourage it."

Cole chewed on his words before spitting out, "She needs more time."

"Does she?" Wu cocked his head in a birdlike manner. "Or is it you who needs more time?"

"We've been over this, Wu," I interrupted. "You admitted I'm my own person. No take-backs."

"You are Luce," he agreed, "but you're Conquest too. You won't be whole until her echoes are silenced."

"How do you propose I do that?" I waited on him to enlighten me. "It's not like I can hold a pillow over my head until she stops kicking. Suffocate her, and you suffocate me too."

"He wants you to harness her power." Disgust thickened Cole's voice. "He wants to control her through you."

Wu didn't disagree, and that made me nervous. "I'm not going to be the one who opens Pandora's Box."

"To win this war, we must use every weapon at our disposal." Wu wasn't talking to me. He was talking over me, to Cole. "Surely you must see that."

"What I see is a terrene that will rise or fall like all the rest. This is not my home, these are not my people, this is not my fight. I have already lost all those things." Cole angled his chin away from me, unable to look at me when he said, "I will fight for this world, for these humans, because Luce asks it of me. I will bleed for her, not for you. You can't win my loyalty. It's already been given, and not to you."

"Conquest owns you." Wu studied Cole for his reaction. "How do you know she's not compelling you now?"

Sickness writhed through my gut, tying my stomach into queasy knots that squirmed. "I would never."

"You might not realize you're doing it," Wu pointed out. "You have no idea what you're capable of. None of us do. None of us will, if you don't try." He shook his head slowly. "How do you know what he feels for you isn't a reflection of what you feel for him? How can you be sure? Unless you master your power, you'll never be certain what's real and what is the direct result of your will."

Giving Wu his back, Cole eased in front of me and cradled my face between his broad palms. I hadn't realized I was crying, that more of my worst insecurities were leaking down my face, until his thumbs wiped away the moisture. He ducked down, putting our faces on the same level.

"I have had a lifetime, several of them, to learn what it is to be compelled to love by Conquest." The rasp of his calloused fingers across my cheeks soothed me. "I would recognize the taint of her in your voice, your eyes, your touch." His thumbs strayed downward, toward my mouth, and they caressed that tender skin too. "Just as I would recognize you anywhere."

Vision blurry, I sniffled and wrapped my hands around his wrists to hold him in place. "Cole . . ."

I'm sorry for who I am, for what I've done, for what I was and might be again.

"Shh." He lowered his forehead to mine, our breaths mingling, my heart racing. "I know."

Two little words, and they were starting to become ours, a means of acknowledging our soul-deep understanding of the other person like we truly were two halves of the same whole.

A throat cleared on the far side of the mountain, but its echo carried to me all the same.

Apparently, Wu was not a fan of PDA.

"You should get back to Portia." I held still, so very still, inviting Cole to linger though I knew he couldn't stay. "I can get myself home."

Wu appeared in my periphery, his forehead pinched and mouth tight. "I'll walk her to her car."

A low reverberation began in Cole's chest and rattled through his throat as he raised his head.

"He did drive all the way out here." I met Wu's gaze over Cole's shoulder. "Or fly." I cocked an eyebrow at him. "I can never tell with you guys."

Wu declined to answer, surprising no one given his stance on charun keeping their own counsel on personal matters.

Heaving a great sigh, Cole withdrew the rest of the way from me, but his meltwater eyes glinted with mischief. "I can give you a ride home."

"Ride." I wet my lips. "On you."

The gleam heated several degrees, as did my cheeks. "Yes."

"I'll just, uh." I pressed a hand to my stomach. "Maybe next time?"

Cole chuckled, a deep and rumbling thing that left me squirming in place. "I'll hold you to it."

I found my hand fisted in his shirt without my permission, reluctant to let him go, but—perhaps taking him too literally—I was in no hurry to remove it. "You do that." I tugged the fabric once then forced my fingers to relax. "Take care of our girls. And our boys."

"I don't like this." His own reluctance to leave me with Wu was anchoring him here when he was needed elsewhere. "You shouldn't be left alone."

Wu cleared his throat again.

We both ignored him.

"They need you." I gave him a playful shove that did nothing but pop my wrist. "Go on. Shoo."

Cole eased back a few steps and let his dragon free. The towering beast dipped its massive head, antlers angled away from my face, and brushed its cheek against mine. The familiar pressure of his tail wrapping my ankle made me grin so wide my face hurt.

An affectionate Cole was an irresistible Cole, scales and all.

Our gazes met for a single instant, but then his camouflage stole him from my sight. A low rumble filled the air while his tail unspooled, the warning aimed at Wu, and I popped his flank. Or at least I think that's what my open palm hit. "Behave."

Wind blasted my hair away from my face, and the leathery creak of his wings grasping for sky ignited an ache in my heart. The intensity of his presence lessened with each mighty flap until I could no longer sense him.

"Come on, Luce." Wu's voice dragged my gaze from the sky. "We should get you home."

"What is it with you guys?" I started walking back to my Bronco, and he fell in step with me. "Do I have a curfew now?" The thoughtful noise he made earned him a glower. "That wasn't a suggestion."

"Of course not." A hint of teeth flashed in his smile. "I left my car near an ice cream parlor. Would you mind giving me a lift?"

Fishing out my keys, I unlocked the Bronco. "Are your arms tired or something?"

His now familiar sigh punctuated the night. "Is that a no?"

Still annoyed with him for pushing my buttons, I was tempted to let him find his own way back. He had no clue how little slack the coterie cut me, Cole in particular, but I wasn't about to explain myself—or us—to him. Plus, the whole partnership thing meant I had to learn how to play nice with him eventually. I might as well start practicing now.

I climbed in and waited for him to settle before aiming us toward Hannigan's. It was a safe bet this was the ice cream shop he meant. Most folks didn't appreciate the fine line between ice cream and frogurt. I parked at the curb, angling my head to the right, mesmerized by the neon signs splashing colors across the darkened sidewalk.

He followed my line of sight. "Would you like to go in?"

"Nah." I flashed back to my last visit and had to admit, "I'm probably banned."

"I could make the purchase for you," he offered. "What's your favorite flavor?"

"You little enabler you." I heartily approved.

After rattling off my order, he ducked in Hannigan's and loaded up two medium cups with enough soft serve to numb the ache in my chest where worries for my coterie resided and enough toppings to make his debit card weep from their weight.

While he paid, I scanned the empty seating area through the giant plate glass windows.

The framed dollar bill Cole had smashed had been rehung in its place of honor. Otherwise, it appeared Mr. Hannigan had used the generous check Cole had written him for damages to restore his business to its pristine, vintage charm rather than modernizing the place. I was still gazing off into the middle distance when Wu appeared at my window with his hands full and an expectant look on his face.

"Walk with me?" I wasn't ready to go home yet, but I had nowhere else to be and nothing else to do. I was all wound up after the visit from Sariah, and I had no outlet for that nervous energy. "I promise I won't tell Cole you didn't escort me straight home."

Sticking it to Cole appealed to Wu if the flash of his teeth was any indication. "All right."

I climbed out, he passed over my cup, and we set out to take a turn about the square.

The Greek revival courthouse at the heart of Canton was the most beautiful building in town, an opinion shared by several motion picture companies who had filmed on its lawn and in its halls. It rose, elegant and pale, from a lush green patch of lawn across the street. We didn't cross to the greenspace but kept to the sidewalk, strolling past the small shops lining the square surrounding the courthouse.

I would have called what we did people-watching, except the hour meant it was more like car-watching as folks blazed through town on their way home for the night.

My footsteps ground to a halt in front of a bridal shop overflowing with jewel-toned fall colors as I savored my last spoonful of froyo. The one-two punch of Mrs. Tacoma's mothball and fruitcake essence radiated from the place, stinging my nostrils, and that last mouthful soured.

"Human mating rituals grow more bizarre with each successive generation."

I reeled my focus in from the tidy boxes stacked on shelves in the back, each one labeled with the name of a bridal party, to study Wu. A second reflection caught my eye first, and I frowned at her, thinking she looked familiar, before the why of it dawned on me.

Who else would have been standing so close to Wu eating froyo like it was going out of style?

No one with any sense. That eliminated the pool down to, oh, I don't know, *me*.

The coterie might be working its magic on my touch-aversion, but clearly there were still dissociative echoes bouncing between Conquest and me if I was no closer to that knee-jerk recognition of self that others took for granted when they saw it reflected back at them.

"It's Kapoor," Wu said abruptly, reaching for the muted phone in his pocket. "What have you got?" Wu snapped to attention. "That is interesting." His eyes met mine. "I'm with her now."

The woman in the glass cocked her head, the thick ends of her ponytail sliding over her shoulder as she strained to catch both sides of the conversation. Mostly she gave herself a headache. A worse one. Barely twenty-four hours passed without a sledge hammer wrecking her temples. One of these days, if the pain got much worse, she might crawl in for an MRI, but she would rather walk across broken glass than be admitted for testing.

After all that focused effort, when a second voice poured into the night air, I met her wide eyes in our shared reflection, suddenly tasting panic that I might have tapped into some wellspring of power within me, only to realize Wu must have worried I was going to aneurism and put his call on speaker.

CHAPTER NINETEEN

"We have a lead on Famine." Kapoor's voice poured into the night. "I need both of you to come in."

"Where is *in*?" I looked to Wu for an answer. "Kapoor is still in town?"

The janitorial work he and his team had been doing for us must be keeping him close.

Wu gave an infinitesimal nod. "We'll be right there." He ended the call and met my gaze. "There's a hotel on Soldiers Colony Road. That's where Kapoor and his unit are staying."

I palmed my keys and gave them a jingle, happy for the distraction. "Let's ride."

We took the Bronco to a boxy hotel slouched off the interstate and had our pick of parking spots. A row of six black SUVs hugged the curb near the farthest corner of the lot, and I almost made a snide comment about how common they were, but it got me curious about how many agents traveled in Kapoor's entourage.

I hung back while Wu lead the charge past the check-in desk to the elevators. Fine hairs lifted all over my body, the sensation of being watched a prickle between my shoulder blades. I pulled on my cop face and kept my motions loose, easy; all the while my mind spun out worst case scenarios.

War had been awful quiet. I hoped this morsel of information wasn't the bait she'd used to set a trap.

The trip to the sixth floor gave me a few seconds to calm my nerves and steady my heart. God only knows what cues charun could pick up from me, given my human upbringing. Knowing what I did about Kapoor, that he was half charun, made me question all our interactions up to this point. Had he read how I felt, what I thought, without me ever knowing the danger of letting my emotions roam untethered?

"Are you ready for this?" Wu stared down at me. "You can watch if you'd rather not participate."

Miller and his interrogation style came to mind at his words. "I'll bow out if you erase lines I'm not comfortable crossing."

"All right." He did me the courtesy of not pretending such erasure wasn't possible and guided me down the hall to the last room on the right. He knocked, and the door swung open under his knuckles. "Special Agent Kapoor."

Special Agent Farhan Kapoor wore faded jeans, boots, and a T-shirt with the FBI logo emblazoned across his chest. The first time we met, he was all boyish charm and black tactical gear. This time, fatigue showed in the creases around his mouth and dark eyes. The overhead lights washed out his tan skin, leaving him sallow and unwell. He looked tired, like he hadn't slept since the last time I saw him, and finding us on his doorstep didn't appear to rejuvenate him.

"You made good time." Kapoor extended his hand and shook Wu's. Noticing how my nails bit into my palms, he let me off with a nod. Call me chicken, but I wasn't eager to shake hands with him after learning the details of his job description. "Good to see you again, Ms. Boudreau."

"Kapoor." My gaze slid past his shoulder to the room beyond. "What have you got for us?"

"Come in, and we'll talk." He stepped back to allow us entry then shut and locked the door behind us. "This is Deland Bruster. He's one of our most trusted informants."

The man in question stepped from the bathroom, and a jolt of recognition sizzled through me. I recognized his face, but I couldn't have put a name to it. He was average height with average looks, nondescript brown hair and eyes. He looked like every other guy on the street, which was quite a feat considering the size of Canton.

"Ma'am." He dipped his chin at me, eyes bright, but his gaze skittered away from Wu. "Sir."

"Go on, Deland." Kapoor hung back, watching. "Have your look."

Heat flashed up my nape at being made the center of attention. Any informant worth his salt would know who I was if he knew what this information meant to me, to us, but that didn't mean I wanted to jump from Canton's frying pan into the NSB's fire on all future interrogations. I was used to being gawked at, but that didn't mean I had to like it, and I sure as hell wasn't volunteering as a traveling exhibit for them.

"Luce Boudreau." Bruster walked a slow circle around me. "It's a pleasure to meet you."

"I'm going to award bonus points right now," I told him, "for not slipping up and calling me Conquest."

"Nah. You're not her. Not yet, at least." The heat of his body warmed my spine, but he didn't touch me. "The potential is there, don't get me wrong, but there's this ... aura. Yeah. An aura." He continued his evaluation, halting in front of me and stabbing me in the chest with his knobby index finger. "You're all tangled up inside, girlie. A hot mess of cables no one can cut to diffuse the ticking time bomb under your skin without you going boom."

His assessment had me replaying War's troublesome revelation: *You are owned, sister, but not by me.*

One other possibility came to mind, but I didn't want to make eye contact with it yet.

I am not owned. I am not owned. I. Am. Not. Owned.

And not, of all people, by *him*.

"You're this tapestry of intent," Bruster marveled. "The past is woven in every strand, your very core is ripe with ancient power, but the fiber spun around the whole is every bit as essential, and it's brand-spanking-new."

I sucked in a breath, too afraid of what he might say next to risk questioning him.

"You're tight with your coterie," he decided. "I see the individual strings connecting them to you, and they're ironclad." His finger dragged lower until it pointed straight at my heart. "This one . . ." He released a slow whistle. "This bond is adamantine."

Sweat drenched my palms, and I had to wipe them dry against my pants. "What kind of bond?"

"The worst kind." His glazed eyes as they roved over my face. "The kind that won't snap even when both halves of it are broken."

"That doesn't make any sense." A bond had already snapped if it was broken.

The faint color in his eyes washed out until he stared at me with blind eyes that saw too much.

"He can't hear you now," Wu murmured. "He's too far away."

I bit down on my lip to keep from pointing out he was right there.

"How is this possible?" Bruster's brows knitted together while he plucked at the air above my chest, the same as War had done. "You are owned. Conquest is owned." The confusion cleared from his expression. "Clever." His graveled chuckles rumbled through his chest. "Very clever." He folded his fingers together then kissed the tips. "You are a masterpiece, and what artist could resist signing their name?"

Senses kicking into high gear, I demanded. "What name?"

"I told you," Wu said again. "He can't hear you."

Bruster continued his narration in a dreamy voice that held traces of such immutable truth that I flinched under his inspection. Nothing I said reached his ears, nothing I did registered in his sight. Wu was right. He wasn't with us. He was tangled in my heartstrings, knotted in my gut, gliding under my skin, a blade that cut away the excess until only the essential remained.

Without warning, Bruster's legs buckled. Kapoor caught him under the arms and lowered him onto the foot of the bed, using his hip to prop the other man upright until Bruster began to rouse from the fugue state that had overtaken him.

"Got what I wanted," he rasped, adjusting his weight until he supported himself with his elbows locked at his sides. "Our bargain is struck."

"Bargain?" I snapped at Kapoor. "What bargain?"

"And the information?" Kapoor prompted him, ignoring me altogether.

"Full report is on here." He fumbled in his pocket and produced a flash drive he offered to Kapoor. "Dates, times, photos, GPS coordinates, the works. You want to see the goods before you go?"

"I trust you." Kapoor passed the small thumb drive over, startling the hell out of me. "Don't look so surprised, Ms. Boudreau. You earned it. This meeting was the cost of the information in your hand."

So Bruster had wanted to meet me. Not just pass on intel, but finesse an introduction so he could get a bead on me. The interest, coming from a man in the business of selling information, gave me indigestion.

"Give it to Santiago Benitez," Kapoor continued. "He'll know what to do with it. Have him send us a copy while he's at it, if you don't mind." Bruster groaned once, slumping, and Kapoor clasped him on the shoulder to steady him. "Give us the quick and dirty version."

"Your girl here isn't the only abnormality this ascension." Bruster twisted on the mattress until he faced us, but his head remained too heavy to hold upright. "War and Famine breached together."

An icy calm unfurled in my chest and fanned throughout my extremities. "How is that possible?"

"No clue." He attempted a shrug that resulted in a faint twitching motion. "All I can figure is whatever hit you with the humanity stick must have whacked them too. Except the shit they're pulling is textbook. Maybe what happened to you weakened the breach site, and the others pressed their advantage."

The voice that poured from my throat resembled mine not at all. "What about Death?"

"There is no evidence to indicate she's active." He wiped a hand over his mouth. "This terrene is going to need an episiotomy after birthing two Otillians at once, and Death would be a damn fool if she didn't wriggle through before the stitches go in, even if it collapses the breach site."

That same imperious tone cracked at him like a whip. "Who owns me?"

"That information is worth more than you've got, girlie, and not just to you."

Chills dappled my skin, a too-late warning the cold place had already overtaken me, and I shifted my weight forward, ready to convince him otherwise. "I must know."

"Bargain with me then." He recoiled from whatever he saw on my face, but he kept the tremble from his words. "Offer me something of equal worth."

"No." Wu noticed the change in me and shifted closer. "I won't let her write you a blank check to cash later. Her favors are worth more than your life, and you know it."

"I know a lot of things, Wu." Bruster rasped out a chuckle. "More every day. Soon your daddy's going to know them too."

"We should be going." Wu stepped between me and Bruster, blocking my view of him. "There's nothing more to learn here."

The clarity afforded me in my current headspace agreed with him, and I curled my fingers around the thumb drive. "You better hope what you know doesn't come back to bite me," I warned Bruster. "I bite back."

Before the iceberg in my chest got any more ideas, we left. The precision with which Wu closed the door behind him set alarm bells clanging in my head.

"Kapoor should have warned us." Simmering fury boiled over in his tone, thawing the ice encasing my heart through sheer proximity. The daddy comment, whatever it meant, had lit a fire under him. "He should have prepared you."

"What is Bruster?" I angled my head toward Wu as we rode the elevator down. "I don't mean his species," I clarified before receiving the talk about how rude it was to ask that. "Is he a psychic?"

"Bruster doesn't read minds or predict futures. He maps hearts. He looks into a person, and the naked truth of them peers back. That's what makes him such a valuable informant. He doesn't have to interact with his targets to learn about them. All he has to do is get close enough to see into them, to follow the tangle of threads in their souls. There's not much he can't learn that way."

"That is damn creepy." I pressed a hand flat over my heart like that might protect what pulsed beneath. "Are there more charun like him?"

"On this terrene? No. He's the last." The ride stopped, and we exited into the lobby. "They were hunted to extinction here. Only the NSB's protection keeps him alive."

I didn't have to ask him why such brutal measures had been taken. No one wanted their innermost secrets exposed. Still, despite the carrot Bruster had dangled before me, I pitied the man his solitude. It was hard being different and alone. I knew that better than most. "Did he look into you too?"

"My father wanted to know the truth of my heart, and he bargained with Bruster to have me read, but that was a long time ago."

That explained his flash of temper at the invasion of my privacy, but I wasn't sure that was what Bruster had been alluding to back there. "Your father sounds like a piece of work."

The more I learned about Daddy Wu, the less I liked what I heard.

Wu's smile was brittle and cracking around the edges, but it was there.

"Kapoor has taken a lot about you on faith," he said, shutting down the topic of his father. "Bruster returning to the area must have been a temptation he couldn't resist." Wu slowed his stride. "Bruster is never wrong, and his kind can only speak truth."

Yet another nail in his coffin. The only thing people wanted less than for someone to know the truth about them was for that person to be honest about what they found. There was comfort in lies, and people dearly loved their comfort.

"Kapoor wanted me read before I became official." One last check against all those precious balances. "He wanted to be certain he was getting what he paid for."

"Bruster has wanted to meet you for some time," Wu admitted. "Kapoor was using you for leverage as a means to other ends. I intervened to keep you separated for as long as possible, but today he took that decision out of my hands."

Wu cast in the role of guardian angel. Who'd a thunk it? "Why the interest on his part?"

Paranoia swarmed me, wondering what Kapoor had tricked me into revealing to the man. I was willing to bet if he played informant for the NSB, he worked with other factions too. All I could do now was hope whatever he'd learned was worth more to Kapoor when kept as a secret than sold on the open market. Or to one of my sisters.

"There are as many factions among the charun who are eager to bear arms against your sisters as there are outliers salivating for the chance to join in the battle and reduce this world to ash." He escorted me back to the Bronco. "You're a powerful symbol cast in either light. Bruster doesn't ask for favors, ever, but he wanted to evaluate you to make his own determination."

As much as I hated to admit it, "Kapoor was right to bargain me away for the information we received."

"It was a strategic choice, yes." Wu glanced back like he could see Kapoor ensconced in his room, buying more of what Bruster was selling. "But if he wants to build trust, earn your loyalty, he must be transparent. With you and with me."

"It is odd he let you walk into that blind. Me, I get. But you? That does not compute."

"You're my partner." He placed special emphasis on *my* but appeared not to notice. "I would have warned you." He shrugged. "Or I might not have brought you to Bruster at all."

"That would make it appear as though I have something to hide." I spread my hands. "I don't." I laughed, surprised when I got what he implied. "You think I do?"

"We all have secrets."

"I can't argue with you there, but you know all mine. Even the one I keep from my coterie."

"Ezra," he murmured without hesitation, as if the name had already been on his mind. "The others don't know about him."

"They might. They keep a close eye on me." I might be letting guilt gnaw on my bones over nothing. I might be endangering them rather than protecting them. I might be doing more harm than good on all fronts, but I was doing the best I could to protect the ones I cared about, and that was all anyone could ask of me. "But I haven't told them."

Wu leaned against the Bronco. "Any particular reason why?"

"I want to bring them answers." I scuffed my shoe on the asphalt. "I don't want to raise more questions. I'm already in doubt in everyone's mind to one extent or another for various reasons." I pulled out my keys. "For once, I want to walk in and say, 'This is a problem I had, and I solved it.'"

"That's not how coteries work." He expelled a soft laugh. "I understand your fear, though."

As much as I wanted to protest fear wasn't the issue, it was a lie, and we both knew it. The deeper I waded into this new world, the higher unfamiliar waters lapped against my throat, and the more in danger I became of drowning.

Ezra had saved me, over and over. And he had abandoned

me, over and over. His hand could be the one that reached out and hauled me onto dry land, or it could be the one that shoved my head underwater for good. Either way, I had three hundred and fifty odd days until I learned for sure. Ezra was nothing if not predictable in his schedule.

Unless I found him first.

The display on my phone glowed, and I half expected the familiar *briiiiiiing*, as though speaking of Ezra might have summoned him, but no such luck. "Boudreau here."

"Hey, it's Dawson. I got an update for you."

Awareness I had no right to his confidence didn't stop me from grabbing this temporary lifeline with both hands. "Oh?"

"Summers mentioned her scene stank of citronella, and it's been bugging the shit out of me ever since. It's an all-natural bug repellent, right? Well, I got to thinking. We have mosquitos in the south until after the first hard freeze, and we're months away from that. Ms. Orvis worked outside a lot given her profession, so I figured she must be using the stuff to keep the pests away from her kids and customers."

"Makes sense."

"The thing is, I remembered why it was pestering me. The Culberson fire had that same grassy scent, but it's every-damn-where these days. Bug spray, mosquito coils, bracelets, patches, you name it. It's one of those smells that outdoorsy people get blind to until someone points it out to us."

"The restaurant had an outdoor patio." The first time I visited, I remembered thinking the built-in benches were a nice touch. "Are you sure you weren't smelling the detonation of a dozen tiki torches?"

"See, that's why I overlooked it. That and—hell, we had multiple eyewitness accounts of the event." Papers shuffled in the background. "Here's the thing, I had my guys run some tests for giggles, and we hit pay dirt. Turns out the Culberson fire had two origins."

"Ivashov in the restaurant with the drip torch and . . . ?"

"Suspect B with a few hundred rounds of homemade accelerant."

"Rounds?"

"As in circular. As in cotton. Probably as in facial cleanser pads."

The tender muscles in my gut clenched as tight as a fist. "What type of accelerant are we talking here?"

"One of my guys is big into survivalist crap. Camps out in the wilds, lives off the land, the whole nine yards. He showed me the pouch of supplies he's allowed to carry during his challenges, and there were these discs he buys from some online retailer. They're waterproof fire starters." A chair groaned, and I imagined him leaning back at his desk. "He starts telling me how much they cost and how some of the guys make their own using supplies they can pick up at the store."

A panicked sound clawed up my throat that he mistook for encouragement.

"What happens is they soak the cotton in an accelerant. Our perps chose citronella-scented tiki torches. Once the material is saturated, they dump the discs in a crockpot of melted wax to waterproof them. The result is a cheap, efficient, and untraceable fire starter."

Waxy Wonders.

Dawson was grocery-listing all those seemingly random items Aunt Nancy had left spread on the table in the backyard. The backyard, which had been planted with jasmine purchased at Orvis Nursery days prior to its brush with flames. The connection with the Culbersons was older, but it was still there. Aunt Nancy had a solid link to the Hensarlings as well.

One I hadn't remembered until now. The family allowed her to harvest cotton bolls the pickers missed for the church kids to use when they made Christmas angels.

Dad still had a few of mine crammed in storage boxes in the attic of the farmhouse.

The cop in me hated coincidence, didn't buy into them, but the child in me, who viewed Nancy as a mother figure, was thrashing her head in denial even as the math started adding up to a grim possibility.

Heart climbing up my throat, I wet my lips. "Have you taken this to Rixton?"

"Not yet," he grumbled. "He's not answering his phone."

"I need to run." I got behind the wheel of the Bronco, and Wu slid in beside me, no questions asked. "Thanks for keeping me updated." I ended the call with an impatient thumb. "We've got a problem."

"So I assumed."

"Sarcasm is your default setting. I get that. I can respect that, appreciate it even, but not right now."

Fingers poised over the phone screen, about to send out an SOS, I remembered Santiago and Miller were both out of commission. With Thom playing doctor and Cole at the bunkhouse with Portia, I had no shadow tonight.

Damn and double damn.

"That was the CFD arson investigator. He's located a secondary origin for the Culberson fire. Odds are good he's going to find evidence that links the Hensarling and Orvis fires to that one too." My hand lifted to my throat like rubbing the column might help me suck in enough air to keep my vision clear. "The accelerant used is a fire starter popular with hunters, fishermen, and other outdoorsy types." I formed the words, I could feel my lips moving, but no sound emerged. I cleared my throat and tried again. "Aunt Nancy makes them for the fishing club. All the members use them."

"That leaves us with a wide suspect pool," Wu said. "What am I missing?"

"I built her a pergola last weekend." A pinhead of ice stabbed me in the heart. "She had trays of plants from Orvis. I asked if she knew the owner, and she said Mr. and Mrs. Orvis, as in the ex-husband's parents, attended her church. That's how she knew about the nursery."

"There's something else, isn't there?" His calm almost shattered mine.

"Ida Bell, a member of War's coterie, also attended church with her." I clutched the wheel with stiff fingers. "The night War came after me, she used Dad as bait. I had stashed him with the Trudeaus, but she got her hooks in him. I never asked how. I didn't want to involve them, and Dad wasn't in any condition to answer questions." That speck of ice spread through my veins. "What if . . . ?"

What if . . . What if . . . What if . . .

The shouting in my head refused to be silenced long enough for me to make sense of my thoughts.

"You believe your aunt may be compromised," Wu said, filling the dark silence. "That she might have delivered your father to War."

I parked at the curb outside the Trudeau house and flung open my door. One leg was on the pavement when Wu grasped my hand and shackled me in place.

"Let me go."

His grip turned bruising as I struggled. "You can't confront her alone."

"I won't leave Dad in there another minute." I twisted to face him. "Or my uncle. We have to get them out."

"Your father has been living there for more than a week without complications." Wu reeled me in closer. "We have time to evaluate the situation before we—"

A snarl rippled through my lip as it curled over my teeth, and I salivated in anticipation of his next protest, of the bite I would take out of him if he tried stopping me.

"We go in together." Gold flared in the depths of his brown eyes in response, a metallic and unforgiving sheen that glittered in warning. "You do as I say, or I remove you from the equation." His long fingers closed around my throat, caging me. His thumb stroked my carotid in a slow and easy glide that turned my blood sluggish. "Understand?"

I held his inhuman stare, scarcely daring to breathe, afraid my heart might stop altogether. "Yes."

"We go in together." Wu pried each finger from my skin as though not squeezing required great effort. "If anyone asks, we'll tell them we ate dinner together."

"I need a weapon." Faster than he could react, I rallied my strength and slid out the open door. I lowered the tailgate, and a sense of relief cascaded through me when I palmed the shotgun. I grabbed a box of rounds and the cleaning kit before rejoining Wu. "Let's skip dinner and say we hit the range."

Wu growled his approval then joined me on the curb.

Call me paranoid, but Sariah's *hello, how are you?* routine had set my skin itching at the start of the night, and it hadn't stopped yet. The only way to scratch was to look in my aunt's eyes and see if a monster looked back.

CHAPTER TWENTY

The Trudeau house, with its cheery front door and immaculate landscaping, looked the same as always. I wanted to laugh off my unease, wanted to tell Wu it was all good, wanted to climb on my air mattress and damn the consequences. But Dad was in there. And this enemy of mine wore so many faces.

"I can go in alone," Wu offered.

"We can't risk tipping her off." I shot down that idea. "You walk me to the door, I invite you to stay for coffee, and we go from there." As far as plans go, mine was thinner than a sheet of paper. "Aunt Nancy can't resist playing hostess. Isolating her shouldn't be hard."

Following coterie protocol, I shot them a group text outlining our plan and tacked on a plea that the guys check in with the rest of my family before catching up to us.

With that final detail handled, Wu and I hit the walkway, two robots going through the motions, and I let us in the house. I checked the kitchen as we passed, but it stood empty.

A voiceover spilled from the living room, and light flickered in the hall as scenes onscreen changed. I crept forward, oxygen a solid block in my lungs, until I drank in the sight of Dad asleep on the couch. I kept inching closer until the steady rise and fall of his chest became apparent.

I glanced back at Wu, gratitude turning my knees to water, and started shaking my head.

No.

No, no, no, no, no.

Uncle Harold stood behind Wu with one hand clamped on his shoulder. I couldn't get a clear read on the other, but the tension stringing Wu taut led me to believe a weapon had been jammed into his spine. Besides the utter stillness with which Wu held himself, he appeared otherwise unimpressed with his current situation. That made one of us.

A smile crinkled Uncle Harold's eyes, but his gaze was … soulless. "Cat got your tongue, pumpkin?"

"Get out of him." The demand cost every ounce of strength left in me. "Get out *now*."

"You don't want that," what remained of my uncle tsked. "I'm all that's keeping him alive."

The pulsing organ in my chest shriveled to the size of a raisin. "What do you want?"

"For you to get your head in the game." A slight movement on his end left Wu gasping. Blood had been drawn. Even with a human sense of smell, the iron-rich scent was one I recognized. "You can't keep playing human." The careful application of pressure sent Wu crashing to his knees, his head hanging loose on his neck. "We need you."

Lacy ice fractals threatened to encase me, to numb my fingers where they gripped the shotgun I had all but forgotten and dull the wailing voice sobbing in my head. But those emotions were fuel to burn, and I had so much kindling. Unable to check the urge, I glanced back at Dad, who hadn't blinked at the uproar. "What have you done?"

"Nothing permanent." His shrug pressed the blade into Wu's pale skin. "I figured you'd want this to go down without an audience." His cackle distorted my uncle's familiar laugh. "Humans, am I right? Can't live with them, can't— Actually I could live without them. Happily."

The elephant stomping on my chest when I contemplated what *nothing permanent* meant to a creature like this made it hard to focus on the threat in front of me when all I wanted was to palm my cell and punch in the three digits guaranteed to bring help screaming up the drive, lights flashing. "Tell War—"

"We had a falling out." He raised his hand and licked a smudge of Wu's blood from his thumb. "If you want to play intermediary, knock yourself out. Maybe you'll have better luck than Sariah."

Sariah as peacekeeper—? Later. I couldn't afford the distraction now. Not when I thought I had her motives pegged. "What happened between you two?"

"War is a killjoy, that's what." He tightened his grip on Wu's shoulder when he began to slump forward and cleared his throat. When he spoke, his voice had shot up an octave. *"Don't plant valerian on Conquest's lawn. Don't domesticate the ubaste. Don't run around setting fires all willy-nilly. Don't murder children."* His opinion of me dropped when I didn't join in the stone-throwing. "You were much chiller before you figured out I'm a—what do you call them again? Skin suit?"

"You're viscarre." Meaning his refusal to leave Uncle Harold might mean that he was . . . No. Not going there. I couldn't and still hold on. "How long have you been wearing my uncle?"

"Since the night War failed in binding you to her."

"You handed my dad over to her."

"I let her borrow him, yes."

Borrow him, as though he were a toy to be passed between them.

"You know how much your dad loves watching Discovery Channel?" His bloodied fingers acted as gel while he styled Wu's hair. "It's like the only thing the man watches other than football, which at least has spandex to recommend it. Anyway, I had an epiphany a few days ago while he was watching a documentary on brood parasites."

Brood parasites were birds who laid their eggs in the nests of other birds, leaving the unwitting parents to raise their young. Often, their victims' own hatchlings got evicted in the process and died from starvation, exposure, or predation.

"Consider me your baby bird." He tipped back his head and gaped his mouth open. "Chirp, chirp."

"I have allergies to dander." And homicidal maniacs.

"Look, I went through a lot of trouble shoving this guy out of his own nest, well, his own body, so you would bond with me." He looked at me expectantly. "That's what sisters do here, right?"

A shockwave blasted through me, shattering the comforting ice. "*You're* Famine?"

"Hi-hi." Famine blew me a kiss. "I'd invite you out for a girls' night on the town, reminisce over some good old-fashioned raping and pillaging, but you've gone straight."

Wu gurgled, a wet bubbling noise, as he slumped forward onto his palms.

"You didn't want this back, did you?" He—no, *she*—kicked Wu in the side. "I liked your old one better. Where is the archduke, anyhow? Now he could take a lickin' and keep on tickin', am I right?" Wetting her lips, she appeared to like the idea and clamped down with dull, human teeth on the trapezius muscle running between Wu's neck and shoulder. "Hmm. Tastes like chicken." After planting a foot between his shoulder blades, she shoved him face-first to the floor. "This one is too lean, smells weird too."

"What did you do to him?" There was no way Wu would have willingly played chew toy.

"I might have poisoned him a little. No worries. I'm immune. The worst that snack will do is give me indigestion." Famine flashed the ornate blade in her hand, bloody teeth glistening. "Pretty sweet, right?"

Gone. There was nothing of Uncle Harold left in there, no spark of the man who'd helped raise me. She had burned him out, reduced him to a costume she wore.

Tears dampened my lashes, blurred my vision, made the room a hazy mess as I brought up the shotgun. But I didn't need clear eyes to hit the target. Uncle Harold, what was left of him, was less than five feet away from me, and I couldn't have missed if I tried.

I pulled the trigger.

An explosion of noise and light filled the living room.

The impact sent Famine stumbling against the far wall, where she gaped and clutched her gut, shock that I had raised a hand against her evident in her features. "War said you ... wouldn't hurt me." Blood spilled from between her fingers. "She ... told me ... I was safe."

"War lied."

"I'm ... your sister." Eyes rounding, her pupils swallowed her eyes. "We're ... family. She said ... she said ... "

"The man you killed was my uncle." The delivery fell flat, the words dull. "*He* was my family."

"I don't . . . understand." Her brow creased in familiar lines, borrowing my uncle's expression. "We're—"

"No," I snarled, stalking over and clamping a hand around her throat. Her protest choked off under my palm. "We're not." I leaned in close. "Why did War plant you in this house?"

"Protection," she wheezed. "Hiding . . . in plain sight."

"We must not have played much hide and seek as kids." I eased off on my grip before she lost consciousness. "Frankly, you suck at it."

"I tried . . . to follow orders." Writhing under my hand, her whine pierced my ears. "But this . . . host . . . and his life . . ." The throat in my grasp swallowed reflexively. "Such a good man . . . an honorable man . . ." Her lip curled at the corner. "Protecting humans . . . serving them . . ." Hatred sparkled in the depths of her eyes. "I had to . . . act. I had to . . . find release."

"War was cleaning up after you. That's why there were two origins with the Culberson fire." The others too, I bet. "Why didn't she extract you after you compromised yourself?"

"I was . . . trapped." Crimson frothed at her lips. "This death too . . . hard . . . to conceal from you."

There would have been no sweeping this murder under the rug, that much was for certain. Uncle Harold's disappearance would have blown Famine's cover. War must have decided the risk of continuing her recon was worth the potential reward, even with Famine crumbling under the pressure of her infiltration.

"This body made . . . tracking you . . . easy." She flashed pink teeth. "All I had to do . . . was sit back . . . and wait for you . . . to call with updates."

No wonder we hadn't brushed up against War. I had been feeding Famine my location this whole time.

"How did you select your targets?" We had yet to discover a link between all three sites.

"War," she gasped. "Coterie."

"You chose locations War had already secured." Making me wonder why she had selected those targets in the first place, unless she really had chosen locations frequented by my family and friends. Or perhaps War's infiltration of this town was so thorough Famine could act out where she pleased without fear of reprisal. "You left her to clean up your mess."

A shuddering spasm rocked her limbs, and her eyes rolled back in her head. I let her hit the ground, unable to stand the contact a moment longer.

Watching the blood darken a shirt my uncle had worn a million times flipped a switch in my head, and the cold place swirled around me, offering the chill kiss of relief from the throbbing ache building behind my breastbone.

An execution might be what Famine deserved, but I wasn't in a merciful mood, and revenge came in as many flavors as there were stars in the heavens. Fingers stiff from the cold, I watched my hands take out my cell and shoot Kapoor a text. The NSB enjoyed using charun as lab mice; well, I had caged him a big, fat rat.

I examined Wu, whose labored breathing concerned me, and Dad, who appeared to be sleeping peacefully, before circling back to stand between them and Famine with the shotgun aimed at her ravaged midsection.

Famine was waiting for me.

"You've grown soft, sister," she panted, blood dribbling from the corner of her mouth. Braced on all fours, she swayed with the effort to stay upright. "These humans have made you weak."

In a move faster than I could track, Famine jerked upright and snapped out her arm, yanking the gun from my hands.

Quick reflexes must run in the family.

Drawing on Uncle Harold's years of experience, she handled the weapon with expert ease and had me in its sights in the span of a heartbeat.

I didn't think. I didn't have to. That was the beauty of the cold place. As long as I operated in that headspace, my body was on autopilot. Going boneless, I flowed out of the path of the slug she fired at me.

There were vulnerable targets behind me who could become casualties of our two-woman skirmish if I let them. But I couldn't think about that right now. Concern for them was a distant drum too far away to hear.

The wound on Famine's side had healed enough to hold in her intestines, but she was too weak to stand or give chase. She was trapped on her knees. That was something. It still might not be enough.

I had loaded five shells in the chamber. Minus the slug in her gut, she had four shots when she only needed one to end my whole world.

The look on her face confirmed she was thinking the same thing. "Apply enough pressure in the right spots, and it will break you."

"That's what they keep telling me." I bounced on the balls of my feet, unsure what my next move would be, uncertain if my hindbrain would guide me or if it would rather show me. "I'm a cop, remember? I work best under pressure."

"No." Her eyes narrowed to thin slits, an expression Uncle Harold had never worn a day in his life. "You're not."

The reminder I wasn't one of Canton's finest hurt worse than if her shot had hit me.

"No," Wu groaned, lost to his fever dreams. "Mercy, Father."

Famine cut her eyes toward him, the gun wavering in her hand, and I charged. I hit her in the throat with my shoulder, sandwiching the weapon between our bodies, and rode her down to the floor. I landed straddling her upper stomach and locked one hand around the barrel of the shotgun, pinning it against Famine's chest with my weight, then swung my other fist in a brutal arc aimed at her jaw.

Contact snapped her head back and left my knuckles singing, but the blow loosened her hold enough I could pry the gun from her spasming fingers. I hurled the weapon across the room, tightening my thighs to keep her trapped beneath me, and cocked my arm to land another blow.

Famine brought up her forearms and took the hit. Rocking forward, she got under my guard. Blood gushed from her wounds as they reopened, but the move allowed Famine to lock her arms around me and yank me flush against her chest. She hauled me over her, hooked her right leg over my foot and her right arm over my shoulder. Famine kicked out her left leg as her left arm hit me hard across my ribs, and we flipped in a messy tangle, leaving her smiling down atop me.

"I'm going to rip this shell apart with my bare hands," she panted, clamping down on both of my wrists to hold me steady while I bucked my hips to unseat her. I managed a minor success and forced her to kneel between my thighs rather than straddling my hips. That would have to be enough. "I will show you your true face before you die."

"That sounds painful." I brought one of our joined hands toward my face while tugging the other across my body until my fingers closed over her wrist. Bringing up my left knee, I sank it into Famine's gut, in the soft spot where her wound had yet to heal, then kicked off her hip with my other leg. The motion sent me sliding back and broke her hold. It gave me precious inches to crabwalk away until I could get my feet under me again. "I'm going to have to pass."

Famine, gasping from the impact to her tender middle, collapsed forward on all fours to catch her breath.

I didn't give her a chance. I soccer kicked her in the mouth, snapping her head to one side. Her elbows buckled then gave, and her face hit the hardwood, followed by the rest of her.

Once I was certain she was down, I backed away to retrieve the gun and held it trained on Famine from a safe distance. About the time my arms started trembling, men and women dressed in FBI tees and black fatigues swarmed the living room. Weapons trained on me, the only threat left standing, they barked orders I couldn't hear over the pounding of my heart.

The shotgun was pried from my grip with such force I suspected the crack I heard was the pinky on my right hand breaking. A swift kick to my knees took out my legs, and the floor rose up to meet me, impact with the hardwood a slap in the face. I didn't fight as my arms were wrenched behind me or when I was cuffed at the spine. I understood the NSB agents were panicky over being crammed into the same room with two of their legendary boogeywomen. At least with my head angled this way, I saw Wu and not . . .

I swallowed hard and tasted bile as the cold place shattered around me, slicing me up on the inside as its slivers migrated through my bloodstream. Hot spikes of emotion simmered in my veins, thawing me enough to register the horrors of the room anew.

Uncle Harold was gone. *Gone.*

I had . . . No. What I had done, I had done to Famine. Not him. Paramedics barreled in and carried Dad and then Wu out of the house.

A woman knelt beside my head, her lips moving, but the dull roar in my head deafened me.

Hours or years or maybe minutes later, the warmth of a wide

palm cradling my cheek melted the remaining frost crystalizing my vision.

"Cole," I rasped. "You're here."

"Of course I am." He traced the curve of my jaw with his scarred knuckle. "Where else would I be?"

Straining, I lifted my head. "Is everyone else—?"

"Sir," a young man's voice broke when addressing Cole. "You need to step away from her. She's not to be released until Special Agent Kapoor arrives."

A prehistoric growl rumbled across the room to vibrate the agent in his boots. Or maybe that was just his knees knocking.

"Apologies, sir," he squeaked. "I don't have clearance to release her."

"I do," Cole snarled in a bass voice that rang through my bones. Leaning over me, he snapped the chain at my spine then popped the cuffs from my wrists before rubbing them until the circulation returned. "Now, leave us alone."

With a panicked nod, the agent vanished into the bowels of the house.

I willed my eyebrows higher to draw Cole's attention back to me, away from that poor guy just doing his job, and to get my answers.

"Rixton is fine. Sherry and Nettie are too." He supported my elbows, easing me upright. "Look at me, Luce." His voice held such tenderness, I ached as he murmured a soft warning. "I'm going to hold you now."

There was no fight left in me when he sat on the floor, none when he hauled me onto his lap, or when he wound his arms around me in a protective cage that insulated me from what I had done.

Thom prowled in sometime later and settled beside us on his haunches. "Your father is stable."

Lifting my head required help from Cole's shoulder. "His heart?"

"Strong and steady," Thom assured me. "He's resting comfortably."

"Mrs. Trudeau is secure." Santiago took position behind Cole, his eyes going cold when he noticed the twisted metal they had used to secure me. "She's at the church." My blank stare must have told him I wasn't tracking. "She had choir practice tonight." He gathered what remained of the handcuffs. "There's no safer place for her now."

And no better support system after the news broke either.

"Wu is being admitted to a private facility." Miller, who arrived last, took position beside Santiago. "The blade Famine used was coated in a neurotoxin. The paralysis is spreading, and respiration is shutting down. His nervous system is on the brink of collapse."

"Let me up." I shoved off Cole's shoulder. "I have to see him."

"They've already left." Miller gentled his tone. "There was no time to spare."

Sinking back against Cole, I wrapped my arms around my middle in a weak attempt to hold myself together. "What will they do with Famine?"

"Contain and isolate." Santiago kept busy with his hands. "She's a hostile and will be treated as such. No doubt she'll end up in some government facility without a name, staffed by people with barcode tattoos on their wrists, who dress for work in hazmat suits."

"That's not what I meant." My fingernails bit into my elbows. "What about . . . her host?"

Calling what remained of Uncle Harold by his name nauseated me. I couldn't do it.

"She will remain with her host until they figure out a way

to separate the two," Miller told me. "She has a form she could assume in this terrene, but it would impede her ability to communicate."

"She killed him because of me," I murmured. "He's dead because I loved him."

Thom stroked the top of my head the same way I often petted him. "You can't go down that road."

Too late. I had been set upon that path, and I had no choice but to walk it to its conclusion.

A steady vibration sparked in Cole's chest and was echoed by the men surrounding me. The reason soon became clear as Special Agent Farhan Kapoor strolled into the room, pinpointed our small gathering, and invited himself to join us.

"I'm sorry about Mr. Trudeau, Ms. Boudreau. He was a good man." His advance stalled out when Miller placed a warning hand on his shoulder. "If there's anything I can do for you or your family, please don't hesitate to let me know."

I'm sorry.

Two little words, morsels really, barely a mouthful, hardly a taste.

I'm sorry.

"There is something you can do for me." I unlinked my arms and sat upright on Cole's lap. "You can let me skip to the head of the line for quarantine. I want to enroll in the academy by the end of the week."

"There's no need." He was already shaking his head. "After your meeting with Deland, the brass decided to treat your hiring as a lateral transfer. You won't be attending the academy. You're moving straight into OJT under Adam Wu's supervision."

That left me with one big question. "What about the testing?"

"With a new specimen in containment, the brass isn't going to be looking as hard at you. I suggested you be allowed to submit to the required procedures in stages, as an outpatient, and they've agreed." He pointed a finger at me. "Keep your appointments, and I'll do my damndest to keep you out of a hospital johnny."

Gratitude tightened my throat. Maybe as far as bosses went, he wasn't a bad one to have after all. "Thanks."

"Get her out of here," he told Cole. "The cleanup crew is about to come in and stage the place."

Climbing off Cole's lap, I shoved my feet under me. "What are you going to tell Aunt Nancy?"

"A home invasion gone wrong fits best, and we try to keep it simple." Experience led him to answer my next question without prompting. "There will be a slip-up at the morgue, and a body will be cremated before anyone can view it. His family will never know the remains aren't his."

The Trudeaus had his and her plots in the cemetery behind their church. Would we bury an empty casket? The urn? The ashes? Or would Aunt Nancy sprinkle his ashes at his favorite fishing hole? Would she keep them on the mantle? Save a portion for herself then divvy the rest up among their children? Would she offer me some? Did I want any?

Shaking off the morbid bent to my thoughts, I attempted to zone back in. "What about Dad?"

"He's been taken to the same private facility as Wu for testing and treatment." Kapoor raised his voice to drown out my protests. "The Trudeaus have been acting as caretakers for your father. We have no idea what Famine might have done to him or given to him during that time."

A greasy ball of fear curled in my gut at what he left unsaid, that he might not be human any longer.

"I would have tasted the sickness in him when I bit him, and there was none," Thom said. "His symptoms worsened after he settled in at the Trudeaus'. Famine must have already been in place at that point. She kept him dazed and compliant. She never let him rise from the healing fugue where I left him."

"It was never your saliva that made him sick," I realized.

"It looks that way." Thom rose from his haunches, his stare fixed on me. "Your father is an intelligent man who spent decades on the force. He was friends with Mr. Trudeau for more than a quarter of a century. He would have homed in on any deviations in his behavioral patterns and questioned them, and Famine couldn't allow that to happen."

Yet Aunt Nancy, the person who knew him best, hadn't been drugged. However, she was in good health. It would have been harder to excuse her sickness, and impossible to explain them sharing symptoms when she had no prior heart condition.

But how had she missed his tells? Or had she? She always kept busy, so I hadn't given it much thought, but had she been busier than usual lately? The baking, the gardening, the Waxy Wonders. How easy would it have been for her to blame any peculiar behavior from Uncle Harold on Dad's relapse? On worry over me after Jane vanished and Maggie was kidnapped?

The devil finds work for idle hands.

How often had I heard her utter the phrase? Whatever she had seen in him, whatever she had noticed, she must have coped through overextending herself to keep her mind off those worries and his too.

"We have no idea what's in his system," Kapoor agreed. "We have the technology and the specialization to treat him. He couldn't be in better hands. The facility is secure, and he will be kept isolated from the charun patients."

"What will you tell him? That he had a third stroke? That

the stress of the situation sent him into cardiac arrest?" I rubbed the drying blood caked between my fingers. "He's a career cop. Hearing he choked when his partner needed him most will kill him."

"I'm open to suggestions." The grim set of his jaw implied he'd done this a million times, that he would have spared the man his pride if he were able. No brilliant solution popped out of my mouth, and he nodded as though he hadn't expected a better fix than the one he had already engineered. "I'll email you a room number, his private line, and directions to the facility as soon as your dad is through admissions."

"Come on." Cole engulfed my hand with his, an unbreakable shackle. "I'll take you home."

While I appreciated the sentiment, I didn't have one of those any longer.

"Hey, Kapoor," Santiago called after the man had turned to go. "Heads up." He lobbed a silver ball the size of my fist at the special agent's chest. "Chain her up again, and see what happens." Knuckles white from strain, he jabbed his index finger at Kapoor. "Luce bows to no one."

A tight fist of emotion seized me by the throat, and I blinked away fresh tears as I received his message loud and clear. He and the others had earned the right to chip away at me, but no damn body else was allowed to touch a single brick in my foundation, or he would bring the whole house tumbling down on their heads.

Kapoor wheezed what might have been an agreement, hard to tell with him doubled over like that, but we didn't wait around to find out if his lungs had worked out how to filter oxygen again.

When we hit the sidewalk, I spotted a black SUV idling at the curb and performed a quick headcount. *One, two, three, four*. The guys flanked me, their steady presence a comfort, but there was no way they would have left Portia at the bunkhouse alone given the intel I had passed on.

Hidden behind the tinted passenger windows, Maggie stared out at me.

The glass was too dark for our gazes to meet, and I was grateful for the barrier that prevented me from reading the expression clouding her heart-shaped face.

"I drove over with Wu." I patted my jeans but came up empty. "I don't know what happened to my keys. They're not in my pockets." And wild horses couldn't drag me back into that house. "Looks like my phone is missing too."

Getting behind the wheel had bad move written all over it anyway. I was not in the right headspace to drive. The only other option, catching a lift in the SUV with Maggie, was out of the question. I would walk before I forced her to endure my company.

"We came in two vehicles." Cole led me down the street, past gawking pedestrians come to rubberneck at their neighbors' misfortune. "Do you need to make any stops on the way?"

I shook my head and let him tuck me in the SUV and drive me to the farmhouse for the last time.

CHAPTER TWENTY-ONE

The covers lifted off my head, static bringing long strands of hair along for the ride, and light spilled over my face. I squinted against the glare, curled in a ball on my side, mumbled profanities, then yanked on the fabric until welcoming darkness once again cocooned me.

The world was less brutal under here, tucked away in my warm bed, in my own home.

Beneath the handstitched, double wedding ring quilt Grandma Boudreau had sewn, I was insulated from the miseries that awaited me once my feet touched the floor.

"You can't hide under there forever."

Suddenly, I couldn't fling the quilt aside fast enough. "Maggie?"

"And Portia," she allowed, her tone somber. "I'm in control, though."

I scrambled upright, folded my legs under me, and she accepted the wordless invitation as I patted the mattress.

"I'm sorry," I blurted as she sat. "I'm so sorry. I had no right to give Portia consent without asking you. I wish I could go back and—"

"Let me die?" she finished.

"No." I churned over my answer. "Yes?"

"I'm not here to say I forgive you, or that we're cool. Most days I'm not convinced I wouldn't have rather died in your backyard." Her fingers wiped under her puffy eyes. "I butted heads with Mom and Dad all the time, over everything, but I miss them. I miss my job, my life, I miss being alone in my own head, in my own body." More tears flowed onto her cheeks. "I miss Justin. I miss what we had, and I miss what we could have been."

"I didn't know what else to do." It came out as weak and as pitiful as I had been in that moment.

"You chose life." She gave up on keeping her face dry and let the rivulets flow. "You did it because you love me. I get that. I do. I would have done the same for you, no question." Her watery laugh slayed me. "I'm selfish too. I would have wanted to keep you with me."

"It all happened so fast." I ran the sheet between my fingers. "I had a split second to decide, and yeah. I chose life. The alternative . . . I couldn't deal. It was all my fault. War, her coterie. You never should have been involved."

"I always knew you were different, I just had no idea how different." She wiped her nose with the hem of her shirt. "I can't blame you for what happened. I saw through Portia's memories how hard you worked to find me, how shocked you were to learn your identity." The tide stemmed. "You can't blame yourself either. This isn't on you. You didn't invite any of this to happen. You're not responsible for what these so-called sisters of yours do any more than I'm responsible for my current predicament."

"You had no choice," I reminded her.

"Are you saying you did?" she challenged. "Something tells me no one asked for your opinion either."

The absolution didn't stick, and maybe it wasn't meant to smooth us over so much as make me think.

"I came when Portia explained about Mr. Trudeau." Maggie dropped her head. "He grilled a mean hamburger, and he never once tattled when he caught us stealing extra cookies from the jar in the kitchen. His fries could have used more salt, and I'm still convinced allowing a marksman to win that laser tag trophy wasn't legal. But he was a good man, and he loved you."

A sob broke free in my chest, and I mashed both hands over my heart like that might ease the ache.

Leave it to Maggie. She always knew the exact right thing to say, her eulogy more fitting than any words that would be spoken at his funeral. I didn't want to hear how sorry people were he was gone. Sorry wouldn't bring him back. Sorry was a two-syllable copout when you had nothing original to add.

"We handled recon on Mrs. Trudeau last night." She traced the stitching on the quilt with her fingertip. "There were concerns after the Uptons that they might both be compromised."

"I didn't . . . " A shiver blasted down my arms. "It didn't cross my mind."

"She's still your Aunt Nancy," Maggie said softly. "She's one hundred percent human."

Grateful tears stung the backs of my eyes that I wouldn't lose her too. "Thanks."

"That's what friends are for, right?" A wince tightened her features, and she sucked in a breath that whistled through her teeth. "I can't stay much longer." She braced her palms on her thighs. "I don't have the strength yet."

"I'm glad you came." I reached for her, and she let me take her hand. "I want to see you again."

"Count on it." A shiver rippled over her, and her posture changed. Her entire bearing altered until I had no doubt she had lost the grip on her body. "Sorry about that." Portia withdrew her hand. "She's getting better, but control takes time."

"Thanks for helping her visit me." I twisted the sheet around my finger until I lost circulation. "Thanks for everything. I didn't get a chance to say that earlier, but I owe you big." I glanced up at her. "I don't know if I made the right call or the selfish one, if there's even a difference, but I know you put yourself at great risk to make it happen. You gave me a chance to save my best friend that I never would have had otherwise, so yeah. I'm in your debt."

"Fair warning, I will be taking that favor and banking it for later. How often does a member of the cadre offer you a blank check?" She patted a breast pocket she didn't have. "I won't be cashing this baby until I'm ready to make a big purchase."

"Stop feeling yourself up and get a move on," Santiago muttered from the doorway.

Portia smashed Maggie's small breasts together. "You want to feel me up instead?"

Reflex primed me to slap her hands down, but it was Portia's body too now.

He lifted his left foot and circled his ankle. "You want me to plant my boot up your ass?"

"He missed me," she announced. "Cuddled with my stuffed pony every night I was gone."

The wattage of Santiago's glower flipped up to full blast. "Thom put that on my bed."

"Mmm-hmm." Portia stood with a shade less grace than she once had, the only indication she was still getting used to sharing too. "That's what Cole told me when I caught him squishing the stuffing out of her."

Thom had been to blame for Cole waking up with the pony that time, but I wasn't about to interrupt them.

Issuing threats was how Santiago told the people who annoyed him least that if they were on fire, he might piss on them to put out the flames. And Portia combatted his aggression with snark just to keep him off-balance enough he didn't notice that maybe she wouldn't stroll past his flaming corpse either.

Bickering all the way downstairs, they left me alone in my room to formulate my plan of attack.

First things first, I checked my email and located the promised information from Kapoor. Figuring I would cut out the middle man, I called the physician assigned to Dad's case instead of his room. Dr. Levine fed me the update I was craving then punted me to admissions to make visitation arrangements.

While I had my finger on the pulse of the system, I quizzed the administrative assistant on Wu. At first, she demurred, all polite but firm on the patient confidentiality front, but I pressed hard with what leverage I had as his partner. With a few clicks of her keyboard, she served up the shock of my morning by informing me he had listed me as his emergency contact. The woman, happy now that I had passed muster, patched me through to his room.

Wu answered on the first ring. "I was wondering when you'd call."

I considered hanging up on him to prove a point but held strong. "How did you know it was me?"

Amusement licked at my ears. "Who else would it be?"

"Your co-workers? Your boss? Your father?"

"There's only you."

Careful not to trigger a landmine, I buried the pity welling in me under a layer of annoyance. He had made his choices, and I had made mine, and we both had to live with them. "Are you guilt-tripping me because I didn't send you flowers?"

He huffed out a laugh. "I prefer balloons."

"I hate to burst yours, but the facility where you are doesn't allow deliveries. I was going to send Dad an arrangement, but they vetoed that idea." And, okay, I might have sent Wu one too had it been allowed to show there were no hard feelings for how things had gone down. "How are you?"

"The doctor told me I can leave in forty-eight hours."

"Nine hours ago, you were paralyzed and couldn't breathe on your own." Charun healed fast, but they didn't heal *that* fast. "What's your doctor's name?"

"Worried about me?"

Yes. No. Maybe. I hadn't known Wu long enough to decide if I liked him, but I was relieved Famine hadn't killed him, and not only because he was my *Get Out of Medical Testing Free* card. "I just want to make sure that quack isn't the same doctor treating Dad."

His soft laughter ended on a hiss of pain, and that was my cue to make a stilted goodbye and hang up before we ran out of things to say.

After yanking on fresh clothes and twisting up my hair, I hit the stairs on a mission. I bumped into Miller and Thom in the living room and cast them a wave as I followed the smell of coffee into the kitchen. For what came next, I required caffeine. Lots of it. I drank it hot, and it burned all the way down, though if I'd hoped the scalding might cleanse my mouth for what came next, I was wrong.

I dialed up Elliot, the eldest Trudeau son, and offered up condolences that burned to ash on my tongue. Oblivious to the truth, he thanked me for all I had done, not realizing his loss was all my fault, and he ended the call after extracting a promise from me to stay with his mother until he arrived.

Jamal, the youngest, who was still older than me, rushed out a few words between panted breaths as he ran to catch his flight. A local friend had called him with the news last night, and he was already on his way home. We arranged for me to fetch him from the airport later, and he hung up without saying goodbye.

Mentally ticking off items on my to-do list, I cut through the living room only to grind to a halt on the threshold.

"Mom isn't thrilled with you right now." Sariah leaned over the couch, holding a dagger similar to the one Famine had wielded to Miller's throat while he sat on the cushions. "And when Momma ain't happy, ain't nobody happy."

Thom stood at the base of the stairs, too far away to help without costing Miller his life. Or, if the warnings were true, costing us ours when he imploded.

Hands flexing open at my sides, I advanced on her. "Lower your weapon."

"Nah." She eased the edge along the underside of Miller's jaw, careful not to pierce the skin, a silent warning I had gotten close enough. "Let's call this insurance."

One wrong move and Miller would be the recipient of an unscheduled tracheotomy. She left me no choice but to listen to her spiel until I figured out how to disarm her. "Maybe you should talk to your dad if your mom's happiness quotient isn't getting met."

"My parents breed like rabbits. Her home life is not the issue." She wrinkled her nose, the gesture so normal it was hard to believe her true identity. "I told you to expect a house call. Ring, ring. Pick up the phone."

"You want to talk?" That seemed unlikely. "Let's start with Famine."

"Ah, so you *do* know about the double breach. I wondered. Sadly, I can't help you there. That's your realm of expertise, not mine. All I can tell you for certain is Famine was given a choice between early entry or her coterie. Mom spotted an anomaly and wanted to take advantage for tactical purposes, but the final decision belonged to Famine."

Miller jolted from the shock. "Famine left her coterie behind?"

"That's why Mom placed her with Conquest. Famine requires supervision, or she goes off the rails, and Mom needed a breather. She has her hands full plotting world domination while managing a full coterie. She doesn't have time to keep an eye on Famine too." A flash of emotion I might have labeled as pity softened her face, there and gone. "Unless Famine's coterie figures a way through without her, she only has the cadre for support. Given my limited understanding of the nature of the anomaly, that's not happening. Death's breach, assuming she can ascend, is their next best chance at breaking through."

Famine hadn't lied. Naively, she had trusted War, her sister, to look out for her. She had trusted War to the point of leaving her own people behind without knowing if she would ever see them again. On some level, she must have trusted me too. The betrayal in her eyes when I shot her proved I had made a believer in Luce Boudreau out of one of the cadre at least.

Tonight, Famine had learned I wasn't her sister. I wasn't her protector. All the love I had shown her had been meant for the man she pretended to be. And I had to wonder if that same evidence of my identity as Luce didn't play into Sariah's interest in me.

"In addition to the free babysitting service, Mom hoped you would provide us with more information on the players in this round since you've been here longest. We learned about the NSB through you, and Adam Wu, but that was about it." She acted like telling me was some kind of favor, and she expected me to be grateful. More than anything it made me curious why Wu rated a mention, but asking would only give her more leverage over me. "Mom was counting on Famine to complete a few months' worth of recon before you caught on, but she's unraveling without her coterie to hold her together. Her impulse control has gone from questionable to non-existent."

The bond between coterie members must be symbiotic in its way. It would explain the connection between me and the others, the comfort they took from my touch and the solace I found in theirs.

"Personally, I'm thankful you took care of a future problem for me." Sariah shifted her weight to get more comfortable. "Do you know how exhausting it's been hopping from host to host to cover Famine's ass? Orvis was sloppy, I'll admit. I kept that host too long. I'm usually not so careless with disposals, so thanks for the help with the cleanup."

I measured the distance between us, still too far to do any good. "Orvis was your work?"

"I liked that body. The setup was pretty sweet too. Out in the country, no nosy neighbors. I didn't even mind the rug rats." The children she had killed and left to burn. "I would have held onto Orvis longer, but after Famine helped herself to a tray of valerian and sneaked out to your house to plant it all over the damn place, I knew I'd have to burn that identity."

And she had. Literally.

Orvis came after the Hensarling and Culberson fires, which left me wondering, "Where does Ivashov fit into the picture?"

"Girl's got to have a host." Her shoulders rose and fell in an easy motion. "I pulled the plug on the Orvis infiltration once I realized Famine had the gall to encourage your aunt to shop at the nursery. It was only a matter of time before you linked that purchase to the valerian in your yard, so I changed hosts and parked the bodies in the basement while I handled the Culberson cover-up."

All too clear, I saw the sequence of events. Her dragging body after body into the small basement room, locking them in, taking the back way out through the cellar doors she locked tight to prevent snooping in case anyone smelled the decomposition in this heat. Leaving the drip torch had been an afterthought to tie all the scenes together.

"I was in bad shape after our little chat, and I did a piss poor cremation job." She patted Miller's cheek. "Lucky for me, the NSB runs a tight ship. They tied up all those pesky loose ends for me."

Without bodies for autopsy, we never would have guessed the Orvis family had died prior to the fire. Had Wu known? Or had his involvement ended after he intercepted the corpses? And did it matter? Yes. The truth always mattered. There was an honesty in death worth preserving for the families left behind.

"Believe it or not, Auntie, I'm on your side. See, I did my recon. I know what's doing above this terrene, and I want no part of it."

A warning prickle climbed up my spine. For all the talk of this world, no one had mentioned what came next. "What are you talking about?"

"I can't give it away for free." A grim smile cut her mouth. "The information cost me too much."

First Bruster and now Sariah. I was tired of all the carrot dangling. I wasn't a damn bunny.

"Most of what you've told me we already knew." Just the broad strokes, but none of her intel was breaking news. "What, exactly, is your proposition?"

"You and I are at an impasse, whether you've realized it yet or not." Sunlight glinted off the blade in her hand as she adjusted her grip. "I ought to kill you. You're the only one who can punch through the ceiling of this world. But you're also the oldest daughter, the strongest, and you're invested in saving these humans. I propose you and I become friends."

"You almost killed Miller." I let her current position speak for itself. "I see the urge hasn't passed. That's not what I'd call friendly behavior."

"We're square. I gave as good as I got, that's all. Ain't that right, buddy?" Leaning over his shoulder, she pressed a quick kiss to his temple. "I wouldn't kill him. That would be counterproductive since I don't want to die." Her gaze zeroed in on me and the precious inches I had advanced toward her. "Have you seen under his hood yet? No? Good. Trust me. That's one latch you don't want popped."

"War will destroy you if she discovers your betrayal," Thom said what we all were thinking.

Sariah winked at him. "Then we'd best keep this our little secret."

Chips of ice hit my circulatory system as I stood there staring at her while she held a knife to Miller's throat. This was a game to her. All of it. And I was so very tired of playing. Chills swept up my arms, and my focus narrowed to the blade in her hand and the fragile column of flesh beneath its poisoned edge.

"I don't expect an answer now." Ready to make her exit, she straightened to her full height and allowed the flat of the dagger to rest against his shoulder. "Mourn your loss and think it over. I'll pop by in a few days, and we can finalize the parameters of our alliance."

Ally with my niece, who had as good as greenlighted my uncle's murder. In what world, and I had learned there were so very many, did she believe me capable of such forgiveness?

I had always been fast, and I had always been strong, and I had never used either attribute to full advantage. Wrapped up in being normal, I had stifled what few charun gifts I could access on reflex. For the first time in my life, I called on both, willed the strength into my limbs and the speed into my soles.

Sariah startled when I appeared at her elbow, and she gasped when I closed my fingers around her throat. Her arm was already in motion, muscle memory stepping into the breach until her brain got on board with what was happening. She altered the trajectory of the blade, sweeping it away from her body, eager to sheathe it between my ribs, but lack of oxygen and my proximity restricted her movements, made her clumsy enough I had no trouble capturing her wrist and squeezing until her fingers flexed open, and the blade thudded onto the floor. I hooked my foot behind hers, shoving her down like my knuckles had magnets in them, and the hardwood was polarized.

"You can't play for both teams." My fingers dug into her pale skin. "You chose your side when you bided your time until my uncle was irretrievable, all so you didn't have to get your hands dirty with Famine. You chose your side when you attacked Miller and rang Santiago's bell." Crimson welled under my nails. "I can't wash the blood off my hands, and neither can you."

"She won't . . . kill you," Sariah wheezed. "She . . . needs . . . you. She'll kill every . . . single . . . person you love . . . to control you."

"I see that now." With the cold came clarity, always. "That's why you're going to help me send her a message written in a language she can understand." Reaching across her, I palmed the dagger. "War must love you a great deal if she's let you live this long."

A pucker marred her brow. "She ... hates ... me."

Only two beings had survived and thrived at War's side. Her mate, Thanases, and their firstborn, Sariah. That spoke of loyalty, of affection, of an attachment rooted deeper than any of them might understand given their sociopathic tendencies. But I recognized love when I saw it, even if it was a paler shade than any I had ever known, and the Freon pumping through my heart had no trouble lifting that blade or bringing it down with all my strength.

Thud.

Crimson wept from the gash in her abdomen, mingling with the phantom stains under my skin, branding me as the villain I was born to be.

Gasping under my palm, Sariah flailed against me, but I kept my fist clenched on the dagger's hilt. I couldn't kill her, not as I was now, but I could do this much. I could hit War where it hurt. Show her how it felt to have your heart bleed.

That snap of emotion alerted me to the fact my rage was burning away the cold place, melting it in the wash of hot blood spilling through my fingers. As the fight drained out of Sariah slowly, her skin began bubbling up, boiling over, the flesh cooking off her bones.

"Get back," Miller warned, yanking me off her with an arm hooked around my waist. "*Move.*"

Sariah's inner monster exploded from her host, and once again I found myself entertaining a super gator in my living room. The beast's stomach hung too low to the ground for me to tell if the dagger had been expelled, but the poison must have been working.

Lurching toward me, she snapped her jaws, but her attack might as well have been in slow motion. The three of us kept her on the defensive, wearing her down, but it was Miller who approached as she collapsed, and Miller who pried apart her massive jaws. The vicious crack as he broke the delicate bones acting as hinges was deafening, and that was before her agonized roar.

"I'm calling Kapoor." I hated that I had favorited his number on my phone, but that was my life now. When he answered, I gave him a rundown of the situation. "You might save her if you make it in time."

Thom shook his head in disagreement or perhaps in warning.

After the call ended, the three of us gravitated toward one another, drawn together because we were stronger that way, and we watched over Sariah as her body twitched.

"We should have questioned her first," Thom said, a half-hearted afterthought.

"She didn't break before," Miller countered, "she wouldn't have broken now."

Thom canted his head. "What do you think she meant about what comes next?"

"We've searched for fifteen years and uncovered nothing but speculation and lore founded in this terrene's major religions." Miller rubbed his jaw. "Sariah is good, but we're better. There's no way she peeked beyond the veil on her own. Only Conquest can do that."

Their conversational tones finished chipping at the ice encasing my heart until the cold place retreated fully and left me to deal with the aftermath. I braced for the surge of guilt over what I had done, the one that would send me stumbling into the bathroom to purge, but it never manifested. I had lost another piece of my soul, but it had been worth it to protect us. And, if I was being honest, the side order of revenge had tasted sweet too.

War had delivered Famine to me. And now I had her daughter. That gave me control over the most pieces on the board. At least until Death arrived. That would tip the balance of power back in War's favor. Unless I got to our final sister first.

"How fast will she burn through the paralytic?" I squatted beside Sariah and checked her pulse. Slow but steady. "Famine claimed she was immune. Any chance that's hereditary?"

Given the cadre's fondness for poison, that's one family trait I wouldn't mind possessing.

"Sariah wouldn't carry a weapon that could kill her. She'll recover in a few hours at most is my guess." He raked his gaze over her before coming back to me. "Otillian biology is too chameleonic for heredity to hold much sway. Sariah is the product of a Drosera mating, and you're no more Drosera than I am. Whatever DNA you have in common with her is in the minority now that War has altered her biology to suit her mate. There's no way to predict how you would react to the poison."

Meaning my niece wasn't fully my niece, a nice wedge of rationality to shove under the door of my mind when I reflected on my actions. Protecting one family, my human one, while cutting down on the other was giving me a complex. "Can you guys handle this while I pack?"

A lame excuse, yeah, but I needed a few moments alone to process the ramifications of moving forward with my little coup. Locking Sariah in a cell would piss off War. That gave me warm fuzzies right there. But if she wanted to play double agent . . . maybe we should let her.

After we microchipped her ten ways from Sunday, of course. Bloodthirsty as she was, I got the feeling it would take more than light stabbing, a little poison, and a broken jaw to rain on her sadistic parade. Hell, Sariah might view waking in an NSB cell under guard as the opening volley in our negotiations. She had made the first strike, after all. She must have known I would retaliate.

"Sure." Miller massaged his throat as though reminded of the pressure from the blade. "We can babysit."

Thom, noticing the same rubbing gesture, cocked his head. "I should bite him, just in case."

I exited on Miller's sigh as he stuck out his hand. Up in my room, I pulled out my luggage and packed nothing but clothes and toiletries. There was no need for mementoes where I was going. The movers, when they came, could pack it all up as far as I was concerned. The one item I lingered over was the old rotary phone. Its hideousness was a comfort, but I had no intentions of relying on it, or the mystery man on the other side of it, for much longer. Come the big two-six, I planned to have run Ezra to ground.

Happy birthday to me.

"Do you need any help?"

The sound of Cole's voice did what it always did, and made me tighten and loosen all over. "I'll take what I can get." And didn't that convey a multitude of meanings? "Has Kapoor made his pickup yet?"

"You missed the stampeding wildebeests?" Cole slung a bag over his shoulder and tucked two more under one arm. "Your hearing must be worse than I thought."

"Ha ha." I punched him in the arm since his were too full to retaliate and almost cracked a knuckle. "What are you doing here?"

His expression shifted through the spectrum before settling on cautious. "Am I not welcome?"

"I think we both know you're always welcome." Traitorous

thing, my heart. It stutter-stepped when he smiled at me like that. "What I meant was—you stayed up with me all night. I figured you'd go to the bunkhouse and crash. Santiago is with Portia, right?"

"He is." Cole angled his head in my direction. "After last night, I thought you could use someone to lean on."

Catching this surly dragon by his tail was irresistible. "I have Miller and Thom."

His shrewd eyes narrowed on my face. "You're going to make me say it, aren't you?"

I linked my hands behind my back, the picture of innocence. "Say what?"

"Use me," he rumbled, meltwater eyes stark in his face. "I want you to use me."

I crossed to him, rose up on my tiptoes, and pressed a brief kiss to the underside of his jaw, the prickly patch of skin quickly becoming my favorite spot. "I would be honored."

A slight curve bent his lips. "I'll meet you outside."

Alone in my room, I strolled the perimeter, ending up at the window Wu had made his perch. Far below, Cole was loading my belongings in the back of his SUV, and I paused to admire his casual strength. Hand pressed against the glass, the chill barrier acted as a reminder of the fragility of his trust, how easily it could be broken.

The house was empty as I passed through each room, flipping off lights and unplugging appliances. When I reached the front door, I leaned my forehead against the wood and listened to the stillness.

"You were the best home a girl could ask for," I told the house. "I'm going to miss you."

After dashing tears from under my eyes, I locked the door behind me and met the guys in the yard.

"Luce and I are going to hold vigil with her aunt," Cole announced with an edge in his voice that had the other two clamping their mouths shut. "Miller, drop her luggage off at the bunkhouse. She can take my room. Thom, you shadow us."

We each went our separate ways, Cole and I reuniting inside the Bronco. I sat there for a minute, gazing out the window at the lovely, old farmhouse where a gruff cop had brought a feral child and made a family with her.

Out of time to reminisce, I drove us across town to Mo Jones' house. Mo-Mo was Aunt Nancy's best friend, and I had no doubt the Jones house was where I would find her. Sure enough, when I reached the sprawling blue clapboard home on the outskirts of town, I counted two dozen vehicles in the yard and enough bodies milling on the low porch to be certain folks from the church had carpooled to be here during her time of need.

The walk up to the front door was one of the longest of my life. I had no right to be here, but Aunt Nancy didn't know what loving me had cost her. As far as she was concerned, I was the dutiful niece who had come home to witness chaos, not the churning heart of the storm.

Cole's fingers brushed over my knuckles, a show of support, but we didn't connect.

Talk about a metaphor for our relationship.

"Lu-Lu," a breathy voice called from down the porch. "Hey, doll face. I wondered when you'd show." A wisp of a woman with light-brown skin and a bald head she'd decorated with henna tattoos that changed each week shuffled bodies aside to reach me. "She's upstairs, third bedroom to your left. I'd walk you up but—" she glanced around the gathering "—the whole community has come out to offer their condolences, and Nan is exhausted from the first wave. I'm doing my best to give everyone an outlet while she recovers."

"Thanks." I looked back at Cole. "I'm going to check on her. Would you mind waiting in the car?"

The crowd would make him uncomfortable and vice versa. There was no reason for him to suffer.

He invaded my personal space. "I'm coming with you."

"He can go up too." Mo-Mo patted his arm, and Cole did his best not to wince. Contact with strangers wasn't his favorite thing either. "I don't blame him for worrying about you after all that's happened. He's a good man to want to keep an eye on you until the monster responsible for Harry's death is captured."

I flinched so hard I rocked backward, right against Cole. Mo-Mo's eyes softened as she measured the two of us, her thoughts clear on her face. She thought I was seeking comfort from my boyfriend instead of reeling from the unintentional blow she had landed.

"Speaking of good men . . ." Her hand lifted to toy with the gold cross at her throat. "How is your father?"

"He's resting comfortably." A stock phrase if ever I'd uttered one. "Thanks for asking."

Breaking away from Mo-Mo, I led Cole through a packed foyer toward a staircase that belonged in *Gone with the Wind*. We climbed up to the second floor, and I would have known where to find Aunt Nancy even without the directions. A dozen women lingered in the hall, handkerchiefs in hand, and their red-rimmed eyes snapped wide at our approach.

"I'm here for Aunt Nancy." I inched toward the door when none of them blinked. The warm presence at my back alerted me to the issue. "This is my friend, Cole Heaton."

The ladies nodded their heads in tandem, a row of bobble head figures tapped by a greater hand, their voices tight and high as in unison they remembered there was somewhere else they needed to be and made their apologies.

"I'll wait for you out here." Cole posted himself at the door. "Take as long as you need."

Grateful he was here with me, that I didn't have to face this alone, I lingered with him, studying the many-times-broken nose, the ragged ear, the jaw harder than a diamond. "They were scared of you."

Mt. Heaton gazed down at me through eyes the color of glacier melt. "That bothers you."

"Not how you think, no." I pursed my lips in search of what I wanted to say. "Their reactions reminded me of when we first met is all. It got me wondering when I stopped being afraid."

Amusement seesawed across his mouth. "You greeted me barefoot in your pajamas. That was all the armor you donned to face down a dragon."

"Yeah, well. I didn't know you were a dragon at the time." I smoothed my hands down my pants, acknowledging the procrastination tactic for what it was, and poised my knuckles to knock. "Never let it be said that I'm afflicted with common sense."

Aunt Nancy offered muffled assent for me to enter, and I shuffled across the threshold into the darkened bedroom. The light was off, and the drapes had been closed. She reclined on the bed, her gaze fixated on the ceiling like there was a whole world up there for her to explore. Her ankles were crossed, and her hands were folded at her navel. Her peaceful repose sent ice crystalizing down my spine, vertebrae by vertebrae.

"I married Harry when I was eighteen years old, fresh out of high school. We've been married forty-six years. Our babies are forty-two and thirty-nine this year. Our grandbabies are ten and six. He was your father's partner for thirty-five years. He was your uncle for fifteen."

As she made her recitation, I drifted closer until I could sit on the bed beside her and hold her cool hand.

"That sounds like a lot of years, a lot of time," she murmured. "It wasn't enough." Her eyes closed, and tears spilled down her temples. "It wasn't nearly enough."

"I miss him already," I said, just as softly. "Dad doesn't know yet. I'm going to tell him when I see him."

Her lips trembled as she mashed them together. "How is Eddie?"

"Resting comfortably," I repeated the company line. "He hasn't woken up yet, but the doctors are hopeful he will regain consciousness in the next day or so."

"That's good." She dragged in a long breath as if reminding her lungs to get with the program. "Are the boys on their way?" Her lids cracked open. "You would have called them. You're always so thoughtful."

"Jamal will be here tonight. I'm going to pick him up at the airport myself. Elliot has to make arrangements for his pets and get the kids packed up, so he'll be here tomorrow morning."

"Has the person who . . . ?" Her fragile throat worked over a lump. "Has there been any news?"

"Not that I've heard." I was out of the CPD loop. The only way I could get updates without making a bad situation worse would be to involve Santiago. And nothing they uncovered would implicate the true villain, whether that was Famine or me, I hadn't yet decided. "I'll ask Rixton to keep you in the loop." He would do that for her sake. "Can I get you anything?"

"No, tater tot," she sighed deeply. "I'm fine where and how I am."

The ballooning sense of dread in my heart kept expanding. "Do you mind if I stay with you for a little while?"

"Not at all." Her lips curved in a faint smile. "I'm just going to rest now."

"All right." I restrained myself from texting her sons with urgent messages to hurry when I had no reason to believe her languor was due to more than exhaustion and heartache. Unable to shake the warning prickles that portended nothing good, I checked on Cole. "Hey."

"Hey." His rigid posture relaxed. "How is she?"

"Not well," I said under my breath, certain he would hear. "I can't shake this feeling I'm going to lose her too."

He gave an understanding nod. "Death forces us all the view life through the lens of our own mortality."

Once again, the assurance she would recover, that I was overreacting, never surfaced, and I was almost glad. I wouldn't have believed him anyway.

"I'm going back in." I checked my phone. "We have about four hours until we pick up Jamal."

"I'll be right here," he assured me. "Go sit with your aunt."

The hours passed in slow motion, the rise and fall of her chest my only entertainment. I had my phone. I could have played a game or watched a movie, but I had this ridiculous idea that my gaze was the only weight pinning her down, that if I looked away, even for a second, she would drift off to wherever she had been staring.

The silent alarm I'd set buzzed in my pocket, and I had a choice to make.

Aware I was being utterly ridiculous, I crossed to Aunt Nancy and pressed a kiss to her smooth forehead. "I love you." The steady flutter of her pulse gave me the strength the leave. "I'll be back soon with Jamal. You won't be alone. I'll send Mo-Mo up to sit with you until we return."

Cole peeled away from the door when I walked through it,

and we made our way downstairs. The house still hummed with voices, music, and laughter. I scanned each room we passed in search of Mo-Mo, but found her on the porch knitting with a circle of their friends.

"I'm going to pick up Jamal," I told her. "Would you mind keeping watch over Aunt Nancy until I get back?" I worried my teeth over my bottom lip. "She just seems . . ."

Without another word, Mo-Mo bundled up her gear. "She'll be right as rain once her boys get here. Those grandbabies of hers always put a spark in her eyes." Her smile widened. "Oh, and John called. He's coming for a visit before work tomorrow."

"That's great." As good and pissed as he rightfully was at me, I hadn't expected Rixton to show up on my doorstep with a shoulder for me to cry on, but a text from him would have been nice. Still, I was grateful he hadn't abandoned my family, even if he had cut ties with me. "That's . . . great."

As Mo-Mo trundled past, I wasted no time heading for the Bronco. I could tell from the stares that Cole was right there with me. We made the drive to the airport in record time, and Jamal, who was the spitting image of Uncle Harold, cupped my cheeks and kissed my forehead. "How is she?"

"I left her napping." I eased from his grip to stand beside Cole. "She was tired when I arrived, there have been so many visitors. We didn't talk long."

"Who's your friend?" Jamal was sizing up Cole, and despite his grim eyes, a tight smile manifested.

"This is Cole Heaton." I touched his arm. "Cole, this is Jamal Trudeau, the baby of the family."

"You must like this one if you're out to discredit me from the get-go." Jamal extended his hand and shook Cole's meaty paw. "I'm glad you're here, man. What Luce walked in on . . ." He ducked his head. "That couldn't have been easy for her.

I'm grateful she has a friend at her back." His brows gathered. "Where's John?"

A baseball bat to the solar plexus would have hurt less. "I haven't spoken to him today."

For several days, longer than any stretch in our partnership. *Former* partnership.

"Oh." Perceptive man that he was, he let the matter drop. "I touched base with Elliot. He'll be here around noon with the fam in tow."

The overnight bag slung across his shoulder was all the luggage he'd brought with him, so we didn't have to wait at the baggage claim. After grabbing him a coffee for the trip out to Mo-Mo's, we piled into the Bronco and drove in heavy silence.

The uneasy feeling that had plagued me since visiting Aunt Nancy started wringing my stomach out like a wet towel. The frenetic buzzing of mourners torqued me further still, and that was before I spotted the white box on wheels with the seizure-inducing strobes splashing color across so many pale faces.

"Sweet Jesus," Jamal breathed. "Stop the car. Luce, stop."

I slammed on the brakes, and he leapt from the Bronco. I had the presence of mind to make sure I wasn't blocking the road in case the ambulance needed an escape route, but the other vehicles got no such consideration from me as I left the Bronco wedged behind four other cars and bolted after Jamal.

We hit the porch at the same time the paramedics exited with a stretcher. The still form under a white sheet required no introduction, and Jamal crumpled. His knees hit the deck, and his palms slapped in front of him. The only thing preventing a total collapse was Mo-Mo, who had seen him coming and wrapped her arms around his middle.

"What happened?" He choked out the demand. "I don't understand. I don't ..."

"Sir." The paramedic nearest him shared a look with her partner, who nodded. "Mrs. Trudeau was diagnosed with stage four pancreatic cancer three months ago. The information was on her emergency medical identification bracelet."

Jamal was shaking his head, but I had lost all mobility.

Cancer.

The answer to an unasked question had just been provided to me.

Guilt had been riding me so hard, I hadn't stopped to ask myself the most basic question. Why would my uncle, a God-fearing man, offer up his soul? What could a charun have offered him that made the use of his body, accepting the taint of what he must have viewed as such evil, worthwhile? There was only one reason why he would have given himself unto Famine, and that was love.

He would have sacrificed himself without a second thought for a member of his family. For his wife? He would have signed any deal, made any trade, agreed to any bargain, if it meant healing her.

This explained so much. Her fatigue, her loss of appetite, her headaches. Signs I had misinterpreted as proof she had been taken as a host were, in hindsight, evidence of her illness. No wonder Famine had risked claiming my uncle even though playing his role within the community, within his family, was daunting compared to the relative ease with which she could have assumed Aunt Nancy's identity. Famine's parasitic nature required sustenance, and Aunt Nancy's body had nothing left to offer.

"Let's get you inside." Mo-Mo stroked Jamal's back. "Come on, sweet boy. That's it. Almost there."

Cole edged around me, accepting the crumpled burden from Mo-Mo, and hauled Jamal upright. When he kept weaving on his feet, Cole lifted him over his shoulder in a fireman's carry and trundled Jamal into the living room, where he deposited him on the couch.

Unable to suck down enough oxygen to keep my lungs pumping, I bowed out while everyone focused on Jamal. I jogged out onto the porch, and when that wasn't enough, I kept going through the yard. I broke into a run at the edge of the road, fleeing the miserable scene, and hit my stride as the graveled drive turned to asphalt. I kept pumping my legs until all I knew was the burn, and I didn't stop until I turned my ankle and took a nasty spill. Palms out to catch myself, I scraped them as raw as hamburger meat on impact.

"Let me take you home," Cole said from behind me.

Of course he had followed me. He hadn't even broken a sweat pacing me.

"I don't have a home," I said miserably. "It's gone, like everything else."

"You still have your father," he reminded me. "You still have us."

Head hanging low, I shook it side to side. "For how long?"

Heavy boots marched around until they faced me, and Cole squatted, waiting for me to find the strength to lift my head and meet the steely determination in his gaze. "For as long as it lasts."

"Mmmrrrrpt."

Thom walked under me, his tail tickling my nose, his wings tight to his spine, and proceeded to bat at a loose thread on my shirt sleeve until I pushed myself back, sat on my ankles. The boxy tomcat must have swallowed a chainsaw to make so much racket, but his purrs soothed me, and they revved higher as I stroked him ears to tail.

"Let me take you home," Cole repeated. "Come home with me."

"Okay" was what he wanted to hear, so that's what I told him.

I don't know how I got to my feet. I couldn't feel them anymore. All I knew was the cat kept nipping me, and if I didn't get my butt in gear soon, I would start losing chunks of flesh to his wicked sharp teeth.

A black SUV rolled to a stop beside us, and a distant part of my brain wondered when Cole had called Santiago for a pickup, but he was riding shotgun. Maggie was behind the wheel. I could tell it was her and not Portia by the tears leaking down her cheeks and the way she flung open the door and her arms, offering whatever level of physical comfort I could withstand. I walked into her embrace, dropped my head onto her shoulder, and hung on until my weight dragged us both to the ground. The guys formed a circle around us, protecting us while I splintered, and it made me sob that much harder.

"We have to end this," she murmured against my hair, long after my tears had dried, but the tone was pure Portia. Maggie had already lost her hold on their body. "The NSB told you to keep playing human. I get that. I really do. You're spot-lit here in town. There was no clean way to extricate you from this situation without raising suspicions. But it's time to circle the wagons. It's time for you to cut ties to this life. It's the only way to protect the family you have left."

"It's time for you to figure out how much of Conquest's power you can tap without waking her," Santiago said from behind us. The cadence of his speech was off, stilted, like he was forcing out each word or wanted to call them back as he spoke them. "You're fast, and you're strong. There has to be more in your arsenal than that. She's in you, a part of you, and if we can figure out how to access—"

"It's too dangerous," Miller interrupted. "She could fracture if she starts digging around in her psyche."

"You think I don't know that?" Violence throbbed in his voice, an unmet need that demanded satisfaction. "I don't want this. I never wanted any of this. But this is where we are, and this is what it will cost to stay alive."

I withdrew from Portia, leaned against the rear wheel, and tucked my knees against my chest.

"Santiago is right." I threw my lot in with his, and Cole recoiled on my periphery while I pretended not to notice. "I'll talk to Wu and see if he's got any suggestions. None of us know what we're dealing with here. I'm an anomaly, but he's got access to all the health records and laboratory findings on the charun in the NSB's program. There might be help there." I linked my arms around my legs. "Kapoor hinted they have an Otillian on the team. I think his exact words were that 'all our information on you and your kind comes direct from the source'. He promised me access, so I'll press for a meeting." Five sets of eyes locked on me. "What?"

"An Otillian on their team, other than you, means trouble." Portia checked with the others for confirmation. "Only the cadre and their offspring are allowed to ascend to Earth."

"Any Otillian who has been around long enough to earn their trust would be a remnant," Miller agreed.

"And that means Kapoor lied, that they've tried converting cadre before you." Santiago glowered. "You might be the most recent in a line of experiments, maybe the only successful one, but still not the miracle he would have us believe."

"We need more information," Cole allowed. "Set up the meeting."

With a game plan solidifying, I found the resolve to stand and dust off my pants. I reached for the SUV's rear door, but Santiago beat me there. He wrenched it open, glaring at me as he slid across the bench seat in the back, like it was somehow my fault he'd surrendered his prime spot up front. Or like he was daring me to comment on the fact that maybe, just maybe, he wanted to be close enough to comfort me in his own way. Mostly by growling at me or hurling insults, but still. It was the thought that counted, right? I climbed in beside him, and he grumbled when I brushed his hip while fastening my seat belt.

"I almost forgot." I reached in my pocket and withdrew the thumb drive Bruster had compiled on Famine. "I got you a present." I passed it over. "Merry Christmas."

"You must have hit your head harder than we thought in that wreck." He accepted what I was offering with a frown. "That or you've got a Santa fetish no one needs to know about."

Leave it to Santiago to ruin my favorite holiday. "Ho, ho, ho."

"This is one of Deland Bruster's thumb drives." Santiago lifted it to his nose, eyes widening. "I can smell him on it." A grin threatened to split his cheeks as he rubbed the stick between his fingers. "Maybe I do hear a sleigh bell or two."

Learning the coterie was aware of Bruster didn't surprise me given the fact the guy had been loitering in town. That was the kind of thing territorial charun tended to notice. But it stung that they hadn't warned me about him.

"Aww." Portia piled in beside me, sandwiching me between them. "Santiago likes you."

"I do not," he snapped. "I tolerate her. That's different."

She drilled the nail on her pointer finger into his forearm. "Is *l-i-k-e* how all the cool kids are spelling tolerance these days?"

"I hate you," he grumbled.

"You do not," she admonished, a teasing glint in her eyes. "You *tolerate* me."

Wedged between the world's most annoying pair of bookends, I met Cole's gaze in the rear-view mirror as he settled behind the wheel. The look we shared settled me better than a warm bath and a glass of wine even before I reached for where his bracelet circled my wrist to feel closer to him.

Miller claimed Santiago's abandoned seat, and Thom, back on all fours, leapt through the open door. He strutted across the console and planted his furry butt on my lap, angling his chin up for scratches. Surrounded by my coterie, another type of family, this one near-indestructible, I embraced the role I had never wanted but destiny seemed determined for me to fill.

For Uncle Harold and Aunt Nancy, for Dad and Rixton, for Sherry and Nettie, I would grant Wu his wish. I would delve into my darkest, coldest places, trusting love to anchor me in this skin. For Miller and Thom, Santiago and Portia, Maggie and Cole, I would leash what lied within. For all those who would view this war through the lens of late night news broadcasts, I would bleed so they remained innocent of the horrors of my new reality.

And above all, I would *not* break.

EPILOGUE

———❖———

Special Agent Farhan Kapoor shoved through an unmarked door into a sterile room decked out with hundreds of thousands of dollars' worth of medical equipment designed with charun biology in mind. The adjustable bed on wheels, silver rails flashing, was about the only staple this place had in common with a civilian hospital room. The patient, dressed in black silk pajama bottoms, propped up with a book older than dirt open on his lap, did nothing to humanize the space.

Now that he thought about it, the guy might be the least mundane item in the room.

Kapoor dropped into an empty chair positioned under a window, closed his eyes for a moment to block out the harsh fluorescence beating down on them, and waited to be acknowledged. The next thing he knew, his chin was bouncing off his chest, and his number had been called.

"I asked you a question." Adam Wu bookmarked his page with a red ribbon sewn into the binding.

"I got three hours of sleep last night." Kapoor rubbed his face with his hands. "That's on top of the two I got the night before." His eyes stung from the effort. "Protecting your girl is running me ragged."

The book snapped shut and was set aside. "How is Luce?"

"Running on autopilot." A lesser woman would have shut down hard after last night, but Luce was about as human as the man staring at him through predatory, golden-brown eyes that reminded him of a hawk. "Harold Trudeau was family, and she pulled the trigger. That leaves a mark. Losing her aunt is going to scar too. She'll blame herself for both deaths."

Wu had no ready answer for that. "Are the security measures in place for the rest of her family?"

"We have units assigned to Mrs. Rixton and Mr. Boudreau. We're pulling strings with CPD to get one of our guys paired up with Detective Rixton so he has backup while on duty." Kapoor crossed his legs. "We're going to keep tabs on the Trudeau boys while they're in town. We'll coordinate with local LEOs to arrange for nightly drive-bys once they return to their homes. Their distance from the nexus ought to take care of the rest."

"Excellent." He reclined on his pillows. "Are there any other updates?"

Kapoor let the other shoe drop. "There's a new addition to the zoo."

Wu titled his head, the angle six degrees past human. "Who?"

"Sariah broke into the farmhouse this morning and threatened Miller. Luce stabbed her with a poisoned blade, the same make as the one Famine used on you." Kapoor had double bagged and tagged the thing after the medics pried it from her gut. The lab had it now, and he wished them luck isolating the venom used so that a stronger antivenin might be created. "Sariah is an independent operator. War might not notice her absence for a few days to a few weeks, but when she realizes what happened, she'll go nuclear."

Wu began peeling surgical tape from his hand and arm. "Tell the doctor I'm ready to leave."

"Are you sure that's smart?" Kapoor winced as Wu removed the IV then started on the leads stuck to the bare expanse of his chest. "You couldn't breathe on your own yesterday."

Hands spread wide, he inhaled until his ribs creaked then gusted out an exhale. "See? Good as new."

Nothing on this guy had been new since dirt was invented. "Are you sure you ought to be cozying up to her?" Luce Boudreau might be good people, but the thing under her skin was an apocalypse waiting to happen. "I figured you'd take on a more administrative role in her care."

Kapoor had done as he was told by insinuating the NSB had an Otillian agent who could open Luce's eyes to her culture, to her past, to the legacy handed down to each charun who took up the mantle of Conquest. But clearly, he had underestimated the depth of Wu's fascination with Boudreau.

Their new recruit would want to meet their "Otillian" agent, and how the hell did he explain she already had?

Never in a million years had he expected Wu to twist their predicament into an excuse to partner up with her. That had been his first mistake: underestimating Adam Wu. A consultation, a quick Q and A, would have sufficed. Now they had an extra alias in the mix, another cover to maintain, and all for what?

So Wu could play with the toy his father had broken? Gods forbid the old man find out what junior was up to these days. What *he* was up to. Then it wouldn't matter if Boudreau was pissed enough to end them over their deceit, odds were good they would already be dead.

"I don't tell you how to do your job." Muscles fluttered in Wu's cheek. "I suggest you show me the same courtesy."

The splash of violence over his face confirmed Wu was too invested to remain objective, a recurring theme where Boudreau was concerned. Too many folks wanted a nibble, just a little taste, but there was only so much of her to go around, and that was before Wu cut himself a bigger slice of the pie.

Kapoor had considered putting a bullet in Boudreau's head to end the problem before it got started. Some days he still considered pulling the trigger. History set a precedent for targeting Conquest first, and for good reason. Without her, the cadre could climb no higher. Their ascension would dead-end. The upper terrenes would remain intact, unblemished by the Otillian blight, and that was all the man doctoring himself ought to care about.

Earth was a battleground, and Kapoor was too damn young to be so tired of fighting.

"How do you deal?" He hadn't meant to ask the question. It popped out all on its own. "You're stone-cold over there, and I'm burning up with fever thinking about what's coming."

Wu remained quiet for so long Kapoor figured the guy wasn't going to answer.

"I have no home, no people, no . . . " The thought trailed into nothing. "What is there to fear when you have nothing left to lose?"

Bleak. That was . . . bleak. "You could die."

He gestured to the room at large. "Apparently not."

"That's why you're fixated on Boudreau," he realized. "She's a fighter." Fate had steamrolled her, but she kept popping up like one of those hinged targets on a midway game. "You like that she's got teeth."

The man smiled, and it was a cold, vicious thing. "You have no idea."

Skin prickling, Kapoor excused himself from the room under the guise of flagging down a nurse. The truth was, he could only handle so much quality time with Wu before his inner monster started nodding its head in agreement. There was a reason Kapoor had made a great hunter, and it was the same reason driving him to make a more permanent mark on society before the beast at his core gnawed through his gut and burst out *Aliens*-style, snapping the fragile threads of his fraying humanity.

The predator in Adam tracked Kapoor's hurried exit with interest. He wasn't hungry. He had eaten six forty-eight-ounce rib-eye steaks raw and sopped up the blood with the buttered rolls on his plates. And, he reminded himself when his stomach attempted a half-hearted growl, Kapoor was an asset.

Expanding his lungs to full capacity made his chest burn, and the rest of his body was riddled with aches and pains too. After lowering the bedrail, he swung his legs over the edge of the mattress and let his feet brush the cold tile before allowing any of his weight to settle on them. His knees cracked against the floor before he registered them buckling, and he hissed out a vicious curse.

All too soon War would discover her daughter was missing, presumed dead, and heads would roll.

Call him sentimental, but he preferred Luce's exactly where it was.

A quiet knock preceded a nurse dressed in pale yellow scrubs. The smile she wore screamed *I can do this. I am a professional*, but her heart hammered against her ribs, her instincts warning her to keep her distance even as her training demanded she rush to his side and attempt to wedge her shoulder under his arm.

"Thank you," he said, polite though her heave-ho routine was making him twitchy, "but your assistance is unnecessary."

"Let me call for one of the aids," she panted. "How did this happen?"

Ignoring the question, he focused past her shoulder. "What is that?"

A plush teddy bear dressed in a black thong, matching assless chaps, his mouth plugged with a ball gag and his chest crisscrossed with studded leather strips, clutched a fistful of colorful balloons emblazoned with a variety of mundane get-well wishes. His other paw clutched a pale blue envelope with squiggles that resembled water doodled across the flap. The contrast was . . . jarring.

"Oh." The nurse appeared to recall the purpose of her visit and flushed fire engine red. "You got a delivery."

A frown gathered between his brows. "Those aren't allowed at this facility."

"The sender was given special dispensation," she explained. "This was one of two arrangements that arrived. I would have come sooner so as not to disturb your rest, but security held them for testing. The balloons are starting to droop, so I brought yours the second it was deemed safe."

"Pass me the card." His hand shot out, and the nurse flinched as if expecting a blow to land. "I won't hurt you." He forced calm into his voice. "Just give me the card, please."

Scurrying over to the plush bear, she lifted the card and placed it on his palm. "Do you want me to open it for you?"

His flat stare told her his body might be flagging, but his mental facilities were humming along just fine. "I can take things from here."

"Yes. Of course." Her gaze touched on the door. "If you're sure you're okay . . . ?"

The envelope held his complete attention, but he assumed by the squeak of her Crocs that she had let herself out. Jabbing his thumb under the flap, he ripped it open and tugged out a white card inked with calligraphic loops and whirls that read *"Feeling yucky and not so ducky?"* Smiling, he cracked it open and kept reading. *"Listen to the rubber ducky, and ignore your quack doctor. I'm cleared to visit Dad tomorrow. I arranged to see you while I'm there. Be a good patient, and I'll bring ice cream. The good stuff."*

Adam lowered the card until he made eye contact with the BDSM bear who was *not* the promised rubber ducky.

Clearly something had been lost in translation when Luce placed her order.

Standing under his own power wasn't going to happen. His lower legs had gone numb while he knelt, and the color in his feet was off thanks to poor circulation from the neurotoxin. His wings were out of commission for the same reason, not that they would be much help in an enclosed space.

Forced to grip the metal railing and hoist himself up onto the bed, he panted through the effort as he settled in on his back. The IV was a tangle under his hip, as were the other tubes and cords. Once he caught his breath, he tucked the card under his pillowcase and mashed the call button.

"How can I be of assistance?" a chirpy woman answered.

"My IV seems to have fallen out," he said flatly. "Can you send someone to restart it?"

"Oh, Mr. Wu." A keyboard clacked in the background. "Mr. Kapoor told us you—"

"He misunderstood." Adam settled against his pillows, eyes fixed on the drooping balloons, fingers twitching with curiosity over the plush bear's texture. He battled the impulse to position it in bed next to him, covers pooled around its pudgy waist, when Luce came for her visit. He imagined the rush of blood heating her cheeks when she beheld her gift and mortification set in. Such a human emotion. On her, it pleased him. "I'm not going anywhere."

Not until she visited him. After that . . .

Word of Famine's capture would reach his father's ears all too soon, and his interest heralded deadly consequences for them both. Adam had come too far, risked too much, to lose her now.

Especially to her precious Ezra.

ACKNOWLEDGMENTS

————————•❖•————————

I owe so many people thanks for helping with this book. It was a beast.

Ella Drake, in particular, didn't bat an eye when I pitched ideas about how to "realistically" make a dragon invisible. Because, you know, they're so realistic to start with. She also helped with many of the tech aspects that make Santiago a more believable computer nerd. I'm sure I messed up things even after she broke them down into bite-sized morsels, but she tried!

Sasha Devlin, my otter half, is like this rainbow I keep in my pocket to unleash on gloomy days. She keeps me smiling and motivated, and she's a wizard with a blurb. She gets me, and that's such a rare thing. I wish I was half the friend to her that she is to me.

Nikki Doherty, my (much, much older) sister (by like four years, which makes her ancient), is always quick to volunteer her help when I need to murder someone. She's also quick to put on her nurse's hat to help me save people. She's used to me DMing her questions that begin with "So, I need to transfuse this guy on the kitchen floor . . ." or "Do tampons really plug up bullet holes?"

Thanks to Megan Prescott at the Oxford Police Department and Assistant Chief Frank Misenhelter at the Hattiesburg Police Department for answering my certification and arson questions.

And finally, thank you to my husband and daughter. They kidnap me from the office, drag me into this bright stuff called sunlight, and generally force me to be present when the work would otherwise consume me.

Okay, so there are three more thanks I owe for helping with this book. Cookie, Lex, and Ollie, you guys are happiness packaged in fur suits. What good is being a writer without office dogs?